Chpt. 20

Sister Mary Baruch

Read All of the Sister Mary Baruch novels from TAN Books

chpt - 20

SISTER MARY BARUCH

Volume 4

Compline

Fr. Jacob Restrick, O.P.

TAN Books
Charlotte, North Carolina

Cover design by Caroline K. Green

ISBN: 978-1-5051-1487-4

Published in the United States by
TAN Books
PO Box 410487
Charlotte, NC 28241
www.TANBooks.com

Printed in the United States of America

In memory of Br. Saúl Antonio Soriano Rodriguez, OFM Capuchin

August 18, 1986 – May 7, 2018

Te Lucis Ante Terminum

To you before the close of day
Creator of the world we pray
That with accustomed kindness you
Would guard and keep us ever true.
May no ill dreams disturb our ease
No nightly fears or fantasies;
Tread under foot our ghostly foe
That no defilement we may know
Almighty Father, this accord
Through Jesus Christ, your Son, our Lord,
Who with the Holy Spirit true
Forever reigns in bliss with you. Amen

Trans. John M. Neale (1818-1866)

PREFACE

COMPLINE IS THE Night Prayer of the Church. Prayed by monks, nuns, religious, and devout Christians since the fourth century, it brings to completion the Divine Office or what we commonly call today *The Liturgy of the Hours*. It is the last hour of prayer.

There is a transition from Vespers, the Evening Prayer of the Church, to Compline, the Night Prayer. After the opening verse, Compline begins on one's knees, with a small penitential rite asking forgiveness for the sins of the day. A hymn is sung, traditionally the *Te Lucis Ante Terminum*, and then a Psalm, often calling on protection from the Evil One who roams about the world, like a lion, looking for someone to devour. The Devil and his minions are defeated in the prayers and blessings of Compline, which ends with the prayer of commending our spirits into the hands of the Lord and entrusting ourselves to the Mother of God...*Hail Holy Queen, Mother of Mercy*.

Sister Mary Baruch loves the Office of Compline and relishes its ushering in the Great Silence of the night, and a time to reflect on the events of the day, or the week, or the year, or even one's whole life.

Those who know her can reflect with her on her Jewish childhood on the Upper West Side of Manhattan; her coming to know the Lord, and her becoming a Catholic, and five years later, becoming a cloistered Dominican nun in Brooklyn Heights, New York. We've met her family, her friends, her sisters in community, and we've met her fears, her compulsions, her struggles to live a life of faith, hope, and love. Her life is not over, but there is a transition from the ambitions and work of her early years and mid-life crisis to a "completion", a compline of sorts, which continues her pilgrimage into Great Silence. The spiritual battle continues, for the forces of Evil confront her in herself, in those whom she loves, in the sins of others for whom she prays and offers penance, within and outside the monastery itself. The years are 2005 to 2007. She likes to end her day after Compline, sitting in her rocker in her cell, praying and writing and telling the Lord all about everything.

Our Lady, Queen of Hope Monastery is completely fictitious; the Sisters in community, her friends, and family are all fictitious. There are some extraordinary events that happen which contemporary monasteries of cloistered nuns may not experience in quite the same way as do Sr. Mary Baruch and the nuns of Our Lady, Queen of Hope. But beneath it all, we find ourselves in the transition times of our lives, confronting sin in ourselves and others, reflecting on God's presence and mercy in our lives, and surrendering to the redemptive love of Christ with whom we move into the peace that comes with Compline at the close of the day.

Fr. Jacob Restrick, O.P.
Province of St. Joseph

The whole life of the nuns is harmoniously ordered to preserving the continual remembrance of God. By the celebration of the Eucharist and the Divine Office, by reading and meditating on the Sacred Scripture, by private prayer, vigils and intercessions they should strive to have the same mind as Christ Jesus. In silence and stillness, let them earnestly seek the face of the Lord and never cease making intercession with the God of our salvation; that all men and women might be saved. They should give thanks to God the Father who has called them out of darkness into his wonderful light. Let Christ, who was fastened to the cross for all, be fast-knit to their hearts. In fulfilling all these things, they are truly nuns of the Order of Preachers. (Constitution of the Nuns, Chapter II, IV)

One

Thanksgiving 2005

*O come, bless the Lord, all you who serve the Lord, who
stand in the house of the Lord, in the courts of the house
of our God.* (Psalm 134, Sunday after First Vespers)

Rocking chairs don't have birthdays, silly goose; they're
just rocking chairs. I'm sitting in mine on this Thanksgiving
night, and it's dawned on me that *Squeak* was forty years old
this year. I don't remember the exact day that I found "her"
on the curb on Amsterdam Avenue and 75th Street. She was
waiting for the garbage truck to pick her up and throw her in
the back to be hauled away and dumped, crushed, or worse,
burned.

Some people have furnished their apartments with furniture left on the curbs of New York. I don't know how
old Squeak was when I rescued her; she still looked young
enough to be redeemed. So I dragged her home to my apartment on West 79th Street. Papa had adopted pieces of furniture over the years; he would know what to do. And sure
enough, he was delighted with my learning how to strip off

the old varnish, sand her down in spots, and re-varnish her with a lighter shade that gave her a brand new look. I liked this style of rocker with a high broad back and wide arm rests.

While her varnish was drying and I was walking home from Barnard College, I passed a store on Lexington Avenue like Pier One, but not as elegant. They had stacks of cushions in the furniture accessories area, and I bought a bright orange seat and back cushion with a brown edge trim, and brought it home for my rocker. I moved the chest of drawers out of the corner and moved my rocker in there with a floor lamp which had a round table built in, perfect for a book and a glass or mug of something. Papa came in to see the finished product and said it "looked spiffy."

I hugged him and kissed him on the cheek, thanked him for all his help, and said that maybe I would name her "Spiffy." He laughed and said, "Rockers don't have names, silly-goose." And off he went to dive into his evening paper.

I remember closing the door quietly, and from out of my book bag, I took a black leather bound copy of the *New Testament*, which I had taken out at the library. I had never read the Christian Bible, and I remember that the first time was when I turned on the light and sat in my rocker. Squeak... squeak.

Oh my, I thought, *this isn't spiffy at all, the stupid thing squeaks*. But it was comfortable. I opened the *New Testament* at random, and my eyes fell on the Prologue of St. John's Gospel: *In the beginning was the Word, and the Word was with God, and the Word was God*. Squeak...squeak.

And indeed, that was the beginning. I came to know the Word that was made flesh and dwelled among us. I met Him in my squeaky rocker, and although she looked rather spiffy, I named her "Squeak."

Its forty years since that happened. Little did I realize forty years ago rocking back and forth in that castaway chair that I would still be sitting in it forty years later in a cloistered monastery in Brooklyn Heights. But here I am, Lord, squeaks and all.

I like writing in my journals in Squeak. It's like being with an old friend. Thanksgiving 2005 is over. It was a sad Thanksgiving in many ways; the first since our dear Sr. Gertrude died, not even a month ago. And close to seven months ago that the Holy Father Pope John Paul died. But we also have lots to be thankful for this Thanksgiving, especially the election of Pope Benedict XVI whom they already say is drawing great crowds to the Papal Audiences. One commentator said the crowds used to come to Rome to *see* Pope John Paul, now they come to Rome to *listen* to Pope Benedict. We are grateful for our new Holy Father and pray for him every day.

Being the novice mistress, I am especially grateful for all the Sisters who live in the novitiate.

Sr. Elijah Rose was one of the first two postulants to enter since I've been Novice Mistress. She is our first African American Sister, although I'm told there was a Sr. Naomi who died sometime in the early 1950s. Sr. Benedict remembers her when she (Sr. Benedict) entered in 1954. Sr. Naomi was a lay sister who was not an extern sister, but lived inside, and did a lot of the menial jobs. She was from Philadelphia originally and used to work for the Hawthorne Dominicans at Sacred Heart Home. It was from them that she saw how work and prayer blended together. She called it "Hawthorne love." She and her brother, Tyrone, shared an apartment off of Huntington Park. He worked as a welder for the Camden shipyards in New Jersey. In 1941, just a year after the Camden shipyards were founded, he was offered a better job in the Brooklyn Yards, so they moved, and Sandra found the Monastery of Our Lady Queen of Hope, and became Sr. Naomi. Sr. Benedict said she was relatively young, but cancer came early. She spent her last months at St. Rose Home in lower Manhattan, and died a peaceful death under the care of "Hawthorne love."

Sr. Elijah Rose also met us through the Dominican Sisters of Hawthorne. She was an RN at Roosevelt Hospital when she entered the Church. She spent several weeks with the Sisters at their Motherhouse in Hawthorne, New York. She took care of a woman patient whose daughter was our Sr. Antonia, and after her mother died, Sister invited "Brenda" to visit the monastery. The rest is history, as they say.

Sr. Leah Marie was my second novice whom I actually met through her Jewish girlfriend from high school, named Leah. Sister's name in the world was Gracie, which certainly brought back many memories for me. Jewish Leah went off to Israel and lives on a kibbutz; Gracie went off to New York Fashion Institute and designed clothes. The "habit" may not make the nun, but it made one student fashion designer very interested in all that it stands for. She became Sister Leah Marie, and wrote to her friend in Israel: "I've joined the Catholic Kibbutz."

By Advent 2005, both Sr. Elijah Rose and Sr. Leah Marie will be completing their third year of simple profession and are approaching Solemn Profession. Rumblings in the community tell me that some of the "Chapter" (the Solemn Professed nuns) think one or both of them should not make final vows, but renew for at least a year. The trauma of 9/11 took its toll on them, as it did on all of us. Three years of simple profession are required by Church law before final vows, but one could renew up to three more years, one year at a time.

I pray a lot for both of them, and for myself, asking the Holy Spirit to enlighten me on what to do. I also needed to talk to each one of them and seek the counsel of some of the other Sisters. The year after they became novices was like it was lived in slow motion. September 11 slowed us all down.

Sr. Elijah Rose lost her much-loved grandfather, Eli, who turned out to have been our apartment building's doorman when I was growing up. I loved Mr. Eli; he always called me Miss Rebecca. I am especially fond of Sr. Elijah Rose because of that, but even besides that, she is a wonderful addition to the community when she isn't overly tired. She is especially good with the Sisters in the infirmary and has a knack for getting them to laugh. When she's tired, she becomes very quiet and pensive. She finds herself sitting still for a long time, a long time. She was also mature enough to ask to renew her vows rather than make Solemn Profession.

After 9/11, Sr. Leah also had periods of depression. Several friends from the fashion institute were killed. It was a real trial of faith for her to come around and pray again. God was hidden in the mess of it all, and she, like many of us,

were numb for a long while, myself included. We couldn't
exactly find God in the rubble. There was a moment during
Lent when I thought she would leave. She didn't come to
the Office in the morning; she couldn't get up. "I just can't
face it; I don't know what to say to God, and the *Psalms* just
don't do it for me."

"I know, Sister, the *Psalms* are something one grows into,
but after many years, they're like a pair of old loafers or
washed out jeans." I thought the clothes analogies would
help.

"What are loafers?" Here she was an actual graduate of the
New York Institute of Fashion, and she didn't know what
loafers were, oy. I remember that next to my saddle shoes,
my penny loafers were my favorite shoes. I could use a comfortable pair right now; they are so much easier to put on.
There's something just not dainty about black Nike sneak-
ers for full-bodied nuns, as Gracie/Leah, the fashionista calls
some of us. Of course, I don't think I was ever as thin as Leah;
Mama would have had her own campaign of Jewish pastries
and huge corned-beef sandwiches to eat between meals! Our
Customary forbids us from eating anything between meals,
all the time, not just for a Lenten penance. It's not bad when
everyone's doing it, but it can be a temptation when nobody's
looking, or you are anxious, upset, frustrated, nervous, or
just a little "peckish," to quote Gwendolyn .

Fr. Wilcox, years ago, heard my confession, and I told
him that "I ate when I shouldn't." He actually kind of giggled at my poor contrition, and said if he had to confess
that every time he ate between meals, he'd spend half his
life in the confessional. I laughed back thinking that was

appropriate. It's rare we laugh in the confessional. It didn't solve the problem, or give me a firm purpose of amendment, but I hope the Lord knows I don't want to cheat on our customs, not even the little things, like not eating between meals. I once told Sr. Bertrand that I fell into the cookie jar during Advent. She thought that was a riot and told me that her first Lent as a postulant was so difficult she wanted to take up residence in the little kitchen.

"I actually told that in confession to old Fr. Blaine, one of our extraordinary confessors; it was during Lent." Sr. Bertrand's lips puckered and her eyes rolled. "And he told me our Divine Lord didn't want me to eat anything between meals."

"And what did you say?"

She puckered up her lips again, leaned into me like she was telling me a deep dark secret. "I told him Our Divine Lord didn't give two hoots if I ate a couple toll house cookies, it was Sister Ambrose I was worried about!"

"She was your Postulant Mistress?"

"Postulant and Novice Mistress both. She was a real stickler for the rules. Do you know she sent a postulant home for reading a letter during adoration? She told her if news from home was so important, she should go home to live with it." Sr. Bertrand made her little humph sound and slouched back in her chair.

"Did you ever find out what happened to her?"

"Nah, she never came back to visit or wrote any letters. I didn't even know her last name. She left early in the morning before we got to say goodbye. That's the way it was in those days, you know."

"Yes, I've heard tell. But look at you, Sr. Bertrand, you're a fine old nun now."

"Who you calling 'old'?" She gave her little guttural giggle. "I never took up residence in the little kitchen, but I've swiped a few toll house cookies in my day, and never told Fr. Blaine again."

I laughed, making a mental note that if I have a novice who suffers from scrupulosity, I would have her talk to Sr. Bertrand about the "old days."

And then there's Sr. Kateri, our first "native American" whose name was Pretty Flower. The Sisters in the infirmary still call her that. Mother had a field day choosing her religious name, but she settled on the "Lily of the Mohawks", Blessed Kateri Tekakwitha. Blessed Kateri was beatified by Pope John Paul II twenty-five years ago. When she was baptized, she took the name Kateri, which is Catherine. So Pretty Flower was pretty happy.

"Sister Pretty Flower has really blossomed in the life," Sr. Gerard told me, thinking her play on words was clever, and looked about at the Sisters in the infirmary kitchenette, who pretended to have not even heard her. Sr. Kateri had three of the infirmary sisters doing bead-work, making rosary bags and belts. Such things? The rosary bags are useful, but who's going to wear a beaded belt? But the Sisters loved it, and I think Sr. Gerard was the most proficient in it. The others were envious of that but wouldn't say anything out of charity.

The only one who didn't take to it was Sr. Bertrand. She was the first to abandon the bead class. "They're too darned small. How do you expect us to thread these things with arthritis? I quit." That was on her first and only day of "bead school."

I tried to assure her that she could do the work with some patience, besides, "don't you want a nice beaded bag for your rosary? Our Lady of Fatima must think they're very beautiful."

"Our Lady doesn't give two hoots about beaded bags; she wants the rosary in our hands, not in a silly bag with a draw string. The only beads she wants are rosary beads."

"Maybe that's what you could do. You could make the rosaries and let the others make the bags to carry them in."

Sr. Bertrand liked that idea. She used to make rosaries and knows just how to twist the metal eyelets. The beads are bigger and she can pray while she's doing it.

Finally, Sr. Sheila is still with us, in her second year of transfer from an active Order. She kept her name, Sheila, and told me this morning before Mass that she is very thankful to be here. We have a wonderful group of simple professed, Sr. Mary Kolbe, Sr. Diana, Sr. Maureen, Sr. Mary Cecilia, Sr. Elijah Rose, and Sr. Leah Marie. The first four will be making Solemn Profession early next year. These four were even delayed earlier profession because of 9/11; a two year novitiate and renewal of simple vows after three years has been practiced under Mother Rosaria.

Sr. Agnes Mary, our former prioress, has moved into the infirmary full time; I'm grateful for that because she needs the rest. She said the other day that she's got a lung condition and is grateful that she's on the ground floor now; no more stairs. She's also warmly welcomed by the "infirmary sisters" who all loved her as prioress.

So, it was a lovely Thanksgiving, Lord, with lots of food, of course, for which I'm always grateful. And then the, what should I call it, Lord? The surprise?

When at the end of Compline, we were singing the Salve Regina (*Salve Regina* is the antiphon sung each night at the conclusion of Compline—*Hail Holy Queen*) and processing to the center aisle and ...CRASH! The new LED light fixture fell from the ceiling and crashed on the altar. We all jumped a foot in the air and gasped for breath. Sr. Kateri dropped her candle stick and bent over to pick it up, when Sr. Myriam, immediately behind, fell over her, and tumbled over. Another gasp from the community, when Mother loudly shouted, "Halt" and we froze in our steps. No one was hurt, thank God. Sr. Myriam, who was crumpled on her side like a poorly executed venia (a side prostration unique to the Dominicans) got the giggles. Sr. Mary George and Sr. Antonia came to her rescue, along with Sr. Kateri who was bright red from embarrassment. Her candle blown out; wax splattered on the marble floor, and the other candle bearer, Sr. Leah Marie got the hiccups.

In a frozen "halt position," Mother very calmly and quietly said, "It seems like our new overhead lamp was not installed correctly. Luckily it did not fall during holy Mass; no one has been hurt, and it would appear to have caused no fire, just a bit of a mess, which can be easily cleaned up. When Sisters are in place again, we will begin the *Salve* again from the beginning."

It was Sr. Bertrand, on a rare visit to the choir from the infirmary, who spoke out without raising her hand, "May we 'un-halt' our position, Mother?" (Sister Bertrand had been a WAC in World War II.)

Mother didn't blink an eye, and without hesitation said, "At ease, Sisters." And everyone gave out a sigh of relief. We were more shook up by the "boom" it made when it hit the altar than the actual accident. We thought we had been bombed. It was a good thing Sr. Gerard wasn't there, as she's expecting the bomb any moment now.

The handful of retreatants in the extern chapel were silent, no doubt frozen too, except for one girl who was laughing, I thought, rather rudely at it all. Sr. Paula, our extern Sister, was in the sanctuary immediately and inspecting the scene, and gave Mother a silent nod that all was okay. She turned, and putting her finger to her lips, shushed the girl laughing. And shaking her head, Sister "tsk, tsked" her way out of the sanctuary.

Sr. Gertrude would have "enjoyed" tonight's accident, I think, as she once told the story of a Kliegl stage light falling on the stage in the middle of a performance. The actors on stage were all shocked, but without breaking character, made an *ad lib* remark about it, and went on with the show. If I remember right, she was describing that to me when I was a novice and telling her about a Sister who dropped a glass bowl of steaming hot potatoes in the refectory. "You jump, you pick up the pieces, and the show goes on." Dear Sr. Gertrude. How I miss sharing everything with her and getting her reflection on it all.

It's been four years since 9/11, and the final curtain came down on her. Somehow I think the shock of 9/11 was a turning point for her, even though she was in her mid-eighties, she could still carry a tune, but the attack on New York was something she never quite got over. It was her heart that gave out in the end.

Well, that's enough for tonight, Lord. I'm all thanks-givinged out!

Your silly goose, Baruch.

Two

Saturday After Thanksgiving

Lift up your hands to the holy place and bless the Lord through the night. (Psalm 134, Sunday Compline after First Vespers)

I HAD MY USUAL Saturday meeting with the novices and postulants in the morning when we'd review the events of the week and look at the week ahead. That maybe sounds more business-like than it is. It's usually a look at the feast days coming up and how we can prepare to celebrate them. We were getting ready for Advent and Christmas.

I told them that Mother Rosaria encouraged our visiting the Sisters in the infirmary during Advent, and gave them a little update on all of them.

Sr. Benedict is now the eldest Sister in the infirmary. She was perhaps the closest to Sr. Gertrude, and would often remind us of "Gertrudisms", she called them. Once very active, her hands are quite arthritic now and her hearing is going. But she is faithful to the rosary and is the most fervent in her prayers for Pope Benedict. She uses a walker now, but is still not very secure on her feet.

Sr. Gerard on the other hand is still going strong in her eighty-eighth year. Her eye sight is failing, but she can still do the bead work. She made it her new apostolate as she's waiting every day for the predicted chastisement. Fatima, Garabandal, Akita, and Medjugorje are her favorite apparition sites. For all her gloom and doom, she is very devoted to praying the rosary, which she leads in the infirmary common room every afternoon at four o'clock. Praying the rosary has been part of all the Marian apparitions since Lourdes. I don't know how the word got out, but Sr. Gerard receives prayer intentions from people all over the diocese. Sister Catherine Agnes helps her respond to the mail requesting her prayers. It's remarkable how the elderly Sisters keep their prayer life going. Sr. Catherine Agnes says it's "because we are free from television, internet, and cell phones." She has never made friends with email. If she did, her password could be SCAR.

SCAR! Sr. Catherine Agnes Russell was Postulant Mistress when I walked through the enclosure door more than thirty-five years ago. I don't remember her ever smiling, and her radar eyes never missed a misstep I made, or so it seemed. I think I thought of her as an enigma; she was in charge of the new Sisters, and "preached" to us about the joy of the life, but her sternness betrayed her words. She was anything but the epitome of joy. But she provided a common "cross" for all of us postulants and novices, which we would whisper about, complain about, sometimes laugh about, and confess about when we went to confession.

Today, I think Sr. Catherine Agnes is one of the most wonderful nuns I've ever known. Isn't it marvelous and strange how God can change everything around. My mother would say, "Such a blessing." And so it is. When I went through one of my crisis periods after my silver jubilee, it was SCAR who comforted me and told me, "There's more than one way to kick the old devil in the pants." She even confided to me that she was tough on us on purpose, because she knew that when everything came crashing down around us, we needed courage and fortitude and perseverance to go on. And she was right.

I think my nephew, Sharbel, might need a dose of SCAR's medicine to get through his present troubles, and I don't know how to help him do that, except to pray, of course, and maybe even do an extra penance, which has never been my forte. Although dear Mother John Dominic used to tell us that we didn't have to look far to come up with an extra penance for a special intention. It was usually standing (or sitting) right next to us. We used to think that was just her quaint piety. Something a "desert mother" would say to you. But it's proven to be true more times than I can count. It's the remembering to "offer it up" that I keep forgetting, but I still pass her words of wisdom onto the postulants and novices. And they look at me like I'm an old nun being quaint.

Sr. Agnes Mary, as I mentioned, is now one of the Sisters in the infirmary, and I often visit her there and can run things by her, and she still has a sharp mind and a wisdom to see through to the heart of things. God has provided again. But I still miss my dear Sr. Gertrude who would sit in the large picture window in the infirmary looking out on our cemetery, and listen to all my woes. She usually had a song to accompany them, and could always pull me out of my doldrums.

I shall pay her a visit before Compline and pray at her grave, along with Mother John Dominic, and Sister Trinity, who was my novice mistress. I call them all the un-canonized Communion of Saints, as I know they still love us and care about what's going on, here on earth, and here in their monastery.

Last September when Rosh Hashanah rolled around, I was visiting with Fr. Matthew, our Passionist chaplain, in the little parlor. I still call him Ezra, which was his name when I first met him forty years ago in Tea on Thames, a little English tea shop near Columbia University and Barnard College. Our friendship is almost as old as Squeak's! He was certainly an answer to my prayers, as I was just coming to know the Lord, in that black leather New Testament, unbeknownst to my dear Jewish parents. (I returned the book to the library and bought my own so I could mark it up.) The words of Jesus were so moving for me, and I didn't have anyone to talk to about all that, especially someone who would understand. And God sent Ezra into my life. He was a Columbia University student and a Catholic convert from Judaism. Sr. Gertrude used to say, "He came tailor-made, darlin', just when you needed it…right on cue."

Ezra became my best friend, but never a "boyfriend," which Mama and the rest of my family could never understand. For many years, Mama blamed Ezra for "converting" me, and I could never get her to understand I was falling in love with Jesus of Nazareth before I even met Ezra from Columbia U. Ezra was my friend, and also my Godfather when I was baptized in May 1970, in St. Vincent Ferrer Church on 65th and Lexington.

The following year, Ezra "ran off" to become a Passionist novice, and received the name Br. Matthew. He served for many years in their African missions, and in retreat work here in the U.S., and at a shrine in Lancaster, England, till he became our chaplain.

We talk about many things when we get together, usually once a month. I want him to meet Sharbel. I think he could give him some good counsel. Well, I don't know that for sure, but he was always easy to talk to for me, and I know how much he loves the Lord. Sometimes it seems like we are too concerned about a lot of other secondary things, like academic achievement and psychological maturity, and social skills, but miss the heart of the matter. As Sr. Gertrude would say, "Have you given your heart to the Sacred Heart?" That's not a sentimental question if you meditate on the Sacred Heart. It's a Heart of love surrounded by a crown of thorns, and pierced with a lance. It puts one at the foot of the cross and the sacrifice of Our Lord, and that's where every priest must find himself. All of us really, for every baptized person shares in the royal priesthood of Christ, at the foot of the cross. Sometimes, I guess, we go in circles to get there, and I'm not sure where my dear nephew is in his journey, but I'm happy he feels confident to share it with me, and maybe I just want Ezra in on it too. I must remember to reserve the little parlor for Sunday afternoon. Hopefully no one else has got it ahead of me. Such problems we should have?

Three

Christmas Night 2005

*Oh God, come to my assistance. Oh Lord, make
haste to help me.* (Introductory verse)

FR. MATTHEW (EZRA) gave a beautiful homily this morning about God playing hide and seek with us. Most of the
time He's hiding, but we search for Him, and can find Him
hiding in the Eucharist, in the sick, in the poor, and today
He lets us find him in a new born babe, hiding in the hay.
I think he must've used that image when he spoke to his
orphans in Mozambique. He probably played hide and seek
with them.

And maybe our whole life is like that…we are searching
for the Lord, and hopefully in the end, we find Him…or
He finds us. The Divine Office is one of those places that
the Lord hides. The antiphons of Advent and Christmas are
some of the most beautiful. They're like the clues to finding
Him hiding in the psalm.

I didn't have any visitors today, so I was able to help out
in the kitchen in the morning, and had a parlor visit with

Fr. Matthew after None. He was having dinner with Aunt Sarah, which he always found to be curious, as she didn't believe in Christmas, but she celebrated it. I told him it was the same with my sister, Sally, who didn't come to visit as she was on a Holiday Caribbean cruise. She was probably praying for bright and sunny days, well maybe not "praying" for that, but hoping for that, and I was hoping for a white Christmas, which we didn't have. Lord, I know You are busy with many things in this world, but wouldn't a light flurry be easy?

I think the novices are all worn out from cleaning, cooking, and decorating. I'm sure a couple of them were praying that it would *not* snow, so they wouldn't have to shovel. I think they were a little disappointed too that we didn't have our regular community recreation. Sr. Leah Marie told me they were looking forward to a peaceful early Compline and off to bed. Well that didn't happen. As you know, Lord, we had a Christmas gift surprise. Fr. Oyster was here.

Fr. Oyster is one of our Dominican Fathers from the Western Province who has something to do with the movie business, and was here in New York for a premiere or something, and stayed on for Christmas at St. Vincent's. We've known him for years. He's our Sr. Regina's first cousin. Reginald Marie Oyster, O.P. Everybody laughs at his name, so he insists we all call him Fr. Reggie, but we love to call him Fr. Oyster. He told us once that the Oysters were a prominent family in the San Francisco Bay area in the early days, like back in the 1800s. Then, he'd slip in that they were known as the Bay Oysters. We all thought that was a riot. He also once mentioned that he was a personal friend of Diane Feinstein,

the Senator from California. Everyone looked over at me,
and I'm told, I blushed. Feinstein is my last name too.
"No relation," I assured them, while blessing myself. "No
relation."

So while we were all very tired, we were always delighted
for a "parlor" with Fr. Oyster. He is very humorous and also
dramatic. It's Christmas night and he was telling us about a
new movie in which a nun is possessed and escapes from the
convent. (*He should tell such a story?* I thought to myself.)
But he had us all on the edge of our seats, describing a scene
when she returns *during Compline*, mind you, and murders
the Superior who was walking in the dormitory hallway
looking for her. She stabbed her in the back with a butcher
knife. We all gasped and looked at our Mother Rosaria, who
leaned back in her chair and blessed herself saying, "Glory
be to God."

We all laughed at the fine acting of Mother Rosaria, who
continued her monologue, "The poor nun should've been
in the chapel chanting Compline with the Sisters and not
roaming around the hall. Sr. Simon, remind me to pad lock
the drawer where the butcher knives are kept." Sometimes
the parlor at recreation is full of hearty laughter. I think Fr.
Oyster enjoyed it more than the movie.

We told him that we would probably never see the film
as it was not our custom to watch movies. This was true,
although we had watched a few on special occasions. After
all it was almost 2006. We had a wide screen television
which we kept locked up in a closet and only brought out
for special occasions.

Compline tonight began around 8:20 p.m.; Sr. Paula, our extern Sister, went out at 8:00 to tell the few retreatants or guests in the chapel that Compline would be a little late beginning. "Mother gave a *pouce*." That's a French word for *thumb*. If recreation was to be extended, Mother would signal Sr. Paula with a thumb up. Before entering the monastery, Mother had been an *au pair* for a French family in New York City and Paris. A "thumb up" (a pouce) was the signal to her from the mother of the family if the children could stay up later than their usual bedtime.

I don't think Sr. Paula ever gave an explanation for it, and our guests probably wondered what in the world a *pouce* was and how did Mother give one. Sr. Paula was an accomplished extern sister who only said what she needed to, and returned without any explanation. "Mother gave a pouce" was enough.

It was just about 8:22, then, with the image of a mother superior being stabbed in the back lingering in our minds, that we were kneeling in the chapel in total silence. We were silently examining our consciences before praying the *Confiteor* asking forgiveness of God, the Blessed Virgin, St. Dominic, and all our Sisters, for the sins we had committed this day.

BANG! BANG! I think we all jumped two feet in our stalls. BANG! Again. It came from the front door of the monastery. It was locked after Vespers. Who could it be? It wasn't a retreatant or guest who was locked out. They were all accounted for at supper time, another one of Sr. Paula's jobs. Sometimes a retreatant would be out, or forget that the door would be locked. And sometimes we had homeless people banging on the door, but not this loudly.

With Fr. Oyster's story still fresh in our heads, I think we all wanted to disappear behind our choir forms. Mother very silently gave Sister another "pouce," and Sr. Paula sheepishly made her way to the front door. Mother didn't wait to hear what it was, but began the *Confiteor* like nothing unusual was happening. I looked over at Sr. Anna Maria, the subprioress who caught my eye, and just shrugged her shoulders. Fr. Oyster was in the extern chapel, and went out to the door with her when he saw Sr. Paula making her way there.

The entrance is far enough away from the chapel that we couldn't really hear what was happening. I only caught Fr. Oyster saying, "Calm down, my boy." And it sounded like someone crying. I thought I half heard my name, "Baruch", but it could have been "broke"…maybe someone's car broke down, who knows. We sometimes gets all kinds of interesting characters knocking on our door. This one wasn't exactly knocking; he was banging. It was very difficult to concentrate on the words of the hymn for Compline. There was a rumble of noise going on while we were singing: *Upon you no evil shall fall; no plague approach where you dwell. For you has he commanded his angels, to keep you in all your ways* (Psalm 91).

By the end of the psalm we didn't hear anything, nor did we hear Fr. Oyster return to the chapel, nor did Sr. Paula return to the choir, which wasn't really unremarkable; she would often miss Compline if her extern duties called for it. Apparently this one did. But it was "all quiet on the western front," as Sr. Gertrude used to say. I sank into my seat

thinking about Sr. Gertrude, and not the Compline reading for Christmas night. She used to love our visits with Fr.
Oyster because he would talk about movies and plays, and
would actually ask her what plays on Broadway she would
recommend. And she would tell him what was playing and
what the reviews were like. He asked to be able to go out to
our cemetery so he could pray at her grave, but Mother said
"no." We don't even let family go to the cemetery; it is within
the enclosure. In many ways, the enclosure is a security and
safety zone for us.

My long distraction was interrupted by the realization that
we were processing out of our stalls for the *Salve* Procession.
I still love our Salve Procession best of all the processions we
do. I got in the habit many years ago of commending loved
ones who have died to the care and protection of the Mother
of God. I put them all "in her train." Her mantle train, that
is, after all we hail her as our "Holy Queen." And *post hoc
exilium*—"after this our exile, show unto us the Blessed fruit
of your womb, Jesus." I've got Mama and Papa in the long
and strong train of her gown. My little sister Ruth, my brothers Josh and David, and my dear friend, Greta Phillips, who
was in my instruction class, it seems like a hundred years ago
now, and was my roommate for the five years before I came
here. She taught me many things about living the faith. Fr.
Meriwether is there, of course, and now Sr. Gertrude, and
Mother John Dominic, and all the Sisters who have died
here. I only mention a few by name, but commend "all of
my beloved dead" to our *Queen and Mother of Mercy, our
life, our Sweetness, and our Hope.* Oh, and of course, my dear
friend from high school, Gracie Price, for whom I first went

into St. Vincent Ferrer Church on 65th and Lexington to
light a candle when she was in Mt. Sinai Hospital. That little
idea popped into my head as I was hurrying down Lexington Avenue to Bloomingdales to buy her something. I had
never been in a Catholic Church, and I thought maybe the
roof would fall in as I was slowly pushing open the heavy
doors of the vestibule, and I walked into a whole new world
I didn't know existed.

Gracie died about three months after that, and my "farewell gift" to her was my "secret": I was going to become a
Catholic. She was my honorary godmother. So I remember
her when we honor God's Mother every night. That was over
forty years ago. I wonder at times what Gracie would be like
and what she'd be doing if she had lived. She'd probably be
a grandmother by now.

Our two white-veil novices led the procession, carrying
lighted candles. We return to our places as we chant the
nightly hymn to our Holy Father Dominic, and Mother
commends all the faithful departed to the mercy of God.
Then, a great silence envelopes us.

I was going to remain in the chapel for the length of a
rosary, when Sr. Paula silently slipped in next to me and
handed me a note. "Come to the little parlor—it's Sharbel."

Oh my, I thought. Sharbel. My one and only nephew,
Sharbel. I had seen him maybe five days before. He is working as a bartender and waiter at a mid-town "watering-spot"
as he calls it. He graduated from Yale last spring, and wants
to become a Dominican, but has huge student loans to pay
off. Apparently his mother, Olivia, is not helping him.

I quickly and quietly made my way out of the chapel, giving a last glance to Our Lord in the monstrance. *"Oh God,
come to my assistance. O Lord, make haste to help me."*

It is highly unusual for any of us to see anyone in the parlor after Great Silence begins after Compline, but it seemed
like a time when our Dominican *epikeia* would allow it.
Charity wins out over the common rule. I quietly opened
my door to the small parlor, and there he sat with Fr. Oyster
in attendance.

"Sharbel?"

"Oh, Aunt Mary, I dun know wa ta do!"

I looked at Fr. Oyster, who gestured "he's been drinking."

I sat down, and could see immediately the anguish in his
eyes, all blurry and blood shot from crying.

"What's the matter, Jack? Are you hurt?" "Jack" is my
personal name for Sharbel. When I first met him with his
father, my brother David, he told me that John the Baptist
was his confirmation name. And he thought that John the
Baptist must've called the Blessed Virgin, Aunt Mary. So he
would call me that. And I asked him what he thought Aunt
Mary called John the Baptist. With a twinkle in his eye he
said, "Jack." So that became my name for him. Although I
really love his baptismal name too. Sharbel. He is a wonderful Maronite saint from Lebanon. His mother, Dr. Olivia
Ghattas, is Lebanese.

"I'm not hurt; I'm only hurting." And he began to cry.
"Mother told me she doesn't wan me to be a Dom—in—
ican or a priest. She says my fahher would hate me."

"Oh, Jack, your father would never hate you. He always
loved you and was proud of you whatever you did."

"God tell that to my Mah-ther, I mean, tell God to tell that to her." He took a couple big sniffs and blew his nose before going on. "I came here because you are my only hope; you have to pray for me, Aunt Mary, and tell God to change my mother's mind. She can be such a beh…oh, I'm sorry, Aunt Mary, I didn't mean it. Do you have any wine in here like when I was here last week?"

"No, we don't have any wine on weekends." Why was I saying that? The weekend had nothing to do with it. We don't have wine any day. He was the one who had brought the wine, reminding me of my mother who always had a bottle of Mogen David in her over-sized hand bag.

Fr. Oyster, who was as silent as a clam, finally said something, "You don't need another drink, my boy, you need a strong cup of coffee. That's what you need." And he looked at me, like I was the waitress in a coffee shop.

"I'll see what I can do." I said very softly, "You wait here." I don't know where I thought they might wander off to.

Mother Rosaria and Sr. Paula were standing in the cloister by the parlor.

"Is everything alright, Sister?" Mother was genuinely concerned.

"Yes, Mother, it's my nephew, Sharbel. He seems to have had a little too much to drink, and came to see me, not realizing what time it was, and was flustered to find the door locked."

"I see."

"Fr. Oyster is with him, and thinks a cup of strong coffee would be most helpful."

Sr. Paula to the rescue. "I can make a pot right away. It's already prepared for tomorrow morning. I'll bring it in. Maybe Fr. Oyster would like a cup too." And off she went towards the little kitchen. (A small kitchen adjacent to the large community kitchen, used as a "service kitchen.")

"Is there anything I can do, Sister?"

"No, Mother, blessed be God. I'll send him on his way. I think Fr. Oyster may be of assistance there."

"That's good. I'll say 'good night' then. Try not to be up too late with him."

"Blessed be God." We say that in place of "thank you." Mother smiled and made her way down the cloister. I headed towards the little kitchen.

Sr. Paula was quietly brewing a pot of coffee and fixing a tray. I quietly sliced a sesame bagel and popped it in the toaster. He might enjoy a bagel and a slice of cheese. I secretly prayed to the Lord while getting two slices of Swiss cheese out of the little kitchen fridge, resisting the temptation to have cheese on a toasted bagel myself. *Maybe Sharbel won't eat it, and we can't let it go to waste, that's almost sinful.* This little scenario is going through my head, while poor Sharbel is in anguish over his mother's opposition to his vocation.

I returned to the parlor, followed by Sr. Paula who went into their side with her tray of coffee, cream, sugar, a bagel cheese sandwich, and a half dozen chocolate chip cookies which she had made yesterday.

Sharbel was looking a bit better, settled down, as Fr. Oyster would say. He drank his coffee black, and gobbled down two cookies. Fr. Oyster was grateful for the coffee too AND the bagel. I kept custody of the tongue, but inside my head

I was shouting, *That's not for you, Oyster Bay, the bagel's for Sharbel. The cookies were for you.*

He only ate one of the halves, and moved on to a couple cookies. I guess recreation had worked up an appetite in ole Fr. Oyster.

"Can I come see you on Sunday, Aunt Mary?" Sharbel's speech pattern was already sounding more sober.

We don't usually have visitors more than once a month, but it was Christmas week, and I knew Mother would agree to it. So I told him, "Yes, that would be just fine. Maybe you could come for None at three o'clock, and we could visit till Vespers."

"That's great; I don't have to be at work till seven. These cookies are really good."

"Well, I'll make sure Sister Paula has a plate full for you on Sunday." And he laughed. I was so relieved to hear him laugh.

"Do you think God doesn't want me to be a Dominican?" he asked as he was finishing off the last two cookies before Fr. Oyster got to them.

"I think we can talk about it on Sunday. A good sign of a vocation, you know, is that there is an obstacle or two along the way. I don't know about God, but I'm sure the Devil doesn't want you to be a Dominican." I smiled.

He laughed his funny way again. "Old Red Legs." I had called the Devil that once when he had come to visit me with his father, and he never forgot it.

"That's right, old Red Legs. He probably doesn't want you to finish that coffee either." And he laughed again, picked up his mug, and gulped it down.

Fr. Oyster was very kind after all, and offered to give Sharbel a ride in his cab to Manhattan.

"Who are you, anyway? Are you a Dominican?"

"Yes, I am. I'm from the Western Province. My name is Fr. Reginald Marie. I'm staying at St. Vincent's."

Sharbel was satisfied and agreed to go with him, as far as the Village, where he was going to meet some friends. He squeezed my fingers through the grille, and thanked me, and said he'd see me on Sunday after None. "Ha! That's funny: 'after none', maybe that's where we got 'afternoon.'"

They went off quietly. I thanked Fr. Oyster, and asked him to put the tray on the turn. The turn is like a large lazy Susan, where one can spin something from the extern parlor to the nuns'. I collected the tray and took it to the little kitchen. Sr. Paula was not there, so I rinsed out the coffee mugs, put the milk away, rinsed off the dishes, and sat down at the table in the little kitchen and prayed that the Lord would take care of everything for Sharbel. He, that's You, Lord, are still playing hide and seek. The half a bagel with Swiss cheese was delicious.

Four

Ash Wednesday 2006

Out of the depths I cry to you, O Lord, Lord hear my voice. (Psalm 130, Wednesday Compline)

UNLIKE ADVENT, PUTTING on the violet of Lent is more somber and has the feel of penance. It's the season that reminds us of our mortality. And this year so far the only death we've had is Sr. Benedict's. I couldn't write about it then because I was too sad. It brought back the grief of losing Sr. Gertrude, maybe because the two of them had been lifetime friends.

Sr. Benedict died February 3, the day after the Presentation. She had been failing for months, and during the Christmas season she had fallen several times, even once with her walker. In all our geographical array, I think Sr. Benedict probably came from the furthest distance, at least among the older sisters. She was from San Diego, California. I know she spoke of an uncle who was a Franciscan and lived at one of the California missions. His name was Benedict. Uncle Ben. We used to tease her by asking her if he was the one who invented instant rice. And she would laugh. I'll always remember her laugh. It was hearty. She once commented that she would be reprimanded by the novice mistress for laughing too loudly. And so she tried to learn to suppress it which only gave her a coughing fit; her face would turn beet red and the novice mistress would say, "Let it out, Sister." And Sister would laugh loud and clear, which she said was contagious, and everyone around her would start laughing.

When I entered, Sr. Benedict was in charge of the altar breads. It was quite a "big business" by monastic standards, but she had been a baker in San Diego, or maybe I should say she worked in a bakery. She was actually quite clumsy in the kitchen and made a mess of things, but the altar breads were different. Only she did the actual mixing of the batter to just the right consistency before it was poured into the molds. She always spoke very reverently of the work, and I think it broke her heart when the community voted to end that work. We did do packaging of pre-made altar breads for distribution, but it wasn't the same. Eventually we even gave that up.

Sr. Gertrude and Sr. Benedict were novices together, and actually met each other before. One could even say it was their friendship that brought them here. Sr. Gertrude's name was Bonnie Chapman, and Sr. Benedict was Margaret Mary Kirby. You would have thought it was the other way around. Bonnie (Sr. Gertrude) introduced Margaret Mary (Sr. Benedict) to St. Malachy's, the Actor's Chapel, on West 49th Street, and Margaret Mary introduced Bonnie to the devotion to the Sacred Heart of Jesus.

Both being alone the Thanksgiving of 1942, the two friends decided to do something adventurous and see a part

of New York Margaret Mary (from San Diego) never saw.
Bonnie (Sr. Gertrude, the New Yorker) took her to see the
Brooklyn Academy of Music on Lafayette Avenue where
they drooled over the billboards advertising the productions
heading there. Even then, BAM, the Brooklyn Academy of
Music, was considered rather avant-garde. This appealed
more to Margaret Mary, (Sr. Benedict) the poetess, than to
Bonnie Chapman, (Sr. Gertrude) the classicalist. They had
a lively discussion and lots of laughs while eating a great
Thanksgiving meal in Brooklyn Heights, and afterwards
while walking around discovered an actual monastery of
nuns right there on Willow Street.

"I still remember opening the door under the ominous
sign: Monastery Entrance." Sr. Benedict shared with me one
afternoon shortly after Sr. Gertrude's death. "We went inside
the chapel, like on tip toes, and wide eyes.

"Bonnie and I were whispering to each other and half giggling at the prospect of running into an actual nun. I had
had Franciscan nuns in grade school, but the sign outside
read: Dominican Nuns.

"I still remember Sister Gertrude's (Bonnie's) first words
garbled in her scarf: 'Oh my gosh, look, the Blessed Sacrament.' And indeed it was, over the altar in the middle of
the grille, as it still is today. We slipped silently into a pew
to pray, and before we knew it, the nuns were coming into
their chapel on the other side of the grille. We could only
hear the swish of their habits and sometimes the clinking
of a rosary. We didn't dare move or sneeze or make a noise.
Only a couple dim lights came on, and we heard someone
say something in Latin, and all the nuns responded...in

Latin, of course. There was another silence, rustle of habits, and a single clear voice sang out: '*Deus in adjutorium meum intende.*'" (*O God come to my assistance*—the opening verse of the Divine Office.)

Sr. Benedict giggled. "Of course, we didn't understand a word at that time, but we were mesmerized by the whole *ambience.* That was my word which I spoke to Bonnie over sixty years ago...we were mesmerized by the whole ambience. I think I was probably thinking of words that would rhyme with *ambience.* Sr. Gertrude was simply awe-struck by the drama of it all." Sr. Benedict stopped talking for a moment, caught up in the memory, or just choked up too much to go on.

I sat quietly and sipped my tea. Sr. Benedict smiled her girlish grin and went on. "We stayed to the very end, and when we were leaving as quietly as possible, there was a nun standing by the door. I wanted to melt and disappear in the floor boards, but Bonnie immediately stepped forward and with her inimical New York accent, put her hand out, 'Glad to meet cha, Sista.' To our surprise, 'Sista' gave us back a broad smile, and in a stage whisper (Sr. Gertrude's expression) she told us she was locking the door, but we were always welcome, and had we ever been here before?

"Bonnie, who obviously assumed the leading role, spoke in her own stage whisper, 'No, Sista, we're from Manhattan, and were just exploring Brooklyn Heights for Thanksgiving; we never even knew there was nuns here.' And with that she waved for us to follow her, after which she locked the door. I looked over at Bonnie and kind of rolled my eyes. I thought maybe we were being held hostage or something!"

I laughed. "That must've been Sister Dominica, the old extern sister the older Sisters still talk about."

"That's right. My, Sister, you have a good memory. Sister Dominica. Well, she moved us into the office entrance where she could talk normal, and offered us a cup of hot chocolate, if I remember right. She told us they were Dominican nuns and that they had adoration of the Blessed Sacrament all night long. We were both pretty impressed and awe-struck. I think that was when I spoke and asked if we could come back again sometime. Sister Gertrude still thinks, well, thought that she was the one, but I was. Anyway, Sister Dominica was very kind and gave us a little square cut-out of their prayer times. It was like a holy card. That was Thanksgiving, 1942."

Sr. Benedict looked at me like she was expecting applause. Instead I just gave one clap. "That's marvelous, Sister Benedict, and to think within two years both of you would be inside as nuns."

"Yes, indeed. It seems like another lifetime. I became Sister Benedict which was my second choice for a name, after my uncle, you know. And Bonnie Chapman became Sister Gertrude of the Sacred Heart."

"That's right. I didn't realize you could submit names… what was your first choice?"

"I don't remember, dear." And we both laughed.

I knew them both, of course, from when I entered, and they surprised me when I somehow learned their ages. They seemed so young and enthusiastic about everything. Sr. Benedict still wrote her poetry, which I must admit was a little obtuse, and didn't always follow a correct meter, and Sr.

Gertrude entertained us with her dancing. I thought how differently the house is today and the stories that our modern novices will tell fifty years from now.

Sr. Benedict of the Heart of Mary began to fail more noticeably after Sr. Gertrude died. She stopped writing her poetry, and her eye-sight was going. The novices would visit the infirmary every week and would often read poetry to her, if she wasn't involved in a jigsaw puzzle or playing whist. Interestingly enough it was the twenty-fifth anniversary of the death of Sr. Dominica, when Sr. Benedict had a heart attack trying to move the card table by herself. She died before the EMTs got to her. We were standing there, silently praying, when they arrived, and I remember, it was the woman EMT who looked up at us from Sister's body, and in a stage whisper said, "She's gone, Sista."

Five

Election in Lent

In the morning let me know your love for I put my trust in you. Make me know the way I should walk; to you I lift up my soul. (Psalm 143, Tuesday Compline)

TWO WEEKS INTO Lent, Mother Rosaria's term came to an end, and we were facing the election of a new prioress. Sr. Anna Maria, the subprioress *in capite,* called for the Chapter to assemble on Wednesday of the second week of Lent, which was a little past the time when Mother's term ended, but when the bishop would be available to preside at the election.

You know well, Lord, that the election of a new prioress is both grace-filled and anxiety-city. Mother Rosaria was not re-electable as she had served two terms. She was a wonderful prioress, in my humble opinion, who served the Sisters with untiring devotion. We were novices together for a short time, and even then she was a great relief for all my nervous anxiety. She was always accident-prone. Well, she was the one who dropped the steaming potatoes! But even during her years as prioress little things would happen that I think endeared her to us. And it always kept her very merciful towards others' mistakes.

The election went into the afternoon, which was a first in all my time. I thought that this time, probably Sr. Anna Maria (subprioress) would be elected, and she got a number of votes in the first ballot, as did I, Lord save us. Sr. Thomas Mary got some votes, but there was one surprise that seemed to me, at least, to be the breath of the Holy Spirit over the whole thing. Sr. Gerard came to the chapter room from the infirmary. "It's my last election. This time, I'm sure I'm electing the prioress who will bury me." She always added a "positive" note to every situation.

"Oh, Sister Gerard, we could all be saying that, don't be so gloom and doom." This was Sr. Catherine Agnes (SCAR) saying this, herself in the infirmary. She was always contradicting everything Sr. Gerard would say. I think it helped both of their blood pressures.

"You're right, Sister, more than half the community could be in the infirmary before the next election." Everyone gave a half-laugh to her half-truth. But it seemed like everyone plunged into a moment of silent prayer. It was almost tangible. I think that's when the breath of the Holy Spirit swept over the room.

By the next ballot, by a large majority, we had our new prioress. Sr. Bernadette Mary. I was so happy because she was my favorite candidate from the beginning. Sr. Bernadette had been infirmarian for a number of years. Before that she was in charge of the kitchen for even more years. She is unassuming and humble. I don't think I've ever heard

her raise her voice or speak uncharitably about anyone. She
was also very prayerful and for years now has had the 2:00
a.m. guard, except for the nights she's keeping watch in the
infirmary. Most all of the voting Sisters knew what a good
infirmarian she was, and if half of them were going to be in
the infirmary, Sr. Bernadette Mary would be a good prioress.

Mother Bernadette for me is like a combination of Mother
John Dominic, Mother Agnes Mary, and Mother Rosaria all
rolled into one. It was truly the Holy Spirit who "rigged"
that election. Such a blessing!

We all have such different, and often fascinating, vocation stories. This should surprise me? As Sr. Gertrude used
to say, "There are no small roles...we're each a 'star' to God
who created the moon and the stars." Well, Mother Bernadette was from Staten Island. That in itself was a revelation
to me, as she never really spoke much about her childhood,
and because I never knew anyone from Staten Island. Oh
there was Clayton Whatshisname who worked in the sorting
room at the Public Library who took the Staten Island Ferry
to and from work every day and talked about it like a kid
would. It only cost him a nickel.

Mother Bernadette told me she rarely went to Manhattan, which I found very strange. How could you not? She's
never seen a Broadway show. But she did spend her Satur-
days babysitting and watching a lot of TV. Her name in the
world was Phyllis Shapiro. I only learned this when I went
into her office for the first time after she was elected.

"Phyllis *Shapiro*, such a name you should have?" I was
taking a chance being so bold, but Sr. Bernadette often
laughed at my exaggerated Yiddish accent. "I never knew

you were Jewish, only now do I learn this; not just 'Mother', but a Jewish Mother at that?"

She laughed her always hearty, but controlled, laugh. "My father was Jewish; my mother was Catholic. My father didn't believe in God; my mother didn't always go to Mass, but she loved the Blessed Mother. I went to St. Christopher's Catholic School on Lisbon Place till high school. They couldn't afford Catholic high school."

I quietly sat and listened. "One Saturday night I was at a neighbor's babysitting; the kids were in bed, so I settled down for a movie on TV. Completely by chance it was *The Song of Bernadette* with Jennifer Jones. I was enthralled. I couldn't imagine what it must've been like for poor Bernadette Soubirous. The movie was better than my confirmation retreat of which I don't remember a single thing; we didn't even pray the rosary. The big gift I got from that retreat was meeting a boy..."

"Oh?"

"No, it's not what you think. He was in one of my silly group discussion things, and he mentioned that his sister was a nun in Brooklyn. Wow, I thought, like Sr. Bernardette when she grew up and left Lourdes. I didn't know there were real nuns anymore. So I came here to visit one cold winter afternoon. I forget why we didn't have school. Anyway, it was Sister Imelda who welcomed me the first time, and even made me hot cocoa. And on my way out, I went through the wrong door, it was a retreatant's door to their enclosed garden, and there she was..."

"Who? Sister Imelda?" I was nearly tongue tied.

"No, Our Lady. That's the Lourdes Grotto in the retreatants' garden."

"Oh, of course. I haven't been in there for years. There's a statue of St. Bernadette there too."

"And two sheep. I was quite young at the time, of course, but when the idea of a vocation kept coming to me, I thought of this place more than any other. And when I learned I could let go of 'Phyllis' and take a religious name, the only name I wanted was Bernadette. And do you know, Sister Gertrude told me that Jennifer Jones's real name was Phylis. Phylis Lee Isley, from Tulsa, Oklahoma. We both had the same first name, even if hers is with only one 'l.'"

"And only Sister Gertrude would have known that!" We both got lost in our thoughts for the moment. I smiled at our new prioress.

"Well, you're certainly a young looking Bernadette, Mother. I remember when we were novices together for a short time before you were professed."

"Oh, I remember that too, and my goodness, I've been going on about my name, what I wanted to say was I want you to continue as novice mistress, and also keep your visits to the infirmary. My, how the Sisters appreciate that. And the novices, well, they couldn't have a better Sister to learn about our life than you."

"Thank you, Mother, that's very kind of you. And of course, I am most happy to continue as novice mistress; they keep me young, I think! I just keep praying we get some more."

"I know, Sister. All the monasteries are feeling the lack of vocations. Our novitiates are shrinking, and our infirmaries are getting bigger. Even there, I don't know how much longer we can care for some of the most aged Sisters. I'll depend on you to keep an eye out for me since I can't be there as much anymore."

And she smiled. Still the infirmarian at heart, I thought to myself. She reminded me of a little girl just for the moment. But that was a deceiving look, she would be a strong prioress ready to face all that lay ahead. Her first happy announcement was the Solemn Profession of three Sisters after Easter! I wanted to shout the "A" word, but I couldn't because it's Lent.

Six

Mercy Sunday 2006

Because with the Lord there is mercy and fullness of
redemption. (Psalm 130, Wednesday Compline)

It's BEEN A wonderful Easter Week, ending today with what
we now call "Mercy Sunday", thanks to Pope John Paul II.
Mother Bernadette raised all of our spirits very quickly; we
couldn't wait till the Sunday after Easter and the Solemn
Profession of three Sisters. It was a special joy for me, as I
came in as Novice Mistress for the final years of their novitiate. Sr. Kolbe, Sr. Diana, and Sr. Cecilia.

Missing from their little group was Sr. Maureen. Sister
had moved to the professed side of the house when I was
assistant novice mistress, so I didn't know her that well. Born
in Dublin, her family moved here when "Moira" was in high
school. She had the loveliest of singing voices and a wonderful Irish sense of humor. She was especially good with the
Sisters in the infirmary, and surprisingly enough, discovered
her gifts and calling was to serve the elderly and the dying.

Sr. Maureen knew of the Hawthorne Dominican Sisters from our talking about them. Sr. Elijah Rose loved the Hawthorne Sisters too and would talk to Sr. Maureen about their special charism of being "servants" of the Lord to those dying with cancer. Our Sr. Bruna went to their home in lower Manhattan the first year of Sr. Maureen's integration year, after which she (Sr. Maureen) asked to renew her vows instead of making Solemn Profession. She would visit Sr. Bruna faithfully several times a week; she often went with Mother. Sr. Maureen was a good driver, something Mother Rosaria shied away from. The drive back and forth gave them plenty of time to talk with each other, and Mother gave Sr. Maureen permission to make a retreat at the Sisters of Hawthorne's Motherhouse in Hawthorne, New York.

It was a retreat, but she told the Sisters from day one that she would be happy to help in their work. There was a male patient who was quite debilitated and needed someone to feed him. He just happened to have been originally from Ireland. So the superior of Rosary Hill asked Sr. Maureen if she would "spoon feed" this old man from Ireland. Sister was more than happy, and began that first evening with supper. She would talk to the Sisters in between times, but also spent a lot of time in their chapel. "They are truly on a hill," she told us when she returned. "I would walk to the bottom of the hill and back again every day. I woke up muscles in my legs I didn't know I had! Buried on the grounds is Mother Alphonsa, the foundress, who was the daughter of Nathaniel Hawthorne. Rose Hawthorne was a wife and mother, and a convert to the Faith. When her marriage ended, she could have fallen in with the literary social life of Manhattan, but she was moved to make a home for women dying with cancer. This soon included men, as well, and the work was begun. Another woman joined her in this apostolate, and they were the beginning of a new Dominican congregation of Sisters.

After Sr. Bruna died, Sr. Maureen realized how much she missed going to St. Rose Home, and how much she felt drawn to be with the dying. Mother Rosaria was wonderful in all this, and realized too that it was a special charism Rose Hawthorne was given, and has passed on to her "daughters" to this day.

And so our Sr. Maureen "crossed the Hudson" and transferred to the Hawthorne Sisters. She was able to be here for the Profession and was a bundle of joy at the reception afterwards. The Sisters could see that it was a providential move. She kept her name, Maureen, and is happy to "be a novice" again.

Sr. Kolbe's family from White Plains were here, which included four sisters and two brothers. Her first spiritual director, Fr. Kelsey, O.P., was one of the concelebrants. Sister's mother homeschools the children at least up to high school. They are a very devotional family. It was from being homeschooled that Sister learned about Saint Maximillian Kolbe and had a strong devotion to the Immaculate Heart. We've also read the works of Sr. Teresa Benedicta (Edith Stein) together. Sr. Kolbe has a keen mind and loves to study, but all in the context of the enclosed life. I think that's what brought her to us.

Sr. Diana, a former French chef, not only made Solemn Profession, but also made enough eclairs to last a week. Well, maybe two days. We were rather jubilant that it was the Easter season, and we would all be on diabetic alert! Sr. Diana is a multi-talented Sister, not just in the kitchen, but in the choir, and in art work. She's discovered iconography since she's been with us. I think Mother is planning to send her off to an icon workshop at one of our monasteries in France. Her family was small next to Sr. Kolbe's and were able to gather in the small parlor.

Sr. Cecilia, our musician, and budding organist, came to us from Sarasota, Florida, by way of Catholic University in Washington. We've been very blessed with Sisters who are talented and love music. Mama actually heard Sr. Cecilia once when she was chantress and intoned the Magnificat. It may have been the only time Mama was here for Vespers, but afterwards she said to me, "Such a blessing, the nun with the voice like Edith Piaf." And indeed, she has been a blessing.

I was afraid we might lose her as the community went into a musical slump after 9/11, but Sr. Cecilia actually helped us get through. I remember the first time she played her clarinet for all of us; it was the prioress's feast day recreation. I think we were all expecting Benny Goodman, at least that's what Sr. Gertrude was hoping for; but instead a classical Bach Sonata for clarinet. She held us all spell-bound.

Sr. Cecilia's uncle was a clown for Ringling Brothers, and we (well, Sr. Gertrude and the Sisters in the Infirmary, and I) always hoped "Uncle Bo" would come visit in his clown outfit. We finally got to meet Uncle Bo. He was dressed very formally in a nice pin stripe suit with a silk, but normal looking, bow tie. He told us he actually made it himself, and called it a "Bo tie." He didn't have a red nose and clown make-up on, but looked very dignified. He was also as charming as can be, and we weren't disappointed that much. He's also getting ready to retire from "the business." It's "too much of a circus." And our small group of Sisters in the parlor enjoyed him very much. He was also very proud of his niece, whom, he said, was the "spitting image of her mother." Sister's mother had passed away before Sister entered here, but if Uncle Bo is right, her mother was a very attractive woman. Sister's two brothers were also here. Neither one is following her in the musical world. They were both ecstatic over computer programming or some such.

Sometimes I can hear Mama in my head saying, "Such a world we're living in. What's it all coming to?" The young generation are all taken up with computers and getting instant information. Will they also learn to play music and listen to slow songs, and dream dreams? Is Uncle Bo part of a world that is being phased out? I hope not. I was snapped out of my day dreaming with Sr. Elijah Rose making a musical entrance.

She briefly joined us in our parlor with Sr. Cecilia's family. She was making the rounds, as it were. She was enjoying it all, I hope. When she asked to renew her vows, I wasn't sure why. I'm still not.

Sr. Elijah Rose is the most extroverted of the three still living in the novitiate. It didn't surprise me that she was making the rounds from one parlor to the other, and would make her entrance singing something. She has a natural and wonderful way with people. She often speaks about patients and patients' families she met when she was a nurse. I wonder if she's also thinking of the Hawthorne Sisters. After all, she knows the Sisters better than most of us do. Lord, I turn all that over to You. Your holy Will be done! But, Lord, I hope it's Your Will that she stays with us. While she's very out-going with people, there is also a deep interior life evident. She's in charge of the laundry right now, which is not the most extroverted job in the house. But she seems to love it. She loves the smell of clean sheets. Maybe that goes back to her nursing days too! She's also good with postulants and aspirants. They are usually sent to help out in the laundry, and Sister isn't scrupulous about keeping a perfect silence. I don't say anything. I remember Sr. Anna Maria and I were not the most silent sheet-folders either. The laundry room was like therapy. And Sr. Elijah Rose is a good "therapist."

I chatted briefly with Sr. Leah Marie before Vespers. She's been the assistant sacristan for the past two years, and loves it, even when there's extra to do, like today. After Mass she didn't make the rounds of the parlors, but went to Sr. Diana's as it had the least people. She and Sr. Diana are the two "artists" among the young sisters. We held off for a couple years, but Sr. Leah Marie also works in the wardrobe, sewing habits mainly, although she's been rather creative with aprons. Gone are the days of plain white or plain black aprons. She likes pastels and specializes in big pockets, something we all like.

Sr. Kateri visited the parlor of Sr. Kolbe. She's been fascinated by the whole concept of homeschooling, and I hope didn't dominate the conversation. But she also had beaded belts for all the siblings; everyone was thrilled.

Sitting here now in Squeak, I can't help but think about how much God's mercy is poured out on all of us, each according to our own needs and temperaments...and indeed, in our weaknesses and failures and fears. It's no small thing to come to know God's mercy in one's own life and how much we need it every day, all the time. No wonder we pray "*Lord, have mercy on us*" so much!

Rocking back and forth, I realize that the Lord also gives us all just a select group of people in our lives, some large, some small. Psalm 91 which we sing every Sunday night at Compline is one of my favorites:

It is he who will free you from the snare of the fowler who seeks to destroy you; he will conceal you with his pinions and under his wings you will find refuge.

The three of them prostrated themselves before the altar six or seven years ago and were asked one question: What do you seek? And they answered, "God's mercy and that of the community." And today they prostrated themselves again and vowed to live our life of holy obedience until death.

Lord, have mercy on us.

Seven

The Assumption 2006

You have laid me in the depths of the tomb, in places that are dark, in the depths. Your anger weighs down upon me; I am drowned beneath your waves. (Psalm 88, Friday Compline)

SPRING AND SUMMER seem to have flown by without much ado. Sr. Myriam had a few inquirers after Easter, but only a couple came to visit. One young woman came for a weekend retreat. Her name was Kelly. She was an architect and lived in lower Manhattan with four other females and one male *housemate*, another new term in my growing vocabulary. Sr. Leah Marie was a good reference for such things. According to Sr. Paula, Kelly had three hands; two attached to arms, and one cellular attached to her left hand. She was never without it. She also let Sr. Paula know she was terribly disappointed that there was no WiFi in the guest rooms. Sr. Paula thought she meant "Hi Fi" and said, "Oh, we don't play music in the guest quarters." Kelly left on Saturday afternoon after Sr. Paula told her the door would be locked after Vespers.

Another unpromising candidate named Arizona came for a weekend and brought her own food with her. Sr. Paula said, "We have very nourishing meals right here; tonight we're having pulled pork which is one of Sister Diana's specialties." Arizona informed her, "I am a vegan." And Sr. Paula said, "Oh, are you from Las Vegas?" Poor Sr. Paula; she should have lessons from Sr. Leah Marie. The "candidates" have to get through Sr. Paula in an unofficial way, before they get to Sr. Myriam, the vocation sister!

Sharbel came to see me after Easter and once at the end of June. No progress with his mother yet, but he was excited to tell me he was going to *do the Camino*. Even Sr. Leah didn't know what that was. Fr. Matthew very conveniently filled us in that it is a walking pilgrimage over the mountains from France to the Cathedral of Santiago (St. James) in Compostela in Spain. "It's a very holy journey," says he. It all sounds rather gruesome to me. But Sharbel assured me he was in good shape for it; he was going with two other guys, and he promised to pray for me at all the roadside shrines. I guess he quit his job; he never mentioned it. He would be gone the whole month of July and would come and tell me all about it on the Assumption, "assuming" I would be here. I don't where he thought I might be!

Today is such a beautiful feast. I offered my Communion for Sharbel, my returning pilgrim-nephew. I had prayed to St. James for him during his pilgrimage that St. James would keep him sober. I read that the Camino could be a little treacherous in spots. Not a word from him all month, so I'm just *assuming* he'll be here this afternoon. Lots of "assumptions."

Sr. Leah Marie, dashing reverently from the sacristy, caught me before Mass to tell me that Fr. Matthew wanted to see me for a moment in the little parlor after Mass. I couldn't imagine what that was about, and of course, it distracted me during the entire Mass, as I was looking at him for signs of illness or stress or frustration. He looked fine, although he could put on a few pounds. I knew he had had two bouts with malaria when he was in Africa; enough for him to return to the States and be told by his provincial that he couldn't return to the missions.

I also worried that he was going to tell me that his provincial was assigning him somewhere else, or he was going back to England, or even that he had been elected provincial himself. All these scenarios were running through my head during the Mass readings. I don't know what to do when that happens. So I tried to do what I tell the novices to do. Just offer up the distraction to the Lord; then it becomes your prayer. I know, it's pretty "lame advice," as Fr. Kitchens once told me during a three day conference he was giving us on contemplative prayer. But I've never found a better solution, so I just keep offering it all to Jesus. I guess in this case, it's also what I put in the chalice and on the paten, a practice Fr. Kitchens himself recommends.

Maybe it was news from Gwendolyn. I hadn't heard from her for several months. She was still living in London, and I know she was in regular contact with Ezra by email. Sometimes he would have a message for me from her. Maybe that's all this was, but then, my distraction turned to Gwendolyn; was she sick, or bankrupt, or going to the North Pole on a penguin expedition? One never knew with Gwen. She was almost eighty years old and still going strong. (I wonder if vegans can eat penguin? Do Eskimos eat penguins? Probably not; are there even penguins in Alaska? I wonder what penguin breasts would taste like? Such distractions fly into my poor head! Oy. *Concentrate on the Mass prayers, Baruch.*)

It must've been something in his homily or maybe just his tone of voice (or my on-going distraction) that brought me back to my first meeting Gwendolyn. I was a student at Barnard College, living at home with my folks and my little sister, Ruthie, and discovered Gwendolyn's little tea shop, Tea on Thames. It was gaining popularity among the college and university crowd, I think because it was quaint, and it was different. Coffee shops were popping up all over, but Tea on Thames was strictly tea. Gwendolyn herself looked like a bohemian artist with printed full skirts of many colors, junk jewelry on both arms and hands, and dangling earrings, but it was her Yorkshire, England, accent that made everyone feel special and like…well, like you were sitting in an English tea shop in York waiting for Sir Lawrence Olivier to walk in and order something eccentric.

She also knew my favorite tea was Earl Grey, and would have a pot ordered before I got my coat off and settled into my seat. Listening to Fr. Matthew brought it all back, as it was at Tea on Thames that I met Ezra. We became regulars very shortly after that, and Gwen silently followed our scenarios, although I had her fooled when I told her I had some big news to tell her. She was sure I was going to announce our engagement, and we wanted her to bake our wedding cake.

"I've got some big news, but you have to promise not to tell my sister." (Ruthie had been introduced to the Tea on Thames ambience, as Sr. Benedict would say.) "I'll tell you after Ezra arrives."

"Well, darling, I think that's so marvelous. I wondered if and when that would happen, not that I'm eavesdropping over your conversation the last five months…it's lovely … let me get you some special tea today." (That meant that she was going to sneak a little liqueur in a tea pot to celebrate.)

So she was quite taken aback when my big announcement was that I was going to be baptized and become a Catholic. Gwendolyn's initial disappointment was instantly turned to great joy, as she also knew we talked a lot about the Faith, and she herself was a 'Yorkshire Catholic' as she proudly put it. Much later on, she told me, she just tucked the marriage thing in the back of her head; thinking how it would be a grand Catholic wedding.

I regained my concentration during the *Lamb of God*. Sometimes the chant just has a soothing effect on me, and I was able to let go of my distractions for those few minutes and re-collect myself, as Mother John Dominic used to say. I would be receiving the Lord in Holy Communion in a few minutes and everything will be just fine. Kneeling there in the silence, I took hold of my rosary crucifix at my side.

Lord, I am not worthy that You should come to me, but free my mind and my heart from all distraction and all impurities. I am Yours, Lord, You know that. I accept all. I pray that Your Holy Will be done in all things.

After Holy Communion, I let myself be absorbed by the Lord's holy presence. Oddly, the words from Psalm 4 at

Compline came to mind: *You have put into my heart a greater joy than they have from abundance of corn and new wine.* And in my mind I added: bagels, rugelach, charoset, Earl Grey tea, and penguin chops.

I smiled to myself realizing how true that is, and I have always been a fan of *an abundance of corn and new wine.* Our closing hymn distracted me from my distraction and two minutes afterwards I was making my way to the little parlor. I entered ahead of Ezra's arrival, switched on the ugly florescent overhead light, turned it off, and preferred to sit in the semi-darkness and wait.

Two decades of the rosary later, Ezra opened the door on his side, and came in, flipping the overhead light on, on his side. I tried not to squint, and tried instead to smile.

"Shalom Shabbat," I said with a smile.

Ezra responded, "And a happy and peace-filled Sabbath to you, Sister *Baruch Atah Eloheneu.*" (Blessed be the Lord.) "Thank you for seeing me on such short notice. I have bad news, but also good news."

I sat speechless for the moment. My hand immediately retrieved my rosary crucifix. My head slightly bowed, I looked up and into his eyes through the metal crisscross bars of the grille. "Tell me the bad news first." I don't know why I said that except that I guess we want to get that over with, and still have the good news to comfort us afterwards. Like eating the required spoonful of lima beans before getting to the cream-puff pastries for dessert.

"I just had word this morning that Aunt Sarah died last night."

"Oh, Ezra. I'm so sorry. Dear Aunt Sarah, may she rest in peace." I blessed myself.

"She loved you, you know...from the very start."

"I know. I think she was always a little sad that I didn't become her niece-in-law. But she was always so understanding and accepting of you...of us!"

"She loved you even more when you became a nun; she told me that...more than once. I don't think she ever told you, but she told me how sorry she felt for you when your family kind of kicked you out when you became Catholic."

"Aunt Sarah was there; I'll never forget that. And you, my friend, she never understood why you had to 'leave New York to be passionate.'" We laughed. That was Aunt Sarah's line when Ezra left for the Passionists novitiate in Massachusetts.

Aunt Sarah was also Ezra's only relative living in New York City. His family lived outside of Buffalo. Sarah Goldman, Ezra's father's only sister, lived all her life on the West Side of Manhattan. She was what we used to call an old maid or a spinster. She was actually a talented seamstress and at one time had her own dress shop on Broadway and 90th Street. Unlike my mother, she never belonged to the Hadassah or any Jewish organizations; she didn't go to shul; and lived a quiet unassuming life. She doted on her favorite (and only) nephew, Ezra Goldman. When he was ordained a priest, she gave him a beautiful gold stole which she made by hand, and embroidered the Biblical verse in Hebrew: "My nephew, Ezra, the priest."

"Coffee, Father?" I was being very polite.

"Thank you, Sister, that would be most appropriate." He was also being formal, as we would with each other, kind of for fun, but his remark reminded me that Aunt Sarah was a great coffee drinker. She rarely wanted to join us at Tea on Thames for that very reason.

"I'll just be a minute or two; hold the good news for now." And I got up and exited the parlor, and scampered down the cloister to the little kitchen. As luck would have it, Sr. Paula was already fixing coffee for someone in the big parlor; so she poured a five cup pot's worth and a couple scones for us.

"Thank you, Sister, I guess there aren't any rugelach left from last week?"

"Fr. Goldman prefers Solomon's rugelach to my scones?" Spoken in her best imitation New York Jewish accent.

I laughed. "Such an extern Sister we should have that you notice everything, oy." It was Sr. Paula's turn to laugh.

"Rugelach for the priest, yes, I was hoping your scones would be on the plate this afternoon when Sharbel visits." (Such an extern Sister, indeed; she didn't forget a thing!)

Sr. Paula daintily replaced the scones with last week's apricot rugelach from Solomon's Deli down the street. I didn't tell her the rugelach were really for me which I'd gladly share "with the priest."

Settled in the parlor again, coffee and rugelach in hand, I reminisced about the first time I met Aunt Sarah. She came with Ezra to Thanksgiving dinner, six months before I became a Catholic. I had not yet shared with my family my "good news." Mama, I'm sure, was already thinking about the reception after Ezra and I were wed under the chuppa (the canopy under which a bride and groom stand in a Jewish marriage ceremony) at Temple Emmanuel on Fifth Avenue. Poor Mama. She was probably hearing the

shouts of *Mazeltov* when Ezra smashes the glass wrapped in
a linen bag, a gift from the Hadassah, and instead heard him
announce in the middle of our pumpkin pie that he had
become a Catholic.

"Aunt Sarah took it all in stride," I said without any
preface.

"Took what in stride?"

"Oh, I was just remembering that first Thanksgiving." We
had often spoken of it in the following years, and usually
whenever we were in Aunt Sarah's company.

"Your poor mother. Never got over it, I think, but they
did become friends years later."

That was true. For one thing, when my sister, Ruthie, died
and I was able to go home and sit Shiva with Mama and my
sister Sally, Aunt Sarah came to pay her respects. "She was
very kind at Shiva, and took care of things in the kitchen.
She was always very kind…" My voice cracked just a bit. I
couldn't swallow my rugelach.

"She was at my first Mass too, sitting up front, proud as
a peacock when I publicly thanked her for being there and
how much it meant to know I was always embroidered on
her heart. And I showed everyone my stole."

We sat silently for at least a minute. Long enough to wash
down the rugelach. I wasn't even at Fr. Matthew's first Mass,
but I later saw the photos and remember remarking how
happy Aunt Sarah looked. I never met his parents.

"So what's going to happen? Is your mother coming
down?"

"No, nothing's going to happen. There's no one to sit
Shiva. My mother never really kept in touch with her after

my father passed. In her meager belongings, I'm told were instructions to be cremated. Can you imagine! That's probably the most un-Jewish thing one can do! But it was all pre-arranged, and the ashes were to be given to me, apparently, to be 'spread at sea' when I'm deep sea fishing."

I just sat with my jaw opened, a little befuddled by this piece of information. "When you're deep sea fishing? When have you ever been deep sea fishing?"

"Exactly. I don't know where she got the impression I went fishing, let alone deep sea fishing." And we both got laughing at the absurdity of it all.

"I've probably told her at times that I've been in deep waters, but I didn't mean literally in the ocean!"

"She did know you always flew when you went to Africa and England, right?"

"Well, I never mentioned it specifically. Maybe she thought I travelled by ocean liner on a regular basis, and could just dump her off the side of the boat one night when no one was looking."

"Oh, Ezra!" And we got laughing. "You wouldn't do that, even if you could…would you?"

"Such a splash she would make… Aunt Sarah in her sewing bag."

"We shall pray for her soul. Poor Aunt Sarah. I'll get Mama and Papa on it immediately." It sounded almost facetious, but I meant it. They were both in my group of un-canonized communion of saints.

The bell for Terce sounded, and I quickly scurried to put everything on the turn for Sr. Paula to collect, and repeated to Ezra that we can do our own Catholic Shiva for Aunt

Sarah, and headed for the parlor door, when I remembered. "The good news! You haven't told me the good news!"

He was half way out the door on his side. "I'll tell you all about it later, but Gwendolyn is coming back after the new year." And the door closed. My mouth didn't. *Gwen is coming home! Gwen is coming home! That's wonderful good news. Thank you, Lord.*

Eight

Same Afternoon

I remember the days that are past: I ponder all your works.
I muse on what your hand has wrought and to you I stretch
out my hands. (Psalm 143, Tuesday Compline)

THE NOON MEAL on Solemnities is always a step up from the
rest of the week, and we may have music instead of our usual
reading. But we had a special reading for the Assumption
at noon, which I've completely blocked from my memory.
A senior moment, perhaps. I was also distracted, thinking
about Gwendolyn's return to New York next year. I wondered what was up. She hadn't been back to visit since a little
after 9/11. That's over five years. I also hadn't heard directly
"from the penguin's mouth," as she would put it. I hope it
wasn't for medical reasons, and if it were, that it wasn't anything serious. Gwendolyn is probably the last friend I have
in the world.

Sr. Cecilia, Sr. Sheila, and I were on the dish-drying team.
We finished up earlier than usual, and nodded to each other
in silence, except for Sr. Cecilia who sometimes hummed

while drying dishes. She's usually excused with a smile as we all know she's a musician, and sometimes they can't get songs out of their heads. And it's like she doesn't realize she's humming. In my day, the humming would have stopped immediately with a glare from SCAR. Sr. Cecilia is progressing very quickly with her organ playing, to all of our delight.

Sr. Sheila continues to do quite well with us and seems very content. While she lives in the novitiate, she doesn't attend novitiate classes and has a regular charge now. She's helping Sr. Aquinas in maintenance, as well as being one of the refectorians, meaning she sets the tables, lays out the serving spoons, and generally straightens things out in the refectory. She's taken to dry mopping the floor as well, which used to be a job for Sr. Bertrand. Sr. Bertrand likes to tell the other Sisters in the infirmary, "I'm a retired crumb-mopper; now I'm just a crummy flopper." She'd say this when flopping into one of the so called "lounge chairs" in the infirmary. She'd peer out at the room over her rimless glasses to see Sisters' reactions, which were minimal after the first couple times. Most acted like they didn't hear her. Only Sr. Gerard would roll her eyes and mumble, "The end is near." The first time I heard her say that I didn't know if she meant the end of the world, the end of her jig-saw puzzle, or the end of Sr. Bertrand, till I saw her, on another occasion, close her right eye, raise her left eye brow, and glare over at Sr. Bertrand flopping into the chair. I can still hear Sr. Benedict telling me, "It's the little things that get on our nerves, otherwise we'd be proud of our sanctity!"

Having finished the dishes, Sr. Cecilia was heading to practice the organ, Sr. Sheila was heading for the mop, the other novices were heading for the chapel or their cells, and I was heading for the back door.

It was a clear day with just enough crispness in the air to remind you that autumn would soon be upon us. I wandered out to the cemetery just to get some fresh air and to remind my cemetery-communion of saints that my nephew, the pilgrim, would be by to see me. The other Sisters don't seem to visit the cemetery so much, so it's usually always very quiet and peaceful here. The din from the traffic outside the enclosure wall disappears from consciously being aware of it. It was rather like a dull hum from Sr. Cecilia.

Mother Bernadette had added several wooden benches under the various trees that decorate the otherwise plain cemetery. I made my way to the one under the oak tree and closest to Sr. Gertrude. I brushed off the pile of leaves making their own cushion of various greens and yellows, and sat down.

Looking out on the grave stones of all the Sisters, I realized that we have more out here than we do inside. Our numbers are shrinking, as Mother Bernadette had said, and we aren't getting as many inquiries or young women coming for retreat who might be thinking of our life, or they turn out to be Kellys or Arizonas. A couple articles we've read in the refectory have talked about the "millennials" coming of age, and not used to making long term commitments. I guess it's a little frightening to think about the enclosure, and that you will spend the rest of your life in one place. I can see a restlessness in our novices, and wonder how it will all turn out.

There was a note in my mailbox after dinner from Sr. Myriam, our vocation Sister, or directress, or promoter, we never know what to call her. She checks the computer every day and makes the initial contact with anyone who inquires by phone, mail, or now, email. She's working with a Dominican Father on creating a "website." Sr. Gerard shivered when she first heard that; she hates spiders, and anything connected with them. "Why does it have to be called a 'web-site?' We aren't spiders." She almost fell out of her chair when Sr. Leah told her, "It's because we're now connected to the world-wide-web."

Sr. Myriam also meets with potential aspirants, and if they pass her initial scrutiny, (and Sr. Paula's unsolicited observations) she may ask other Sisters to sit in on a parlor with the young woman. Her note was inviting me, or asking me, to meet a young woman tomorrow afternoon, along with Sr. Catherine Agnes (SCAR) and maybe one other. I like doing that. It's been a long time now, but I remember when I first met with the novice mistress and Mother. I think I must've tripped over all my words and probably appeared young and foolish. I smile now, because that's what we're looking for—young and foolish. Not foolish in the way the world thinks of that word, but in the sense of the ancient monks and nuns who left everything to live for Christ alone. The world thought them to be foolish. To give "it" all up. "It," of course, stood for lots of things: a husband, children, a family, a career, travel, money, fun, adventure, grandchildren. "It" is a big word indeed.

My family, well certainly my mother and brother and sisters, thought I was foolish for giving "it" all up. After all, I

had been a student at Barnard College; I had a future ahead
of me; I was a product of the '60s, and we were re-inventing
womanhood. Papa was probably the only one who understood that there is a call deeper than the call of the wild
world, deeper than the ordinary fleshing out of a livelihood.
I didn't know his secret, or how he knew, but I knew there
was a deep spiritual part of him that was deeper than the
other fathers I'd met. Mother John Dominic saw that deep
part of him too, and knew just how to reach it…to touch it.
It's that deep part which opens us up to faith and to God's
glorious grace. Maybe Papa saw it in me because he knew
it in himself. Such thoughts I should have in the cemetery?

I had to laugh at myself, sitting on my wooden bench
under the oak tree, self-analyzing everyone else. That was my
brother David's job. He was the psychiatrist with an office
on Park Avenue. He thought I was the most foolish, and
couldn't speak to me or visit me for thirty years. And then,
God began to scratch away at the mound of the world's dirt
over his deep spot, covered over with a lifetime of…of what?
The world's promises for happiness? Or as Sr. Leah Marie
once put it so astutely, "All the trinkets of contemporary
hedonism." (My goodness, I thought, little Sr. Leah may
have designed clothes, and donned junk jewelry, but she
thought deep thoughts under her once technicolored hair!)

David never married except to his career, and in one
"foolish escapade," fathered a son. Maybe not "foolish" completely, as Sharbel is the son, and Sharbel is a fine young
man who wants to be a priest. And now his mother thinks
he's the foolish one, for throwing "it" all away. Her "it" is
mainly, I suppose, being a doctor and living a prosperous

life in David's duplex on the Upper East Side, left to him in his father's will. She is herself a neurosurgeon living in the Hamptons on Long Island. She's also a devout Catholic, according to Sharbel, but I guess she misses seeing that deep spot that goes so much deeper than a wonderful career, or the lobes of the brain. Maybe he prayed to St. James to do some brain surgery!

I stretched out my legs, which felt really good. It's something we don't do in choir, the refectory, or the community room. I should pray more earnestly for Sharbel's mother, Dr. Olivia Ghattas. I've only met her once and was rather impressed with her. I love that she named her son Sharbel. We read the life of St. Sharbel many years ago in the refectory, and I've had a kind of devotion to him ever since. His name in Arabic (I think?) means "Sharb—story of" and the "el" is God. *The story of God.* It's wonderful to think that we are each like a chapter in the Story of God. And it's a true story, that's what makes all the difference. That's the "it" that makes our lives so mysterious…so foolish.

Sr. Gertrude, her grave not far from my out-stretched feet, saw "it" that way too. For her, our life was a great drama and our "stage" was this old stone building with wooden floors that creaked in places, but got us where we wanted to go. The set had many lovely rooms, but the chapel was center stage. Our cells were our dressing rooms; even the grille in the parlors she called the "lovely curtain" that separated us from the audience.

Sr. Gertrude lived out of the deep spot, but she hid, like stage make-up, behind her theatrics and her Broadway musicals. "It's the Lord living in you that knows the whole plot and how it will end. Let Him be the Director, the Producer, and your Leading Man." And she would laugh. The deep spot.

Fr. Matthew (Ezra) once mentioned in one of our more spiritual chats that he's afraid lots of priests and religious lose sight of that deep spot too. He didn't call it a "deep spot" but the interior depth within the soul. I used to call it "my quiet place." I still call it that, and thank You, Lord, I still go there…my inner space. It's such a blessing! I hope it has deepened over the years; I know it has, because the surrender to You, Lord, is in that place within us, which is deeper each time we give in. This is a kind of quiet place too, the cemetery. Makes us remember the days that are past…and what is to come.

A chilly breeze suddenly passed over the open field of graves, and the thought that a cup of tea would *hit the spot* right now. So I made my way back to the monastery, checking Sr. Myriam's note in my pocket… *Hummm*, I hummed. The girl's name was Havana. I thought to myself, *My goodness, Baruch, girls have funny names these days.*

Nine

Tea for Two

Lord, make haste and answer; for my spirit fails within me. Do not hide your face lest I become like those in the grave. (Psalm 143, Tuesday Compline)

AN AFTERNOON TEA would be lovely, even more so because I would have it in the infirmary. We can't just sit in the refectory and have a cup of tea and chat like "in the world." But one could have a cup of tea anytime in the infirmary. Sr. Jane Mary, our former prioress, always welcomed the company. I think she was the loneliest of the infirmary Sisters maybe because she had been a strict prioress and didn't have that grace of warming up the Sisters. I've had a few "hard knocks" from her myself, but I've learned to let go. She did the best she could at a time that was very strange or difficult—those years of renewal after Vatican II.

We also knew that she had been a young widow when she entered, but never knew the whole story or what wounds she carried with her. She didn't fit in with the jig-saw puzzlers, Whist players, or beaded baggers, but she liked to read. I

67

knew that from my years as librarian, when she was prioress. She was actually the one who introduced novels into the library and a few secular magazines like *Time* and *National Geographic*.

So I found her by the picture window, her latest novel sliding off her lap, as she nodded off, and jumped awake. "How 'bout an afternoon tea, Sister Jane Mary?" My presence behind her chair gave her a second jump, and startled her even more by my reflection in the window, but she laughed at herself. "I would be delighted."

She got up and went with me to the infirmary kitchen where I turned on the new electric tea kettle, and grabbed a couple mugs.

"Humph, those ugly old mugs, let's have real tea cups; something with a little elegance."

I smiled. I had forgotten she was originally from Canada and was from a rather well-to-do family. She would have grown up with elegance. "Indeed, we shall, my father never drank his tea in a mug; he said it 'demeaned the brew.'"

So we sat at the kitchen round table with an ugly plastic oil-clothe table cover, in gaudy autumn colors, and sipped our tea in elegant tea cups with saucers.

"My nephew is coming after None. He wants to be a Dominican, you know, but he's loaded down with college loans, so he's working for a couple years."

"Oh, yes, he's your brother's boy, as I recall?"

"That's right. His mother's also a doctor on Long Island."

"How nice." She sipped her tea and looked at me over her cup. "He'll have to get a canonical dispensation, you know."

I stopped sipping. "A dispensation? For what? College loans can be paid off."

"He's illegitimate, my dear."

I nearly spit my tea clear across the table. "Sister Jane Mary!" I was more shocked by her tone than the implication, but I never even thought of that; I didn't know that. It wasn't his fault his mother wasn't married. "Whatever do you mean?"

She spoke without any emotion, like she always did, like she was teaching a class on the eschatological significance of the habit. "Well, unless Canon Law has changed, and it may have, my dear, a boy born of an unwed mother is an impediment to the priesthood." I gulped the rest of my suddenly un-elegant tasting tea. "But a dispensation is easily had. I had a friend in Montreal whose son applied to a Benedictine abbey in France, and he had to get a dispensation for that very reason."

I recovered quickly from the initial shock. "Oh, then, he won't have any problem. Besides, he's a good boy."

Sr. Jane Mary just half-laughed. "His moral character is not the problem, my dear."

I wished she wouldn't call me "dear" so often. She's beginning to get on my nerves. So, looking very elegantly at my wrist watch, "Oh dear, look at the time. I'm almost late for None."

"Go, dear, I'll take care of the dishes."

Good, I thought, *that'll give the old bag something to do. Oh dear, I'm sorry, Lord, I know You love the old bag with an Infinite Love.* And I laughed at my uncharitable thoughts, thinking of our line from the Confiteor at Compline: *I have sinned in my thoughts, and in my words, and in what I have done and what I have failed to do.* I was thinking about that as I genuflected, holding on to the form at my side. I knelt, waiting for Mother to begin the "*O Sacred Banquet*" (the antiphon written by St. Thomas Aquinas, prayed before each hour of the Office in the presence of the Blessed Sacrament). Looking at Our Lord in the Holy Eucharist, I calmed my nerves and knew He would work everything out for Sharbel. I wondered if he was in the extern chapel. I wondered if his father, my brother, David, was listening in, as it were. If all those who go before us, listen in. If they know what we are doing. I know they are all in Christ now, and perhaps that's a big part of Purgatory. Sometimes I smile to myself thinking Mama and David are now Catholics. There must be such joy in Heaven and in each one's soul when we come into the fullness of truth and the best part, that the Truth is a Person. Does that surrender, that falling into the arms of Christ, happen immediately upon death? Is the "choice"...the "yes" to God then? And is Purgatory our being made ready for the fullness? Purified of all our penalties because of our sins, but purified as well of all our ignorance, unbelief, sarcasm, and mistakes. Mama probably looked around at Purgatory and said, "Such a blessing."

I try not to think too hard on these things, but to cast them into the Heart of Jesus, and to pray for their salvation, and to offer up my little penances for them. I can't do anything as heroic as the saints we read about; I'm too weak and schlepping my own baggage around.

So I don't know if David knows about us, especially about his own son. But I like to think that he does. If that's true, than Mama is Sharbel's biggest intercessor or will be one day. I mean, she can talk to the original Sharbel who was such a miracle worker. Again, I can hear Mama saying, "We should know such people in Heaven?"

Sr. Anna Maria, the subprioress, began the *Oh Sacred Banquet*, which means that Mother is occupied elsewhere. "... *and a pledge of future glory is given to us.*" We are reminded of Eternal Life every time we pray the Office.

None is a little hour and goes quickly. I waited for a minute afterwards before quietly leaving my stall. I didn't see Sr. Paula at the Office, which is not unusual for the little hours, she's kept pretty busy with visitors and guests. I popped into the little kitchen to see if she was there, but no such luck. Maybe she was already taking coffee and chocolate chip cookies to the parlors. So I quickly made my way to my "reserved" parlor, passing a scouring Sr. Annunciata whom, I presume, was not happy the parlors were all taken. She turned slightly to see who it was entering the little parlor. I kissed my scapular. It's our way of saying "excuse me." Or a little penance if we make a mistake. I'm afraid I did it out of spite because she looked to see who reserved the parlor she probably wanted. I realized I was not in a very charitable mood; maybe I was just anxious about my parlor with Sharbel.

I opened the door, and he was not there. So I sat in the creaky old wooden chair that begged to be retired. Maybe he got chatting with Sr. Paula. I heard the single chime for the half hour from the grandfather clock in the cloister corner. Hmmmm. Where could he be? Maybe the subways were having problems. Maybe he forgot the time. Maybe he forgot the day. I went through my litany of "maybes."

I was able to enjoy a lovely gift we were given in honor of Sr. Benedict. It was from her prison pen pal of thirty some years ago. He was released from San Quentin in the year 2000. He would send some very nice items to us as gifts. We have at least ten coffee-table books on various subjects in the library, all given by William Watson III. William got a decent janitorial job at a Catholic high school somewhere in Wyoming. Sr. Benedict was so proud of him. She announced that "he was now a contributing member of society in Wyoming." At least four of us said, "Wyoming? Where *is* Wyoming?" I wasn't too sure myself, as Mama used to say, "It's one of those square states west of the Mississippi."

Willie Watson from Wyoming, we began to call him. One year, for her Golden Jubilee, Willie subscribed Sr. Benedict in one of those Fruit of the Month Clubs. Every end of each month, we got a crate of some sort of fruit for the next month. Sr. Benedict would write to him and rave about each fruit. She didn't tell him she broke out in hives over the strawberries, but the rest of us enjoyed them.

A week to the day that Sr. Benedict died, a large box arrived with a card. "In Memory of my Best Friend and dearest Sister Benedict. With love from William Watson." It was two beautifully framed portraits of Pope Benedict XVI. He knew how excited and thrilled she was when he was elected pope. Mother put one in the cloister right before the refectory entrance, and one in the extern parlor, so it would seem like we were being visited by himself. And Mother added, "And it reminds us that we have Papal Enclosure."

I sat staring at Pope Benedict, all by himself at the moment, and wondered where that nephew of mine could be. It was quiet in there without any visitors so I prayed the Divine Mercy chaplet, something which I'm sorry to say, I don't do very often. I know the poor world needs lots of mercy. I thought of my sister, Ruthie, and my two brothers, Josh and David. And many people at this very moment are in need of an out pouring of God's mercy. I wondered what Willie Watson of Wyoming (wherever that is!) was doing right now. Sr. Benedict probably has a poem in her file somewhere about "I'm just a roaming in Wyoming." After a half hour, I ran out of mercy and left.

I went back to the little kitchen. Sr. Paula was rinsing the plates and cups from the other parlors.

"Did you see my nephew, Sharbel, Sister? He was supposed to be here for None and meet with me afterwards."

"No, Sister, I didn't see him at all, and I've been in and out of the front parlors all afternoon. Did you check the phone?"

"Oh, I didn't. That's a good idea. Thank you, Sister. If he shows up, please call me or come get me; I'll be up in the library." I headed down the cloister for our little public phone room. Mother Bernadette, bless her, had it painted after scraping off the wall paper from a hundred years ago. It was one of the first things she did. It also had a voice-mail recorder connected with the main phone in the front entrance. I checked. No messages.

Well, he wasn't in the best of shape when I last saw him. He probably forgot. And I headed for the library to check the computer there. We had graduated to email. Maybe ten of us had our own email account. The community computer was on its own carrel in the corner of the library behind the one row of books. Sr. Antonia had reorganized the library since my day. It wasn't quite as "homey" as I tried to make it. But the computer was convenient. I don't think Sharbel knew my email address, and I know I didn't have his, but I would check anyway.

It had been a while since I checked any emails, and the machine wanted my username which I thought was SIS-TERSHALOM, and then my password, of all things. And they didn't match. So much for that. I uttered a few unsavory words I didn't know were lying dormant under my coiffure. I left the library disgruntled over the world of technology and my afternoon shot when I could have done something... something spiritual. I about-faced back into the library and over to the very bottom drawer of the librarian's desk. I used to have a little stash of butterscotch candies there, just in case someone got a fit of coughing or something in the library. The drawer was empty! In the corner of the desk was the box with the "books-out" cards in them. I curiously looked through to see what Sisters had what books out, which was none of my business, of course, but an old habit from when I was librarian. I suddenly felt "naughty," as Mama would say. Guilty. A snoopy old busy-body at my age! Lord, have mercy.

I put the cards back neatly in the box, and made my way out again. I thought, *Well, at least I'll have a whole bag of sins to bring to tonight's Compline: thoughts, words, deeds.* And omission. I usually can't think of any sins of omission. Fr. Meriwether didn't express his humor very often, but I'll always remember in his class on "sin" he told us, very straight-faced, that "sins of omission were sins we were supposed to commit and didn't."

I went down a back staircase, and out to the side lawn. There, sitting all by herself in our glider-seat was Sr. Annunciata. My first reaction was to turn around and go back and out another way, to ignore her.

But I didn't. She looked very much alone on the old glider whose green and yellow was chipped and peeling. At least it still glided back and forth without jerking or getting stuck. I went over to Sister with my best smile, "Mind if I join you, Sister?"

She was taken aback. But returned my smile, and brushed off the leaves on the seat next to her. "Aren't you cold, Sister? It's a little nippy out here."

"Not yet...I like the cold." A bit of a silent pause, and I jumped in, "I'm sorry, Sister, for taking the small parlor this afternoon if you were planning to visit with someone. I was meeting with my nephew who never showed up."

"I wasn't expecting company, Sister. I'm sorry if I gave you that impression. I had just come from seeing Mother to ask her permission to go to the funeral of my niece, poor girl, she hemorrhaged after child birth, and they couldn't save her."

"Oh, that's awful, Sister. I'm so sorry to hear that. How old was she?"

"Sixteen...they used to call it 'sweet sixteen.'..remember? I think I was just feeling very hurt when I passed you in the cloister. So don't fret about it."

"Isn't it funny, well, not 'funny' but strange, you know what I mean, that we can get very attached to our nieces and nephews. I guess they're like the children we never had."

"Yes, I think that's true. Billie was my only niece...my sister's only child."

"Billie?" (*Such a name for a girl?* I'm thinking to myself.) "Wilhelmina was her name, but they called her Billie."

"Oh, gee, Wilhelmina is such a beautiful name."

"I know." She paused for a moment and looked at me. "That was my name."

"Wilhelmina...such a beautiful name, Sister, but we won't call you Billie."

"Thank you, Baruch, and we won't call you Barry." We laughed at our sudden silliness.

I suddenly felt very close to poor Sr. Annunciata. I didn't really know her very well. She was close to the little circle of German Sisters when she entered. She was a novice after I was solemn professed, but she's not much younger than me. She never frequented the library, at least when I was there, and I just misjudged her, I think.

"Well, Sister," I said getting up from the glider. "I am a little chilly. If you need a companion to go to the funeral with you, I would be honored."

"Thank you, Sister. But Mother said 'no.' I guess a niece is not immediate enough family."

I sat down again without saying a word. A full minute passed before I muttered, "I'm so sorry, Sister. I know what you're feeling; I've been there."

Sister took my hand, "I know you have, and I've always admired how you've gotten through those moments, especially 9/11. I accept Mother's refusal. Our life is really separated from the world, and times like these are powerful reminders. My being here and praying is the best thing I can do. You can be my companion in prayer." Her eyes were lined with tears ready to fall.

"And so I shall. And I'll put the infirmary sisters on it; you know they have a rosary group that prays together every afternoon at four o'clock.

"Thank you, Sister…now you better go in or you'll catch a death of cold."

I smiled and did as she said. I bypassed the little kitchen and went first to the infirmary and then to the chapel. I'm glad that "feelings are not facts" as I was feeling something very ominous about my dear, one and only, nephew. And feeling just a little proud that I didn't have any sins of omission in my bag…yet.

Ten

Thanksgiving 2006

He has put into my heart a marvelous love for the faithful ones who dwell in his land...I will bless the Lord who gives me counsel, who even at night directs my heart. (Psalm 16, Thursday Compline)

THE NOVICES WERE all busy in their community room making decorations for the refectory; the simple professed Sisters were helping Mother Bernadette make turkeys out of apples with toothpicks and cocktail umbrellas. The infirmary Sisters suspended the beaded bags industry and were feverishly making beaded napkin rings for the refectory, in an array of autumn colors. Mother herself locked her office door and was in the infirmary helping with the beaded napkin rings.

I only found this out by a surprise visit to the infirmary. Sr. Paula was down with the flu and confined to the infirmary for the first time in her monastic life! Poor thing. Sr. Anna Maria was filling in for her, sitting at the front desk for the various and sundry visitors. We would normally be "closed" on holidays, but Thanksgiving brought with it lots of food, mostly pies and a couple already-cooked turkeys. I think people think that we are half starved in the enclosure or that we never get treats, like candy. With all the candy we get, we should all be diabetics by Solemn Profession. Well, we do try to be abstemious—a favorite word of Sr. Catherine Agnes (SCAR). Since her arrival in the infirmary five years ago, however, I'm surprised she hasn't broken out in pimples, like an adolescent. She must have befriended a lot of people in her younger days as she's inundated with boxes of Walt Whitman Samplers.

I offered to help with the beaded napkin rings, to be politely dismissed by Sr. Gerard. "Thank you, Sister Baruch, but we can handle it. Besides, Mother is helping."

I suddenly had a twinge of guilt, wondering if I came across as pushy to them or always needing to control things. I know that wanting to control things can be a tendency of mine. Mother Jane Mary pointed that out to me after my fortieth birthday. Learning to control our tongues comes early on, and can be mastered with a few blunders and lots of mercy and forgiveness along the way...controlling one's thoughts is something else. I was happy to learn years ago that St. John Cassian underlines it as a difficult monastic practice. It's quite ancient, going back to the desert fathers who would say, "Sit in your cell and watch your thoughts."

So I simply whispered an "I'm sorry...they look beautiful." And moved on to Sr. Paula's room. I had the urge to curtsy to Sr. Gerard, but I controlled the urge. I'm getting better at that too, as I'm taking pride in my humility. Mother Bernadette looked up at me with an assuring smile and nod.

Sr. Paula looked awful in an oversized flowered bathrobe and a night veil. She was sitting in an infirmary geri-chair working on a puzzle she called Sudoku, putting groups of nine numbers in order.

"You're the only one to come see me except for Mother who was in right after Mass. Today of all days, I should be out front for all the turkeys."

"Not to mention the candy they bring."

It took a few seconds, but she got it, and laughed. "Especially Mrs. Gobblebee." And we both laughed.

"Oh, I've forgotten about her....Does she still come around?" Mrs. Gobblebee lived in the Flatbush neighborhood of Brooklyn. She used to come with her mother who was a friend of Mother John Dominic. Every year they would bring one or two cooked turkeys to the monastery. It became a tradition. She pronounced her name with a long "O", but we always jokingly called her Gobble Gobble Gobblebee.

"No, she died a few years ago, and after that there wasn't even a single drum stick." And we giggled like high school girls.

"Well, I'm glad you're here and getting some rest." Sister swallowed and looked up at me and nodded.

"I don't like the flu. I don't feel bad except for my head, chest, and stomach."

I laughed. "Well, thank goodness your feet don't hurt." And we laughed some more.

Changing the subject, Sister Paula plunged ahead, "I still haven't seen that nephew of yours. Have you heard from him?"

"No, I haven't. That's what's got me worried. I think it was the day after the Assumption that he called and apologized, but said he was terribly sick from his trip. He was thinking of going to New Haven or Alaska with his 'buddies' when he felt better. He would see me before the holidays. I don't know if he means today or Christmas. And New Haven or Alaska? These young people certainly like to travel! I was going to suggest London, and maybe he could help Gwen pack, but I haven't heard from him or from her." We soaked in a moment of silence. "What's going on with you?"

"Not much. I'm feeling better, blessed be God. But tell me, Sister Baruch, what do you think of that Havana?" Havana was the aspirant.

"Well, I've only met with her once. Sister Myriam seems happy with her. I did find her a little strange, but I'm not sure how. I can't put my finger on it."

"Oh, I'm glad to hear you say that. I find her strange too, and I've met a lot of strange birds coming in and going out of that door, but she takes the cake."

I laughed. "You certainly have, and you know just how to handle them. What is it about Havana you find strange?"

"I can't put my finger on it either, like you said. Maybe she needs glasses, but she has a funny way of looking at me. My mother used to tell me about a friend of hers who was 'wall-eyed', like one eye isn't looking at you, but the other one is. And then, she seems nervous, and laughs a lot, not that that's so strange, others have that nervous laughter too, but she's…well, she's kind of rude, you know. She was the one laughing when the lamp crashed on the altar. And, this is silly, but she never calls me 'Sister' and you know me, Sister, I'm not one for formalities, but once she kind of brushed me aside to get to the parlor, and completely ignored me.

Didn't say excuse me or nuttin." Sister stressed the double negative with a head nod.

"I noticed the 'Sister' thing too, now that you mention it. She never called me or Sister Myriam 'Sister.' Maybe she didn't grow up with nuns, and didn't learn all that."

"It could be. Some of these young girls coming to visit just stare at you. I half expect them to stand there with their mouths open saying 'duh...' "

She did a perfect imitation. And we laughed so hard, Sister got choking and red faced. I dashed out of the room without a word, returning two minutes later with a tall glass of orange juice.

"Oh, thank you, Sister Baruch, I shouldn't laugh so hard." She took two big gulps, licked her bottom lip, adjusted her veil, and leaned back with a sigh.

"I'd better go check on the novices in the refectory. Is there anything I can get you, Sister?"

"No, thank you. I don't feel like eating anything, which is not a good ailment to have on Thanksgiving Day!" Thinking for a couple seconds. "Are there any others besides Havana looking at our life?"

"Only a Kristen...Kristen...Atkinson, I think her last name is. That's Kristen with a 'K'. She hasn't been to visit yet, but has emailed Sr. Myriam a couple times and wants to come. She's a senior at Notre Dame, I think."

"Well, that's impressive. We used to have girls coming almost every other weekend it seemed, and on retreat over the holidays. This year, nobody."

"I know. Mother says all the prioresses were commenting on it at their last meeting. Now, you get better, and eat lots of turkey."

"Gobble gobble." Sr. Paul waved with her hand under her chin.

I stopped at my office to check the voice mail. The first was actually from my sister, Sally. "Sis, Mitz and I are going to Brooklyn Heights for dinner at friends not far from your place, may we stop in and say hello?" Well, that's nice. I haven't seen her in months, and have never met Mitzie, so that should be very interesting.

There were four more messages; three asking for prayers for various intentions including unemployment, a deceased gold fish, and varicose veins. The final one, however, made my day: "For Sister Mary Baruch...Aunt Mary, Happy Thanksgiving. Maybe see you after Vespers? Jack."

I called my sister right away. She wanted to come right when we were having our dinner, so she said, "Well, how about 2:30? We're supposed to be at our friends by 3:30 or 4:00."

"Two thirty is perfect. Maybe you can stay for None; it's at 3:00."

"We'll see. Mitz may really enjoy that. Okay, we'll see you around 2:30...oh, we'll have Pancho with us, I hope that's okay?"

"Who's Pancho?"

"He's our little adopted Mexican baby."

"Oh, wow...of course, that's wonderful. See you then. I'm excited to finally meet Mitzie and now Pancho." I hung up shaking my head. The names people give to their kids today! Sr. Cecilia's Uncle Bo, the circus clown, just became a grandfather. Sister was reading a letter to us from him at recreation: "I'm so happy and proud of my new granddaughter, Granola." The Sisters just sat there in unbelief.

Well, I thought, at least Pancho is a real name. I think it was Pancho Villa who was some general or big shot in the Mexican Revolution. But I don't think there's a Saint Pancho, and I'm sure there's not a Saint Granola. And I was laughing out loud which is a strange feeling when you're alone. But I was happy—this Thanksgiving, my two nephews were coming: Sharbel and Pancho. Made me think of Mama and what she would say...and about Thanksgivings on W. 79th Street...and I ran off to the chapel for a quiet hour alone with the Lord...lots to be grateful for...lots to pray for.

Eleven

Same Afternoon

> *O Lord, it is you who are my portion and cup; it is*
> *you yourself who are my prize. The lot marked out for*
> *me is my delight: welcome indeed the heritage that*
> *falls to me!* (Psalm 16, Thursday Compline)

THERE WAS INDEED a lot to pray for. My immediate thoughts, however, were about Sally. My older sister, Sally, was always thought to be the most intelligent of the Feinstein girls, something which I overheard once and never forgot all these years. She was always more studious than Ruthie or I. She graduated from Barnard College and worked almost immediately as a journalist, first in Philadelphia and then in Chicago. She was a "newspaper woman" according to Papa.

Mama had always thought Sally would marry a rich Jewish man and give her a half dozen grandchildren to brag about at her Hadassah meetings. She realized I was never going to stand under the chuppah, and Ruthie was married twice, once at City Hall and once at Coney Island on the beach. Both were a "wash up" (Mama's words). Sally never seemed to have any boyfriends that she'd bring home for the holidays, but she had regular steady roommates. When she gave up being a journalist and started a business with "her partner," Ruthie explained the situation to her. Mama would say, "My three daughters: the thespian, the lesbian, and the Dominican. Oy, such a blessing I should have in my old age?"

Mama mellowed, I think, at the tragedy of the "thespian's" sudden death by a drug overdose. I wasn't quite the black sheep in the family anymore. She liked the irony of that expression, especially after seeing our white habits.

Going home to sit Shiva for Ruthie also brought a reconciliation with my sister whom I hadn't seen in twenty-five years. She didn't understand my life, and I didn't understand hers, but we were still sisters. What can you do? I knew I could simply pray and lay it all before the Divine Heart of Jesus, and that I've been doing. I know my atheist brother, David, was thinking about spiritual things in his later years, and maybe Sally would be too. I know that makes all the difference in the world. How can you talk about love, sacrifice, chastity, virtue, and purity without a faith in God? If one doesn't have a relationship with God, I was thinking to myself while drying the dishes, what does one base "being good" on? Sally's life was a dilemma to me that I couldn't talk about with anyone. It was something we never talked about in community.

Mama could be very funny about it all. I suppose, it was her way of coping. I think parents must have a hard time not blaming themselves if things don't turn out like they thought they would. I certainly didn't turn out as Mama planned. Once, I remember, when Mama was here and was probably feeling her Mogen David elderberry wine, she scratched at that wound. "I wonder what I did wrong, Becky, that Sally never fell for a fella."

"I don't know, Mama, but I know you can't blame yourself. We make our own choices in life, you know. Look at me. Do you blame yourself for not going to shul more or not taking Hebrew lessons?"

That made Mama laugh. "Oy, such questions. You and your brother, my children, the psychiatrists." And she'd take another sip of her wine. She had gotten quite comfortable in the extern parlors visiting her prodigal daughter, the nun. "Shul? I should go and listen to that Rabbi go on about raising your family to follow Torah?"

Mama didn't care for Rabbi Liebermann, or rather, she didn't care for Mrs. Liebermann. I never understood why. I know he separated from his wife, and their one son was in and out of juvenile court. I think he even spent some time at Rikers Island. Talk about a place needing God's mercy!

"Your father was the one for Hebrew, not me. I learned the prayer for lighting the Shabbos candles from hearing my mother pray it, and she learned it from her mother. I wonder if Sally is lighting candles for Shabbat? Shabbat Tabatt, it's her giving those mutts haircuts that gets to me. After all the money we spent, the best women's college in New York, and her great jobs for big daily newspapers, and she gives it all up to have a beauty salon for dogs, for heaven sakes!" Mama would stomp her foot.

Sally and Mitzie started what they called an "Upscale Canine Grooming Salon." Apparently it is a thriving business, and they make lots of money "giving those mutts haircuts."

"A beauty salon can make lots of money and be very prestigious." I didn't know what I was talking about, and don't know why I was defending Sally.

"Helena Rubinstein, may she rest in Cosmetic Heaven, made lots of money and was very prestigious. The only mutts in her salons on Fifth Avenue, mind you, were miniature poodles probably groomed in Paris."

I had to laugh. Mama was right. But I thought Sally very clever nonetheless. "I don't think Sally and Mitzie have a Fifth Avenue salon kind of place, but they probably have lots of poodle clients."

Mama sipped her wine and peered at me with her smiling eyes sprouting crow's feet despite the efforts of her friend Helena. "I wonder what Mitzie looks like? A basset hound? Or a cocker spaniel?"

"Oh, I hope not a basset hound; they have such droopy eyes." And we got giggling back and forth through the parlor grille, which helped distract Mama from playing out the guilt trip. I don't think Mama ever met Mitzie in person.

After Mama died, Sally and Mitzie sold the business, moved to New York into our old apartment, opened a small shop-salon, and travelled a lot. Sally herself was not particularly religious and told me more than once that Mitzie was the "spiritual one." But I had not yet met the spiritual one before this afternoon, and wondered myself: basset hound or cocker spaniel?

Thanksgiving dinner was very pleasant, thank you, Lord. There isn't too much variety to our life, and Thanksgiving dinner fits its own "template." A new word I learned from Sr. Antonia and her computer. The apple-turkeys were all cute standing on their spindly toothpick legs. The stuffing was still my favorite part, as growing up we never had pork sausage or bacon bits in our quasi-kosher stuffing. And Sr. Simon and Sr. Diana turned out the most delicious buttermilk biscuits. Sr. Leah Marie and Sr. Elijah Rose baked the pumpkin pies and made a big deal about them being "organic pumpkin." We all smiled and a few made yummy sounds, but I couldn't taste any difference from non-organic. I would have added some organic nutmeg…that was Mama's secret ingredient. I also had a small sliver of mincemeat pie, as a "penance" in preparation for my meeting Sally and Mitzie. I hate mince-meat unless it's really ice-cold.

Mother Bernadette added a rosé wine to the menu which added a nice touch and made everything festive. The music, selected by Sr. Cecilia for the second year in a row, was the score from Tchaikovsky's *The Nutcracker*. It was her sly way of introducing Christmas, like Santa coming at the end of the Macy's Thanksgiving Day parade. We've yet to work on her liturgical sense of Advent!

It did, however, send my mind back to the first time I saw *The Nutcracker*. Papa took his "three princesses," ages 8, 10, and 13, Ruthie, me, and Sally, to the New York City Ballet production at Lincoln Center. Afterwards, Papa took us to Breyers Creamery on Broadway where we all got ice cream sodas and talked about what we wanted to be when we grew up. Sally was going to be a famous author of romance novels, or a high school English teacher; I was going to be a stewardess for Pan Am and fly all over the world; and Ruthie was going to be a ballerina and dance the Sugar Plum Fairy in *The Nutcracker*.

But this Thanksgiving, I had Sharbel and Sally on my mind, and meeting Pancho and Mitzie. I also offered up the truffle at dessert time which followed upon the mincemeat pie and prayed that it would all go smoothly and that Mitzie wasn't too dog eared or have a loud bark.

At 2:10 we were done with dishes and everyone was running off to take a nap which I wish I had planned on, but grabbed a coat by the back door and made a quick visit again to the cemetery. No time to make the rounds, I went directly to Sr. Gertrude.

"Happy Thanksgiving, Sister Gertrude. I hope you've had a marvelous one if you all do that sort of thing." I spoke like that just to her as I know she would get a kick out of it. I'm almost positive they don't celebrate American holidays in Purgatory.

"My sister Sally and her 'friend' and their baby are coming to visit me in twenty minutes, and I just wanted to let you know, and hope you can inspire me to say the right things. Tell Mother John Dominic and Father Meriwether, oh, and Ruthie, yes, by all means, tell Ruthie if you're able to do all that." I paused to think what else I needed to say. "I sure miss you, Sister. But you know that. I'll offer up my truffles for you tonight." (I hoped she couldn't see that I had my fingers crossed under my scapular, just in case.) I spun around and hurried back into the monastery, and making sure no one was watching, I checked my reflection in the cloister window to make sure my coiffure was straight before heading for the parlor I had reserved. *Deep breath, Baruch, and smile.*

I quietly opened the door and there they sat...Sally, looking more and more like our mother, her dirty-blonde-colored hair brushed back and held in place with a mother of pearl comb, next to her a younger-looking, very attractive woman with a brown and yellow scarf atop a tailored burnt yellow jacket and brown skirt, and next to her sitting quietly on the chair, a short-haired, bulging-eyed Mexican Chihuahua wearing a tiny tilted black sombrero with red tassels and a rhinestone collar...Pancho!

Mitzie and Sally immediately stood up, and Pancho gave out a tiny bark. I bent over in a profound bow laughing. I stood up and managed to talk, "This must be my Mexican nephew!" And they both joined me in my laughing.

I went up to the grille with my best smile, "Mitzie, I'm so happy to finally meet you; I'm sorry I'm laughing; I thought...I thought..."

"Don't think a thing of it." And in a whisper she said, "Just don't tell Pancho he's adopted." We all laughed again. I put my fingers through the grille to squeeze hello to my sister's.

"Please, sit down. And Happy Thanksgiving."

Sally said to Mitzie, "Well, are you satisfied now? I told you she was a real nun. Look at her. It's the real thing."

Mitzie was quite the more refined and had the situation completely under control. "I'm more than satisfied. I'm delighted. But you're much younger than I was picturing..."

I smiled. *Smooth operator*, I thought. "Thank you, I'm actually three years younger than Sally, but nearly fifty years without make-up and eight hours of sleep a night, do help a great deal." (I rarely get eight hours of sleep, but I can be a smooth operator too.)

"Not to mention the 'thing,'" says Sally pointing and making a box with her hands above her forehead. *Not a smooth operator. She may be the smartest, but certainly not the smoothest.*

"Well, I know you're rushed for time, but I hope you'll come back when we can have a real visit. I don't know anything about grooming dogs…is Pancho here one of your clients?" I was digging into the skin between my thumb and index finger, under my scapular, to keep myself from laughing. It was a trick Sr. Gertrude taught me.

"Oh no, Chihuahuas don't take much grooming, that's one reason we got him. He's also easy to travel with." Sally held up her soft weaved oversized bag, Pancho's travel bag.

I laughed. "Mama used to bring that bag here with her. She never had a Mexican Chihuahua in it."

"I know, probably more like a flask of Israeli wine."

"Flask? She'd have a whole bottle of Mogen David with her."

"Such a mother we had?" Sally said, trying to be funny, but was close to choking up. Mitzie came to the rescue.

"We're having dinner with clients actually, well, they're not the clients, their long-haired shih tzu is a client, but Aaron and Rivka Stein are our friends."

"Rivka? You know what Rivka is?" I said to both but aimed at Sally.

"Of course, I know, Rebecca Feinstein." To Mitzie, "Rivka is *Rebecca*, and that was Becky's name before."

"Oh, how 'bout that. But I rather like Baruch as a name. Did you choose that or was it given to you?" *This Mitzie IS a smooth one.*

"It was given to me by my first prioress, Mother John Dominic, who was a gentle lovely woman. Our father liked her very much too; he'd come and visit with her, not with me, but with her!"

"You must've had a very interesting life, Bec…may I call you Becky? Or would you prefer Baruch?"

"Sister Mary Baruch would be nice." That's all I said. In a quiet, even-toned voice.

"Oh, I think I like that too. I've never known a real nun I can call by her real name." Mitzie smiled, with the most perfect teeth I've ever seen.

"Aaron and Rivka have been here," Sally got in. "They knew one of the nuns who died last year. Their granddaughter did a paper on her a couple years ago; I think she wrote poetry."

"Oh, that would've been our Sister Benedict. Poet Emeritus. She worked for a poetry publishing house a hundred years ago in the City."

Sally smiled. She softened the tenseness she came in with. I think she was nervous about me meeting Mitzie or vice-versa.

"How do you know them?" I thought was a polite and simple inquiry.

"We met them on an Alaskan cruise actually. We were still living in Chicago, but struck up a conversation with this friendly couple in the buffet line at breakfast. The conversation came around to dogs…I don't know how that happened…"

"Rivka asked what we did in Chicago, remember. And you (Mitzie) told her we owned a dog salon."

"Oh, that's right. And Rivka thought it was the most wonderful occupation to have. It turned out that they were great dog lovers, and even had a Pomeranian in the Westminster Dog Show."

"We had been to that show several times, at Madison Square Garden. Well, we became good friends; exchanged numbers and all that, and when we came to New York again for the show, they invited us to stay with them. We did that at least three times. We cut their dogs' hair for them when we were there. They had four at the time, remember?"

"Hummm," nodded Sally. "You can imagine they were thrilled when they learned we were moving to New York. Free haircuts!" She sounded like Mama for just a second, except Mama would have added, "for the Stein mutts." I couldn't help but laugh.

"What's so funny?" Sally sounding like Sally again.

"Oh, you just reminded me of Mama."

"How? Oh, I know, probably about the 'hair cuts'…she could never understand why I gave up journalism for canine grooming."

That made me laugh even more. "That wasn't all she didn't understand." *Oooops, Baruch, you put your foot in your mouth this time.*

"What do you mean?"

Well here goes. "She didn't understand about you and Mitzie, you know, about your…your lifestyle." Pausing more a moment for that to sink in and staring at the corner of the grille. "Of course, she didn't understand my lifestyle either; I think we both threw her for a loop." We all laughed, even Mitzie.

"Poor Mama," Sally chimed in, "the only 'lifestyle,' as you put it, she understood was Ruthie's and look how that turned out." The laughter became a sullen hum.

Philosophical Mitzie was weighing in, "I don't think she understood Ruthie's life either. Oh, she had a romantic idea of the life in the theater, like most who aren't in the theater have, but she never understood the, what would you call it? The underbelly of the life. The drive, or the passion, is always there, although I suppose that comes and goes quite dramatically, pardon the pun. There's a lot of cut throat competition, rejection, heartache, and politics...it's also a 'big business' at the other end of it all. There's a dark side to it."

Mitzie was certainly waxing eloquently, as Sr. Gertrude would say. Thinking to myself for a second, I thought Sr. Gertrude probably didn't really know that dark side of the theater to that extent, or she held onto the passion part and transferred it across Broadway and across the river, into Brooklyn Heights!

We all sat lost in our private thoughts for a ponderous minute.

Looking at me, Mitzie continued, "I dare say, your mother certainly never understood your life, and when she finally came to accept it, she didn't grasp the deeper parts of it, but that's okay, isn't it?"

"You're right. I suppose that's true about everyone's life. I don't understand your life or haven't even thought what the dark side of what that may be…" (They kind of laughed.)

"Most people never do. I'm not sure that we do ourselves." Now Sally was getting philosophical. "We're a couple old ladies who are great friends, have a business together, and try to enjoy life, and take care of each other. The 'passion' isn't the dominant driving force."

"Since you brought it up," Mitzie jumped in, "I've been dying to meet you and talk about a few things. Like…well, I've been striving to live a celibate life for some years now; it's an ascetical practice I've learned from a spiritual teacher I've had, and it was all quite new and difficult in a way, and then Sal mentioned she has a sister who is a Catholic nun, who probably knows all about it, but she doesn't talk to you. That was before Ruthie's death."

I was not shocked by the direction of the conversation, but perhaps somewhat surprised. Mitzie was not at all what I had pictured in my poor head. My hand automatically moved down to grasp my rosary crucifix. *Lord, I'm gonna need Your help here.* I smiled.

"It's a bigger discussion than we have time for today, and you've got to get to the Steins and cut Rivka's hair." She laughed.

"Rivka's the lady; Madame Chow is the dog."

I laughed at myself. "I bet you it's not long before Rivka has you cutting her hair too."

"Such friends we should have?" Sally sounded just like Mama, and we laughed at our kind of 'private joke.'

"Maybe a key word we can think about till the next time we meet is that word 'passion.' It seems like we all have shaped our lives, or followed our passions, and I'd like to think about it, and tell you about my passion. That may help you understand a little, and I'd be grateful." Looking at Sally, "It was something I could never really do with Mama, you know."

"That sounds marvelous," Mitzie said before Sally could say anything. But Sally smiled and agreed that would be very interesting. The Mexican pooch had fallen asleep on the hard chair in a puddle of sunlight coming through the single window in the parlor. There was a quiet peacefulness in the room. *Sally WAS an old lady*, I thought. And she's my only living relative.

"What are you having for Thanksgiving dinner?" The Jewish sister inquired.

"Having? We already had it. What everyone else has on Thanksgiving—all American roasted turkey, stuffing with pork sausage, yams, creamed green beans and mushrooms, and pumpkin pie. Oh, and mincemeat pie." I grimaced.

"Ah, yes, your favorite," Sally teased. "Well, I brought you a tub load of charoset; I know it's not Pesach, but it tastes so good all year round. This was Mama's recipe, you know. It's got nutmeg and raisins in it. I bought some for you and some for Rivka and Aaron. Where's the nice little nun who brings us things?"

"You mean, Sister Paula. She's down with the flu, poor thing. I can take it from the turn. Thank you so much; we'll have some tonight with leftovers. It's perfect. I hope the Steins enjoy it as much."

"We're probably having roast pheasant…" Mitzi said a little cynically.

"Well, just pray it's not roasted Pomeranian."

"Sister Mary Baruch! You're awful." And they got up laughing and joking with each other about former dinners at the Steins. Sally put the plastic containers of charoset on the turn. Pancho Villa was yakking up a tantrum by now, his sombrero slipping down under his chin, hiding his rhinestone collar.

This time it was Mitzie who put her finger through the grille to "squeeze" goodbye. "It's been wonderful meeting you, Sister, I'm looking forward to the next time."

"Me too, Mitzie. Don't eat too much Pomeranian, and Sally, if they have mincemeat pie, give it to Pancho Villa here." And off they schlepped with pooch underarm, still barking at the rudeness of suddenly being woken up, no doubt.

How sad, I thought, *and they don't even know it.* Life without the joy of knowing the Lord. I hummed to myself a line from Psalm 4 that we sing at Compline after First Vespers of Sundays or Solemnities: *"What can bring us happiness?" many say. Let the light of your face shine on us, O Lord. You have put into my heart a greater joy than they have from abundance of corn and new wine…and homemade charoset…*

Twelve

Close to Vespers

*And so my heart rejoices, my soul is glad; even my body
shall rest in safety.* (Psalm 16, Thursday Compline)

DEAR SR. ANNUNCIATA saw me coming out of the parlor,
carrying my containers of charoset. She walked with me
silently to the little kitchen.

"Have you ever had charoset, Sister? It's usually served at
the Passover Seder, but it's delicious anytime."

"Oh, no, I don't think I have; we weren't allowed to
play with the Jewish children in the neighborhood, or they
weren't allowed to play with us; I never knew what came
first. But we certainly couldn't eat your food."

"Well, you'll have to try a little right now, that way you'll
know if you want some for supper." (This was good Jewish-
Mother logic.)

"Oh, do you think so? It's in between meals…well, maybe
just a little taste." Her 'strict observance' flew right out the
open kitchen window. I got a couple paper plates that had
oversized turkeys decorating the whole plate, and scooped

99

out a large spoonful for each of us. We sat at the table in the little kitchen.

"Uuuummmmm, this is quite tasty," as her lips smacked together. "I can taste nutmeg in here." *Wow*, I thought, *those Gentile taste buds are right on target.*

"You're right; there is. That was always my mother's secret ingredient. All charoset usually has fruits, like tart apples, nuts, and honey. It represents the mortar the Hebrew slaves used to make bricks."

"I know your mother used to bring your special foods to you when she would visit. So this must be a real treat for you."

"She did…and it is. My sister, Sally, brought this for me, for Thanksgiving. Mama would be proud of her; I hope she's watching it all."

"Watching all of what, dear?"

"You know, my sister and her friend coming to visit with me, and my sister making charoset from her recipe. Sally was never one for the kitchen."

"Well, she certainly out did herself with this one. Do you think I could have just a little more to make sure I'll want some tonight?" She sounded like a little girl asking for another candy. I scooped another spoonful.

"Thank you, Sister, you're too kind." She took a mouthful. Her eyes were actually sparkling with delight. "I'm sorry if I haven't always been so kind to you."

That took me aback a little. "Whatever could you mean, Sister? You've always been very….kind to me, to everybody."

"Well, I've always been very polite, I think, but my thoughts weren't always so kind. I was afraid of you."

"Afraid of me? Gracious, Sister, I hope I never did something to make you afraid of me?"

"No, it wasn't you at all. It was me. My father was very anti-Jewish, and told us to be careful of Jews, they're up to no good. Like I said, we were never allowed to even play or walk to school with the Jewish kids. I don't know what I thought they would do to us, but I grew up suspicious of Jewish people. And then…"

"And then what?"

"And then I entered the monastery and one of the other Sisters, one of the German Sisters, you know, I think it was Sister Boniface, may she rest in peace, told me to be careful, the librarian is Jewish. That was you. So I never went into the library."

"I know. I noticed that. None of the German Sisters did, I think because when Mother made me librarian, I moved out the printing press and all the stuff that Sister Hildegarde, the book binder, had had. And Sister Boniface loved Sister Hildegarde, so she never forgave me."

"I know. She told me about that. She made it sound like Sister Hildegarde had just died the day before, and I think it had been a couple years."

"It was. Like they were waiting for another book-binder to enter who spoke German. Mother John Dominic told me to move the old stuff out."

"I didn't know that part. Holy obedience covers a multitude of sins." She was actually licking her fork. I couldn't help but laugh.

"That's certainly true, Sister. If it wasn't for obedience most of us would have flown the coop years ago!" And Sr. Annunciata thought that was hysterical.

"That's true for me too. I once got so upset over Mother Jane Mary correcting me for something, I don't even remember what it was now, that I thought 'I'll show her; I'll leave.' It was obedience that stopped me in my tracks. I had promised Our Lord I would obey her."

She leaned back in her chair, putting her finger on her pudgy little nose, and said, "Do you know when I stopped being afraid of you?"

"When you came into the library the first time to return a book?"

"Well, yes, it was. But the book I was returning was one you had checked out for me and put it in my mailbox. I don't know how you knew I loved trains, but there it was—an illustrated book about locomotives. I thought it was so kind of you to do that. That if you could do that, what did I have to be afraid of. I also thought you had a lovely voice when you were chantress, and seemed to fill the choir with some special feeling. I said that once to Sister Gertrude whom I knew would know what I meant, about filling choir with such a sweet sound. And Sister Gertrude said, 'Of course, my dear, that's because she's Jewish. It's God's special gift to us.'"

"Thank you for telling me that, Sister. It's beautiful. And I can just hear our dear Sister Gertrude saying it. Here, have another spoonful of charoset."

Sr. Anna Maria popped in right at that moment. "Sister Baruch, your nephew is here."

"Oh, Blessed be God. I'll be right there. Here, Sister (handing her the spoon). Don't eat it all at once…save some for supper. And say a prayer for me." And off I went, turning back after three steps, went over and kissed Sr. Annunciata on the top of her head. And dashed down the cloister to the small parlor.

I didn't know what to expect when I saw Sharbel, but it certainly wasn't what I saw. I was maybe expecting a neat shirt, maybe even a tie, and his big all embracing smile, but there he was in torn jeans, a sweat shirt, and under his left eye a bloodied scratch surrounded in black and blue. Even his nose looked a little off centered, and his hair was a mess.

"Sharbel! What happened to you?"

"Oh, Aunt Mary, I'm sorry. I must look a mess. I fell going up the subway stairs. It was good there was no one else coming down. I think I was mugged, 'cause my bag with my wallet was gone when I went to get out."

"What did you do? Sit down, Jack, let me get you something to drink. Coffee or tea or milk maybe?"

"I don't want anything right now; I just want to see you. I told the cops I had an aunt who was a nun in Brooklyn, and he told me his uncle was the pope. He didn't believe me. I guess I caused a little bit of a scene at the turnstiles getting out. I jumped over one cause I didn't have my subway card, or my wallet, or any I.D. I thought he was going to arrest me, and I told him my aunt was a nun, and she was expecting me before Vespers at the monastery; that's where I'm going. "

Before he could go any further, Sr. Anna Maria knocked and opened the parlor door, and a New York City police man came in, holding his hat, as I recall.

Without any introduction he said, "This young man claims he's your nephew, is that right, Sister?" (I could just make out his name on his uniform over his shield: O'Brien.)

"That's right, Officer O'Brien. I'm sorry he's caused you so much trouble, but I thank you for bringing him here. I believe he's been mugged and doesn't have his wallet or anything. What can I do to help?"

"You've done a lot already, Sister, by identifying him. We found his wallet. He wasn't mugged, he fell on the stairs and lost his bag with his wallet and a few other things he shouldn't have in there." He glared at poor Sharbel who was looking very contrite and frightened. "He kept saying his aunt was a nun, as if that was supposed to make everything all right! I said to him, if that's a lie, young man, you're in a lot of trouble. If it's true, I'll say a prayer for you."

"You said you'd eat your damn hat! Pardon my French, Aunt Mary."

"That's all right, Sharbel. Your father spoke French too."

"Well, Sister, is this really your prodigal nephew?"

"Yes, Officer, he certainly is; I'm his father's sister." I don't know why I had to put in a genealogy, but it actually helped.

"And his father's name was 'Feinstein', is that right? Dr. David Feinstein?" He said all this without looking at his note pad; I was quite impressed, given the circumstances.

"Yes, that's right. Did you know him?" That was going out on a limb, but what the heck?

"I never met the man, but my wife did. She was his patient for a time."

"Oh, I see."

"I understand he died on 9/11? I'm sorry, I shouldn't…"

"That's okay. You're right; he did. He was having breakfast with our mother for her birthday."

"I'm so sorry to hear that." And looking at Sharbel. "I'm sorry, kid, I didn't believe you. Make your old man proud of you, and stay away from the sauce."

Sharbel just sat there looking like a deer caught in the headlights. Officer O'Brien, still with hat in hand, scratched his head and looked back at me.

"So you must be a Feinstein too?"

"That's right, Officer, the proud daughter of Ruben and Hannah Feinstein, even if I'm the black sheep!" Big smile. And two seconds later, he burst out laughing.

"This is too grand to believe, wait till I tell my wife. Her maiden name was Leibowitz, if you catch my drift! I was the black sheep too for marrying a Jewish girl! When she was having troubles with depression and stuff, she wouldn't go to a non-Jewish doctor. She was afraid of them!"

And we both laughed, leaving Sharbel a little bewildered by it all.

"Before you have a family portrait taken, can I have my bag back?"

"Here it is, Shar-bell, I never heard that Jewish name, and I grew up in New York."

Sharbel didn't rebound, but like a perfect gentleman, stood up and thanked Office O'Brien, and put out his hand. "Thank you, Officer, I'll remember to watch the sauce."

Office O'Brien shook his hand, and turned to me, "Say a prayer for me, Sister, the streets aren't safe out there anymore." And he turned to leave.

"I will, Officer, and thank you for bringing Sharbel here safe and sound. And remember…" He was almost out the door, "your hat, Officer O'Brien, they're delicious." He laughed, putting it on his head and gave me a little salute. And I of course, saluted him back.

Sharbel just looked at me wide-eyed. "You are incredible!"

"And you are incorrigible! What's this 'sauce' he was talking about?"

"Oh, you know, that real spicy tomato sauce they put on pasta."

"Uh huh. Was that called Johnny Walker or Jack Daniels tomato sauce?"

"Aunt Mary! You never cease to amaze me."

"My dear nephew, I did have a life before I came here."

He laughed and clapped his hands. "When you were a black sheep?"

"Baaaaah." And he laughed even more. "And it's almost time for Vespers. Can you stay?"

"I'd really love to, but I've got a new job, so I'd better rush to get home and cleaned up…Sometime soon, okay, I've got to tell you all about the Camino, and…and I've got something for you." He put his finger through the grille for me to squeeze. "Good bye, Aunt Mary, and thank you a million times over." And he headed for the door.

"You're welcome…and Jack?"

"Huh?"

"Happy Thanksgiving." And he was gone. I headed for the chapel, my head full of everything.

I am really happy and thankful now to just be sitting here in Squeak before supper. It had been quite a day. I'm looking forward to our special Thanksgiving recreation. The novitiate joins the professed and we talk about the day. Maybe I will tell them about Pancho, but not my real nephew!

Lord, every day is Thanksgiving Day for us when we live under the same roof. How privileged we are to celebrate the Holy Sacrifice of the Mass every morning and to be here day in and day out, not needing to rush anywhere because we are always at home. Thank you, Lord, for bringing this black sheep into this chorale.

And now, Lord, I'm looking forward to our simple supper of soup and turkey sandwiches...and Sally's charoset... if there's any left!

Thirteen

Immaculate Conception, December 8, 2006

Inviolata, intacta et casta es, Maria. You are inviolate, undefiled
and chaste, Mary. (From a Final Antiphon at Compline)

IT WAS HAVANA'S second "interview" with the unofficial
vocation team, headed by Sr. Myriam. My first interview
with her was nearly four months ago. I noticed right away
the "wall-eye" Sr. Paula mentioned, as well as a kind of snide
attitude, but she may have been nervous, and I remember
my emotions were rather scattered in August too. So this
would be a better interview, I told myself.

Havana Elenita Sanchez was born in Miami of Cuban
parents. Havana was their hometown from which they had
escaped, and to honor it, they named their little girl Havana.
She said her friends call her "Vanna, like Vanna White on
Wheel of Fortune." She touched the grille and said "ping."
None of us had any idea what she was doing.

We had never heard of Vanna White or *Wheel of Fortune*, which surprised her. I guess people who grow up with

television can't imagine living without one. We didn't ask what the "ping" had to do with it.

"So, Havana, you think you'd like to be a cloistered nun?" I thought we might as well get right to the point.

"Yeah. I've been coming here a long time and really like it." I restrained from looking over at Sr. Paula who was sitting in for the interview. Maybe Sr. Myriam thought that Havana might have a leaning towards being an extern Sister, and invited Sr. Paula to sit in on this interview. Or maybe Sr. Paula had expressed her concerns about her to Sr. Myriam. I didn't know.

"Did you go to school here in Brooklyn?" I continued, sounding very professional, I thought.

"Yeah."

Sr. Myriam broke into this "in depth conversation" and added, "Tell the Sisters what you've been doing since you graduated from high school."

"Oh yeah; I work for a cleaning business called Maid to Order. We are teams of four or five, and we clean apartments real fast like; my specialty is kitchens and bathrooms. I like scrubbing." And she let out a kind of laugh, which made us all laugh with her. Maybe the "ping" had something to do with making things sparkle.

"So, you like making things sparkling clean?" *Not a bad trait,* I thought to myself. It was something I was never compulsive about, but I appreciated it in others. When our Aunt Ruth visited us from south Jersey, she could "ping" all afternoon in the kitchen.

"And do you live at home with your parents?" This was Sr. Paula's initial inquiry. I could tell she wasn't the most enthused about Maid to Order Havana.

"Yeah, I live with my mother and brother, and my grandmother. My father died about five years ago. My grandmother, Nonna, talks to me a lot about religion and stuff; she's the one who told me about you all here."

The interview seemed to go on endlessly, and in the end, while we found Havana rather awkward and unsophisticated in religious matters, despite Nonna's talking about it all the time, Sr. Myriam gave her an application. It is the Solemnity of the Immaculate Conception, so if she enters, it certainly wouldn't be till after the new year. She still has to come for a two-week aspirancy inside before that. We decided that wouldn't happen till after the new year either. In the meantime, she was free to visit as often as she could. She lit up with delight at that suggestion and added that she'd try, but the weeks before Christmas were Maid to Order's busiest time. We all shook our heads like we understood perfectly; it was our busy time too, Sr. Paula let her know.

Afterwards, I had the chance to talk to Sr. Paula in the little kitchen. Sr. Paula remarked, "That was my first time interviewing someone for the life."

"I know, funny because you probably know all the aspirants or inquirers better than any of us do; you've let them in and let them out from the chapel probably for years."

"I know. It struck me when we were talking to her that I've never seen her with anyone, like her mother, or her grandmother who told her about us, or not even a friend. Of course, that doesn't mean anything. She's not an unattractive girl, would you say? Except for that funny eye." And Sr. Paula tried to do it with her eyes, but only went cross-eyed, which gave us both a suppressed fit of laughter.

Sr. Paula was putting clean mugs on a tray and looking through the cupboard at her boxed cookies, pulling down a box of good old fashioned Oreo cookies.

"I wasn't feeling so well yesterday, so didn't want to bake up a batch of oatmeal cookies; I know Sharbel likes them." (She remembered that he was coming to see me this afternoon.) "These will have to do." She looked over at me for my approval. I'm glad she reminded me, without her knowing it. I completely forgot Sharbel had called and left a message that he'll be here an hour before Vespers.

"Yeah, they're *made to order*." And we laughed till the bell for Sext sounded.

"Ooops, there's our 'ping.'" And off we went silently to the chapel.

My poor mind found it difficult to concentrate on the psalms. I couldn't get Havana out of my head. I wondered if we were prejudiced against her because she didn't appear or sound too intelligent. And she never called us "Sister," which isn't a matter of intelligence, but then, maybe it was lost in the culture. She seemed perfectly fluent in English even though she lived with a mother and grandmother whom I presumed only spoke Spanish. She didn't seem to be the least knowledgeable about our life, but then who really is when they come? Maybe she isn't familiar with the internet like most of the young women coming today.

I was looking forward to a quiet afternoon before my visit with Sharbel. I hadn't seen him since Thanksgiving, less than two weeks ago. At least no more home deliveries by a police officer.

My quiet afternoon after dinner didn't happen as Sr. Kateri asked to see me for a minute. I wondered if she was coming down with something as she looked a bit piqued.

My office in the novitiate is really a converted cell, so it's not the most spacious room to meet with people, but I had a couple nicely padded arm chairs in a corner with a small table between.

Sr. Kateri (Pretty Flower) was near the end of her second year in temporary vows. She stilled lived in the novitiate, but was close to moving over to the solemn professed side.

"Come in, Sister, and have a seat." I was at my desk for the moment looking for a ball point pen in case I had to write anything down. I joined her in the chairs.

"Thank you for seeing me, Sister. I know this is supposed to be a time of great silence, but I was prompted during the Office to see you; maybe it was Our Lady since it's her feast day." She smiled.

"Yes. Is there something on your mind?"

"Well, I don't know how to say it, and maybe this really isn't the time. Maybe I should wait till our regular meeting next week; you're busy, and I've got to…to order more beads for the Sisters."

"Just come out with it, Sister. What's bothering you?"

"I don't know if I should go into integration. I don't know if I should make final vows, really. I don't know if I should stay." She put her head down; I could see her hands were trembling just a little.

I didn't say anything for the moment. Just let her calm down. Then, quietly, "There, that was easy to get out. Have you been thinking about this for a long time or is it something more recent?"

"I'd say more recent; maybe since Thanksgiving. It first really kind of hit me when I was making those apple-turkeys for the tables…like, 'what am I doing here?' I asked myself. I could be teaching nuclear engineering to grad students, and instead I'm sticking toothpicks in apples. There are days when I …" and she stopped.

"Yes? There are days when you…?"

"When I don't want to sing the psalms and miss going out and doing things with my friends. Doesn't that sound awful?"

"No, it doesn't sound awful. It sounds pretty normal to me. I have those moments too."

"You do?" She looked at me like it was the most amazing thing I ever said in my whole life. "And what do you do?"

"Oh, I take a deep breath usually, and go on. It's also normal to begin to doubt yourself when you're getting close to solemn profession. Sometimes it happens before, and sometimes afterwards…and sometimes both times."

She sat listening. Her face relaxed from the tension she carried in with her, and her hands weren't trembling.

I went on. "There are times when all the reasons we came here don't seem to work anymore, if you know what I mean." She nodded yes. "It may be a sign that we aren't meant to be here, or that we aren't meant to be here anymore. I think we're all meant to be here in God's plan for the time that we are. But we shouldn't act on certain 'feelings' too quickly.

Our feelings are quite fickle, as you know. You've had other times when you wanted to pack up your beads and head for the reservation." She laughed at my poor example, and nodded 'yes' again.

"A wise old nun once told me, when I was ready to pack my bag and head for the subway to Manhattan, to give it two weeks. Pray quietly. Ask the Holy Spirit to show you the way. And sometimes, it helps to look back and think about why we came. It certainly wasn't for a career in nuclear engineering, or library science, or classical music, or beaded bags and tooth-picked turkeys...it was for something more, or I should say, for Someone more."

She was silent; her head down for a moment, then she looked up at me and smiled. "You're right, Sister, thank you, I mean, Blessed be God." She took a deep breath and found a big smile on her face. "My turkey fell apart before we even prayed grace." And I laughed with her.

"It helps, Sister, to be able to talk about it, like you've done. So don't be afraid to come to me at any time. That's what I'm here for...that and to make tea for the Sisters in the infirmary. Come and help me; the beaded-bag Sisters are working overtime, you know, before the Christmas rush. I don't know how they got so many orders for bags..."

Sr. Kateri got up at the same time that I did and left with me for the infirmary. When we were in the cloister, she leaned towards me and whispered, "I put an ad for them on our website." And stepped up her pace to beat me to the infirmary.

Passing by the picture window, I looked out on the cemetery, and to my happy surprise, there was a light snow falling. I stopped for a moment to look at it and to look in the direction of Mother John Dominic's grave. I smiled and winked: "Two weeks."

Sharbel never came.

Fourteen

Christmas Night 2006

Ecce complete sunt omni a quai dicta sunt per Angelum de Virgine Maria. Behold, all the things spoken by the angel of the Virgin Mary are now fulfilled. (Nunc Dimittis antiphon after First Vespers of Christmas)

WELL, DEAR LORD, Happy Birthday. My Advent Heart has been especially full this Advent; I think maybe the first time really since 9/11, five years ago. I don't know if it's age or circumstances. I suspect it's the combination of both. I love the fourth week of Advent, or I should say, the five days before today; it's like we relive the week with Our Lady, every day bringing us closer to the birth of her Son.

In many ways, Lord, it's been a difficult year. I don't want to dwell on the times of death since they are all too present the older one gets, but in a different way than Easter which celebrates Your conquering death and bringing us a whole new life, Your own birth into our poor world is the beginning of our redemption.

Isn't it amazing how we never get tired of meditating on the mystery of the Incarnation? Every day, three times a day, when we pray the *Angelus*, and when we pray the Joyful Mysteries of the rosary, but the week before Christmas we have The *O Antiphons* to carry us along throughout the day. Four nights ago: *O Radiant Dawn, splendor of eternal light, sun of justice: come, shine on those who dwell in darkness and the shadow of death.*

That's really all of us, but the shadows of death become longer the longer one lives. It struck me four nights ago that we are immersed in a huge love story. And with all the extras that take up so much time, we can move through these days with joy and peace, and basking in the splendor of the Radiant Dawn that came upon us this morning. Christmas morning in the monastery. There's nothing quite like it. I hope the young Sisters all get sunburned from that radiance!

Three days ago I got a phone call from Sharbel. He was very busy at work and would be working on Christmas Day, but could he come by this afternoon and give me my present? Years ago that wouldn't have happened, but Mother Bernadette said it would be fine. I've also shared a little of my anxiety over him with her since she became prioress, so she was more than fine about it; she was magnanimous, like Our Lady's soul that magnifies the Lord. The week before Christmas are really Marian days, I think, and maybe it was Our Lady who prompted Sharbel to call me. I was elated, as I've praying extra hard for him this Advent.

I didn't have to reserve a parlor; they were all free. He said he would come for None and stay till Vespers. So after None, I made my way to the little parlor and opened the door, and there he was sitting in the same chair he had sat in when Officer O'Brien brought him here. Except today he looked like a different boy. He sported a neatly trimmed dark beard which framed his face in a most handsome way. His half Lebanese and Jewish features blended together. I thought if he wore a robe and hood he would look like one of the apostles; like "John" perhaps, the Beloved.

"Aunt Mary of the Advent Heart."

His greeting brought tears and a big smile to my face. "Jack, how handsome you look. I think John the Baptist would be envious of your beard." And he laughed as he stood to squeeze my fingers through the grille.

"Before I forget, my mother sends her greetings. I thought maybe she would come with me, but I guess brain surgery goes on right up to the holiday."

I didn't know if he was being facetious or sincere. "It was nice of her to send greetings; that means a lot. I don't think I've been her favorite un-relative in the world."

Sharbel put his head back and laughed. "You are so clever with words; I would never have come up with 'un-relative.' But it's true, isn't it? She should be your sister-in-law, but she's not, and yet, I'm really and truly your nephew." I silently tucked that in the back of my head to share later with Sr. Jane Mary.

For Sharbel, however, I just giggled a little and let it go. I moved the conversation in a different direction. "You know, I've never heard a word about your pilgrimage, or your other expeditions, or where things stand in regards to the Dominicans, and all that." Maybe I had moved into too many different directions!

"Well, I have a little Christmas gift for you." And smiling, he took a small gift wrapped box out of his tweed overcoat draped over the other chair. "I'll put it on the turn, but don't open it yet."

"Okay. I'll wait till Sister Paula leaves."

"Sister Paula?"

"She's our extern Sister; you've met her before, several times. She's bringing in a pot of coffee and something to nosh on while we kibitz." I knew he would enjoy a little Jewish slang.

He had pictures in the other pocket of his overcoat. "These aren't very good because I didn't have a camera with me; they're all from Robby's phone actually. Robby was one of the guys who walked the Camino with me."

There weren't too many pictures of the countryside or the mountains, mostly group photos of three or four of them at cafes or restaurants.

"Well, it looks like you were all having a jolly time."

"We were. We stayed mostly in these youth hostels along the way, but usually went to a nice place to eat. We were starved by the end of the day's hike."

"And apparently thirsty." Every photo had bottles of wine on the table or in their hands.

"Yeah, that too. We drank a lot of wine…every night, but we also sang and sometimes danced, and talked about the crazy people we met along the Way."

"Oh, I thought it was a pilgrimage."

"It was, Aunt Mary, it was. We also prayed. Actually we sang the rosary every day when we were walking. It was really cool; I never sang the rosary, do you?"

"No, I don't think we ever have. Sometimes we kind of get into a sing-song monotone, but it's not really singing. What melody did you do?"

And as he was trying to demonstrate the melody of the Hail Marys, Sr. Paula knocked her usual discreet knock, and came into the extern side of the parlor with a tray with the usual Pyrex coffee pot, and a plate with six slices of fruit cake. She smiled at Sharbel. "Merry Christmas almost, Sharbel. I hope you like fruit cake."

"Wow, thank you, Sister Paula, I haven't had any fruitcake at all this year."

"Well, eat up, I've got enough in the back to feed us till Easter." He laughed as he wasted no time taking a piece and sticking it in his mouth.

"My, you're looking very Omar Sharif," noticing the new bearded look.

I laughed this time. "That's funny; that's how my mother described you to me before I ever met you."

"I know. She used to say that to almost everyone. She made me watch Funny Girl with her one afternoon before one of our trips, so I'd see what she meant." He drifted off for a moment, putting another bite of fruitcake in his mouth. "I sure miss her."

"I know. I do too. We used to celebrate Chanuka and Christmas together. She always liked this little parlor, you know, and usually had a bottle of Mogen David in her bag."

"Oh, I know. She would have loved El Camino, except for the walking part."

And we laughed. "May I open my gift now?"

"In a minute. Look at this picture. See what I've got around my neck?"

"Yes…it looks like; I'm not so sure…it looks like a clam shell or something."

"That's right. That's the official symbol of a pilgrim. Kind of like a sacramental."

"That's interesting; I didn't know that. There's always so much to learn in Catholicism, oy." Sharbel laughed.

"The shell is actually called a scallop. The Scallop of St. James became proof for pilgrims in the middle ages that they made it to Compostela, but a priest I met on El Camino was telling us that it goes back to St. Augustine who tells the story of meeting a little boy at the beach pouring sea water with a scallop into a hole he had dug. When St. Augustine asked him what he was doing, the kid said, 'I am emptying the sea into this hole.' And St. Augustine used that to talk about the immensity of the Trinity and our trying to empty it into our head."

"The hole in our head?"

"Yeah, like that." He laughed. "Did you know that Pope Benedict includes a scallop shell in his coat of arms and so do Prince William and Prince Harry? Even before Christian times, pagans used to make a kind of pilgrimage to the sea on the same route, for fertility. The scallop for them was a symbol for fertility…and so the Birth of Venus has her coming out of a scallop."

I just sat in amazement and let him go on. It was actually very interesting, and his enthusiasm about it was refreshing.

"It's symbolic, I think, of lots of things…new life. Even, like St. Augustine's story, you can think of the water poured on a baby's head, is pouring the immensity of God into a little soul." He paused enough to pour his coffee and eat another slice of fruitcake.

"This fruitcake is really good. Anyway, the shell became for me like the rosary. I filled it with all my intentions each day. And a few times I used it to scoop water from a stream, but mostly to hold on to and pray. You see, we really were pilgrims."

"That's beautiful, Jack. If I remember right, when I was baptized, Fr. Meriwether used a metal, silver I think, scallop to pour the water on my head."

"And the immensity of God was poured into your soul."

"That's right. That's a beautiful symbol, isn't it? I bet some nuns' veils used to resemble scallops...I wonder why it was chosen to symbolize that one reached the relics of St. James at the end of the pilgrimage?"

"Well, this same priest—he walked with us for a couple hours one day and had Mass for us in the evening at a little outdoor shrine at one of the hostels—he told us that one story says that St. James rescued a knight who had fallen into the sea, and was covered in scallops, and another one that the horse carrying the relics of St. James to Compostela fell into the sea, and when they got him out—to save the relics—the horse was literally covered with shells...scallops, that I guess protected the relics. The priest liked that story best; he said wearing the scallop or having it on your backpack, or both, was a protection from evil. I guess there are lots of stories about the Devil attacking pilgrims on El Camino."

"Oh my, did you...do battle with the Devil?"

"Well, Aunt Mary, you know me. I've been battling the Evil One, it seems, for a couple years. Between you and me, I don't remember some nights on the Camino if I had too much vino. I try to watch it, you know, and always make sure I've eaten something before I drink, but like…once I start, I don't want to stop. It wasn't like that every night, but when we'd start off again in the morning, I was always a little hungover and didn't remember some of the stuff they talked about which we supposedly talked about the night before. Funny how that happens."

"Your Aunt Ruthie used to talk about that too. I think she called it 'black outs.' Well, I'm glad you were with others who wouldn't let you wander off on your own in the middle of the night, or falling into the sea like the poor horse."

"Yeah, we kind of pledged that we would watch out for each other. Todd, one of the other guys, had problems when he drank too. He wants to be a Franciscan. We talked a lot about our vocations. He's also from a pretty rich family, and it's his father who's opposed to him being a Franciscan. Besides, we had our St. James' scallops to protect us."

Another long pause, and another slice of fruitcake. I silently prayed, grateful that he was here and able to share all this with me. Ruthie was never so honest about it all.

"Todd and I used to pray Compline together, usually after a half a bottle of wine, but we did well. He had been on retreat at a Franciscan friary in Ohio, and they had these small Compline books. We tried singing parts, but didn't do a good job of it; sometimes we got a fit of laughing over our Gregorian chant…I hope that wasn't sacrilegious?"

I didn't know if he was asking me or just stating the fact.

"There's a line in Psalm 4 which the Church puts on our lips every Saturday night: '*You have put into my heart a greater joy than they have from abundance of corn and new wine.*' The joy you had, even trying to sing the psalms, is a gift of the Holy Spirit poured into your souls."

"After an abundance of new wine." And he laughed. "Well, not really an abundance. I remember our praying Compline.

"And where is this Todd now? Is he a New Yorker?"

"No, we were at Yale together. He's with his family in Ohio. I told him he should come visit after the New Year, and I'd introduce him to my aunt, a cloistered nun."

"Well, that would be very nice. You'll have to come for Compline!"

"Yeah, that would really be awesome." He kind of stuffed a half slice of fruitcake into and mouth and garbled, "Now, open your Christmas gift."

I went to the turn and retrieved the beautifully wrapped box in shiny red foil paper with a red and white bow. There was a little gift tag: To Aunt Mary...From John the Baptist.

I opened it slowly and carefully, which drives most people nuts, but I like to save the paper and use it again if I can.

I opened the lid, and turned back the white tissue paper, and there lay a beautiful ivory scallop.

"That was my St. James Scallop; I want you to have it."

I was suddenly too choked up to say anything. It still had the worn-looking cord, but the shell itself was like new. I gently took it out of the box, and put the cord over my head, and let the shell rest against my heart.

"It's like a pectoral cross," I managed to get out. "It's beautiful, Jack, thank you so much, but don't you want to keep it? It protected you on your pilgrimage."

"I want you to have it, and to think of me every night when you pray at Compline: *Protect us, Lord, as we stay awake; watch over us as we sleep.*"

"I will…I will. Of course, I can't wear it into Compline, but I can put it in my habit pocket. It will be my special intention for you every night." After a minute of silence. "I have something to give to you, if you let me." And with that I took out my pocket rosary. "Your father gave this to me for my birthday. It's from Israel. The wooden beads and the crucifix are made from wood in Bethlehem. I think he would love to know that you have it, and you can pray for him on it." I looped it through one of the openings in the grille, and he took it, holding it like it was precious jewels.

"It's not going to break, Jack. They are pretty sturdy. They've landed on the floor enough times, and once I even stepped on them."

"Thank you, Aunt Mary, they are very special, coming from my father, and from you. It's the best Christmas gift I could receive."

"And so is my St. James' scallop." I lifted it up to my lips and kissed it. We both sat for a silent minute holding our Christmas gifts. "Now tell me, Jack, are you spending Christmas with your mother? And how's she doing with the whole vocation thing?"

"I'll be there for Christmas Eve and Christmas day. She's having a little Christmas Eve 'Soiree', she calls it. I won't know most of the people there; doctors and their wives from the hospital. She doesn't talk too much about my wanting to be a Dominican. I think she thinks it's just a phase I'm going through. There will probably be a handful of doctors' daughters at the soiree. Kind of like Thomas Aquinas's family, well, maybe not quite that drastic. I'm not being kidnapped and held in the family tower, but she thinks I just need to fall in love with the right girl and get married, and then go to medical school and live happily ever after."

"And what are you thinking? What do you pray about?"

"Oh, I still want to be a Dominican. More than ever. That was my intention for the Camino. I kept looking for a sign, but nothing extraordinary happened. Todd wants to enter the Franciscans this next year, but he can't decide which ones. His father won't pay off his student loans either, so he may not be able to go yet. I need to get a better job this year; it's not really good for me to work in a bar."

Going out on a bit of a limb, I softly asked, "Do you think you may have a problem with alcohol?"

"Oh, I don't think so. I gave it up for Advent. I can quit whenever I want to, and I just have to be careful if and when I do have a drink. I fell into a drinking crowd at Yale, you know…"

"Yes, but Yale has been over for a couple years." I didn't say anything more.

"I know. Two thousand seven will be a good year, a new beginning."

"Well, we'll both pray that it will be. And it looks like you didn't have any problem with the fruitcake nobody likes at Christmas!"

He laughed. "It was really good…for fruitcake, that is!"

"Would you like me to ask Sister Paula to wrap up the whole cake; better yet, let me get you a whole one; we've probably got two dozen! You can give it to your mom on Christmas Eve."

"That would be awesome."

I smile at him thinking, *Everything is 'awesome' to his generation, but I suspect the fruitcake fits the bill.* "I'll be back in three minutes." I left quickly, and headed for the little kitchen. Luckily Sr. Paula and Sr. Diana were both in there mixing up something or other.

"What's that around your neck?"

"Oh, I forgot." Taking it off and putting it in my pocket. "It's the pilgrim shell my nephew, Sharbel, had when he did the Camino; he gave it to me for Christmas."

"Oh, that's St. James' Scallop; Princess Diana loved them; her family had one on their coat of arms." Only Sr. Diana, of course, would have known that. "I think it's a sign of grace and new life; what an awesome gift before the new year."

"Yes, awesome. Sharbel also found the fruitcake awesome. Sister Paula, do you think we could spare one he could take to his mother for Christmas Eve?"

"Oh, sure, let me get one just like it; it has a really pretty lid too. I'm glad he liked it; I thought he would; it's loaded with Kentucky bourbon."

Fifteen

News Year's Day 2007

Magne Pater sancte Dominice, mortis hora nos te cumsuscipe, et hic sempter nos pie respice. Great Father, holy Dominic, take us up with you at the hour of our death, and always watch over us lovingly here below. (Antiphon honoring St. Dominic, Compline)

LORD, IT'S BEEN quite a day and what a beginning of a new year! How can I even begin to describe it! Sr. Immaculate Heart was telling us at recreation that her great nephew was trying his vocation with the Camaldolese hermits in Ohio, and that he loved the solemnities because they didn't have work and had more time for prayer. Of course, You know all that, but I thought how wonderful that would be. We seem to have less time for prayer and lots of extra things to do for a Solemnity. I'm not complaining, Lord, it's all worth it, especially like today, when we honor Your Mother. What a wonderful way to start the new year. The day when we wonder what the new year, 2007, will hold. The year, Lord? Little did we know how the afternoon would unfold!

I had an extra hour this morning when the novices were having chant practice and I wasn't needed anywhere else, and Sr. Precious Blood asked me to fill in for her hour of guard because they needed her to help in the kitchen. It was wonderful, Lord, because I had You all to myself. I started my new year's resolution, as You know, reading from *Divine Intimacy* every morning. Makes me think of those times when I wish I were a Carmelite and had two hours of mental prayer every day. But I think You provided this extra hour for me today. Thank you, Lord. I offered my Holy Communion this morning, as You know, for Gracie Price. Every New Year's I remember my New Year's Eve with her and her Mom and Dad, when we prayed the rosary together and drank champagne when the Ball fell in Times Square...1966... the year I became a Catholic and the year Gracie went to Heaven. My gift to her was my secret that I was going to be a Catholic and I wanted her to be my godmother. Dear Gracie.

After my Holy Hour, I had some free time. The novices and aspirants were cooking up a storm in the infirmary kitchenette to make a new year's surprise for the infirmary Sisters; the simple professed were in the main kitchen, and so I was totally free. I didn't have any real visitors, and so with Mother's permission, I called over to Fr. Matthew. I wouldn't call Fr. Matthew a "visitor." After all, he lives here. He didn't have any company either, so we had planned to get together for a parlor after Terce; however, all the parlors were occupied, so we had our little new year's "chat" in the sacristy. We have two sacristies, one for the priests and one for the Sister Sacristan; there is a large turn joining the two rooms so the priest can talk to the sacristan. It's not the most private of places, but I taped a note up on the door on my side: "Occupied till Sext. SMB." I had already told Sr. George, the sacristan, and got her okay. The note was for other wandering nuns.

"Happy New Year, Fr. Goldman," I began when I slid the turn around to create the open space between us. He was seated in a sacristy chair, making him look like a midget priest.

"And *L'chaim* to you, Sister Feinstein of the Adverse Heart." I laughed as he would tease me with that title, my real title being "of the Advent Heart."

I dragged a chair over to the turn, so we'd be on the same level. "Thank you, as always, for the beautiful Mass this morning. You haven't lost your voice yet, you know; you must have cantor genes in your DNA."

He laughed. "Perhaps. Aunt Sarah always said I missed my true vocation."

"To be a cantor?"

"No, she had Broadway in mind, or radio broadcasting."

"Well, the Lord had other plans, thank God. Speaking of Aunt Sarah, what did you finally do with her ashes?"

"You promise not to tell anyone?" I held up three fingers like a Girl Scout pledge. "I have them in my bedroom closet in a nice box that looks like a carrying case for a chalice. I should tell you that just in case I kick the bucket before I dispose of them."

"Oh my, that's awful."

"Well, I think I have a few more years ahead of me."

"I don't mean you, I mean Aunt Sarah in your closet. Is it sacrilegious or uncanonical or something? In your closet? Oy."

"Not really. I don't know about the Jewish side of that. Cremation would never be done to begin with; what to do with the ashes afterwards would not even be a question. I just don't know what to do. I thought about asking you to ask your sister to take her along on her next cruise and dump her overboard when no one was looking."

"Ezra!"

"Well, she wants to be buried at sea, remember. I can't put her in the cemetery here; it is consecrated ground and Aunt Sarah wouldn't be comfortable." (He looked at me for my reaction to his quip, but I was thinking, Sr. Bertrand should be here to respond to that one!)

"So I have an appointment with a Rabbi Judith Collingswood next week to inquire about a potter's field kind of arrangement in a Jewish cemetery."

"Collingswood? Doesn't sounded too kosher to me."

"It must be her married name. Imagine, a Reformed Jewish woman rabbi married to a Presbyterian." And we both laughed.

"Poor Aunt Sarah. I think you should go dig a hole somewhere in Central Park in the middle of the night and bury her there. She never went to shul. She went to Central Park...remember she told us she'd go to the Boat House for coffee. Ah! The Boat House...rent a row boat and drop her off the side."

Ezra didn't respond immediately. He was thinking...or remembering.

"That's not a bad idea, but it's too cold out right now; the ground's probably frozen solid, and the lake is frozen. I'll see. I don't think she'd like the murky water at the Boat House;

she liked their coffee, that's about it. But the Park might do. In the meantime, maybe Rabbi Collingswood will have the right answer. By the way, I checked Canon Law about the question you had about Sharbel. The impediment of illegitimacy no longer exists in the new code. So no worries."

"I wish that were the only worry I had. We had a nice visit on Christmas, as you know. He gave me his pilgrim's scallop. I have it under my guimpe. He's looking for a new job; he thinks his mother is trying to set him up with a romantic interest. He had stopped drinking for Advent, but I don't know if that lasted. He says he wants to be a Dominican, but I don't where he really is with the whole vocation thing."

"Give it time, Sister; you know it takes time, sometimes, to work things out. It's a different world they're coming from than we came from, and we thought ours was pretty wild!"

"It *was* wild, in its own way. Remember Woodstock! But you're right."

"So how are the girls?" (That's how he'd refer to the novices when speaking just to me.)

"Oh, they have their ups and downs too. We do have two aspirants with us right now; you've seen them when they come for Communion. Havana Sanchez from Miami, but living here in Brooklyn for a number of years with her mother and grandmother—a little strange, but surprisingly she's also a real charmer—and Kristen Atkinson, she'll graduate from Notre Dame next spring. She seems very promising. Her family lives in Irvington, New Jersey. I'm not sure how they are about the whole vocation thing either. I think they were expecting Kristen to go on to Law School; the

CHAPTER FIFTEEN 133

father apparently is a big shot lawyer in the City, pardon my slang. Sometimes I catch myself sounding like Ruthie."

"Or your Mother!"

"Such a mother I should sound like?" Ezra laughed his old young-man laugh.

"And what's your new year's resolutions, Fr. Goldman?"

But before he could answer, the fire alarm sounded; both of us jumped and nearly fell off our chairs. There's an alarm right in the extern sacristy. I jumped up and rushed to the door.

"Oh my!" is all I said, as I opened the door, and looked past the chapel to the cloister and saw smoke pouring out and around the corner. I shouted back at Ezra, "It's coming from the infirmary. Oh my. Oh my. I hope the Sisters are okay." And I rushed off, letting the sacristy door slam behind me. I didn't even genuflect as I passed the Lord in our beautiful solemnity monstrance.

The smoke was very thick, and I could hear Sisters coughing, and running down the cloister. Sr. Barbara, the infirmarian, was pushing Sr. Gerard in her geri-chair out to the back door. I knew there was a side door in the infirmary which was meant as a fire escape, and hopefully that's how they all got out. I went down the cloister and through the little kitchen and through the refectory, and out another door, as Sisters were coming as fast as they could down the stairs from the professed dormitory. *The novitiate!* I thought. It's just above the infirmary, so I dashed up the back stairs, I ran down the corridor to the novitiate and saw Sr. Leah Marie and Sr. Kateri grabbing things, and I shouted, "Leave it all, get yourselves out." The smoke was beginning to pour up the stairs and into the novitiate. The alarm seems to scream louder and louder.

"Oh, Sister Baruch, it's awful; there was an explosion in the infirmary kitchen," Kateri could just about get it out. "The old sisters started to yell and panic, it was awful."

"I'm glad you were there to help control things."

Mother's voice suddenly came over the p.a. system which was very startling in itself, as we never use it. "Leave everything behind, Sisters, and evacuate the building. The back door is clear…move towards the back. Leave everything."

I didn't even have time to think what I had that was worth saving…a clean habit maybe; my journals…Squeak. Oh my, Squeak! I dashed back up ahead of a wave of black smoke, and bounded into our cell. Squeak was oblivious to anything, of course, but I threw the books on her seat onto the floor, dragged her out of the cell by her back, and in a grand swoop, hoisted her onto my shoulders. That nearly knocked me down the stairs, along with a wave of guilt. I heard again Mother's admonition: "Leave everything." But I couldn't leave Squeak to be burned up like firewood. I was taking her back because obedience is at the heart of everything. But then Sr. Elijah Rose was bounding down the stairs. I couldn't go back up. So I turned Squeak around, grabbed the back, and dragged her down the stairs.

"Let me help you, Sister," came the reassuring voice of Sr. Elijah Rose, who grabbed onto the rocker legs. The sweat was pouring down the back of my neck; I thought I would dislocate my shoulder at one point, but we barreled on, and together we made it to the back door.

Another wave of guilt hit me; there could be Sisters crawling on the floor to get out, and I'm saving a stupid old rocking chair. At the bottom of the stairs, I dropped Squeak just outside the door, inhaled a breath of cold fresh air, and bounded back up the stairs. Sr. Elijah Rose ran over to the other door and charged into the cloud of smoke holding her scapular up to her nose.

Rushing back up the stairs, I nearly fell stepping on my tunic, but grabbed the railing in time and hoisted up my skirt. A waft of smoke came down the stairs and hit me with a sudden choking sensation; my eyes were burning, and I felt my stomach flip; I was afraid I was going to throw-up. I felt like my forehead was red as a lobster. I tried not to open my mouth, but that didn't work. At the second floor landing, the hallway going towards the library was still clear, so I ran, open mouth, coughing as I went, holding up my scapular and tunic. It was the first time in thirty-five years I ran down this hallway. "Are there any Sisters here? Sisters? Sisters?"

Sr. Antonia came running out of the library nearly crying. "The books…all the books. What will happen to the books?"

"The books will be fine, Sister, get yourself outside." I didn't know that for sure, of course, but the library was at the other end of the fire; certainly it will be contained, I prayed, before it reached this end. I followed Sr. Antonia down the far end stairs and outside. I've never been so out of breath in my life. Gasping and breathing in the fresh air was marvelous. We grabbed each other's hands and ran around to the back entrance to join the others.

I learned later that the chapel was full of smoke; Mother had unlocked the enclosure door, and Fr. Matthew came

through, and went immediately to the monstrance and
removed the luna holding the Sacred Host, then to the
tabernacle, and grabbed the ciborium. He came through
the nuns' sacristy, and quickly set the ciborium down on a
vestment case, and unlocked the little case on the wall with
the holy oils, put them in his pocket, grabbed a purificator,
soaked it with holy water from the bucket on the counter,
held it to his nose and mouth, picked up the ciborium again,
and made his way down the side cloister through a cloud of
smoke and out the back door. The fire had not reached the
sacristy or chapel, but the smoke was filling the cloister like a
dense fog. The monstrance left behind was empty and silent.
Sister Paula saw it, ran up the altar steps and grabbed the
monstrance and wrapped it in her apron and made her way
out. There was blood running down the front of her tunic.
We nearly collided in the cloister.

"Sister, you've got blood all over your tunic."

"I fell going up the stairs to direct the two retreatants who
were running down the wrong way. I'm alright."

Sisters were coughing and gagging from smoke inhalation, but they were able to stagger out into the fresh air,
as we heard the fire engines arriving, their sirens screaming
through the once silent air that normally surrounded us.
People were hollering obscenities outside the wall; I think
the traffic was all tied up. Over the enclosure wall, we could
see the hook and ladder rising above the infirmary windows,
the smash of glass, and the sudden gush of water blasting
through the window. Oh what a sight it must be making.
More windows smashed. A distant scream heard.

Other firemen with masks rushed into the building, down the short hall and directly into the infirmary, knocking over the little table lamps in the corners. One burly looking fireman with a reddish beard helped Sr. Catherine Agnes (SCAR) down the stairs, holding on, till she swooned into a faint, and he scooped her up in his arms and rushed toward the open door, his heavy boots pounding on our wooden floors. He put her in Squeak, which was conveniently by the door, and he rocked her and bent her over and back again. She coughed, opened her eyes, and looking at the bearded one, asked, "And who, pray tell, are you?" And oddly enough, she laughed. And he laughed, kissed her on the cheek, and took off towards the burning building. SCAR patted Squeak's arms, and rocked back, breathing in the cold air, patting her cheek where she had been kissed. It assuaged my guilt a little; Squeak was there to hold up SCAR and help her get her breath back.

Sr. Antonia and I had come down the far end stairs, around the corner of the building. I had run from the novitiate, assured that no one was in there. Panic struck me, however, as Sr. Elijah Rose was not back after I saw her charging into the smoke and up the stairs. I interiorly felt enraged, *That stupid girl; she shouldn't do that! She never thinks...*but before I could holler, there she was, carrying Sr. Jane Mary, in her own arms, down the stairs. I don't know where she got the strength. Sr. Jane Mary was holding on for dear life, tears rolling down her ashen face. I think Sr. Elijah Rose was singing to her. (I was right as I asked her later what she was singing to Sr. Jane Mary in a scene forever emblazoned in my memory! And Sr. Elijah Rose told me: *"Mama's little* *baby loves shortnin, shortnin, Mama's little baby loves short-nin bread.*" Only now do I laugh out loud at it all. Of all songs for a strict, former prioress, proper Canadian; she was being comforted by Sr. Elijah Rose's soothing rendition of '*Mama's little baby loves shortnin bread!*') Not only that, but my esteem for Sr. Elijah Rose swelled my heart. She's a native New Yorker, our former Nurse Brenda Hubbard, and here she is in a full Dominican nun's habit carrying an elderly sister down the stairs, singing a song she must've remembered from her own childhood. Funny, how tragic moments or really scary moments can bring our poor lives into focus, and even change our rage and/or fear into tears of admiration! How much today's young ones are giving up…the young ones! The young ones! The aspirants. Where were they?

I didn't see them anywhere, and they had been in the infirmary. Another moment of panic shot through me like an arrow. I was just getting my breath to holler "Havana!" when I saw them making their way out the door. Havana seemed to stay cool and collected in the midst of it all, look-ing like she was in a daze or sleepwalking, (*maybe she's in shock, Lord?*) while Kristen was in a panic mode becoming manic about where to turn. Poor thing, she had only been with us inside since three days after Christmas. She's proba-bly sorry she ever left Irvington, New Jersey. They were the last to make it out, we thought, holding wet tea towels up to their noses and mouths.

Kristen hollered when she saw me, "Sister Agnes Mary… poor Sister Agnes Mary." Our former prioress came out in the arms of a fireman, his mask slung off and hanging behind his neck. He looked like he was kissing her, and smacking her.

As soon as they got to the outside, he lay her on the ground and continued his mouth to mouth resuscitation, but her head fell to the side. She was gone. Her veil and guimpe were pulled half way off, and her cropped white hair framed her face, showing no sign of struggle. I paused in utter amazement. She looked totally at peace. *Lord, have mercy on her soul. Dear Sister Agnes Mary…*Sr. George was by her side, and took her hand and kissed it. "She's at peace now; she has seen the Lord." Mother Bernadette hurried over to her, and gasped when she saw her face, her eyes still open in the blank stare of one who has just died. Mother exclaimed, "Get Fr. Matthew." Ezra was already on his way there.

Another boom startled us, and part of the second floor ceiling collapsed into the infirmary common room, smashing the plaster statute of Our Lady of Fatima, just missing Sr. Barbara who had returned with a fireman and was trying to drag out the metal box with the meds in them. She actually had a mask on over her coiffure, shouting orders, or directions, at the fireman.

Many Sisters huddled together by the body of Sr. Agnes Mary, as we counted each other and prayed out loud the *Memorare* to Our Lady as the smoke subsided, and all we could hear was the water gushing from the hoses, and grown nuns weeping into their scapulars. Dear Sr. Cecilia, almost by instinct now, intoned the *Salve Regina*, and the small group gathered around the body of Sr. Agnes Mary joined in the singing amidst coughing and weeping.

I counted. The novitiate Sisters were all here, and thank God, were helping the older Sisters. Sr. Leah was missing, but came hurrying back with several pitchers of water from the refectory and paper cups, and another wave of admiration struck me; she did that on her own, not thinking of herself. Mother Bernadette was moving rapidly among the Sisters, counting them all by name.

Fr. Matthew, kneeling on the grass beside the body of Sr. Agnes Mary, anointed her with holy oil, truly "extreme unction," and I saw his hand blessing her, and hopefully giving her the Apostolic Blessing. I stood silent for a moment, feeling very much alone, but united to Our Lord, and in that moment prayed my prayer. *Lord, have mercy on her soul. And Lord, however I go, please let me receive the Apostolic Blessing.* I was instantly comforted and happy to be a "Bride of Christ," an image I rarely thought of, but somehow knew it in that instance. I was so happy, Lord, to be a Catholic and to be united to You. The panic and fear disappeared, and I took a deep breath and looked around at these women who were my sisters all these years, in this monastery we call 'home.'

Sr. Leah suddenly came into focus, handing me a plastic glass of water. "Are you all right, Sister?" Her voice was full of compassion and concern.

"I am, Sister. I am." And I wrapped my arms around her and hugged her, causing her to spill water all down the front of both of us. And we looked at each other and laughed. Everything was okay. The Sisters gathered around the body of Sr. Agnes Mary sang the Compline antiphon to St. Dominic: "*Great Father, holy Dominic, take us up with you at the hour of our death, and always watch over us lovingly here below.*"

I caught sight of Sr. Annunciata sitting alone in a folding chair, holding Our Lord in the ciborium which Fr. Matthew had handed to her. Her head was slightly bowed, but she was fine. I took my half glass of water over to her. She was very grateful. "I'm so parched, thank you, Sister Baruch."

"Tell Our Lord thank you for me." And I left her puzzled, no doubt, at my request. There was a firemen and two firewomen (I learned later the correct title is "firefighters") administering oxygen from small portable cases to the Sisters still coughing. Sr. Jane Mary, still kind of wrapped in Squeak's wooden arms, was breathing and still coughing; Sr. Elijah Rose knew just how to bend her to maximize the good air. Kristen was helping poor Sr. Gerard; she had gotten a cool wash cloth to lay on Sister's forehead, and I noticed she was patting Sister's shaking hands very kindly. Havana stood off from the crowd without any emotion, it seemed, and just watched.

"Havana, go with Sister Kateri and bring woolen blankets out for the Sisters; it's cold as the dickens out here." I surprised myself by my own shouting. But she took off immediately, looking for Sr. Kateri.

But it was old Sr. Gerard from her geri-chair—her veil all askew, the washcloth on her forehead and her hands shaking—who shouted, "Sister Bertrand! Where is Sister Bertrand?" A tear flowed down old Sr. Gerard's chubby cheeks. Her nemesis was missing from the crowd.

Sixteen

Same Afternoon

*O spem miram...O wonderful hope, which you gave to
those who wept for you at the hour of your death, promising
that after your death you would be helpful to your brethren!
Fulfill, Father, what you have said, and help us by your
prayers.* (Antiphon honoring St. Dominic, Compline)

Mother Bernadette heard Sr. Gerard call Sr. Bertrand's
name and spun around, looking over the small groups of
Sisters and firemen. "Sister Bertrand?" She grabbed on to
the arm of the closest fireman and said, "One elderly sister is
unaccounted for...Sister Bertrand. I must go find her."

The fireman held her back. "Don't go, Sister, I will go,"
he said, putting his mask on as he moved towards the side
door and the stairs leading up to the infirmary. Smoke was
still pouring down the stairs. Mother brushed him aside, her
handkerchief over her nose, "I must find Sister Bertrand; I
must."

"Stand aside, Madame, I insist, or I shall get the chief to
help me?" He bounded up the stairs alone, "Sister Berkman?
Birchman?"

Mother hollered after him, "Sister Ber—trand, as in Louis Bertrand," as if that would help. And under her breath added, "I am the chief, here, Lord, am I not? You take care of everything." Mother was suddenly very anxious, and called the Sisters who were close by to come together and pray the *Memorare* again for Sr. Bertrand.

I joined the little group, praying for her with all my heart. One suddenly realizes how precious and dear one is when you lose them. Sr. Bertrand was certainly a "pip" as Mother Rosaria used to say. But she was our pip, and she was lost in a deadly fire. I felt the urge to run back up the stairs with the fireman.

I thought of dear Mother Rosaria, and thanked the Lord she was at our monastery in West Springfield for the Christmas season. She needed the rest. She will be so upset when she hears of our fire and the Sisters who have died, presuming Sr. Bertrand is among them.

Fr. Matthew was conferring with the firemen, who were collecting their gear. The smoke was almost gone; the smell of burnt wood, and old carpets, upholstery, and fire-hazard drapes lingered in the air. The fireman who went in search of Sr. Bertrand came back out alone. He spread out his arms like a priest at the opening prayer.

"No Sister Berkman." Sr. Gerard cried out and held her arms out in a full orans position and howled, "Oh Lord, have mercy on our Sister Bertrand."

The Sisters became suddenly silent. Even the water gushing from the hoses stopped, and the ladder was slowing moving back into place. The Sisters silently huddled together; the few around the body of Sr. Agnes Mary held on to each other. I think we all had our heads down, bowed in silent prayer, when from atop the monastery, from the front corner of the roof, came what sounded like a "hoot owl:"

"Yooouuuuu wwhhoooo? Yooooouuuuu wwhhoooooo?" We looked up, and there she was from the roof garden, waving her white scapular and "hooting" at us. Sister Bertrand was alive and safe and "on top of it all."

Mother Bernadette, with a fireman's helmet put on over her veil and a fireman's jacket, and her newly acquired friendly fireman went up through the debris to bring her down.

When she appeared coming out the door five minutes later, the Sisters gave a spontaneous round of applause and ran over to welcome her. Sr. Bertrand was waving like the pope come out on the balcony.

The first words out her mouth were, "What the Sam Hill is going on?" And we got hysterical laughing. "My one new year's resolution was to pray the rosary on the roof-top garden, even in the bitter cold. I was all wrapped up in two army blankets, and on the glider seat with the left over snow, and I heard a boom and sirens. I thought, 'O Lord, another terrorist attack, and I'm on the roof.' So I crouched down in the corner where the tomato plants used to be, and prayed my rosary."

We all quieted down, listening to her every word, amazed at how Divine Providence intervenes in every moment of our lives. Sister hated the roof garden, and never went up there after 9/11. Today she did!

"I could hardly meditate on the fourth glorious mystery for all the sirens."

And we laughed again. Sister Gerard was up and out of her geri-chair, walking over silently with her arms open, and enveloped Sr. Bertrand in a huge bear-hug. I don't know why, but we all applauded again.

Sr. Agnes Mary's body was quietly taken inside with the help of two Brooklyn firefighters and a canvas stretcher they had with them. Her body was laid to rest on a couch in the community room. Mother got everyone moving back into the monastery; she called the doctor, and the coroner, and made her way up the stairs to look at the damage. A temporary infirmary was already being put together using the end of the professed floor which had a number of empty cells. Two unused cells in the novitiate would need major work, but no one was injured.

The bell for Vespers tolled like nothing had happened. The chapel was undamaged. There lingered the smell of the smoke, but Our Lord was back in the Solemnity Monstrance. I think we all welcomed Vespers with a New Year's urgency to be silent and pray. Granted, Vespers had a tinge of solemn gratitude, sadness, and peaceful reverence about it, like we knew we were safe and enfolded in His Solemnity Heart. We were able to begin our suffrages for Sr. Agnes Mary. It was all quite amazing. What a way to begin the new year!

Our recreation tonight was probably the most unique New Year's recreation we've ever had, but then, it was a most unique new year's day. Mother knew the best way to hold "it" all together was to follow custom, and so like every new year's night in the past, we drew our patron saints for the year, and our prayer intentions. These have always been done with reverent humor. They seemed more poignant this night after all we had just been through.

I was happy to draw St. Michael the Archangel. It's the first time I've ever drawn him. There always seems to be a mysterious link with the patron we draw each year, or so it has seemed to me. So I wonder what more this year could possibly hold in which I will invoke and have the special intercession of St. Michael, Archangel. My devotion to the Holy Angels hasn't always been the most fervent, but I decided then and there that would change.

The aspirants, Havana and Kristen, were given the charge of keeping guard (Eucharistic adoration) so we could all be together for recreation. Mother spoke briefly about the tragedy of Sr. Agnes Mary's dying from smoke inhalation. She had very weak lungs to begin with, and so just a little smoke would have been too much for her to handle, as indeed it was.

"Sister may have had weak lungs, but she was strong of heart. When she was prioress, as we all know, she was magnanimous of heart at a very difficult period during the renewal. She often spoke to me, when she first moved into the infirmary and I was infirmarian, that she offers everything to Our dear Lord, whatever sufferings He wants to give her, but she said she prays that He will be merciful and not let her linger too long, but draw her up quickly into 'the fire of His Divine Love.' Those were her exact words, Sisters, 'the fire of His Divine Love.' So while today's fire was certainly a tragedy we shall long remember, I cannot but help think Our Lord answered her prayer, and took her quickly, as the doctor said it would have been."

Those were comforting words from Mother Bernadette, and we all nodded in agreement. The infirmary Sisters were with us tonight, not in a separate group but mixed in with us in our recreation circle. They would have temporary cells in the professed dormitory till the infirmary was repaired.

Sr. Catherine Agnes (SCAR) spoke up, "Thank you, Mother, for those beautiful words and the sentiments they carry. We shall all miss our Sister Agnes Mary dearly, but we are also most grateful to you all who helped save our lives."

Sr. Jane Mary from her wheelchair raised her hand as if in a toast, "Here, here!" And surprisingly we all did the same. Sr. Jane Mary, still holding the floor, added, "And to you, Sister Elijah Rose, Blessed be God."

And we all responded, "Now and forever."

With that Sr. Paula arrived clankity clank clank, pushing the metal cart with Martinelli sparkling apple juice, a white porcelain tea pot full of hot cocoa, and three bottles of New York's Moet champagne, a gift, as the card read, from our community's "Yorkshire Penguin." Gwendolyn had sent us a case of champagne for Christmas. "To add a little sparkle to your New Year." Little did she realize!

Sr. Simon, who would move into the infirmary this new year, had prepared a couple dozen homemade soft pretzels with and without salt. This was such a nice change from the usual cake and ice cream. Soft pretzels were a wonderful way to start off a new year, especially after a difficult and hard beginning.

We were 18 hours late, but we filled our glasses with something, and sang *Auld Lang Syne* and wished each other a healthy and happy new year. Having news of the fire,

Sr. Rosaria shortened her stay at West Springfield and left immediately to come back. She arrived just before recreation and to our delight spilled champagne down the front of her coiffure. Sr. Cecilia played *O Holy Night* on her clarinet and we all joined in the singing with quiet voices. Finally Sr. Elijah Rose recited a poem written by Sr. Benedict in her memory and for Sr. Agnes Mary and all our faithful departed. It was a fitting way to end the recreation, as we kind of drained our glasses, and made our way to the chapel for Compline. No pouce was needed.

Seventeen

Epiphany 2007

Alleluia. Omnes de Saba venient, alleluia, aurum, et thus deferentes, alleluia, alleluia. Alleluia. All those from Sheba shall come, alleluia; they shall bring gold and frankincense, alleluia, alleluia. (Nunc Dimittis antiphon for Epiphany, Compline)

IT HAS BEEN a good week, Lord, a week of recovery. The Gregorian chant of the Requiem Mass for Sr. Agnes Mary's funeral was both beautiful and somber, but in a hidden joyful way. The rising and falling of the phrases on the waves of the chant are so peaceful like the ebb and flow of the ocean. I had shared with Fr. Matthew the words of Mother Bernadette about Sister's prayer that she would be quickly drawn up into the fire of divine Love. He based his homily on those sentiments.

Our procession to the cemetery passed right over the very spot where she died, although that's probably not true. I think she died in the arms of the fireman carrying her out of the building. Not a bad image to have. We stood around her grave, as we always do, and sang our final *Salve Regina*, the Marian prayer we sing every night at Compline. It completes our day; it also completes our earthly life.

We were fortunate to get workmen in two days after the fire to begin to repair the floor and ceiling. The report from the Fire Chief said the fire was caused by a gas explosion from the oven, which caught the table cloth in the kitchenette on fire and spread rapidly through the kitchen and out into the common area because of the draft, which also caused the flames to rise. It was both the "gas" part and the "draft" part which mystified us. Someone had opened a window, which was peculiar because it was the infirmary, where the slightest draft was anathema, and it was the dead of winter. It also amazes me how the firemen can determine all those causes. Although, I think he came and talked to the Sisters in the infirmary. A fire doesn't just start on its own.

Havana and Kristen had not begun to cook yet and don't know who opened the window. No one apparently was actually in the kitchen when the gas explosion happened.

The Dominican Third Order and many of our kind benefactors gave us "a ton of money," the words of Sr. Elizabeth, the bursar. New beds and mattresses, chairs, and a beautiful new carpet were all quickly purchased for the renovated infirmary. The Sisters are hoping to move back in soon. A new electric stove and oven were purchased, and the new round table in the kitchenette would be left without a table cloth. (*Thank you, Lord.*)

An email from Gwendolyn confirmed that she would be here on January 20. She had business matters to clear up and would be staying with us in the guest quarters, grateful that we had room for her.

Mother announced that we would have recreation this evening in the large parlor, as "one of the three wise men would be visiting us, with a very special gift." The novices and I couldn't decide among all our Dominican Fathers and Brothers who were the three wise men, let alone a single one. They were all "wise men" to us; some more wise than others, we joked.

Dishes were done quickly; I think we were all anxious to know who the wise man was who was coming to visit, and whether he was bringing gold, frankincense, or myrrh.

We were all gathered in the big parlor, quietly chatting among ourselves. I was seated between Sr. Sheila and Sr. Kateri, who was hoping it was a Fr. Bergman who was a nuclear physicist. And I was hoping it was Fr. Ambrose, our former chaplain, home for the holidays.

We were all happily surprised when the parlor door opened and a very attractive woman in a full length mink coat and mink hat walked in. Most of us recognized her immediately: Rhonda Lynwood, the famous Broadway actress and movie star. Sr. Antonia, of all people, let out an audible gasp of delight, "It's Myrtle Pine from *Lonely Heart Legacy!*" Indeed, it was, although Myrtle Pine was her name in the movie which was all the rage around 1965. It was a romantic tear-jerker which ended with Myrtle entering a convent of nuns in Montreal.

Rhonda Lynwood had been nominated for an Academy Award, and while she went on to star in a number of other films, it was *Lonely Heart Legacy* that made her famous.

And walking in 30 seconds behind her was Fr. Oyster, who opened his arms in a grand gesture, "Sisters, Happy New Year, and please welcome Rhonda Lynwood."

We actually stood and applauded. It was amazing. Sitting down again, I whispered to Sr. Sheila, "I wish Sister Gertrude were here to see this."

It was not unusual for us to get visits from various stars of stage and screen, as Sr. Gertrude would have said, but Rhonda Lynwood was certainly one of the most famous. She was at least in her mid-seventies, but looked fifty, and still had a deep melodious voice.

"Sisters, thank you for that warm welcome. I can't tell you how thrilled I am to be here. When Reggie, ooops, I mean Fr. Reginald, here invited me to join him, I couldn't think where else in all of New York I would rather be."

I think Fr. Oyster blushed and with a less than melodious voice explained, "Rhonda and I are in town for the premiere of a movie in which she makes a cameo appearance."

"I'm the star's grandmother, if you can believe that!"

We all laughed. I'm not sure why, except she thought it was hysterical, and it seemed like the polite thing to do.

Sr. Antonia raised her hand, like we were in school, and got Mother's attention to call on her. She spoke very excitedly.

"It was your role as Myrtle Pine that made me want to be a nun." None of us reacted adversely to Sister's outburst, but stared wide-eyed at Myrtle herself.

"How very kind of you to say that, dahling. Other nuns have told me that too. And I must confess to all of you, it was Myrtle Pine that made me want to become a Catholic! I had played other very romantic roles in my younger years,

but the role of Myrtle Pine was a difficult role to—how do
we say today? …wrap my mind around. I had no faith in
anything really, except all the glamor that comes with Hollywood, and I needed to get into this character. So I studied
the *Baltimore Catechism*, and would sneak into the back of
the chapel of the nuns in Hollywood when they were chanting their prayers. I think it was there that the moment of
grace happened." She said that very thoughtfully and put her
head down for a moment. We all just sat silently waiting for
her next line. I wondered if she was thinking or praying or
simply remembering.

"So you see, Sisters, the conversion that happened to
Myrtle Pine really happened to me. I had become a Catholic
three weeks before we shot the final scenes when she enters
the convent in Montreal."

We gave out a collective sigh, then after a silent pause,
Mother Bernadette spoke, "Thank you for sharing that with
us; I would imagine there are more than a few nuns who
would credit you with their thinking of a vocation. We are
a small community compared to the grand abbey where Sister Myrtle entered." We all kind of snickered as Sr. Myrtle
was not Myrtle Pine's religious name, but Mother couldn't
think what it was. It was Sr. Antonia again who filled in the
blank, "Sister Solange Marie, Mother, she was Sister Solange
Marie."

"Indeed, thank you, Sister. Sister Solange was one of my
favorite nuns too."

We were talking about her like she was a real character,
and we couldn't believe Sr. Solange Marie was sitting in front
of us in a mink coat, forty years later!

Wanting to change the subject no doubt, Ms. Lynwood looked about the drab and unpainted parlor. "This is a beautiful monastery with a wonderful location, as I'm sure you know. But do you know that I've been here before?"

"No, we didn't know that." Mother voiced the surprise for all of us.

Slipping off her mink coat and letting it fall draped on the back of the chair, and removing the mink hat, she shook out her ash-blonde hair and said, "I was a friend of your Sister Gertrude, and when I learned she passed away, I just happened to be in New York for a television engagement, and I came briefly to pay my respects at her wake."

I remembered that. We all had commented on the woman swathed in black with a black net-veil covering her face. We all thought it was probably a Broadway actress. She met with Mother Rosaria in the parlor who never revealed to us who she was.

"I owe a great deal to your Sister Gertrude. I was her understudy in an Off-Broadway show; I can't even think of the name of it now. It was my first part ever in a Broadway, albeit Off-Broadway, show. Bonnie Chapman was the lead actress, big enough to have an understudy, mind you. And I was she. I was a wreck every evening, afraid that Bonnie would not show up. Bonnie said I was nervous because I was not confident in my character, our character, and she taught me how to kind of relax and meditate, for lack of a better word, on being the character. 'You have to forget yourself,' she said. It was that simple. Forget yourself. And it worked. One Saturday matinée Bonnie called in with laryngitis and couldn't possibly go on. I made my debut, as it were, and thanks to Bonnie's confidence in me, I had the confidence. I've been forever grateful to her."

We all sat kind of speechless. We knew Sr. Gertrude for many more years than Rhonda did, and we knew the real Sr. Gertrude who said of herself that she was "always an understudy, never the leading role." It was Sr. Paula who added, "Sister Gertrude taught a lot of us to have confidence…to forget ourselves and to cling to the Lord."

I was sorry Havana and Kristen were not there, but glad that Srs. Elijah Rose, Leah Marie, and Kateri were there taking it all in. It takes both courage and confidence to persevere in our life, and sometimes that's most needed years later when we realize we aren't playing a role, but are in this for real.

Fr. Oyster was surprisingly silent during all this, sitting back with a big happy smile listening to it all. Then he leaned forward and seemed to be addressing Mother more directly than all of us.

"Rhonda is here on a kind of secret mission." We all inched silently towards Mother, our radar turned up to high. He turned toward Rhonda and became silent. We shifted our attention back to her.

"Well, it's a very delicate matter, and I didn't think Fr. Reginald was going to raise it so soon." She smiled but looked rather scornfully at him. We didn't know whether to love him or hate him at that moment.

"Actually, it's very short notice, I know, but I would love to make a retreat. I've never made a real retreat; I mean without conferences and some spiritual exercise every half hour." We all snickered under our guimpes.

It was Sr. Paula, the extern suddenly turned guest mistress, who blurted out, "You can stay with us! There are no retreat-ants till two weekends from now." In unison (it seemed), we turned from Sr. Paula, to Rhonda, to Mother.

Before anyone could respond, Fr. Oyster spoke again, directing his words to Mother. "That is the delicate part, you see. Rhonda is followed by paparazzi wherever she goes. This is not immediate, but sometime in the next couple months."

Silent until now, Sr. Bertrand spoke out without raising her hand, of course, "Papa who? Who's razzing her?"

Fr. Oyster laughed, "It's nobody's papa; it's the photogra-phers and gossip columnists who follow celebrities around. Even to get here unnoticed, we left through the kitchen entrance of the Waldorf and grabbed a cab."

"Well, I'll be dern tootin." Sr. Bertrand stomped her foot. She had gotten a whole new zest for life having been saved from the fire, her moment of celebrity.

Mother quietly intervened, "Go on, Father."

"We were hoping there would be a way that Rhonda could make her retreat, for a week or ten days, or perhaps even longer…" And he hesitated. You could have heard a pin drop at this point.

"Inside." Kaboom. Silence. Only Sr. Bertrand seemed to be listening close enough to get it.

"Inside what?"

Rhonda regained her voice back. "Inside the cloister with you. I know that's probably impossible and against the rules, but I wanted to at least try, and Father here thought there might be a way around it. I could never go to Holy Angels in Hollywood; the paparazzi already hang out there and wait for me to come out from Mass. I need to be hidden away where no one knows me. Flying into New York yesterday, I thought of Sister Gertrude, and of you, and well, I just ran it by Father Reginald over dinner last night." ("At the Waldorf" some of us heard Sr. Bertrand mumble under her breath.)

"We know this is highly unusual, and we don't need an answer right now, but hope you can discuss it among yourselves and get back to me." Fr. Oyster was sounding like her agent, a role he no doubt plays with great confidence.

At that point, we all held our breath, knowing Mother would lower the "Absolutely Not" boom, but to our surprise, she said, "I will discuss it with my Council and the community, and we will get back to you within 48 hours. Will that work?"

"Thank you, Mother, that's more than I hoped for. I shan't be a problem; I can be as quiet as a mouse, and you wouldn't even know I'm there."

We all smiled, thinking of Sr. Solange Marie. The conversation turned several directions before Mother reminded us that it was time for Compline. We all thanked Rhonda Lynwood for coming, and promised we would keep her in our prayers.

Eighteen

Friday After Epiphany

It is the Lord who grants favors to those whom he loves; the Lord hears me whenever I call him. (Psalm 4, Sunday Compline)

THE MONDAY MORNING after Epiphany, Mother called the Council together at 10:30 a.m. This consisted of Mother, Sr. Anna Maria, the subprioress, myself as novice mistress, and Sr. Thomas Mary and Sr. Catherine Agnes (SCAR) as elected members.

"Well, I guess our 'wise man' from the west didn't leave us with a gift, but with a dilemma. It is a highly unusual request, and I hope you've all been thinking about it."

SCAR was the first to offer an opinion. "I don't think we should allow such a breach of enclosure. Nor do we want to set a precedent. We are not a retreat house; we have very nice rooms outside the enclosure that would do just fine."

Sr. Anna Maria tended to agree with that, underlining that we don't want to set a precedent.

"I don't think we're setting any precedent," I joined in. "She wants it to be highly secretive. No one needs to ever know; so there's hardly a precedent."

"That's true," Sr. Thomas Mary added, "but there's the whole canonical question to consider; our Constitutions are quite clear."

"Well, I did a little research earlier this morning." Mother Bernadette took over the floor, or in this case, the table. "The regulations in *Venite Seorum* (a papal document on the enclosure of nuns) are very clear, with a possible loop hole of persons engaged in instruction or a service to the community, and for other reasons, an indult would need to be granted. There are really more regulations regarding our leaving the enclosure than about who may come in. We know that prelates, visitators, priests and servers for liturgical reasons, physicians or others whose skill is required, with the permission of the bishop, may enter." None of us said anything yet. We were all familiar with these.

"When the community filed out for Compline, I lingered behind to say goodbye, and it was then that Fr. Oyster and Ms. Lynwood filled me in on another part of the puzzle. Apparently, Ms. Lynwood has been diagnosed with terminal cancer. This has not yet been made known to the public. She told me I could share this with the community. She has less than six months. She has lived a devout life, but not always a sinless one, is how she put it. She wants to do penance and to get her life reconciled and in order with God. She knows that is not possible to the degree she would like were she on the outside." We sat in silence for a minute.

Mother resumed speaking, "You're all right; it would be most unusual and extraordinary. I just think we are being called to an act of charity. Many of our monasteries are facing dire situations with decreasing numbers entering and our infirmaries overflowing. As you all know, we are coming onto hard times just in maintenance, and the future is going to call for more and more repairs. We are faithful in our observance, I would say, without comparing us to others or bragging to ourselves. I wish there were something we could do to help Ms. Lynwood in her time of need."

"You're right, Mother, and our living an enclosed life is what we are doing for her, and for the whole Church for that matter. That we do is itself a grace for her. And so it is a grace for her to want what we have. If she comes inside, we take that away from her…one of the Fathers would say, 'we stop preaching to her.' And that would not be charity." I was suddenly feeling very convinced of this, but knew there must also be a way to reach out to her without pulling her inside. I sunk into my quiet place and closed my eyes.

"Well, there are plenty of retreat houses up and down both coasts; half of them are empty, I hear." This was the positive insight of Sr. Thomas Mary, who was most aware of our maintenance issues, but not the most pastoral in her solutions. She thinks we should close half the place down and cram us all together in the west wing where we'd get more afternoon sunlight. She prays for the boilers and hot water tanks.

"Sister Mary Baruch's friend will be occupying the best guest rooms; I don't suppose we could ask her to share?" That was Sr. Anna Maria, the subprioress, whom I thought was my friend. It wasn't so much in what she said, but the way she said it. It pulled me out of my quiet place in time to hear Mother come to the rescue.

"No, that wouldn't work out; as Fr. Oyster put it, she really needs privacy. I don't know if there are Trappistine or Carmelite monasteries that might be able to take her, or hermitages that I hear are quite lovely, but she has a special attachment to us, or so it seems." Sr. Thomas Mary let out a little exasperated humph.

Mother sat back in her chair looking at each of us. "I just don't know what we could do." I raised my hand like we were at a monastic council seminar.

"Sister Mary Baruch?"

"Well, Mother, there is the Cave. We've used it as a hermitage for ourselves, but it's really outside the enclosure. It hasn't been used in a couple years for retreatants, as I recall, but I think it could be fixed up. It was the chaplain's quarters years ago, remember, before our time actually. There was a parlor added when it became a family guest quarter. There's a bedroom and bathroom with shower, a study, a little kitchenette, and a parlor with a grille where she could meet with anyone with perfect privacy. The stairs go up to the sacristy, and if Father Matthew would be willing, she could have his far end pew off to the side. It's quiet and hidden from the rest of the chapel. No one in the extern chapel would see her."

We sat silent for a long pause. Mother spoke, "That's a brilliant idea. The rooms do need some work, but we have like a month before she plans to come, if we agree. It's very private, as you said. There's always the chance that someone will recognize her, and there are the altar boys on Sundays…"

"The altar boys wouldn't have a clue who she is." This was SCAR's offhand remark. "You could always give her a postulant's veil and a pair of glasses or something; anyone peeking around that corner would think she's a Sister from another congregation on retreat. I think Sister Baruch has solved our problem." She smiled…a rare event.

"I shall run it by Fr. Oyster, but I think it would work. It would require a Sister to bring her a tray at least for the main meal; there is a turn in that little parlor. She could do breakfast on her own in the kitchenette."

"There's also no Wi-Fi or television or computer outlets down there, so she will go through withdrawal on her own." The wise words of Sr. Paula who seemed to know about these things.

SCAR joined in again. "I remember when it was the chaplain's quarters. Fr. O'Toole lived there for a couple years. He used to call it *De Profundis*… *'Out of the depths'*; but Mother John Dominic named it *The Cave*. It doesn't have any windows, you know, except the small one in the bathroom which looks out on the stone foundation under the enclosure wall."

"And what about fire regulations?" Sr. Thomas Mary, always finding something to use as a monkey wrench.

SCAR rebounded. "That was taken care of. One can exit through the sacristy, or through the door at the top of the stairs off the bathroom, which connects to the boiler room, and up other stairs to the extern hall which is locked from the outside." There was so much wisdom hidden beneath that unstarched guimpe.

So the problem was settled after Terce. After None, Mother called us all back in and confirmed that Fr. Oyster and Rhonda Lynwood were both thrilled with the idea, and Rhonda said she could play the part of a visiting Sister with great aplomb. We all smiled, pretending we all knew what 'aplomb' meant. We knew she could do it—she was Sr. Solange Marie after all.

"Now, Sister Mary Baruch, you are charged with being her guardian angel, that is, the liaison between her and the community. You have permission to speak with her in the private parlor there at any time. You can arrange for the younger Sisters to bring her meals, and between now and when she comes, perhaps you and the novices can spiffy up the place a bit. Sister Paula can help her with the choir books in the chapel, if she's interested in following along."

Sr. Paula and I nodded to each other, and in unison said, "Yes, Mother, blessed be God."

"It is most important, Sisters, that no one mentions this to anyone, including relatives and friends or Third Order members, or volunteers, that she is here. I will make all this known to the entire community this evening at a special community meeting. Are there any questions?"

"No, it sounds like you have it all worked out," Sr. Thomas Mary sarcastically responded. "Let's hope Sister Baruch won't be passing out autographs."

"Our help is in the Name of the Lord," was Mother's only response. Sr. Catherine Agnes (SCAR) looked at me and put her index finger up to her lips, a gesture any Sister under fifty would know immediately. But did she mean for me not to respond back at Sr. Thomas Mary's sarcasm, or that

I in particular shouldn't breathe a word to anyone? Probably both. SCAR knew me too well, I chuckled to myself, delighted at the prospect of being Rhonda Lynwood's guardian angel. And the immediate "Oh no" feeling that I wouldn't be able to share this with Gwendolyn who would arrive in a few days, or my sister Sally, or Sharbel, who might not even know who Rhonda Lynwood is! Such problems I should have?

* * *

Mother filled in the community with the news at our community meeting that evening. Afterwards, on my way to the chapel, I noticed my office phone blinking. To my surprise, there was a voice mail for me from Sharbel's mother, along with her number and the request to call her at my 'nearest convenience.' Sharbel's mother has never called me, and this gave me an immediate anxiety attack, not literally, but interiorly. I hadn't really heard from him since Christmas. I carried his gift scallop in my habit pocket every night for Compline to remind me to pray for him. Fr. Matthew told me not to reach out to him, but to let him get in touch with me. He might be going through a crisis and is embarrassed or intimidated to talk to me about it. Embarrassed, I could understand, but I don't know why anyone would be 'intimidated' to talk to me! I'm just a little unknown nun hidden away in a cloister in Brooklyn Heights... with a rocking chair and a clam shell in her pocket.

I called Dr. Ghattas's number immediately, and got an answering machine, so I left the message that I called and would try again. Sr. Anna Maria popped into my office, which was unusual, to give me some correspondence she hoped I would answer for Mother, a job I had been doing for the last three prioresses. But I think it was more to chat about Rhonda Lynwood.

"The one who's going to have to keep her mouth closed is Sister Paula. Sr. Extern Chatterbox." Sr. Anna Maria was being her usual cynical self.

I laughed, not so much in agreement, as in the way Sister said it. "I think we'll all have to practice custody of the mouth, including you...and me!" We laughed. It had been a long time since we had a good laugh together. Sr. Anna Maria and I knew each other before we entered here; we met while both on retreat. She was much more confident about everything, and knew the vocabulary much better than I. She talked about 'vocation discernment,' something I had never heard of, even from Fr. Meriwether. Sr. Anna Maria entered six months before I did, but we were still novices together for a year and a half. She helped me 'discern' SCAR's meanings when I would be corrected, which seemed like several times a day. Anna Maria was our *Laundry-mistress* (my name) for many years. Neither of us was very good about keeping the silence when we were folding sheets. But I felt like one could talk more naturally in the laundry than in the library where I was *Book-mistress*. There was something sacred about the library...but the laundry room?

Things changed when Anna Maria became subprioress, not for the worse, it just changed. It may have been just that we were both advancing in the life and what we thought was restrictive or unnatural just became normal for us. But I like it that I can still talk to her in a way I don't talk to anyone else. Like, we've grown up together in the life. I told her we'll have to get together so I can tell her all about my meeting with Sally and her friend. Sr. Anna Maria had met my sister when she came to pay her respects when I was sitting Shiva for Ruthie.

The next morning, I tried calling Sharbel's mother before Terce, and another "leave a message after the beep." I thought for a moment: "hospital." She didn't say that, but why would she be calling me?

We didn't have class as it was still the Christmas season till the Baptism of the Lord, which gave me a free afternoon to read, to run the dry mop through dust ball heaven under my bed, and spend an extra hour in the chapel before Vespers, trying to meditate on forgetting myself, and what needed to be done in "the Cave" to make it ready for our secret retreat-ant. I was making a mental note of things to do.

While Mother was in a lenient mood, I asked permission to make a phone call after Compline. I explained very briefly the urgency that Dr. Ghattas seemed to have when she left a message. Mother quickly agreed, and I made my way to my office and closed the door behind me.

To my relief, a woman's voice answered the phone.

"Dr. Ghattas?"

"One moment, please, may I ask who's calling?"

"It's Sister Mary Baruch, Sharbel's aunt in Brooklyn Heights."

"One moment, please." A young, very pleasant voice, I thought.

"Sister Baruch?"

"Yes, is this Dr. Ghattas?"

"Yes, Sister, it is; please call me Olivia. Thank you for getting back to me."

"You're welcome; is everything all right with Sharbel?" I came right out with it.

"I'm not sure, to tell you the truth. That's why I called you. I have not seen or heard from him since before New Year's."

"Oh my."

"He has disappeared like this before, but only for a day or two, and he'd call or show up at home. I called his work two days after the New Year, and they had no idea where he was, but I was to inform him if he wasn't there by the weekend he could kiss his job goodbye."

"Did you call his father's duplex? Maybe he's finally moved in, and just doesn't think, you know how young people can be." Here I was sounding like the expert on millennials.

"No, because I know he's sublet the apartment for the income. I called you hoping you would know if he'd run off to a Trappist monastery or something." She didn't giggle, nor did I, well, not too loudly.

"I'm sorry, Doctor, uh, Olivia, but I wish he had, at least we'd know where to look."

"Well, maybe you would. I wouldn't know where to begin. Do Trappist monasteries even have telephones or internet these days?"

"I don't know. But it certainly is worrisome, isn't it. I haven't seen Sharbel since Thanksgiving and Christmas." I didn't fill in the circumstances with "Officer Krupke" bringing him here.

"He has disappeared before, as I've said, but never this long."

I hesitated before saying it, but let it out, "Have you contacted the local hospitals?"

"I have actually. At least all the ones in the Metropolitan area, even Bellevue."

"Oh my. And nothing, huh?"

"No...nothing. Please let me know if you hear from him or if he appears on your doorstep."

"I will, Doctor, you can be assured. Did you try the hospitals in New Haven? Maybe he's back at Yale with his old college friends or fraternity or the pilgrims he walked the Camino with, or something." I was hoping I wasn't sounding too desperate.

"I didn't think of that. Thank you, Sister, that's a good idea. We would be very relieved if that's so."

"We?"

"Winona and I. That was Winona who answered the phone."

"Oh, is she your secretary?"

Dr. Ghattas laughed. "No, that's Sharbel's girlfriend."

"Oh." That was all I could say. "Please let me know if you find him. Good night now. God bless." And I hung up the phone in slow motion. I let my hand reach down into my pocket and touch the shell. *His girlfriend! Oy vey!*

Getting the Cave ready helped to distract me. And so it began. We dusted, swept, vacuumed, and even repainted the bathroom and little kitchenette. We had Michael put in a working space counter, with a microwave (something Fr. O'Toole never would have used), a toaster, and a new half size refrigerator. There was a small table in the kitchenette, and one in the parlor as well. The parlor had an old wooden floor that creaked and was stained and faded in various spots. We scrubbed the floor, but then Sr. Leah Marie suggested we move the Oriental rug from the reading room next to the library to the parlor in the Cave. It would fit perfectly, cover the floor, and give it a certain warmth. Of course, that meant getting Sr. Antonia's okay, which was easier than anything, as she'd wanted to get rid of that rug for years, and anything for Sr. Solange Marie! We could have moved half the library down stairs if we had asked!

Sr. Paula donated a faux Tiffany lamp from an unused retreat room upstairs, which added color and warmth to the parlor. I moved the old-fashioned picture of the Sacred Heart which Sr. Gertrude had in her cell to the bedroom, and prayed to Sr. Gertrude to help me prepare my heart to be a good guardian angel. Sr. Gertrude had been elevated to the "patroness of self-confidence through self-forgetfulness." I needed both.

Finally, we added a little table and wooden arm chair to the nun's side of the parlor, and even re-stained the inside of the turn and added a round oil cloth mat on the bottom. The Cave was ready for its cave woman.

Nineteen

Baptism of the Lord 2007

He who dwells in the shelter of the Most High and abides in the shade of the Almighty says to the Lord: "My refuge, my stronghold, my God in whom I trust." (Psalm 91, Sunday Compline)

IT WAS A lovely day, even if it's sad for me to see the Christmas season ended. I wish it still went to February 2, the Presentation in the Temple, but they didn't ask me. It was a quiet Sunday here; we actually undecorated the tree in the community room and put our other ornaments away till next year. Everything in its proper box, clearly labeled. We were good at that.

I met with the "vocation team" after None, and we unanimously decided to wait on Havana's entrance until after Rhonda Lynwood's retreat. Perhaps if it was someone else, like Kristen, we wouldn't hesitate, but Havana has a way of stirring up trouble, at least that's what I think along with Sr. Paula, who isn't on the vocation team, but has let her sentiments be known. We like Havana and just don't want to take a chance on indiscretion while Rhonda is here.

When we told this to Mother, she said we should not let Rhonda's retreat dictate the rest of our lives; if Havana was to enter earlier, that's fine. We also didn't know till then that Rhonda would not be coming till Shrove Tuesday, which this year is February 20. That's more than a month from now. Apparently she needs to take care of some things in Los Angeles, see her doctor, and make up a phony excuse for the gossip magazines. Fr. Oyster told Mother the story was that Rhonda was travelling to the Far East. (I guess for her, Brooklyn, New York, *is* the far east!)

Also, according to Sr. Myriam, Havana's grandmother told Havana that she should enter on February 2. Havana was very pious in her own way, and thought this was the perfect day to make her "presentation in the monastery." Sr. Myriam says, "She is very charming in a wonderful Latino way, if I may say that. There is a kind of zest for life that permeates the Latino soul." Sr. Paula would just shake her head and say, "I don't see it, and I bet she doesn't know a word of Latin."

Although Sr. Paula and I don't think Havana quite has that verve but tends to be moody, I would have to deal with all that when she enters. She passed the psychologist's interview with reservations. According to him, Havana is very smart and speaks several languages fluently. She is also stubbornly independent, which I made note of. And "being an only child in a dysfunctional family could prove to make community life challenging for her."

That is interesting as I thought she once said that she had a brother, but maybe I misheard or am thinking of someone else. The Maid of the Month Club, or whatever that is, gave her a good reference and said she is a hard worker. Sr. Paula calls her the "Ping girl."

On another subject completely, I heard from Sally right after the fire. Apparently our fire made the evening news, and she and Mitzie were concerned. Mitzie enjoyed meeting me so much and wanted to come back for another visit soon. They were off on a Caribbean cruise soon and was there any chance that I could have Pancho come live with me for a week? I laughed out loud and assured her that Mother would never allow that. I had visions of Pancho running and yapping down the cloister with his Mexican sombrero on.

"Not to worry. We can leave him with the Steins, and maybe we'll just pop in to say hello when we drop him off."

"That would be fine; it would be helpful if you'd call ahead." *People think we're like the monastic welcome wagon or something*, I was thinking rudely to myself during my hour of guard that afternoon. I was feeling very distracted and could hardly even remember what day it was for what mysteries of the rosary let alone meditate on them. Gwendolyn, Rhonda Lynwood, Sharbel, Winona, Sally, Mitzie, Pancho. Pancho! *Poor Pancho*, I thought. We could fix up a hidden retreat quarters for a movie star, but not an insignificant chihuahua. But Rhonda Lynwood would not be yapping on the stairs leading to the sacristy with a sombrero on, but wearing a dignified postulant's chapel veil, and a mink coat! These were my crazy thoughts, and it was the Baptism of the Lord, one of the new luminous mysteries Pope John Paul has given us, but I didn't remember which one it was. Was it before or after the Wedding Feast of Cana? Was Rhonda going to sing too loudly in the chapel, and would I have to correct her? And where was my mysterious nephew these days? What does his mother mean: "he disappears?" What kind of a name is Winona?

Lord, forgive me for all my distractions. I offer them all to You because You know I cannot do anything about any of them. Don't let me turn my heart away from being the "welcome wagon" because it's always You, Lord, that we meet, and I want to always welcome You whenever and however You come to me. I also know, Lord, that You call me to be more hidden and silent than I ever have before. I want my life to be lived entirely for You and in You. I want my poor soul to be a newly renovated cave where You can take refuge. I believe in You, I hope in You, I adore You, and I love You. I entrust to Your Sacred Heart all those for whom I pray. Help me, dear Lord, to listen to Your every word, for You are the Beloved Son in whom the Father is well pleased. Amen.

There was a quiet in the chapel that is probably always there, but I'm not always attuned to it. I know the Lord is present in a deeply hidden way in the Eucharist, and that He is present by grace in the depth of our souls...my soul. He is found in the quiet place, that "cave", within me where He was drawing me to Himself when I was a child, and pulled me into His presence one chilly Saturday morning when I went to light a candle for my friend. Just knowing that brings a peace which the whole world cannot give.

I can't kneel as long as I used to, and sometimes I doze off in my stall and drop my rosary. But this afternoon, I settled into my choir stall and just smiled at the Lord, and I didn't fall asleep. It's at moments like that that I can't imagine what my life would have been like without the Lord. How "blessed" I am to be all His.

Thinking of Sally, perhaps, I thought that really it's all so simple. I believe there is a God, and that He has revealed Himself to us, His creatures. He is Love and love by its very nature wants to reveal itself. I believe He has spoken to us. My whole Jewishness is filled with that truth. God has given us His word and revealed His will. Perhaps that was what my bat-mitzvah was all about, but I didn't realize it so much then. And most of all—He has revealed Himself in Jesus, His Word Incarnate. Christmas. And more than "revealed." He gave His life to unite us to Himself and make of us an Offering of Love. And that Offering of Love—His death and resurrection—is real and present before me in the Most Blessed Sacrament of the Altar. The Resurrected Jesus is still with us, really and truly, all over the world, in every conse-crated Host, He is present among us.

The chill comes when I realize this is the Truth. As the Lord said, "This is the will of My Father, that they come to a knowledge of the truth." That's what makes all the difference.

It's not a matter of feelings or emotions and even less so of illusion or escape; it's a matter of the truth. And the Truth is not a thing, or an object of the intellect. It's a Person…a Beloved Son of a Loving Father and that Love is given to us. The Blessed Three.

My hour with You in the Blessed Sacrament passed very quickly, Lord, or so it seemed, when my distractions were dissolved in Your peace. The familiar sight and sound of the Sisters coming into the chapel did not take away the peace, but absorbed it somehow. And we lifted up our voices and hearts, hopefully, in the Church's Evening Prayer. It marked the end of the Christmas season.

There was soup for supper and warm bread and cheese. And we began reading a new book in the refectory, which makes a simple meal special. And at Compline I put all "my people" in the train of Our Lady, Mother of Mercy, Our Life, Our Sweetness, and Our Hope.

It was a lovely day.

Twenty

January 19, 2007

Hear, O Israel! The Lord is our God, the Lord alone! Therefore, you shall love the Lord, your God, with all your heart, and with all your soul, and with all your strength. Take to heart these words which I enjoin on you today. Drill them into your children. Speak of them at home and abroad, whether you are busy or at rest. (Deuteronomy 6:4-7, Reading at Compline, Sunday or Solemnity after First Vespers)

BESIDES GETTING THE Cave ready, the novices were helping with the finishing touches on the renovated infirmary. Sister Sheila was a big help in organizing everything. She jokingly whispered to me, "I feel like a Benedictine: ora et labora et labora." The extra "labora" was good for all of them, myself included. I supervised the stripping of an old wooden table which we then refinished, making it look better than new. Sr. Gerard and Sr. Simon were setting out a brand new jig-saw puzzle of wild animals and five different shades of jungle vines and leaves was being laid out in 2,500 pieces. Another table in another corner of the room had six new chairs with padded cushions around it. This was for the Native American beaders who were now attempting larger bags and decorative book covers. Sr. Kateri was creating her own designs. She seems happier and over her slump.

After stripping the old table, I had the morning free—or so I thought, till Sr. Paula came to find me and announced that my sister and another woman were in the small parlor. So off I went, probably smelling of turpentine. I left on my old faded denim work apron and had my sleeves rolled up, for effect. Before opening the parlor door, I realized that I was doing that out of vanity; I wanted them to know I "worked" at things like refurbishing furniture. Sally would be impressed because Papa used to do that. Mitzie would just be impressed. I had my hand on the door knob when I thought, *Isn't this silly? Look at you, Baruch, a regular old "ping girl."* I caught Sr. Paula on her way to the enclosure door, and told her to tell my guests I'd be five minutes. I put the apron back where it belongs, rolled down my sleeves, straightened my coiffure, washed my hands in the little kitchen, and made my entrance. The vanity wasn't entirely dissipated, I wanted to do a twirl like Loretta Young making a grand entrance. But instead, I gave them a big smile.

There sat Sally. Mitzie was standing by the framed picture of Pope Benedict, and before even saying hello, she said, "I've always wondered why the popes wear Jewish yarmulkes. Oh, hello."

"That's an interesting question. I used to wonder that too whenever the bishop would come by. It looks like a yarmulke, and my father used to wear a white one like that for Passover, but it actually developed in the middle ages when clerics received the full tonsure."

"Tonsure?"

"Yes, they had the back or crown of their heads shaved as a sign of entering the clerical life. It marked when a layman became a member of the clergy. The skull-cap, called a *zucchetto,* was worn for warmth. Only later did it begin to stand for different kinds of clergy, and different colors were used. The pope wears a white zucchetto since the time of Pope Pius V who was a Dominican, and thus wore white. Pretty neat, huh?"

"Zucchetto...sounds more like an Italian soup." Leave it to the Jewish sister to equate it with food.

I laughed. "You're not too far off. The word actually means 'small gourd' or more, 'small half a pumpkin, or little pumpkin.' The Italian word for pumpkin is zucca."

Mitzie found her way to her chair during my little lesson in ecclesial vesture.

"My goodness, Sister, how do you know all that?"

I smiled, looking over at Sally, "Such things I should know? Actually, one of our young Sisters was a student at New York Fashion Institute; she's always been interested in clothes, especially ours," I touched my bandeau. "When she was a novice, as a class, we read together a fascinating book called *The Church Visible.* It gives a history of all the ecclesiastical paraphernalia, some of which have Jewish roots, like the zucchetto."

"That's quite interesting I would think." Mitzie taking the lead.

"Oh, it is. All throughout the book, Sister Leah would say, 'Totally awesome stuff.'"

"And what do you call this?" pointing to my bandeau.

"We call it a *bandeau*; it's simply a head band as part of the veil. It's soft, and gives a neat appearance while hiding all one's hair." I was waiting for her to say "totally awesome," but she just smiled and took it all in.

"So where's the little Mexican mutt?" Oh dear, I hope I wasn't sounding too much like my mother.

It was Sally's turn, "Oy, we dropped him off at Rivka's first, so we could use coming here as an excuse to get away."

"I see."

"It's not that we don't like Rivka, but she tends to go on and on. What do you mean 'mutt'? He's a pedigree Chihuahua."

"I know, I'm sorry, I was just thinking of Mama sitting here like she used to do. She called all your....ah, clients 'mutts.'"

"I know. I'm sorry she never got to meet our baby."

"Your baby? You mean Pancho? He's a dog for goodness sake." I said it with more exasperation than aggression or attack.

"I know, but he seems like our baby."

It was Mitzie again, the more spiritually-minded one who asked, "Do you think dogs go to Heaven?"

Well here we go, I thought to myself. I smiled first. "No, dogs don't go to Heaven because they don't have immortal souls like we do."

"What do you mean?" Sally was getting into the conversation.

"I guess a lot of what we say and do and believe is really about our souls. Our soul is not just the, what would you call it? The animating principle between what is living and non-living. In this sense we could say that everything that is alive has a soul…it's the life principle. And in that wide meaning of soul, Pancho has a soul; it's what makes him to be alive, not a stuffed animal, but a living creature. Oh…even the word for 'soul' in Latin is *anima*. Anyway, even fruits and vegetables, trees and plants, have what we would call vegetative souls, unlike rocks, mountains, water, air, minerals, you know…dirt and soil, the earth. Plants are alive…there are certain qualities to distinguish them, like they grow, and need nourishment, usually water and sunlight. They are also usually stationary, or rooted in one place."

They both sat silent and staring at me quite attentively. "I'm sorry, it's a long answer to your question, and I'm only half way there. Would you like some coffee or something?"

"Not at the moment, go on." (I guess Mitzie is the one who decides things as she didn't even consult Sally.)

"Well, moving up the ladder of living things, you could say, next come the animals. They even carry the *anima* name. They have everything the vegetative souls do but more: they have locomotion, and they can know; they have sense knowledge, some of their senses are even keener than ours, like Pancho can hear pitches we can't, and smell things we can't. Well, you know, there's a whole world of animals to study—they have sense knowledge, and what we call animal instinct. Like the plants, they need nourishment and reproduce, but they are much higher up on the scale of living things. That's why Pancho is your pet, and not a rock."

"I used to have a pet rock." This was Sally, the most intelligent of the Feinstein girls, confessing she had a rock for a pet. I just looked at her a little dumb struck.

"I'll get Sister Paula to bring in some coffee." And I got up and made a quick exit. I was afraid I was going to burst out laughing. Sally and her pet rock. I wonder if she gave it a name? Luckily Sr. Paula was in the little kitchen, watering the plants, which I thought was very apropos. She was happy to make a pot of coffee and had just made a loaf of banana walnut bread.

I ventured back to the parlor. They were having an "animated argument" over whether a rock could be a pet, which I thought was good; it clarified the things I was trying to say. They calmed down as soon as I sat down.

"Coffee will be here in a couple minutes. Now, back to our souls. So we could say there is a vegetative soul, and an animal soul, but what about us? Our souls have all the qualities of the two below: we need food and reproduce, we have locomotion, and sense knowledge. But we also have two very big differences from the plants and animals…we have intellect and free will. By that, I mean, we can know things other than what we know from the senses; we can also abstract from the sense knowledge of something, and have a universal concept." Pausing to let this sink in, we were all lost in our thoughts for a moment. I remembered a great movie. "We don't have movies in here, except on rare occasions, usually a visit from Father Oyster."

"Father Oyster?" They both said it in unison! And thought that was hysterical.

"Well, we had a showing of *The Miracle Worker*, with Anne Bancroft, and what's her name? She played Helen Keller."

"Patty Duke." Mitzie the movie goer. "I remember seeing that when it first came out; I think it won the Academy Award."

"Yes, it came out in 1962, I think. Ruthie and I saw it. Did you?" to Sally.

"Oh yeah, great film. She was like an animal before Anne Bancroft came along."

"Precisely. But she wasn't an animal. She was human, but because she was wounded in her senses, being blind and deaf, she hadn't made a universal concept yet. That was the point Fr. Oyster was making, that when she 'got it' with the concept of 'water' remember? After that she was able to give names to everything, and communicate with words."

"Yes, it was an amazing movie. I remember."

"Our intellects can reason things out, abstractly. We can make judgements about things; we can speculate and make up things in our imagination; we can form images of things that don't really exist, except in our minds. We communicate with words. And we can give words to nonmaterial things like patriotism, honor, kindness, respect, and so on. Animals cannot know things these ways. When you left Pancho with Rivka, he's not sitting in the corner right now wondering 'Where have those two gone again? Are they off to Alaska or Europe this time? What time will they be back? I shall just hide under the coffee table and brood.'"

"Who's going to feed me at 5:30 sharp?" Mitzie added to my litany. "What's the second thing again?"

"The second thing is free will. This is really the huge human difference. We have a will...we are responsible for our decisions and actions, once we reach, as we say, once we

reach the age of reason. The intellect is the faculty for reason, and the will for action. Actually—more profoundly, the
intellect is made to know what is true, and the will moves to
what is good. We know and we love…and love is free; it's an
act of the will. You can't make anybody love you."

Deep in their thoughts (I hoped), Sr. Paula made her
grand entrance once again with a tray of sliced still warm nut
bread, a tub of clotted cream, and a pot of Starbuck's French
roast coffee…a Christmas gift from Fr. Matthew.

"Hmmmm." Sally was on her feet and heading towards
the table. "Hi, Sister, thank you so much for this; we don't
deserve such special treatment. That bread looks absolutely
scrumptious."

I'm sure that helped to make Sr. Paula's day. We aren't
always so expansive in our gratitude for all she does. She
smiled big. "The bread just came out of the oven. It's a new
recipe I'm trying out for a special guest."

"Oh, and who might that lucky visitor be?" Sally, the
investigative reporter still hidden in her bones. Poor Sr.
Paula looked over at me like a guilty puppy, but before she
could spill the beans about Rhonda Lynwood, I saved her,
"Lady Gwendolyn Putterforth is coming tomorrow."

"Oh, how delightful. I remember you were always very
close to her, and Mama, and Ruthie. Gwendolyn. Didn't she
own the tea shop uptown? What was it? Tea for Two?"

"Tea on Thames. And 'yes' to all of the above. She was
especially good to Ruthie who was her opening number at
her Penguin Pub in the Village."

"Oh, that's right." Sally was more involved in the clotted cream, fixing a plate for Mitzie, who just sat there and let her wait on her. Or so it seemed.

"Sister Paula," I said to change the subject, "what's the best part of being human besides nut bread and clotted cream?"

"Oh that's easy. It's our souls, made in the image of God." And she laughed as she made her way out the parlor door. "But I hope we have clotted cream in Heaven," and she closed the door behind her.

"What did she mean?" Mitzie turned her attention back to me. I was waiting for Sally to offer me some coffee, but she never did.

"Well, clotted cream is a good on earth and…"

"No, I mean about the image of God."

"Oh!" I laughed at myself. "What we were talking about before. Our souls have these spiritual faculties which do not come from the physical part of us, like the five senses do. And so there is part of our soul which knows and loves, and this is how we are created in the image of God who knows and loves, more than that, God who is Truth and is Love. Our free will comes from God who wills that we be free to love…we are not programed like a computer, or live out of instinct like an animal." This was getting a little tedious and repetitious, but I think it was necessary to repeat.

"So, you see, there is part of us that is not material in any sense, but spiritual. And this is our immortal soul… immortal because it can't die, only 'things' break down and stop being alive."

They were both engrossed in that thought while delighting in the nut bread and clotted cream.

While they had their mouths full, I went on, "Animals, as cute and loveable as they are to us, even obedient and with some senses more acute than ours, do not have these faculties apart from bodily life. So in other words, no, Pancho cannot go to Heaven. Only human beings and angels have intellect and free will...that's the spiritual part of us. God created us this way. Isn't it wonderful!" I was lost for a moment in my own expounding on it all.

"I understand the spiritual part, like you say. It's really who we are, more than our bodies which are always changing or getting sick and will one day die. I think I'd like another piece of that bread." And Mitzie was on her feet and heading to the table. "Do you want some, Sister Baruch?"

"No, thank you, Mitzie. I'll save it for noon time. I will have a little coffee, if there's an extra cup there. Just put it on the turn."

After a pause while she poured and figured out how to turn the turn, I went on. "Our bodies are also important, and who we are, albeit, the most changing part of us. But we are human persons; our bodies are not like old coats we can throw off and put on a new one when this one gets old."

"Ah, that's the whole eastern thing, you know. I once had a spiritual teacher who said that very thing; that the body was just a shell, an old coat we shed at the end of our life, and get a brand new one. It's reincarnation. Do you believe in reincarnation?"

"Oh no, not in the least. We are unique creations of God, and whole and entire, body and soul. We are incarnate creatures, however, using that word...we are infleshed spirits, and if you think about it, although I don't believe we throw off the body and get a new one, in that eastern teaching, it is the soul, the spirit, that doesn't die, but continues in another life. A new life. And that life will be complete with glorified, resurrected bodies. That's what we celebrate at Easter, of course. In Christ comes a whole new spiritual and physical way of life."

"And maybe that's where karma comes in?" This was Mitzie still. "Like you make up in a new life for the mistakes of the past life; there's like a progression going on."

"Yes, I understand, and used to think a lot about that. Heaven is not a step on the Karma Ladder. It's doesn't have any place for this free will I mentioned. There's no sense of one's unique individual existence as a creature of God. A Hindu or Buddhist would say that's all illusion. On the other hand, beginning with the Jews and in all of Christian belief, the body is something holy. What we do with our bodies matters. There is great reverence given to the body after death." I let that soak in for a minute, lest my Starbuck's coffee gets cold. We seemed to have saved Fr. Matthew's gift for the guests. Now that's bad karma if ever there was such a thing.

I wanted to say more about the reverence given the body, but I knew they weren't ready to hear that yet, and I hate it if I sound like I've climbed into the pulpit. But so far, they've been very attentive, so I went on more about the soul, "When we say we are made in the image of God, we mean that we can know and love, that we have intellect and will. And so God does too, since you cannot give what you don't have, God gives us a share in His very nature. Of course, this makes God very personal, not simply a cosmic force or huge energy or even the mind behind the design. (Thinking of David, my brother.) David had come to conclude that; you'd find that very interesting, Sally. Our big atheistic brother came to realize that there must be a great Mind behind the design of the universe. He was always a 'mind person' himself, of course."

Sally drained her coffee and nodded in agreement. Mitzie was up and refilling her cup.

Looking to Sally, "This would be more up your alley—if God is personal, and knows us and loves us because He has intellect and free will, like we do, then He also communicates with us using words, that reveal the mind and heart of God."

"Yes, that's quite fascinating, isn't it? I've always loved words, as you know. All those years working for the newspapers..." Sally was deep in thought. "And going to Barnard, well Becky, that's for both of us; we were English Lit. majors, and that certainly plunged us into a world of words."

I let her own words swim around the room and back again.

"Sometimes I think, or have thought a million times in the past, that if this is all true—if God is real and has really spoken to us, don't you want to know what He says?" Total silence; not even a sipping sound.

They didn't respond to that, but I hope I planted a seed there that they will think about. Sometimes it comes down to that very simple point: There is a God, and He has revealed Himself to us His creatures. My great uncle Sol, the Talmudic scholar would agree with me that far. He spent his life pouring over what God has said. I made a silent interior little prayer to him, for now I know he knows the fullness of Truth. "*Uncle Sol, help me!*"

I took a last gulp of my coffee, and went on looking at Sally, "We're using words right now, of course. And we know from our Jewish backgrounds, our heritage really, that God reveals His mind and heart, or His will in words. Because of the written word, people say, Jews are People of the Book."

Sally, who was not particularly religious, said, "We call the word His Torah, or His law, I remember that being drilled into us. The Torah is written and was given to Moses after…?" She looked up at me through the grille.

"After the Passover, of course. God saves His Chosen People and then makes a covenant with them, binding them to His Will…His Law…His Torah." Sally almost clapped her hands, and looked proudly at Mitzie as if to show her that she knew her Jewish history. *(Thanks, Uncle Sol.)*

Mitzie had become totally silent and drank her Starbuck's French roast without a comment. But she was thinking. Or she was simply letting the "sisters" bond in their Jewishness. "You've given me a lot to think about, Sister Mary Baruch!"

I knew that would be a good time to close. "My goodness, look at the time." I held up my arm revealing my tiny round "nun's watch" as Mama once called it. "I have got to collect the novices and go to prayers." I was being Sr. Mary Fibber again as I didn't have to collect anyone; the novices got themselves to prayers, but it was a way to begin an exit.

"Oh, we're sorry. We didn't mean to keep you so long, but it was certainly worth it, wasn't it, Sally? I love talking about religion and philosophy. None of our friends ever want to get into it all. They think I'm a little touched because I find it all very interesting."

"They think you're touched; what would they think of me!" I stood up and spun around. I remembered doing that some years ago now when I met David in this very parlor after a 35 year absence. He used to joke and call me Sr. Ophelia at the nunnery. Sally and Mitzie laughed as they got themselves up and piled their dishes on the turn. "Maybe I'll just wrap the rest of this nut bread up in a napkin and take it with us, if that's okay." (Mama reincarnate, I thought!)

"That's fine; I'll tell Sister Paula you loved it so much you couldn't let it go."

"We're leaving tomorrow for the Caribbean. Please pray for nice weather." This was Mitzie asking for prayers.

"And a safe sail. I'm always half afraid of those cruise ships," added my sister, Sally, who was also looking more and more like Mama. She even had the beginnings of slumped shoulders like our mother. She had neatly wrapped the bread in a paper napkin and put it in Mama's old bag. I wondered if Mogen David was hiding in there too. But I got serious.

"I will pray for both. Beautiful weather and no ship wrecks! Thank you for stopping, and come back and tell me all about your trip."

"We will. We will." They were both very joyful as they waved to me on their way to the door. It was Mitzie who had the final word, waving to our picture of Pope Benedict, "Goodbye, Ben, nice yarmulke, but poor Pancho, no immortal soul."

Twenty-One

Still January 19

O Lord, you are good and forgiving, full of love to all who
call. Give heed, O Lord, to my prayer and attend to the
sound of my voice. (Psalm 86, Monday Compline)

AFTER THE DISHES, we have an hour of grand silence which
I happily spent sitting in Squeak and praying my rosary. I
usually do spiritual reading then, but my conversation with
Sally and Mitzie was still replaying in my head, and I was too
distracted to read. The rosary helps to calm my mind. I'm
not usually meditating on the given mysteries, but the slow
repetition of the Hail Mary has a soothing effect.

I was thinking about the *Magnificat* that we sing every
evening at Vespers, and how I missed singing it in Latin,
which we still do on feasts and solemnities. Our Lady sang
it in Hebrew, of course, but the Latin Church sings: *Magni-*
ficat anima mea Domino. My soul magnifies the Lord. There's
that word *anima*. Mary's soul and body were so pure, free
of all sin, because she would bear within her the *incarnate*
Word of God, and name Him Jesus. Her body was purer

than the Ark of the Covenant which was laden with the purest of gold, seven times refined.

I wasn't meditating on the mysteries of the rosary, at least not in their proper order, but just thinking about the body and soul of Mary which takes us through the Annunciation and Visitation and then to the Assumption. Mary's body was even preserved from corruption, and when she "fell asleep in death," the Lord raised her body and soul into Heaven.

Then I thought of the prayer that I love but don't always remember to pray, called the *Anima Christi*...Soul of Christ. We pray: "Soul of Christ, sanctify me. Body of Christ, save me." The human body and human soul of Christ belong to a Divine Person. The Divine Word had/has a body...that glorified body is alive at this very moment. And He has given us His body and blood, soul, and Divinity.

I could never say all that to Sally and Mitzie, but maybe it begins with thinking about the soul, and the body. God's grace can sneak in there...Our Lady can make her way into their thoughts, or so I prayed. I asked Mary, Our Jewish Mother in Heaven, to intercede. I rocked and prayed.

I also prayed for Gwendolyn who would be arriving tomorrow, and as always, I pray for the postulants and novices and simple professed. God has touched each of their souls in such a beautiful and unique way. I know they each have their struggles and coming to terms with themselves. Living a cloistered life is still a very radical thing to do; probably more so today than when I first crossed the enclosure door. Well, it was radical for me too, and I'm sure for the generation before me. I think the bottom line is a complete and radical surrender to Jesus, which is always a big leap of faith...and sometimes that doesn't appear to be such a leap till after we've made it...even years afterwards. I suppose married people go through this too. There are times when I get lost in wondering what my life would have been like if I hadn't become a nun. And there are times when I'm terribly distracted imagining a life of travel and meeting all kinds of people. If I had gotten married and had a half dozen kids, I'd take them to all the neat cultural places in New York and London and Paris and Copenhagen. I don't know why Copenhagen comes into my distraction, but it does. And Amsterdam where I imagined windmills on every corner and people clopping around in wooden shoes. And sometimes I get in a kind of sad mood, feeling lonely maybe, or sorry for myself, but this afternoon, I'm rather content to be rocking in Squeak and praying for those I love in the afternoon silence.

We had a free evening without recreation. It was nice to have that quiet time to do whatever you wanted. After dishes, I made "a visit" to the Blessed Sacrament for just five minutes. That's all it takes sometimes to offer everything up to the Lord again. I didn't rehash my conversation with Sally and Mitzie or plan the next one, or think about what I should have said. I just let it rest. If they can think about having souls, that's a good beginning. I thought about Rhonda Lynwood coming, and wondered what she was thinking about her soul and thought it was wonderful that she wants to make a hidden retreat from the world of fame and fortune to prepare her soul to meet the Lord. And I thought of Gwendolyn arriving tomorrow. She's even older than Rhonda Lynwood. I wonder if she's coming home to get her soul in order. And I thought about all of us, because none of us know when the Bridegroom will come, as He says in the gospel. Is my soul ready?

I quietly slipped out of my stall, genuflected with a little umph coming up again, as my right hip is getting stiffer these days. I stood in the cloister like I was waiting for a bus, trying to decide if I would go to the library, to the infirmary, or just go to our cell. The infirmary won as I hadn't really seen the new furniture and carpets in the evening with the new lamps lit. One lamp, so they tell me, goes on and off when you clap. Imagine that! Sr. Bertrand will have a field day with that one.

Sr. Gerard and Sr. Bertrand were assembling the new jungle jigsaw puzzle, separating all the straight-edged pieces first, both of them mumbling to themselves in the process. Sr. Jane Mary was settled in one of the new recliners. She was reading a hardbound book and put it down in her lap as I walked by; she smiled but said nothing. Sr. Catherine Agnes and Sr. Annunciata were sitting together in front of the picture window looking out at the side lawn and the cemetery. Sr. Simon was dozing in her chair. All seemed very serene in the new infirmary.

"Chamomile tea, anyone?" I quietly inquired in the middle of the room. Two hands went up, and one voice, "Forget the chamomile stuff; it's like drinking straw. I'll have peppermint decaf." Sr. Bertrand hath spoken.

"Me too," "Me too," the other two changed their minds. So peppermint decaf was the unanimous tea of choice. I went to the kitchenette, and Mother Bernadette was there, already boiling the water.

"Peppermint, right?"

"How'd you know that, Mother?" And she laughed.

"I made the same inquiry two minutes before you arrived. But I'm glad you're here; I received a nice email from Gwendolyn Putterforth today. She's not coming for a short visit, you know. I don't think she's well; she didn't say one way or the other, but she asked if there was a chance she could stay in a guest room for a couple months, or could I recommend a friend or benefactor close by who might have a furnished room to rent."

"Oh my, Mother, I didn't know that. What did you tell her?" I was searching through the cabinet with teas on every shelf, except peppermint decaf. Till I found an unopened box.

"Well, I wanted to talk to you about it first. I know she is your close friend, and really, she's been a close friend of the monastery for all these years. And very generous to us." Mother stopped pouring the water into the mugs for a moment. "I thought about all the fuss we made over Rhonda Lynwood, whom we don't even know. And Gwendolyn was not asking to come inside, but to be a guest in one of the retreatant rooms, and I think that will be fine. Do you see any reason why it wouldn't be?"

Dunking the tea bags rhythmically, I looked at Mother Bernadette and smiled. "I think that's the sweetest thing I've heard in a long time. I would be thrilled for her to be here, and I won't be visiting with her all the time."

"That's settled then. I'll email her back tonight, but if she doesn't receive it in time, you can tell her our decision when you see her tomorrow. I wouldn't want her long-term stay to interfere with your own life, you have your hands full with the novices…"

"And with Sister Myrtle Pine," I added, putting the tea on a tray with a saucer of Lorna Doone cookies, a recent favorite with the infirmary Sisters.

"Myrtle Pine, indeed; I'm counting on you to keep it all peaceful and undercover. I hope we haven't bit off more than we can chew."

I thought that was a curious statement of Mother's, but immediately reverted back to Gwendolyn. She hadn't said anything to me about staying here. Well, after all these years, she knows the chain of command. I gathered up the tray and headed into the infirmary common room.

"Tea time," I announced. I had a flash back of Gwendolyn bringing a pot of Earl Grey to me and Ezra, and saying the same thing, "Tea time." I left the Sisters with their tea, and quietly made my way out of the infirmary…with two Lorna Doones in my pocket.

Twenty-Two

January 20, 2007

Turn your ear, O Lord, and give answer for I am poor and needy. Preserve my life, for I am faithful; save the servant who trusts in you. (Psalm 86, Monday Compline)

"I'VE COME HOME to die, M.B.," were her first words out of her mouth. My best friend and godmother, Gwendolyn Putterforth, returned from London, England today, and came bounding into the parlor to see me.

"Gwen, Gwen, look at you! You don't say hello or Happy New Year; you tell me you've come home to die—well, it doesn't look like it's in the next couple minutes. Come here and let me see you."

Gwen stuck both hands up and fingers through the grille. Her stiff upper lip quivering when saying, "I'm sorry, M.B. Happy New Year to you—blimey, you look marvelous and haven't aged a day. I knew I should have been a nun!"

"Well, listen to your Jewish-mother-goddaughter, you need to get back to some old fashioned fat-filled American cooking and find those pounds you seem to have lost." She laughed, blousing out her (now) oversized Irish knit sweater and tweed skirt. Her scrawny looking neck was partially hidden by an icy-blue colored silk scarf sporting a penguin in each corner. Her wheat-colored hair was swept back and held in place by brass penguin barrettes.

"Well, honestly, Rebecca Feinstein, I can't believe how marvelous you look. Don't any of you age in this life?"

"Of course we do; we just have better ways of hiding it." I pointed to my coiffure. "Now before you go into your song and dance, I've spoken with Mother, and she told me your request; she also spoke to her council, without me because she said I would be prejudiced, and we are happy to make the two guest rooms at the far end of the guest wing upstairs yours for the next three months."

She lowered herself into the wooden chair closest to the grille. "I'm flabbergasted, love, and overwhelmed with joy. At my age and in my condition, I could never afford to rent an apartment, and the thought of a furnished room in a dowager's basement depresses me. I would do that if I had to, mind you, I'm not proud. I just picture a little old Italian lady with white hair in a bun, and an apron full of flour over her house dress, renting the room of her son who died in the war."

I had to laugh at her fantasy "landlady". "Well, we don't have our hair in buns, but we are pretty much old ladies with white hair. We do have about ten young ones too that keep us busy."

"And you've got our favorite priest, right on the grounds, whom I haven't seen since he was in England. He emails me, which is more than I can say about certain white-haired nuns, but how's he doing? Between you and me and Pope Benedict," nodding to the picture on the wall, "Ezra was looking quite poorly at times."

"Oh, I think he's fine. He's slowed down and could put on weight. His bouts with that malaria took a lot out of him apparently. I see him about once a month—we have a pot of tea together." I knew that would bring a smile to her.

"Earl Grey, of course! But you don't have my 'penguin pups' (a homemade designed black and white cookie) to munch on."

"That's true, but there is that little kitchenette off of the guest dining room. There is an electric oven in there, so who knows?"

"Oh, that would be such fun. Making penguin pup biscuits again. The young Sisters would love them." Speaking a little softer, like it was a secret, "The place isn't buzzing with vocations, is it? It's the same in England, which is maybe even worse."

"No, not even a big retreat business anymore, if that's the right word for it. It's not a 'business', but it helped out and kept many of us busy." Lost in my thought for a moment. "We have dozens of beaded bags for sale!"

"I saw them in your little gift nook or whatever it's called. If there were one with a penguin on the side, and maybe ten times larger, I might be tempted."

"You'll have to tell that to Sister Kateri; she'll probably do it. Speaking of penguins, how's little Vicky doing?" Vicky is a stuffed toy penguin Gwendolyn gave to me on my entrance day, which I returned 35 years later after Gwendolyn's taxidermy real penguin was stolen.

"Vicky is a little worn for wear, I'm sorry to say, but she keeps me company and gives me comfort. That's partly why I'm here."

"Do tell." I shifted quietly in my wooden chair, reaching for my left side, and holding my rosary crucifix in my hand under my scapular.

"It was lovely being home in England, as I've written more than once, even if my sister didn't let me retire, and put me to work, which I didn't mind. She has a great little club going in Soho, but I wanted a cottage near York or Leeds, in the Great Green Hills of Yorkshire. Big city life. Or I should say, late big city life, takes its toll on you."

I just nodded as if I could identify with what she was saying. I never lived anywhere outside of New York or Brooklyn, although a cottage in green hills, anywhere, sounded 'lovely' as Gwendolyn would say.

"Jacqueline and I got along as long as we were busy working. She didn't know how to relax and began to criticize me for taking it easy, as she put it. I was very tired by night fall, just when business was getting ready to begin. I was the maître-d' of sorts, greeting people at the front door, sometimes checking IDs. It was delightful as I met lots of lovely young people, and had lots of fun with visiting New Yorkers, some who even remembered Penguin Pub, imagine!"

"Did any remember Ruth Steinway?"

"They did! They did! There was a theater couple who lived on Sullivan Street in the Village who were, they told me, regulars at the Pub, and came especially to see Ruthie. They came to pay their respects when you were sitting Shiva at your old apartment. You probably met them. They liked my sister's 'joint' they called it, but it didn't hold a candle to 'the Pub.' I treated them to free drinks!"

"You were like the maître-d' with the mostess…the Lady Putterforth."

Gwen laughed, making her penguin earrings jingle around and kicking her in the neck. "That was part of the problem. Jacqueline was all business, not hostess with the mostess. She threw a fit whenever she saw me giving free drink tickets out to certain people, or talking to them for too long. It held up the queue, like she thought they were queued up to the corner to get in. She rejected any of my suggestions for different piano players and singers. She wanted me to go over there to help her after my great success with the Pub, and then rejected every suggestion I made. But that was Jacqueline; I knew that; I knew her. And then…" She stopped and was lost in thought.

"And then…what?" Squeezing my hand around my crucifix.

"And then, I passed out one night, and the young people around me kind of panicked, or so she said. One chap was on the tack enough to call for an ambulance on his mobile, and off I went. London General."

Sr. Paula knocked and made her usual quiet entrance, which gave us a moment to catch our breath. She had English tea and her attempt at 'new year biscuits' she called them, to impress Gwendolyn, who was still the maître-d' with the mostess, and raved about how clever they looked, "and how colorful." Sr. Paula was pleased as punch. I half expected her to curtsy when she left.

"She must've put a whole bottle of red food coloring in these biscuits; what are they supposed to be? Flames of fire?"

"Kind of. They're the descent of the Holy Spirit blessing the new year."

"Oh dear." That was her only reaction as she stirred a little Coffeemate into her tea, and took a bite of the descent of the Holy Spirit. "Oh my, they're delicious, M.B.; have you had one? They're quite good; they're really just cinnamon biscuits with little red hots which surprise the pallet."

"I'm glad you like them. But as you were saying…you went to the hospital, and?"

"And I was kept overnight for tests and observation. It could simply be exhaustion or dehydration, or something more serious. So they played the vampire and took lots of blood." She smiled at her attempted humor and went for a second flame of fire.

"And…?"

"And I have leukemia, my dear. Not acute yet, and with modern medication, I have…I have 'time.' The more advanced and, well, experimental treatments are more here in New York than London. So I've come home to die." As she dove into her third biscuit.

I couldn't say anything. I felt the frog settle into my throat. I never learned her British stiff upper lip when confronted with sad news. I put my head down and closed my eyes for the moment. It's my way of praying without words. It's the few moments needed to accept things as God's loving will in our lives or someone else's. Gwen knew me well enough not to say anything more. She took refuge in her English tea like good British people do. It's their best therapy.

The frog shrunk enough for me to talk. "I'm glad you've shared all that with me. And I'm really glad you've chosen to come home to deal with it all. You were always there for me, you know, and always have been, and I want to be here for you, I hope you know that."

I think the frog had jumped through the grille and into her throat. She couldn't say anything, just nodded, as I saw the tears roll down over her quivering upper lip. Fingers through the grille was the only "sisterly embrace" we could do in this monastery parlor which held the joys and sorrows, laughter, tears, and prayers of many an inhabitant for a hundred years or more.

"And now I must go and freshen up in my new boudoir, Penguin Place."

She knew that would make me laugh, and she was right. We both laughed and brushed aside the tears at the same time.

"This is a place for Penguin Prayers too, you know. So we're happy you'll make your nest here." We both stood at the same time, and without more chatter, made our ways to our separate doors.

"Welcome home, godmother." And I closed the door behind me and headed for the chapel where "us penguins" gather to pray and give everything over to the Lord.

In manus tuas, Domine, commendo spiritum meum. (Into your hands, Lord, I commend my spirit. Compline response to reading.)

Twenty-Three

February 20, 2007, Shrove Tuesday

I will praise you, Lord my God, with all my heart and glorify your name for ever; for your love to me has been great: you have saved me from the depths of the grave. (Psalm 86, Monday Compline)

SR. ELIJAH ROSE never ceases to amaze me. Yesterday we had a novitiate meeting to discuss the arrival of Rhonda Lynwood, whom she and the other Sisters in the novitiate knew of, but not like their parents and grandparents did. I don't think any of them ever saw *The Lonely Heart Legacy*. Sr. Elijah Rose was more excited about a Mardi Gras party and thought we should "pig out"—her words, not mine—on all the sugar and fat we'd be giving up for Lent. And she told us about going to New Orleans for the last night of Carnival. She was not a Catholic at the time, she assured us, and "had an awesome time." I didn't want to hear about just how awesome it was, but they ate something called "King Cake," and she had the Infant Jesus in her cake, or something. I was drifting in my thoughts about other things. The conclusion was that she would be happy to make a "King Cake" for us, if we wanted one. Sr. Leah Marie and Sr. Kateri were caught up in the moment; Havana kind of made a face and said she didn't get the big deal Shrove Tuesday was, and what does 'shrove' mean anyway.

I explained the practice of the early Church when penitents were "shriven" of their sins the day before Ash Wednesday, and then did forty days of penance before receiving the Eucharist again on Easter. We talked about how we could practice better silence during Lent and finding more time for prayer. Recreations would be reduced so we'd have that extra time for prayer and spiritual reading. I encouraged them to take advantage of the extraordinary confessor we'd have this afternoon to be "shriven" of their sins and to choose something to fast from during Lent as a penance, other than the desserts and meats we would not be having during Lent. Doing something extra sometimes is more pleasing to the Lord than giving up. They wanted to know "like what?" *Sometimes millennials can be a little clueless,* I thought.

"You know, like visiting the Sisters in the infirmary. Staying longer in the kitchen to help with dishes other than your assigned job. Even little things, like smiling at a Sister whom you don't particularly like." They thought that would be one of the hardest things to do, as they're used to ignoring the Sisters who bother them.

"I'm waitin' for Sister Jane Mary to smile at me first— no way am I gonna do it first," confessed Sr. Elijah Rose. Another surprise, as she was probably the friendliest extrovert of all the Sisters in the novitiate. Sr. Leah Marie was the shyest, and so it would take a real effort for her to smile, not because she didn't like people, or like a particular Sister, but because she was afraid they didn't like her, and that's why they didn't smile first.

"The older Sisters aren't used to looking at each other and smiling like we are. They were formed with stricter 'custody of the eyes.' They weren't even permitted to look out the windows."

They thought all that was amazing and didn't quite get the ascetical reasoning behind it. My own struggle as a young nun was the not eating between meals, and not having desserts during Lent. One can only eat so many apples, and even those weren't always so available. One thing that hasn't changed, however, I thought, is that we are penance enough to each other. Mother John Dominic used to say we sandpaper each other. That was true enough.

I reminded them when they took her dinner tray down, to try not to engage Miss Lynwood in conversation, but again, one can be friendly, and smile, and assure her of your prayers. We even had a little "sign language" which said that, so we didn't have to break the silence. As Sr. Leah assured us again, "It's awesome."

I had the afternoon free and would try to go to confession early. I was to expect Rhonda Lynwood to arrive around three o'clock. Fr. Oyster would be bringing her himself, and it turns out that he's the extraordinary confessor, so they might arrive early, and I should be on the alert, according to Mother.

Rhonda's basement quarters were dust-mopped, and I had a nice *horarium* (the house schedule, literally 'the hours') done in calligraphy and in a cheap frame, on her desk. I brought in a second chest of drawers as I figured she would have more clothes to deal with than we do. I had her chapel veil laid out on the bed, and I thought she might like my black knit shawl which had belonged to Mother John Dominic. It can get a little drafty in the chapel. Everything looked in order. I thought she will probably find it all very austere compared to what she's used to, but that's what she wanted.

Sr. Leah Marie poked her head in the doorway. "May I come in, Sister?"

"Of course, Sister, come on in; I'm just checking that everything's ready for our retreatant."

"That's nice. I wonder if she'll be wearing her mink coat?" And she smiled. (Probably only Sr. Leah Marie would think of that and would want to see the inside lining and how it was constructed!)

"Well, if she does, I'll have to tell her not to leave it in the chapel. Sister Paula might want to 'borrow it.' Can you imagine!" And we both laughed. "What's on your mind?"

"Well...Mother just put up a note that the extraordinary confessor is going to be Fr. Oyster."

"That's right; she told me that too just an hour ago."

"Well...you see...I was wondering...it's, like, extraordinary, right? One doesn't have to go if you don't want to, right?"

I could see she was anxious about it for whatever reason and assured her: "That's right, one does not have to go to an extraordinary confessor. It's usually someone we don't really know, like a diocesan priest from the Bronx or Queens."

"Oh, that's good, I like Father Oyster and just feel funny about going to him for confession; besides, I can wait for old Father Wilcox. I like him." And she showed great relief in her face.

"That's fine, Sister. It's good because its right before Lent begins, but it's also okay if you want to wait. "

"Thank you, Sister. I'll wait then. Havana told me she's not going either; she doesn't believe in confession." And with that Sr. Leah exited as quickly as she had come in.

I smiled to myself…this was a private 'mission' of Sr. Leah to tell me that. I didn't remind her that we had all gone to Fr. Oyster for confession during Advent last year. It was just to tell me about Havana. Another bump in the road. She doesn't believe in confession, in making the venia, and isn't "sold" on Eucharistic adoration. Her grandmother told her it was a waste of time. I had yet to meet this theologian-grandmother, but that was one of my Lenten resolutions.

I had permission to meet with Gwendolyn for the hour before Sext, which I was looking forward to. We hadn't really met during the month since she moved into the upstairs guest rooms. I would peek at night though and was happy to see she was in the extern chapel for Compline almost every night.

The small parlor has an ominous feel to it when nobody is on the other side of the grille. I sat alone taking in that emptiness, waiting for Gwen to arrive. There were no outside windows in this parlor; the only light at present was from a small lamp on the corner table. I didn't like the fluorescent ceiling lights, much too bright.

I thought about Mama who used to prefer this parlor to the other larger ones. She used to like to sit up close at my right side of the grille, and would usually begin speaking in a kind of stage whisper. She would revert to normal speech very shortly after; I think it was the starkness of the room. Ruthie thought it was like the visiting room in a prison.

The middle parlor was airier and had the framed picture of Pope Benedict reigning over the otherwise bland wall. This parlor used to be called St. Rose, but now it's called Parlor Number Three. There were just three chairs on my side and four chairs on the visitors' side. The turn was right next to the corner where Mama would sit. It was turned in to my side, as I noticed how worn the oil-clothe cover was.

I silently began to pray a decade of the rosary with my side rosary, but I was thinking about these walls and the old saying "If these walls could talk." These walls were over a hundred years old. I think they went from plain white paint to a green wall paper with thin felt stripes. I never saw them, but the older Sisters used to mention it, and that it was rather nauseating, but one would never say so, so they remained till another prioress had them stripped and the walls painted an egg shell white. In my time, it was Mother Rosaria who had them painted again. Beige on the two sides, and a darker tan color on the back wall where the door was. Mother Bernadette added the oriental carpet, thinking it would help with the noise level, but we're still debating that one.

I was meditating on Mama's going on about her cruise with David and Sharbel, when the door opened quickly and Gwendolyn fluttered in and was all excited.

"M.B., you won't believe who I just saw! I was coming over from Ezra's quarters, and there was that Dominican priest with the funny name, Father Crab or something, and

standing there with him, dripping in a full length fur coat…
you won't believe…was…"

"Rhonda Lynwood." I smiled.

"How did you know? It looked like he—they—just
arrived. He was carrying two suitcases, which I don't think
belonged to a priest, unless Father Crab is into Louis Vuit-
ton carry-ons. Were they going to see Ezra? I was so flabbergasted, I didn't say anything. I may have said 'Hello, Father
Crab' but went on down the stairs. She didn't say anything."

"Well, you might as well know, but must promise not to
tell a single soul. Rhonda Lynwood is making a long retreat
here, but it's top secret."

"Oh my golly gee willikers, love; she'll be here with me? I
can't believe it."

"Calm down, Lady Putterforth. Rhonda is staying downstairs in the former chaplain quarters; it's not in the enclosure but still very quiet, private, and out of the way."

"Well, isn't that something. I must say, she's still quite
stunning for her age, isn't she? I remember wishing I was
her when I first came to New York. She was a smash hit in
London too, and summat of a sensation; she was married to
an English bloke, you know."

"No, I didn't know that. And if you just saw her it means
I have to go. She'll be looking for me to show her to her
rooms. I'm her 'guardian angel.'"

"Blimey!"

I laughed. "Maybe we could meet later this afternoon?"

"I can't. I have to go into Manhattan to a new doctor
attached to Sloan Kettering. But I'm doing fine, love, *my*

rooms are perfect; we can get together sometime later in the week."

"Maybe. We don't usually have parlor visits during Lent, but you're an exception, maybe."

"Maybe? I hope I am; besides, I want to hear everything about Rhonda Lynwood."

I laughed. "There isn't anything to tell. She wanted to make a private retreat *far from the maddening crowd*, to quote another of your English blokes! Remember, not a word to anybody."

We squeezed fingers through the grille and parted. I regret having told her, but what was I to say? She's the one who ran into her on the stairs. Sr. Paula was discreetly waiting for me outside the parlor door to tell me that Rhonda Lynwood and Fr. Oyster would return at two o'clock. "I've already put her bags in the Cave. I will meet her at two o'clock and take her down to her rooms; you could be in the parlor down there any time after that, if you'd like."

"Thank you, Sister. I'll be there shortly after 2:00."

I called up to Gwen's room, but no answer. She must've gone out already. So I went to the chapel. I had time to think about my sins. Sr. Annunciata was the Sister making adoration, but I think she had dozed off in the chair. We now have a wooden chair with arms, which is much easier and more comfortable for the older Sisters, but also easier to fall asleep in. The Sisters in the infirmary that are able take a turn at adoration, especially during the day. Mother mentioned at a council meeting some time ago that we might have to cut back on our hours of adoration. We might have to let go of the all night adoration.

I hope not, Lord. There should be one place here in Brooklyn where You are adored day and night; where there is a place of silence amidst all the crazy noise outside. Sometimes I close my eyes, and I can still picture walking down Fifth Avenue at Christmas time, and the mass of people on both sides of the Avenue. The hustle and bustle of New York...it took a while, didn't it, Lord, for that to run out of my soul, and for me to settle into the stillness and silence here. I have to be patient with the young Sisters. I know the hustle and bustle still rustles around in them. And Sally and Mitzie... and Sharbel...and Rhonda Lynwood. How different our life is inside these walls, but we all have souls that long to see Your face, as the psalmist puts it. Each and every one unique and precious to Your eyes.

It's in those quiet moments that I think about certain truly "awesome" truths, like the Incarnation. And that You, Lord, know us and love us each individually and uniquely as if we were the only one You created. And that you ceaselessly gaze upon us with the look of love. Even in our weaknesses, our sinfulness, our slothfulness and sand-papering each other, You love each of us with an Infinite Love.

If the Sallys and Mitzies of the world could know and believe that, they would want to be pure of heart and body, because You have told us that the pure of heart will see God. It seems, Lord, like the whole world these days is caught up in a whirlwind of noise, lust, greed, and underneath it all a despair with life. Ruthie covered that up with her humor and being busy. Like our self-worth comes from what we do, what we accomplish, or how much money and independence we have. Even in our life, sometimes, Lord, You know, we drag those ambitions in with us. And yet...You love us when we're young and full of energy, and You love us when we're old and doze off in front of the monstrance. It's not so much what we "do," even in our prayer and praise, but that we belong to You. That we let You love us.

Sr. Annunciata jumped in that startling way we jump awake at times. She mumbled something to herself, or maybe to the Lord, I couldn't hear. She looked around to see if anyone else was in the chapel, and when she saw me, she smiled and gave a little wave. And I waved back.

The bell for Sext broke the silence which had settled on me. The Sisters would be coming in for the Little Hour, and then dinner, or as Sr. Elijah Rose continued to call it, "lunch."

Dinner on this Shrove Tuesday was potato and ham soup, chicken cutlets and macaroni and cheese, and little bags of potato chips. And lemon meringue pie. I think that was a gift from Gwen. We all have our ways of showing our love.

Twenty-Four

Shriven

But you, God of mercy and compassion, slow to anger,
O Lord, abounding in love and truth, turn and take
pity on me. (Psalm 86, Monday Compline)

BLESS ME, FATHER, for I have sinned. It's been at least a
month since my last confession. I know I should have gone
two weeks ago, but I, well, I forgot it was Friday. I am in
Solemn Vows, some days it seems like two weeks ago, but
recently, it's felt like a hundred years. I worry, you see, and
sometimes there's just too much to worry about.

"Worrying isn't a grievous sin, Sister; it's very natural."

"I suppose so, but it shows my lack of trust in our Lord.
I know He will take care of everything, if I let go of trying
to control things, or have others always agree with me. I'm
not always right, and then, I get down on myself for being so
stupid, or immature. Sometimes, Father, I pout like I'm a ten
year old girl. And then my pride kicks in, and I don't want
the young Sisters to see me pouting, so I put on a happy

face, but it's all a sham sometimes. I am still very lacking in humility, and full of self-centeredness and vanity. I like…"

"Yes, Sister? You like…?"

"I like to look at my reflection in the windows off the cloister. I'm sure that's vanity, but also a kind of pride. I love our habit; I always have since before I even entered, and I just like to see myself in it. I don't know if that's a sin."

(Father was silent)

"I…I murmur in my head about the other Sisters and a couple of my relatives; I worry about them, but then murmur instead of offering it up. I pass rash judgements on the other Sisters, and am full of distractions sometimes which I don't try to stop. I am not really poor except in not giving of my time; I sin against chastity by thinking about others' sins in that area, but I try to distract myself immediately, usually by thinking about food, like what we're having for supper. And I'm sorry for any way that I have been disobedient to the prioress, or to our life."

"Have you disobeyed the prioress?"

"Not in anything asked of me or of us. I guess I'm more unfaithful than disobedient, in little things, Father, little things, like not eating between meals and keeping silence in places. Oh, and one more thing, once this past month I wanted to run away, but that only lasted 30 seconds, maybe. I know that's not really a sin, but I felt guilty about it while the Lord showers me with blessings, and I forget to be grateful. For these and all my sins past and present, I'm truly sorry and ask a penance of you and absolution."

Fr. Oyster gave a little "canned" fervorino, and a decade of the rosary for my penance. He also told me to be careful of becoming too scrupulous, and only then, on my way out, did he say, "And Sister, if you know who will be taking care of Rhonda Lynwood, tell her to be compassionate and patient with her; she is a broken woman."

I thought about that during my decade of the rosary. I wondered if he knew who I was all along, or did he say that to everyone, and poor Rhonda Lynwood, whatever could she be broken by and how would I be in a position even to be compassionate and patient?

I greeted her when Sr. Paula brought her down to her rooms. She was quite taken by it all, I think. She didn't speak, but had a lovely smile. Sr. Paula left us in the parlor and I began to explain our horarium to her. I told her I would meet with her here again after Vespers and show her how we will do things to bring her supper. It will be put on the turn. She should make a list of things she can't eat, if there are any, and coffee, tea, milk, and juice will be on her own, and to let us know when her supply is getting low. I tried to be warm and welcoming, and when I left her, she had a kind of sad, drawn, look on her face. Poor thing, I couldn't imagine what's going on in her head.

We gave her a chair and prie-dieu in a corner of the sanctuary opposite where Fr. Matthew sits. She'll be quite hidden from the main chapel, and have a clear view of the Blessed Sacrament in the monstrance. We've had other religious Sisters there before, so anyone who might happen to see her would think she's just a visiting Sister. Her chapel veil will be her disguise.

Knowing Sr. Paula, she's probably sitting with her for a couple days to help her navigate her way through the books.

I settled into my own stall after all that, happy that it all went well. Thinking back on my confession, I didn't think I was scrupulous, but conscientious, and then felt just a little guilty because I forgot to mention how exasperated I was becoming with Havana. And there I was murmuring again, this time about Sr. Myriam for almost insisting that we accept Havana as a postulant. She knew Sr. Paula, for whatever reason, was opposed to that—she told Sr. Myriam so. That caused hard feelings between them. Sr. Myriam is the Vocation Sister, and Sr. Paula is the extern; she had no business telling Myriam how to do her job. Sr. Paula gave in and stomped away, and pouted for the rest of the afternoon. I didn't mention that I took delight in another's Sister's pouting because I didn't feel so alone. Sr. Elijah Rose pouts too, but she makes it seem like she's being silent, which, of course, is one of her biggest challenges. She and Sr. Leah Marie seem to be getting on each other's nerves more than usual. And even Sr. Kateri lost her patience with Sr. Gerard who didn't want to use red beads in her design. Sr. Jane Mary, who usually never said an uncharitable word, lost her temper and yelled at Sr. Barbara for leaving a window open, causing a cold draft. Sr. Barbara assured her that the window was never opened at all. She would check with Sr. Thomas Mary if the furnace was working okay as it was chilly in the infirmary.

Sr. Thomas Mary lost her patience because the furnaces were all running at top speed and the Sisters in the infirmary should stop complaining and put on sweaters. And Sr. Barbara snapped back at her that they were all wearing sweaters and woolen habits, and knitted gloves, which wasn't true.

It was probably a good thing Fr. Oyster was here and we could all go to confession before Lent began; maybe we'll be more charitable with each other. In the meantime, I left a note for Havana in her stall to meet me in my office after None.

To my surprise, Rhonda was in her seat in the extern chapel sanctuary. No mink coat, but, according to Sr. Paula, a very nice cardigan sweater over a modest cotton blouse and a brown corduroy skirt, and like us, a quiet pair of black walking shoes, nicer, no doubt, than our Nikes. (Oops, envy, an hour after confession.) According to Sr. Paula, who was probably enthralled that "Sr. Solange Marie" was sitting in our chapel, reported (to me) that Rhonda pulled out her own genuine reading glasses. *Well, thank the Lord, they weren't sunglasses*, I was thinking to myself.

I watched Havana read my note, and she looked exasperated and shoved it in her pocket. She looked over at me with a forced smile, or so I took it. I didn't smile back. *Was I becoming my own version of SCAR?*

I did pray for her, however, asking the Lord to give me compassion and patience with her; I also prayed for Sharbel for some reason; he came to my mind. One of my "worries" I think I will probably continue to confess!

* * *

Havana quietly knocked, then came into my office. "*Laudetur Jesus Christus.*" I spoke our traditional greeting when entering a room.

"Whatever," was her response. So much for being fluent in languages; Latin apparently was not one of them.

"Havana, you know the correct response to that."

"Yeah, but you said it in Latin."

"That's right. I thought you knew Latin. Please, sit down. I understand you're having a difficult time with some of our regular observances, and I'm not talking about Latin. A very simple one is that we address each other as 'Sister.' It's especially important for you to remember that with the older Sisters. It's a sign of respect for them."

"Yeah; I'll try to remember."

"Yes, 'Sister', I'll try to remember."

"What else?"

"What else, 'Sister?' We have the practice of going to confession, usually every two weeks. Before Lent and Advent, we have extraordinary confessors, like today."

"Do ya hafta go?"

"Do you have to go, Sister? And no, one is not obliged to go; one can go to any priest or wait till the regular confessor, but it's highly suggested." Havana just stared at me. "Do you have a spiritual plan or resolution for Lent?" She just continued to stare.

"We allow the novices to have an extra hour of adoration each day, divided up in time if need be."

"I don't want any extra time....Sister." I nodded approval.

"It's come to my attention that you find Eucharistic adoration a waste of time; is that right?"

"Who told you that? That blabbermouth little Leah?"

"It's not important; the question is, is that right?"

"My grandmother told me you can't always be sure that's really Jesus, so be careful; it could be idolatry."

"Is that right? When did your grandmother tell you that?"

"I dunno, sometime after Christmas, I think."

"Well, I can assure you, Havana, that our Eucharist is valid. And much of our life, as you know or are finding out, is centered on living in the real presence of Our Lord in the Blessed Sacrament. If spending time with Him is a waste of your time, you might not be suited for this life."

Havana just stared at me. No emotional reaction one way or the other, which I find very strange. I made a mental note to talk to Mother and the House Council about this.

"Anything else?"

"No, Havana, not at the moment. Father Oyster is still in the confessional. You're excused."

"Thank you." She stood up quickly.

"Thank you, Sister." I repeated. But she didn't repeat it. I could feel my indignation rising up the back of my neck, making it stiff. The back of my eyes were burning. It's rare, if ever, I feel my temper that "hot," as they say. But I dismissed her with a hand wave before I spoke out. I stood up and moved around, and back again and sat down and stood up again and headed out the door towards Mother's office.

I passed Sr. Elijah Rose coming the opposite direction. She made a sign to speak, and we stepped into an alcove in the cloister.

"Sister, our...our retreatant was asking for you, according to Sister Paula."

"Thank you, Sister, I was just going there." Which of course, wasn't the truth, although I was planning to go there after seeing Mother. I could see Mother at any time, I better see what Rhonda wants, so I headed downstairs to the Cave.

Rhonda was waiting for me in the Cave's parlor, and smiled when I opened the door.

"Oh, Sister, I'm sorry, I locked myself out of my room. I didn't know the door would lock automatically, and I forgot to take my key with me."

"There should be a spare key on the hook by the stairs. You'll also have a key to the sacristy, which will be locked during the day. So you are very safe and secure down here. Sisters can come through a door across from our door to this parlor; we will only come in to put your meals on the turn. There is an extension phone on the table in your living room; that's only for inside calls. I left my extension there which is for my office. You can always leave a note for me on the turn in the sacristy; Sister Barbara will get it to me. Sister Paula will help you for the first couple days to get your books organized for the office. She can also pass notes on to me. If there's anything you need, just let me know. And Welcome. We're all praying that you have a fruitful and grace-filled retreat."

"Thank you, Sister, you're all being so kind. I promise, I won't be a bother to anyone. The Cave is a rather ominous name, isn't it? It kind of scares me."

"I know…but you could call it the "Intersanctum.""

"Intersanctum…hmmmm, I don't know if that's much better. It sounds like a scary television show."

"Well, you're right below the sacristy and the chapel actually; the Blessed Sacrament is just above the ceiling in your living room. Maybe you can come up with a good name for here."

"I shall...it's like the Death Hollows." And she got all choked up.

"More like Sleepy Hollow. It's so quiet down here, you won't even hear the noise of the traffic outside. But you just be comfortable for now. I'm pretty sure we're having pancakes for supper tonight." I said that to make her laugh, but it didn't work.

"You're so nice, Sister. I'm glad they gave me someone to talk to...it's so quiet here. I don't know if I'll survive. I haven't lived without a phone, a television, a phonograph."

"Oh, you'll get used to it, but I imagine it will take a few days...it's kind of like withdrawal." And that made her smile. *She probably knows more about 'withdrawal' than I do!* "And if it's driving you crazy, you can always talk to me; I have permission for that, so don't feel like you're ever imposing."

"Thank you, Sister, I'm feeling more comfortable already. Let me see, now, Vespers is next, right?"

"That's right, and then there's about 45 minutes of silent prayer time. Just for today."

She smiled. "Do I have to wait till the bell rings to go to the chapel?"

"Oh no, you can go to the chapel at any time, day or night. My first prioress used to say, 'Our dear Lord waits for us there all the time.'"

"That's beautiful. Well, I may go up now then. I do want to put on a warmer sweater though, it's chillier in there than I expected."

"I know, it usually isn't as cold as it seems. I'll leave you now…"

"Thank you, Sister, and I'm looking forward to them."

"To Vespers?" I asked, perplexed that she would use the plural.

"To the pancakes!"

"Me too," I said and left her then, smiling to myself. My mood had suddenly changed; I was not furious and outraged at the likes of Havana, but I still went down to Mother's office. But it was locked. She was probably in the parlor with Fr. Oyster, so I went to the library and prayed on the way that the Holy Spirit would put my finger on a good Lenten book, something…something unusual.

Twenty-Five

Ash Wednesday 2007

My soul is waiting for the Lord, I count on his word. My soul is longing for the Lord, more than watchman for daybreak. Let the watchman count on daybreak and Israel on the Lord. (Psalm 130, Wednesday Compline)

LORD, TODAY WAS probably the most unusual Ash Wednesday I've ever had here. I remember years ago how we began with a stricter silence, and the meager meals we had as part of our fast. No butter on the table. And no visitors in the parlor until after Easter. That part changed some years ago, although we don't encourage visitors, and the novices don't receive guests.

My first surprise was my sister and Mitzie were here at 10:30 a.m. I met them in the small parlor right after Terce when Sr. Cecilia came to tell me they were here. Sister was filling in for Sr. Paula, who was back in the infirmary again.

"Well, this *is* a surprise. Happy Ash Wednesday."

"Sister Mary Baruch, we're sorry we didn't phone you ahead of time. We didn't realize it was Ash Wednesday till

we noticed some people on the street with dirty foreheads."
Mitzie gestured to her forehead.

"We're going to the Steins for lunch," my sister put in,
"and thought we'd pop in on the way; it's been awhile, and
we brought you something from St. Thomas."

"From St. Thomas? Thomas Aquinas?"

"No, St. Thomas, Virgin Islands' St. Thomas." Mitzie
laughed. Sally didn't seem to get the humor of it.

"Well, that was very nice of you. I hope it isn't something
one can eat."

Sally laughed at that. "Hardly, it would be rotten by now,
besides I'm sure you get plenty of rice and beans here." She
laughed again thinking that was a riot.

"We had a lovely time on the cruise, (looking at Sally) and
the food was hardly anything like rice and beans."

"The meals on board, yes, they were scrumptious. I meant
that little café we ate at which unsettled everything, well you
know…"

Mitzie picked up the ball again, "We went into a charming church, well, it wasn't really a church, it was a cathedral.
What was the name of it?"

"I don't remember; it had a double name," said Sally the
former journalist, known for remembering details.

"Peter and Paul?" I guessed.

"Yes, that's it, the Cathedral of Saints Peter and Paul. It
was quite beautiful inside, and there was a gift shop, naturally…every place has a gift shop! And we bought you this."
Sally pulled a white box out of her bag and put it on the
turn.

I opened it, and it was another shell; a huge ribbed like coral shell blended with pink and blue shades fading into each other, and covering the 'inside' was a painting of Our Lady of Guadalupe.

"Thank you very much…this is really beautiful, and so kind of you to think of me. I love Our Lady of Guadalupe. My, it's like I've begun a collection of shells."

"Do you already have one like this?" Mitzie looked almost disappointed.

"No, not at all, and not this pretty. Sharbel gave me a scallop from his pilgrimage in Spain. The shell is the symbol for the pilgrim." I took a chance and added, "Do you know who Our Lady of Guadalupe is?"

Mitzie, the budding theologian, "Well, that's Mary, isn't it?"

"That's right. She's actually dressed in the garb of an Aztec princess in Mexico around 1530 something…" and I told them the whole story of Our Lady and Juan Diego.

"That's really incredible…and it still exists? This toilsome?"

"Tilma. Yes, it does. It's in a basilica in Mexico City."

"Oh, we'll have to go there, Sal, I've got to see this thing for myself."

Sally smiled. "They probably have a website; you can see it online."

"Yeah, but it's better to see the real thing."

Before a debate started, I added, "You remember all we talked about the soul last time you were here?" They hummed a "yes." "Well, more stupendous than this tilma of Saint Juan Diego, he was just canonized, you know, four years ago, more stupendous is the soul of Mary. For one thing, her soul was completely free of sin, unlike our souls, and every soul since Adam and Eve sinned, she was untouched by what we call Original Sin. We call her the Immaculate Conception."

"Oh, I always thought that meant when she got pregnant with Jesus." The budding theologian again.

"A lot of people think that, but it's actually when Mary was conceived in the womb of her mother, St. Anne."

"But why was that?" Finally Sally asked the big question.

"Because God had chosen her before she was even conceived, from all eternity actually, but in time...before she was conceived, He chose her to be the Mother of His Son." They didn't say anything, and they were not budging, so I interiorly breathed in the presence of the Holy Spirit, and went on.

"I think the big difference between Catholicism and Judaism or Islam or any New Age kind of religion, and the ancient ones like Buddhism and Hinduism, is that we believe, from revelation...that God Himself has revealed this...that God is One, and within the One God there are what we call three 'persons'...kind of like each of us, we, you, are one woman, let's say, because the word 'person' can be ambiguous here... you are one, but there is the 'ego' or 'I' that refers to all of you; then there is your mind, that knows this 'I' more than anyone else can, because only *you* can know *you* that way... and you love, and that love is you too...like we talked about before, there is you, and the you who knows herself, and the you who loves. Each is related to each other, but you are one."

They sat totally silent (*Thank God*), and I think were following my explanation. I thought all those years of conferences and classes…and prayer…are paying off!

"The 'mind' or knowledge God has of Himself, we call the Word. There is only one 'thought' in God, the Word, which is also God; it's the perfect image of the Father, as St. Paul puts it. And God loves…this is the Holy Spirit, who is God. So really, God not only loves, but He is Love. These three make up the One. We can call them different names, like Lover, Beloved, Loving…or Thinker, Thought, Thinking. Or Father, Son, and Holy Spirit. Or First, Second, and Third Person."

It was uncanny, but at that moment, Sr. Cecilia knocked lightly three times and opened the door on my side, with a tray holding a pot of coffee, two mugs, and a pitcher of milk. And surprisingly a plate with four rugelach on it, left over from yesterday. She put the tray on the turn. "Thought you might like these." She smiled and left as quietly as she entered.

"Well isn't that sweet of her, but can't you have coffee with us? And look, apricot rugelach." Sally suddenly became alive again. "That's not the Sister who usually waits on us."

"No, Sister Paula is under the weather. That was Sister Cecilia; she's filling in for her today."

Having poured the coffee and sitting down again, Mitzie wanted me to "go on."

"Well, like I said, the big difference between Catholicism and Judaism is the Blessed Trinity. We don't believe, like we talked about before, that our souls go through cycles of reincarnations, but only one Incarnation, and that is God's

Himself. The Son, the Beloved, the Word, the Thought, the Second Person, who is fully and completely God, took to Himself a human nature, that is, a real human body and soul, and this took place, in the virginal, immaculate womb of Mary. We call her the new Eve, or the Second Eve…interesting, isn't it, that she's portrayed on a shell? Like the birth of Venus."

"That's absolutely fascinating, Sister Baruch, I mean, Mary Baruch, I never heard it all put that way. You've explained it all so easily." That was Mitzie complimenting me; Sally sat wide-eyed with half a rugelach in her mouth.

Mitzie sipped her coffee and stared off into space. She was thinking.

"Don't you want some rugelach?" Sally was suddenly concerned about my not eating.

"No, thank you. I would love some actually, but today is Ash Wednesday. We're fasting today. It's the first day of Lent, you know."

Not really hearing this exchange, Mitzie came back to earth. "So does Jesus leave this Trinity when he comes to Mary's womb?"

"That's a very profound question. No, Jesus could not by His very Divine Nature 'leave' as you put it, the Trinity, but He, the Second Person of the Trinity, not the Father or the Holy Spirit, but the Son, took a human nature to Himself."

I let Mitzie think about this for fifteen seconds, then went on. "You know, the very first thing I read when I picked up the Christian Scriptures for the first time was the genealogy of Matthew, sounding very Jewish. But then, I flipped ahead and read what we call the 'Prologue' of the Gospel of St. John. You should read it…it refers to Jesus, not by name, but as the Word. *'In the beginning was the Word, and the Word was with God, and the Word was God.'* It's quite profound. My Jewish heart kind of leapt for joy as I knew God through His Word in Torah and in every blessing our Mother would recognize." I glanced over at Sally. "St. John says everything that was created, that came into being, was in this Word; everything, in other words, everything that is, *is* in the mind of God." Pause and let that sink in. *"And the Word became flesh and dwelled among us."*

"That's Christmas," Mitzie kind of whispered to herself.

"That's right, although the Word became flesh in Mary's womb nine months before Christmas; we celebrate that day too—it's the Annunciation, on March 25, nine months before Christmas. Christmas is the birth of the Word."

"He was just a baby…but also God." Mitzie was thinking deeply.

"Yes. I said the Second Person, we call Him, of the Blessed Trinity took to Himself a human nature, but He didn't lose His Divine nature. So the theologians explain that Jesus is a Divine Person, but with two natures…He is God with a Divine nature and a man with a real human nature. So, even as an Infant, even in Mary's womb, He knew who he was. And everything he did in His human nature, is the action of God. That's quite mind boggling, if you think about it."

Mitzie bit the rugelach in half. "Wow…I've got to think about that. I never heard it all put that way." Sally didn't want to be left out of the picture, "Uh, me either, Becky, that's quite marvelous the way you put all that."

I was almost bowled over by that compliment. Never would I have dreamed I'd ever hear that from my older sister, the most intelligent of the Feinstein girls.

"Next time, we can talk more about it. You originally wanted to talk about celibacy, and I kind of put that conversation off; see...for me, it's all connected to who Jesus is...everything is...this whole life, being a nun and all that, makes no sense if Jesus isn't all that I just said. If He isn't God made man, God made visible, and God who is still alive in a glorious resurrected body, than what are we doing here? But that's for the next time. We're spending the next forty days, you might say, getting ready to celebrate that resurrection. And...(I paused)...how we come to belong to Him." I stopped. My Dominican soul wanted to go on, but I knew to stop. It takes times for these truths to sink in, and I was grateful Sally and Mitzie listened so attentively.

They said they were off to the Steins. "Madame Chow is due for her haircut," quipped Mitzie. They thanked me, wished me a happy Ash Wednesday, and Sally, having put the remaining rugelach in her bag, waved goodbye. "We'll be in touch."

"Thank you again for my beautiful shell. I love it..."

I didn't know what to do with it; a passing thought wondered if it was meant to be an ash tray. I shuttered for a moment with the image of someone snuffing a cigarette out on Our Lady of Guadalupe. Not knowing what to do with it, I put it on my shelf next to Sharbel's scallop, and asked Our Lady of Guadalupe to take care of the three of them.

Twenty-Six

Ash Wednesday Afternoon

> *O Lord, it is you who are my portion and cup; it is*
> *you yourself who are my prize. The lot marked out for*
> *me is my delight: welcome indeed the heritage that*
> *falls to me!* (Psalm 16, Thursday Compline)

NOT A PEEP out of Rhonda Lynwood. She was either in the chapel or in the Cave, or the Intersanctum, or the dungeons below. (I chuckled to myself.)

I was grateful to have a free afternoon, and after dinner (lunch), I thought an Ash Wednesday nap would be very nice. I know that doesn't sound very penitential, but I don't mean a lie-down nap, but a "Squeak-nap." Before heading to our cell, I checked voice mail in my office. Sometimes Mother actually leaves me a message instead of a note. But to my surprise: "Hi, Aunt Mary, it's Jack. I'm back in town for a couple days. Thought I would come see you around two o'clock, if that's okay."

I immediately reserved the small parlor, and went to the chapel to make a visit. I also dashed over to the infirmary to see how Sr. Paula was. It was truly "nap-time" there, including Sr. Paula sitting in her lazy-boy with a book on her lap. I didn't have the nerve to wake her.

I eventually made my way to the parlor with ten minutes to spare. No one was in the little kitchen, so I left a note on the counter that I was having a visit with my nephew at two o'clock. I called Maxine Truffle, a lay volunteer sitting at our front desk, to let her know I was expecting a young man named Sharbel, and I would be in the small parlor.

I didn't know anymore what to expect when Sharbel was coming to visit. But I was both excited and anxious to see him.

Five after two, the door opened, and there he was, all smiles, like we were old pals. And I hadn't seen or heard from him in over two months. The prodigal pilgrim.

"Aunt Mary, I'm glad you got my message; I'm sorry, I know it was late, and I didn't know if you were allowed to have visitors on Ash Wednesday."

"We normally don't, but you're an exception, and my, my, my—look at you!" He was looking much better than past visits, and sporting a full but well-trimmed beard.

"I know. Do you like it?"

"Oh, yes, it makes you look very monastic." (*He probably thought I was going to say "romantic."*)

"I know. My mother hates it, I think for that very reason. She says she named me Sharbel because she loves the name and the saint, but I don't have to look like him!"

I laughed. "You have a long way to go till that happens. The only pictures I've seen of him show a snow white beard, like down to his waist." An exaggeration, but gave him a good laugh. "Where have you been? Do you know your mother was worried sick over you?"

"I know, she let me have it. But I sent her a letter from France and told her to let you know I was a pilgrim again."

"No, she didn't let me know, but she's probably had a lot on her mind. So tell me, what's going on? Why and where were you in France?"

"Gilbert, one of the guys I met on the Camino, and who kinda hung out with Robby and me, anyway, he entered a Benedictine monastery in France, and invited Robby and me to come to his clothing. That was in the east central part, near Lyons. We stayed at the monastery for a couple nights. Gilbert, now Frere Polycarp, gave us a map with all the monasteries in France. We bought Eurail tickets and took off."

"And you only went to monasteries?"

"Nearly 'only.' We went to a couple hot spots in a couple cities—oh, and we went to Lourdes for four days. I meant to send you a postcard from there, but I never got around to it; I'm sorry, Aunt Mary. I prayed for you there especially, and for Mother Bernadette."

"That's very nice, Blessed be God, and I will tell her that. You're a lucky young man to be able to afford a couple months in France."

"Well, I make good money off my dad's duplex, you know. My big conflict right now is that I think I want to be a monk instead of a friar. You can imagine that sent my mother off the deep end! Even worse when I told her, and maybe in France."

I don't know why, but it all made me laugh. *Poor Olivia,* I thought, *upset that her son wanted to be a Dominican in the*

Province of St. Joseph, namely, the east coast, and now he tells her he may move to France and be a monk!

"Your poor mom!"

"Poor Mom, nothing. She could afford a chateau in France, and visit me twice a year."

"Sharbel!" I said using his real name. "I can sympathize with your mother a little; I'd never get to see you!"

"Oh sure you would; monks from other countries can go home and visit every couple years."

"Well, that's all very interesting." I paused and looked closely into his eyes, "And you were alright in every which way? I'm sorry, I shouldn't ask, but I did rescue you once and have been concerned."

"I know you have, and I'm depending more than ever on your prayers. I don't have to have my mother's approval, but I would like her blessing. And, well, France is wine country, you know, and Robby and I may have over done it a few times, but we never got in trouble. One guest master almost kicked us out for making too much noise. We were staying in like retreat quarters."

"Oh my. I can just imagine. Well, I'm glad you're home safe and sound. Oh, well, what about Winona? Did you tell her about wanting to be a monk?"

"Winona? Oh sure, she's thrilled about it, but hopes it will be somewhere here."

"But isn't Winona your, uh, girlfriend?"

"Winona? Heavens no. She was in our group on the Camino too. Gilbert even invited her for his vestition, but she couldn't get away because of work; she's a nurse. How do you know Winona? Has she been here?"

"No, I spoke to her once on the phone. She was very concerned about your whereabouts. Funny she never mentioned the vestition thing."

"Oh, she probably didn't even know I was invited. What do you mean, you spoke to her on the phone?"

"Your mother had called me to see if I knew where you were; that was a voice mail. When I called her back, Winona answered."

"Well, I'll be. She met my mom after the trip. Both she and Robby and one other girl from New York all came over one night to my mom's for dinner. My mother, come to think of it, was very friendly with both of the girls, and gave them her phone number. I think *she* thought I was interested in them and had probably forgotten about being a priest. It was more wishful thinking on her part."

"Well, you might begin there, and let your poor mother know you and Winona are not an item." The way I said it made him laugh. "So, what are you are going to do now? Become a hermit in Lebanon?" That made him laugh even harder. "Such decisions you have to make; are you here to stay?"

"Not really, I want to visit some monasteries here; the one advantage is we speak English here, ma soeur."

I laughed.

"I was going to buy a car, but then decided it would be better to rent one. I'm leaving for Oregon tomorrow."

"Oy vey. You're driving to Oregon?"

"Isn't that exciting? I am. I'll pick up Robby in Ohio, so I won't be making the trip alone. He's interested in being a monk too. There's a new monastery in Iowa that still celebrates the Latin Mass and chants the Office in Latin. We visited their motherhouse in Germany. But I wanted you to know, so you can pray for us."

"Of course, I will, Jack. I always do. Now, your mother knows about this trip, right?"

"Well, she knows Robby and I are driving to Oregon. She thinks we're both crazy and irresponsible, but I think she envies our youth and energy. Besides, she's still so wrapped up in her work, she won't even miss me."

"I see." That's all I said. I could see beneath that exterior charm and handsome beard, a wounded little boy who maybe never knew the love of his mother. But who am I, Lord, to know any of that? Such big life decisions looming before him, and he's really kind of alone. I resolved then and there to pray for his mother too.

"I wish your father was still alive. I think he would have enjoyed a road trip with you. He loved to travel, as you know."

"And Grandmamma. My happiest childhood memories are with the two of them." And he couldn't go on.

"And 'Grandmamma' doted on you, you know."

"I know." We both sat silent for a minute. "You probably think I'm crazy and irresponsible too, but I love the Lord, and want to do His will. I know you of all my family understand what that means. I'm just not sure which path that is, but I hope you'll pray for me to find out."

The bell for None quietly tolled. "I will. And, Jack, I do understand. Someday, when you come back from your trip, I'll tell you all about it. AND you know your Aunt Sally lives in our old apartment."

"I know, but I've never met her. Grandmamma used to say she was a 'barber for mutts.'"

We both laughed. "I know, I know. How I miss her! She would have loved a wine-tour through France with you!"

He laughed. "And meeting the French monks."

"I can just see her eating cheese and croissants, and…"

"Bragging about 'my daughter, the nun!'" We both laughed. It's good to laugh. I don't think Sharbel and I have laughed so much. I wanted to go on, but was squeezed for time.

"Can you come to None?"

"I will, and then I'll take off. Back to the Island before rush hour."

"Well, my dear nephew, *Barukh atah, Eloheinu*. God bless you, and keep you safe in all your travels. Thank you for coming to see me. You've made my day…you've made my Lent!"

He headed towards the parlor door. "And Sharbel!"

"Yes, Sister Mary Baruch?"

"Keep off the sauce. Amen."

Twenty-Seven

Ash Wednesday Evening

Out of the depths I cry to you, O Lord, Lord hear my voice!
O let your ears be attentive to the voice of my pleading.
If you, O Lord, should mark our guilt, Lord, who would
survive? But with you is found forgiveness; for this we
revere you. (Psalm 130, Wednesday Compline)

THE EVENING MEAL was vegetable soup and bread. Good bread. Sr. Diana was following in Sr. Simon's footsteps. We have no recreation on Ash Wednesday, and would have an early Compline. I didn't have that on Rhonda's schedule, so after dishes, I rang her extension and told her to meet me in her parlor.

She opened the door looking very wretched, like she had been crying for hours. Her eyes were wrinkled and puffy.

"I'm sorry if I've disturbed you, Rhonda. I just wanted to let you know that Compline is early tonight, at 7:30."

"You're not disturbing me; I'm sorry, I must look a mess. Just a little crying spell."

"Well listen now. We don't have recreation tonight either, so why don't I fix us a couple cups of chamomile tea, and we can have a chat…I'll be back in less than ten minutes."

"Do you think so? That would be so nice. Goodness, it's only my second night here and already I'm a train wreck."

"You are not a train wreck. It's not easy getting used to a different place, let alone one so…so quiet."

I didn't know if "having tea" with Rhonda Lynwood counted as "taking care of her," but it seemed like a sensible thing to do. Gwendolyn calls it "tea therapy." It's a popular British remedy for the blues, and I've seen it work its charm in the infirmary many a time, so I interiorly invoked *epikeia*, and headed up the stairs to the infirmary kitchenette; it was closer than the little kitchen. There was already a little tea therapy going on in the infirmary, so the kettle was hot, and open on the counter was a new box of decaf black peppermint tea…perfect, better than chamomile. A little jar of milk, and a pocket full of sugar packs, and off I went back down the stairs.

Ronda was most grateful. We sat at our respective tables in this little parlor, which was actually quite cozy at night with the tiffany lamp and oriental rug. We dunked our tea bags; that's all part of the therapy, I decided.

"Is the silence getting to you?" I thought that was a safe opening.

"Oh no, I love the silence, but it does make you think, doesn't it?"

"I suppose so, yes, it allows you to think deep thoughts; I never quite thought of it that way."

"That's kind of you to say. You've been living in this silence for maybe twenty years?"

"Now *you're* being too kind. Try about forty years! Funny, I remember when I was a teenager, I used to go to my 'quiet place,' I called it. Even in a lot of noise or people, I'd practice that, like on the subway or in the park. I think I found my quiet place especially after my brother, Josh, died in Vietnam. Death has a way of doing that." I hoped I hadn't trod on sensitive ground too quickly.

"You know," Rhonda hesitated. "You know I'm living with a death warrant. My oncologist in L.A. originally said I had six months to a year, but before coming east, my latest pet scan shows that I'm full of it, and he now says 'two or three months' and he told me the symptoms to look for."

"I'm so sorry to hear that." (Dunk your tea, Baruch. How does one respond to something like that?)

"Having the cancer isn't really my problem, I don't think. But the knowledge that I'm going to die changes how I think about everything else. And my sins, Sister, all the sins of my life are pouring into my memory. Sins from long ago, that I'm not even sure I confessed or was really sorry for." She dunked her tea bag and dribbled all over the table. "Oh, look at me; I'm such a mess."

"Father Matthew is a wonderful confessor, Rhonda, and he's always here. He's our chaplain, you know. He's very sympathetic. I've shed a bucket or two of tears in his presence." That made her smile, and calmed her down enough to sip her tea.

"Maybe while you're here, a general confession would be very…very…what? Very healing and comforting for you."

"I've made general confessions, and I'd like to do that. I will. Fr. Reggie has been wonderful too in that regard, but I have never talked about some things to...to another woman, let alone a nun. There are things I don't think Reggie...I mean Fr. Reginald, can really understand."

"I suppose so, but then, a priest doesn't have to really understand, but to forgive. To absolve us when we confess and say we're truly sorry."

"I'm sorry to get all weepy with you."

"Oh, Rhonda my dear, you get as weepy as you want; you can cry buckets if you like, and maybe that's part of your being here. This house would probably float away in the flood if it collected all our tears over the years."

And that made Rhonda smile again, even gurgle a giggle. She looked at me with her mascara running down in black rivulets, reminding me of Mama's tearful face when she came to tell me about Ruthie. How sad, I thought, that we women paint our eyes with black inky paste to look more...what? Rhonda would be even more lovely without any makeup. Oh well.

"You've all lived such holy, quiet, prayerful lives that you have nothing to be afraid of when you die and Jesus welcomes you into His arms...*Enter good and faithful servant into your Father's house,* or something like that. But my life has not been holy, quiet, or prayerful; I'm so afraid now, and wish I could start over, or at least make up for all my unfaithfulness. It's like I've half killed myself...for what. To be loved? Loved by men...loved by the multitudes who applaud and scream when they see me. It's all so vacuous in the end." And she started to heave a little sob, and wipe her eyes with an egg shell white linen handkerchief trimmed in lace, smudging all the dripping mascara. What a sight. Poor Rhonda.

I didn't jump right back with a response, but let her own words sink into both our minds. "Being afraid, or a better word, 'fearful' is not so bad. The Scriptures say that '*the fear of the Lord is the beginning of wisdom.*' I think that's the kind of fear you're feeling right now, and the wisdom is beginning."

"Do you really think so? Lord, I hope so. Knowing that I'm going to meet my Maker in a very short time, makes the time that remains very precious to me. I don't even want to look at a television, gab on the phone, flip through senseless magazines full of scandalous stories and advertisements. I loved doing all that, wasting hours on hours. And when I think of the millions of dollars I've wasted on cosmetics, and publicity, and endless, endless chatter and gossip, oh my. All that for what? For my own self-aggrandizement. The fabulous, beautiful, Rhonda Lynwood. If people really knew the real me. But God knows the real me." She broke down again and the rivulets overflowed.

"I'll be right back." And I dashed out the door; she probably thought I was scandalized and abandoning her, but I simply sped through the locked door to the enclosure, which she didn't know was there, and went to a "common supply closet" and grabbed two boxes of Kleenex and returned.

"I forgot to put these in your room. There's plenty more when you need them. Do you need a tooth brush?"

She suddenly thought that was hysterical, and laughed while she blotted her face and blew her nose. "I have my own. It's electrical and costs over a hundred dollars...see what I mean!" The tears started again.

"Well...you do have lovely teeth." They were also exceptionally white; I didn't know how she did that, and didn't think I should ask.

She changed to laughter again. "Thank you, Sister. I probably bought my dentist's summer house with all the crowns and implants I've had." And she made a big smile like a horse with sparkling teeth.

"Our mugs are empty. Now, you take all the time you need. There's early Compline, if you want to come, and then, unfortunately, the Blessed Sacrament is reposed for the night too. Sister Bertrand, one of our eldest Sisters, says we're putting Jesus to bed for the night. But He fills the chapel with His presence from the tabernacle, day and night. And right through the ceiling here. But try to get a good night's sleep, you'll feel much better in the morning." (I was sounding like Dr. Feinstein, M.D., instead of Sr. Mary Baruch, O.P. How easily we play into roles.)

"Thank you, Sister. I hope I can talk with you some more. Don't worry. I have my Ambien with me."

"Ambien?"

"It's a little sleeping pill. Works wonders. Would you like to try one?"

"Not tonight, dear. I usually conk out as soon as my head hits the pillow."

She giggled and blew her nose at the same time while I gathered our mugs and made a quiet exit. "See you in the morning. Don't worry about being at Matins; we don't expect it. Sleep in!" (I had morphed into my SCAR role, but without the threat of disobedience. SCAR was so wise, I thought. Mother should have made her Rhonda's guardian angel.)

I returned the mugs to the infirmary kitchenette and by happy coincidence Mother Bernadette was in there drying dishes.

"Mother, just the one I want to see."

She smiled, looking at me over her frameless glasses. "Uh oh."

"Nothing bad, Mother, well maybe one thing is, well maybe both are, not really 'bad-bad' but of concern."

"Let's have a cup of tea." Ah ha, Mother was into tea-therapy too! We fixed our cups (no mug for Mother) and sat at the new round table which now had no tablecloth but a white vase with artificial sunflowers.

"Two things, Mother. First, I'm just coming from the Cave where I just had tea with Rhonda. She's pretty weepy at the moment. I think she's coming to face her life, which I know she came here to do, or maybe she wasn't expecting that so forcefully, but she's facing her fears. I couldn't find you to ask permission to take her some tea, and I spent time talking with her; listening mostly, but talking."

"This new peppermint tea is lovely, isn't it?" She was thinking before speaking. We both sipped. "Sister, I asked you to look after Rhonda Lynwood, and so you already have built-in permission to talk to her. I'm seeing already how unusual it is to have her here. Exceptional really, but some-how I believe it's all in God's Providence that this has hap-pened, and that we're being asked to be here for her. You know, she only has six months to live."

"Actually less, Mother, she told me tonight. New tests have shown it's a matter of a couple months."

"Oh dear, what a burden that must be, and it may be an added burden on you, Sister, which I don't want to impose."

"It's not a burden, Mother, and I'm just happy you've assured me of your permission; there's always 'such a blessing' that comes with obedience."

"You're right, and you have my permission, even if you have to speak during Great Silence. You wouldn't have to handle the tea thing; she can make tea for the both of you in her kitchenette. You can bring her a supply; perhaps some of this peppermint. You have a lot on your plate already, Sister, so let me know if this is too much of a burden."

"I will, Mother, but it isn't. As you know pretty much, my one sister died of drugs and alcohol; my other sister has lived her own life without faith in God and His Torah, to put it in a Jewish context; my mother and brother never visited me for over twenty-five years, and my best friend and roommate confesses her sins to me in a post-mortem letter. I can handle a little burden."

"Indeed, you can, Sister, and maybe God has put Rhonda here for that very reason." She sipped her tea, and smiled at me again. "You know, people think we all live on Cloud Nine, I suppose, free of troubles and always at peace with each other, apart from the trials and sins of the world. And there's a little particle of truth in that, but we also live life more intensely, and I truly believe, are called to bear the burdens of the world, like Our Lord did, so He continues to do that through us and in us. It's like…" and she hesitated. Sipped her tea. "It's like we are a holocaust."

I didn't say anything for the moment. "That's true, Mother, I've often thought about the Holocaust, and all that happened to…to my people. It's beautiful what you just said, that our lives are given over for others. It's like our way of living out St. Dominic's charism of 'preaching for the salvation of souls.' We just 'preach' without words, or maybe with words, sometimes a lot of words, but more just by living this life day after day."

"Ummm hummmm. I've watched you over the years, you know, Sister Baruch, especially in the infirmary when I was infirmarian. You have a way of letting others share their burdens with you, especially the older Sisters. Dear Sister Gertrude loved you, you know. She loved your being Jewish. I'm not sure if it reminded her of New York and the whole world of show business that she came out of, but did you know, she once said to me when you had left for Compline or something: 'There's our own Edith Stein.'"

I couldn't respond as I felt the tears mounting behind my eyes. After a moment, "Sister Gertrude never said that to me, but she liked to talk to me about St. Teresa Benedicta of the Cross. (Edith Stein's religious name when she entered Carmel. She was taken out of the monastery and died at Auschwitz.) I think she identified with her too."

"You're probably right. Now, what's the second 'not-bad-bad' thing on your mind?"

"Oh, yes, I nearly forgot. I'm concerned about Havana. I don't think she really belongs with us, and I'm hoping she will come to that conclusion herself, the sooner the better."

"Yes, I agree. I think we all see that. Maybe we could invite her mother and grandmother for a little… what?"

"A little tea-therapy. I've never met either one, and that may be just what she needs. A word from her grandmother carries more weight than anything I've ever said to her."

"Well, I'll leave it to you to make the arrangements. A tea party in the parlor during Lent—what is our life coming to! With Rhonda Lynwood camping out below in the Cave! Say your word, Sister...you know... your word."

"*Oy*, such a life we should have?"

Twenty-Eight

The Morning After, Daybreak

My soul is waiting for the Lord, I count on his word.
My soul is longing for the Lord more than watchman for
daybreak. Let the watchman count on daybreak and Israel
on the Lord. (Psalm 130, Wednesday Compline)

LORD, I THOUGHT I would have the morning to myself. But I guess You had other plans for me. A note from Sr. Paula on my way to the refectory for breakfast after Mass: "Can I see you, love, for five minutes after Mass? G." I had missed my last chat with Gwen on Shrove Tuesday, so I headed to the little parlor instead of the refectory, secretly hoping there would be a sesame bagel left when I eventually got there. Solomon's Deli gave us three dozen bagels yesterday. I think maybe they think 'Ash Wednesday' is like a feast day, or maybe they know it's a fast day, and think we only eat bread on fast days. Either way, I was grateful and couldn't shake the thought of them during my thanksgiving after Mass.

Gwen was already sitting in the chair close to the grille.

"Thanks, M.B., I just wanted to ask you for your prayers. I'm seeing a new doctor at Sloane this morning. It's ironic, because he's from London's Harding Cancer Center. I came back to the U.S. for cancer care, and my doctor's from England! He's here doing research on a new experimental treatment. They only take so many patients for these studies, and I'm one of them."

"I hope that's good news. It sounds a little like you're gonna be one of his guinea pigs or something."

"I suppose there's a thread of truth in that, but he's had marvelous results in the U.K., so it's not something brand new. He's a pukka oncologist. I just hope it's not anything involving chemo, and sitting for hours with an I.V. in my arm."

"I know. That must be such a cross for people."

"My car service will be here in a jiff...I'll let you know how it all goes. Prayers, please. Ta-ta." She was quite chipper about it all. "*Ta-ta*," I said to the empty parlor, repeating "*pukka*" to myself, and hoping I remember it to look it up in the dictionary. Pukka...

I said the *Memorare* for her right there in the parlor, and then took off for the refectory, a little chipper in my walk. I was not disappointed.

The Simple Professed were due to visit the infirmary this morning. They were supposed to do any "chores" that needed done by any of the Sisters or the infirmarian, but they usually wound up helping with a jigsaw puzzle or watching the bag-beaders at their trade. There was never a competition among them for popularity with the older Sisters, and the three of them seemed to get along amicably, till just recently. It might be my own subjective perception of things, but there was an invisible sheet of ice developing between Sr.

Elijah Rose and Sr. Leah. They were losing patience with each other. Sr. Elijah Rose would complain if Sr. Leah was too slow; Sr. Leah would complain that Sr. Elijah Rose was showing off.

I went to my office and found Havana's home number in her file. I called and got the answering machine. I didn't leave a message as I didn't want to make Mrs. Sanchez anxious. I didn't really know how she or Havana's grandmother felt about Havana's being here. Neither of them were here when she entered and began her postulancy. I was just sitting at my desk wondering about things, when my phone rang and startled me.

"Sister Mary Baruch."

"Sister, I'm sorry if I'm disturbing you. It's Rhonda."

"Good morning, Rhonda, you're not disturbing me at all; what can I do for you?"

"I baked a few cinnamon buns this morning, and wondered if you'd like to try one. If they're good enough, I can bake up a batch for the whole community. I'm not used to baking anything and…"

"I'll be down in three minutes." (Maybe I was too quick to respond. Hot cinnamon buns; thank goodness I didn't give up baked goods for Lent, right? Lord?) "Tea is fine in the afternoon and night; I'll bring some good coffee down from the little kitchen." I think I was feeling anxious about Gwendolyn, and cinnamon buns would be just what the pukka doctor ordered!

Rhonda was waiting for me and put on the coffee right away. The smell of the cinnamon buns gave the Cave a whole new ambience! Finally settled down in the parlor…

"It was so kind of you last night to listen to all my woes. I hope I didn't scandalize you."

"Scandalize me? Don't you worry about that. I am a New Yorker, you know. We aren't exactly immune from the ways of the world growing up." I hoped that didn't sound too arrogant.

"That's very kind of you. I had an apartment for a few years in New York. I loved the energy of the city. I like the whole east coast actually, and have a lovely big house near Newport, Rhode Island, not quite one of the famous mansions, a little north on Ocean Drive. It's called Waters Edge. It's the most peaceful of my houses."

"Houses?"

"Oh, yes, I have three, well four, counting a little cottage in Switzerland, but one in L.A. which I use mostly when I'm working on a film; a little ranch house in Malibu, which I use to get away from L.A.; and Waters Edge, which is really a 'grand estate' in Rhode Island. I'll probably go there from here, although my doctors are in L.A., so I don't know where I'll go." She smiled.

"Oy. Such problems we should have?" I said in my best New York Yiddish.

That of course did the trick and made her laugh.

"I thought I detected something Jewish in you! How marvelous. My second husband was Jewish and from New York too."

"I know...Stanley Feldman."

"You're right, how did you know that?"

It was my turn to laugh. "Like I said, I'm a New 'Yawka', dahling. My sister Ruthie used to read all the movie and theater tabloids like they were the Bible. We'd talk...and then, even in here, Sister Gertrude—your pal—kept up on your career. But I think it was Ruthie who told me about Stanley Feldman. I think she called him a 'second rate screen writer' and didn't give the marriage a year."

Laughing, she said, "Your Ruthie was quite right, well, about the second rate screen writer. But ah, he was a charmer and a real knock out, if you know what I mean. I'm sorry, Sister, I shouldn't talk that way to you."

"Knock out? I get it. One of my earliest best friends— gosh, I haven't thought about this in a hundred years—my friend Gracie, used to use that word to describe the boys in school. She was very pretty, and very popular, and was always asked out by the 'knock-outs' but it didn't affect her any."

"Smart girl. Did she ever marry one?"

"No, Gracie died of leukemia when she was in college. The disease really knocked her out, so to speak. She's my honorary godmother. It was because of her, in a way, that I became a Catholic. But that's another story for another time."

"Well, I'd love to hear it sometime. My Stanley knew he was a knock out, and unfortunately, half of Hollywood did too. He cheated on me a lot."

"Oh, Rhonda, I'm so sorry to hear that."

"Yeah, I don't think men know what they do to us; they sweep us off our feet and six months later they're sweeping us under the rug. Your sister was right about it not lasting. I was glad to be rid of him, actually. I was making a ton of money, and he was becoming a leech."

She stared off into the empty space and got all teary eyed. "He's also the cause of one my biggest sins..."

I just sat silent, letting my left hand move down to grab hold of my rosary.

"But that's another story for another time. How are the cinnamon buns?"

I licked the sugar icing from the corner of my mouth. "They're deee-licious, Rhonda. Maybe I should test one more to see if they're all alike." She smiled with delight, while actually my curiosity was running wild in my head, wondering what the big sin was, and then I felt guilty for even wondering that, and wondered why Ruthie never told me anymore, and Sr. Gertrude certainly wasn't given to Hollywood gossip, so I would just have to wait.

She went back into her kitchenette. I thought of Gracie again, and how she would not be so impressed by the 'knock outs' who asked her out. I laughed to myself thinking of Sidney Bergman, two inches shorter than me, a flat top haircut with horned rim glasses and protruding ears, a little left-over acne, and who was my date for the senior prom. Fat Sidney; the kids called him 'Shrimp' which was funny because he was strictly kosher, and certainly not a 'knock out,' but boy, could ole Shrimp dance! And I, Rebecca Abagail Feinstein, was his best jitterbug partner.

"What's so funny?" Rhonda said on returning with fresh coffee.

"Oh nothing, I was just remembering someone from my past. The cinnamon buns are wonderful, Chef Lynwood. What's your favorite main dish?"

"Oh, that's easy. Whole grain brown rice and shrimp."

She probably wondered why I thought that was so funny!

* * *

Afternoon

After our meager Lenten dinner, Sisters Elijah Rose and
Leah Marie were washers at two different sinks. Havana was
drying by Sr. Elijah Rose's sink, and seemed rather agitated
by something. If she found a grease spot or participle of food
not washed off, she would hold it up to Sr. Elijah Rose and
point to the spot like she was personally annoyed by it. Sr.
Elijah Rose was distracted by something and would just huff
when she had to rewash it. It wasn't like her to get irritated;
if anything, she would laugh at little things. But not today.
Maybe it was the Lenten fast.

I was able to retreat to our cell for the hour after dinner and sat in Squeak and closed my eyes. I think I dozed
off for a few minutes. I was feeling guilty about eating the
cinnamon buns, even though I'm legitimately excused from
the fast because of age (ahem), but I do try to keep it as a
penance, and I've failed already. Lord, You've got to help me.

When I went down for None, there was a note in my
cubby-hole. "I want to tell you about Stanley. Can we have
tea again? Rhonda."

I managed to smile and interiorly kick myself for immediately feeling put upon, then I wondered, "Stanley? Who's
this Stanley?" I remembered. Stanley Feldman, the second
husband who happened to be Jewish and a New Yorker.
I jotted down a short response, "I'll come down after our

supper, as we don't have recreation this evening." I slipped it to Sr. Paula before going into the chapel.

I was still feeling guilty when I knelt down before the office began. Lord, I am sorry for being so impatient and only looking after myself. The poor thing only wants to tell me about Stanley Feldman. For this I came into the monastery? I'm sorry, Lord, You know what You're doing. Sister Gertrude would tell me it's a scene You're directing, and in His Divine providence, I'm in it. I smiled and looked up at the monstrance. But You were silent. I hope You were smiling back.

Immediately after None, I went to my office. Maybe Mrs. Sanchez was home now. I called, but again, no answer, and I didn't leave a message. Well, she must be at work, or maybe she's away, I thought to myself.

I went to the infirmary to get one of the boxes of decaf peppermint tea, and Sr. Annunciata was putting the kettle on.

"A little 'tea therapy' with someone, Sister?"

"That's about right; I'd never quite thought of it that way, but you're right. It's Sr. Catherine Agnes; she's feeling down in the dumps, so I told I'd join her for tea before Vespers."

"Oh, I'm sorry to hear that. She's okay, though, isn't she? Just feeling a little blue?" I hadn't noticed SCAR looking 'down in the dumps' as Sr. Annunciata so delicately put it.

"She's fine. I think she's just a little lonely. She's still pretty sharp upstairs, you know, and sometimes the infirmary Sisters can be a little dull."

"You have such a way with words, Sister!" I laughed. "I'm sure the tea and your conversation will boost her spirits."

"You're welcome to join us, Sister. I know Sister Catherine Agnes always enjoys your company; she's told me so."

"Thank you, Sister, that's very kind of you, and I would, except I'm having a little tea therapy with our retreatant in the Cave after supper, and have work to do first; in the meantime, I came in to steal some decaf peppermint."

"Oh, God bless you, dear. How's that all going? I couldn't believe, well maybe I shouldn't even say it, but I couldn't believe the Council agreed to let her make a long retreat here with us. She's not well, I understand?" Sister was fishing for information in that subtle way we do it.

She stopped talking by rummaging through the boxes of tea in the cupboard.

"Peppermint, Lipton's Decaf, Twining's English breakfast, Lemon mist—oh, look—here's Earl Grey. That would be nice for a change."

(*Watch it, Sister.* I'm thinking. She's found my secret stash!)

"Yes, that is a nice change. And Earl Grey is one of my favorites; that came from Gwendolyn Putterforth." None of that simple confession deterred Sr. Annunciata.

"Oh, good. Is Earl Grey a Jewish tea?" She said it without rancor and totally, I'm sure, in her ignorance of tea. I actually laughed.

"No, Sister, the Earl was not Jewish nor is his tea! Not that I know of, anyway. Although, I think it's the 'bergamot' that makes black tea Earl Grey, and bergamot does sound very Jewish, doesn't it?"

Sister just stood there dunking.

"If Sister Barbara comes in, tell her I took a box of peppermint tea."

"I will, and enjoy your tea with Rhonda Lynwood. She'd probably like some Earl Grey too. She probably knew lots of Jews in Hollywood."

"Yes, like Stanley Feldman."

"Who?"

"No one, Sister, a man standing."

"Huh?"

"It goes better with a little milk or cream, Sister, not a squeeze..." It was too late. The Earl got doused with lemon. I couldn't bear it anymore.

"Enjoy your tea, and tell Sca...Sister Catherine Agnes that I'll come visit her soon." And off I went back to my office till the bell called us to the chapel for Vespers.

Twenty-Nine

The Annunciation 2007

Lord my God, I call for help by day; I cry at night before you. Let my prayer come into your presence. O turn your ear to my cry. For my soul is filled with evils, my life is on the brink of the grave. (Psalm 88, Friday Compline)

THE WEEKS OF Lent seem to be moving along too quickly, Lord. I thought it was the season when we were supposed to slow down and listen to the silence! I know, I'm being just a little facetious, but I know You understand. You're also showing me how selfish I can be with my time and how impatient I can be with others. Have I always been this way, Lord? Well, if so, help me, Lord, to be grateful for all the interruptions you've allowed in my life.

First, Rhonda, who wants me to call her 'Ronnie.' I just can't do that, Lord. So Rhonda was all apologetic again for missing our appointment, she called it. But that same night was the beginning of an almost routine "tea therapy" in the Cave, after Compline. It's been a real sacrifice, as I cherish that silent time, and at the beginning I felt put upon, and guilty because it was during Great Silence. Because of that, it was the ideal time. In the Cave's little parlor we had our own grand silence, and Rhonda began to unload a lifetime of sin and infidelity.

"Stanley was more interested in money and travel to exotic places to shoot stupid scenes for the stupid screen plays he was writing. My first husband, Eric, was a loser from the start, and lost interest in me when the rest of Hollywood was buzzing around his head. It was an easy marriage, Las Vegas style, and an easy divorce. Then Stanley came into my life. I was in rehearsals for *Blue Bonnet*, the Broadway drama that didn't make it through the out of town try outs, but Stanley was an assistant director of lighting, and so would go to the cast parties. That's how we met. He was not just a knock-out, Sister, he was a charmer. He had that New York Jewish humor that kept me laughing through the depressing reviews we were getting. Anyway, one thing led to another. Stanley said I should stay in New York, that's where all the action was. So I stayed. And we got 'hitched' downtown at City Hall. I wasn't a Catholic yet, mind you, and Stanley's shadow never crossed the threshold of a synagogue."

I'm thinking to myself, she certainly can go on with endless details. How do I kindly ask her to get to the point? Fr. Wilcox, I remember, used to get impatient in confession if I went into a lot of background details, and he would say, "Just the sins, Sister, just the sins." So I smiled, and gave it a try. "Just the sins, Rhonda, just the sins."

She blinked a couple times, then took a deep breath and said, "I got pregnant, and Stanley didn't want the baby. He even accused me of not being careful, and maybe it wasn't even his, and he wasn't about to settle down and be a father."

I blinked and took a deep breath and let her go on.

"I was thrilled and frightened at the same time. I didn't want to become a mother without a father, and be without a career, and without a family nearby, and on and on. I don't think I ever really prayed about it, or thought about it being a real human being with a soul and everything." She paused and averted her eyes from me, and in almost a whisper confessed, "I had an abortion."

I don't know why I wasn't shocked. Maybe it was the build-up which made me almost guess what she was going to say. Maybe because we've heard and read and prayed so much about it for the last thirty-some years, since 1973, that even the word doesn't shock us anymore. I don't think I even showed shock on my face, but a kind of droopy sadness. I was a little more shocked when she went on and told me it wasn't the only one; she had three. She wept telling me, and even told me how old they would be now, and that she was afraid that God didn't forgive her.

What does one say at times like this? I can't imagine the anguish and guilt one must feel after they realize what they've done, not just to the baby, but to one's own deep sense of being a woman. Isn't there something in us that's part of our soul, our nature, that makes us to be unique creatures of the Creator-God? We participate in that divine act in our very bodies. How she must have suffered all these years, I thought. In my day it was simply "the pill" that was the newest big sin; we never really talked about abortion, certainly not at home, and I don't remember it being part of the "girl-talk" at school, even among the newborn feminists from Barnard. Of course, I lived a pretty sheltered life. And when I came to know and love the Lord, I was thinking and reading and talking about other things.

"Rhonda," I began almost at a whisper, "I can't imagine how horrible you must feel. I'm happy you were able to get it out and share it with me. I had a dear friend who was never able to do that, and she must've felt like she carried the burden and guilt of her sin all by herself." I paused there, thinking of Greta, and remembering the times she would quietly weep at Mass, and I just thought she was moved by the beauty of it or the closeness of the Lord.

"I want you to know that I will help you carry that guilt, and that with you, I will bring it all to the Lord. And you know, Rhonda, when we do that, the Lord floods our soul with His mercy. He loves us so much that He took all our sin upon Himself and as our dear Sister Gertrude once told me, He annihilates our sins—if we are truly repentant, and you are, and He forgives and wipes those sins away. I presume you've confessed them, and the Sacrament of Penance has absolved them, and replaced them with Divine Mercy. Isn't the Sacrament of Penance the most wonderful sacrament there is, after the Eucharist, of course, and Baptism, of course?" My little sacramental litany lightened Rhonda's guilty doldrums, and she actually smiled.

"Do you really think so? I mean, I went to confession when I became a Catholic, and I'm sure I mentioned these sins, but I didn't see then what I see now. I mean, they were little babies, with souls, forming in my body."

"Well, I'm sure you were fully forgiven and absolved, but it's okay, even more, it's good to confess them again in a general confession. What a difference your faith must've made in your life."

That remark just started the flood of tears all over again. Apparently, the third time was after she was a Catholic. But she said she didn't realize the gravity of the sin. The "gospel of the world" was still very strong in her mind, is the way she put it. That "tea therapy night" was a big break through, thank you, Lord.

Every night was not a catharsis, thank You again, Lord, or I would have been wrung out completely. Rhonda also shared how daring and exciting it was to become a devout Catholic in the world of Hollywood. I was able to share a little of my conversion with her, which she found fascinating, how things happened kind of in the reverse. I became a Catholic and only some years later entered the convent (as she put it) and she entered the convent, via a movie role, and it became so meaningful for her, it brought her to the faith.

"My third husband, Jimmy Wainwright, was a drummer and played with a jazz band, well, a quintet, to be exact, called The Angles. They thought it was a clever name because they were all Anglos, from England, but living in Los Angeles. Jimmy was from Cheshire actually, like the cat."(She laughed. I laughed.) "He was a Catholic, and we actually met at the nuns' monastery in Hollywood. I was filming *Wind Struck*, and was able to go to daily Mass before being on the set, but Jimmy was there on Sunday, and I recognized him, which was probably the most flattering thing that can happen to someone in Hollywood. I was used to it, but he was a simple drummer in a band."

She's off again, I thought, Detail City. Maybe it was part of her being an actress; one had to paint the scene, or so Ruthie would say when she was going on about something.

"I had been to a bar mitzvah, as I recall, Sol Cohen's son, one of the producers for *Wind Struck*. The Angles were the live band, and they were good. I was struck by the drummer's, what would you call it, spaced out look. He was in another world. He also had gorgeous black hair that flopped over his eyes and would swing back and forth with the beat."

I smiled at the details; I thought Jimmy Wainwright probably looked like my brother, Josh, who didn't play the drums, but could get lost in another world, singing a song. Ruthie thought he looked like Johnny Ray.

"We got married in a little Catholic chapel in Cheshire. It was my first real wedding, you know. His family were so happy for him, and that we came all the way to England for the wedding." In a kind of faraway afterthought, she added, "We went to London, Paris, and Rome for our honey moon."

"Did you and Jimmy have children? I don't remember reading that you did."

"No, Sister. We tried. I became pregnant probably three times, and lost the baby all three times. I thought God was punishing me for having the... having the you know what." She wasn't even able to say it now, she had become suddenly so emotional again.

"Jimmy was good to me. But our careers were so different. He was out most nights. I would go to his gigs once in a while, but if I was filming, I was done in by the end of the day. And sometimes I'd be out of town for weeks at a time.

Jimmy was alone a lot. His little jazz band were also kind of into stuff, if you know what I mean."

"You mean like marijuana and other assorted drugs?" Here I was over 30 years a nun, and I was sounding like I knew "the scene." Well, I did have an inside look from Ruthie, and Gwendolyn would talk about "stuff." I wasn't completely naïve.

"Yeah, I wish it were only pot and martinis. Speaking of martinis, I don't suppose we have a cocktail hour here, like on weekends?"

That made me burst out laughing.

"I only said that to make you laugh, and it worked!"

"It worked. I can just imagine if we went from Vespers to Beefeaters Gin."

"It would be more interesting if you went from Beefeaters to Vespers." And we both got laughing.

"Actually, I do miss the olives." And Rhonda laughed even harder.

It was a happy break from the seriousness and intensity of the conversation. Poor Rhonda didn't have much luck with her husbands.

"Jimmy got into cocaine, and it was all downhill from there. It broke my heart. Of my three husbands, he was the love of my life."

"Did you get a divorce?"

"No, I couldn't bring myself to that, and anyway, before that word was ever spoken, Jimmy…I was out of town at the time, in Vegas, for the premiere of *Conquering Loon*, and he…he…overdosed and died." The flood gates opened again.

"I'm sorry, Sister, you've lived in such a different world, you wouldn't understand. Jimmy was not a bad person…he…"

"I have lived in a different world, as you put it, but I do understand, Rhonda. My little sister overdosed and died too."

"Oh, Sister, I'm so sorry to hear that."

"She was an actress, you know. She never became a star, but she had the passion for it, and it got spent in the wrong direction. Drugs. How sad it all is."

We sat in silence for a few moments. Rhonda looked her age despite her plastic surgery. I had told her early on that she didn't have to wear makeup, false eyelashes, or even lipstick. We were just us; she didn't have to be all made up. I said it in a kind way, and she understood, and actually looked healthier and younger without it all.

"How did you deal with all that?" asked the grand actress with taunt crows' feet sprouting out from her eyes.

"Oh, I prayed. I always prayed for Ruthie, but somehow my prayers meant more now. It confronts us with all the big questions, you know. And Mama. As tragic as it all was, it brought my mother here for the first time in thirty years. She was able to accept my life. Ruthie used to visit me over the years, and kept my mother and me kind of connected that way, and when Ruthie died, Mama didn't want me to find out from anyone else. She came here. I think it hit Mama too…the big questions, and maybe I was somehow a strange answer to some of them, I don't know."

"That's such a touching story, Sister. The big questions. I'm being smacked in the face with them right now, aren't I? When Jimmy died, I fell into a deep depression. I couldn't really pray. I think I was angry at God for letting it all happen. The da...darn drugs. Oops, I almost slipped."

I had to laugh again. "Rhonda, you are so funny! I think people think we are made of meringue, and we're really... well, I can't think of a comparison, but we're not all sugary and fragile. We're pretty tough dough when it comes to life...in the end, it's the Lord who makes all the difference and makes any sense out of life. Our life, or your life."

"I can see that, in just the short time I've been here. The silence and constant prayer really must have an intense effect on you. It toughens you up; I can see that. It doesn't make one oblivious to the sins of the world, but lets you...how would you say it? It lets you carry them and, in a way, makes up for them."

"I don't know about making up for them, but maybe we do penance for them because we confront it all in ourselves too, you know. The selfishness of the world-run-riot, is present in the human soul. And we surrender, God willing, to the redeeming love of Christ who takes away the sin of the world...we pray that every day, don't we? The best you can do, the only thing you can do, is cast it all into the Heart of Jesus. Jimmy Wainwright, Stanley Feldman, the babies you didn't have, the depressions and messes you got into—cast it all into the Sacred Heart."

Rhonda sat silent, staring at me. I hoped I didn't sound like some Protestant Evangelist on television, calling her down for an altar-call. Gwendolyn used to tell me about them. She would say they were very engaging preachers, emotional, and must've moved a lot of hearts, and that's good, but they didn't have the sacraments.

"Thank you, Sister. I can't tell you how much that has helped me. I've lived a wretched life, especially after Jimmy's death; I abandoned the Faith for a few years; I couldn't pray, go to Mass, or talk about any of it. I did some horrible things, but even worse, I think, I drowned myself in the obsession for fame, recognition, applause, and all that...that..."

"Crap!"

"Sister!" And we burst out laughing again.

"I'm sorry, Rhonda, I didn't mean to scandalize you. We're not meringue, but we're not devil's food cake either." We laughed even more. "If I may ask, how did you come back from it all?"

Rhonda didn't answer immediately. There was all the nose blowing and eye patting first.

"There were two things. This may sound a bit self-aggrandizing, but I was alone in my house in Malibu. It was a Saturday night, and I was alone, but decided to buy a whole pizza for myself, and I had a bottle of Merlot, which wasn't so unusual, and I put in a VHS of *Lonely Heart Legacy*, and I found myself crying my eyes out at the end, you know, when Myrtle Pine enters the convent. It touched my soul again like when I filmed it. And I knew I couldn't blame the Lord for everything that happened in my life, and that I was missing out on the best part. I guess I knew, as you put it, that the faith was not the meringue of life, but the sweetness of the cross, when we live it. I didn't know how to make a 'come back,' but the Lord did! I had to embrace suffering and find in it a sweetness I never knew.

"I went back to Beverly Hills the next day, and went into the chapel of the Dominican nuns on Hollywood Blvd. It wasn't Mass, but there was a priest talking to them; I think they were on retreat. And…you're not going to believe this, but he was telling them how much God loves them, and brings them to Himself through strange doors, like Myrtle Pine when she went to the convent. I sat in the pew stunned. It was like God had hit me over the head. His talk was all about mercy and forgiveness, and when he ended, and the chapel was silent I, like, came to. And I'm sure it was all grace now, or my Guardian Angel, but I went to the side entrance and into the office, and there was a lay woman there, and I asked who the priest was giving the talks, and was there any way I could talk to him? She was very kind, and told me to wait. She called a number, and talked to him, and hung up, and told me how to get to a door on the outside, but inside the gate, to the priest's quarters, and he would see me there. I went and knocked on the door…"

(*Rhonda and all her details, but these were really enthralling!*)

"I just blurted out that I was Myrtle Pine, and I wanted to go to confession. That was it! He invited me into a private sitting room, and put on a purple stole, and closed his eyes, and said, 'And what do you have to bring to the Lord today?' And I let it all out. That was nearly twenty years ago…"

It was my turn to sit silent and stare. "That's an incredible story, Myrtle, I mean Rhonda." We laughed a relaxed laugh. "Did you ever know the priest's name?"

"Oh indeed I did…and still do."

"Who was he?"

"Father Reginald Oyster!"

Thirty

The Next Night...After Compline

Upon you no evil shall fall, no plague approach where you dwell.
For you has he commanded his angels, to keep you in all your ways.
They shall bear you upon their hands, lest you strike your foot
against a stone. On the lion and viper you will tread, and trample
the young lion and the dragon. (Psalm 91, Sunday Compline)

WE'VE GOTTEN USED to Rhonda Lynwood being with us,
Lord. Only one or two Sisters seemed to keep up an air of
disapproval. I hope she will be able to stay with us till Easter,
but we will see. She's lost a lot of weight, and hasn't been at
the morning Office as often. So we will see. I was happy to
arrange for her to meet with Ezra in her little parlor, rather
than the tight space of the confessional; she was open to face-
to-face. I told her she didn't have to go into all the details she
did with me, but a general confession of her sins would do it.

I was actually rehashing our conversations during meditation, which I suppose would be considered a distraction,
but it helped me to review my own life, and I want to be
renewed, Lord, in living every moment for You. You are the
love of my life, as she put it about Jimmy. It's more difficult

to think that I'm the love of Your Life, Lord, but You keep telling us that.

And, Lord, I'm sorry for dwelling on all of this. All Rhonda's details kept creating images in my head which were hard to shake off. I appreciate so much more our silence and enclosure for it protects our imaginations from running wild with words and images. I guess, Lord, that's the power behind *Lectio*, too, if we let Your words and deeds fill our minds. I remember in my early days, we didn't even get a daily newspaper, but today we are subject to all the scandals making headlines, which can be like little explosions of impurity in our minds, for which I'm truly sorry, Lord. I must pray more for priests who hear hours of confessions every week, and can't let all the penitents' sins not affect their own striving for purity. I also know how important it is to keep the confidence of the one who shares their weaknesses and sins with you. It's like the "seal of confession" in a way, and I'm doubly humbled, Lord, that Rhonda felt confident to share her burden with me, even in all its sordid details. Poor Rhonda…poor people living in the world surrounded by all the forces of evil. It gives new power behind our prayer every day at Compline: *Protect us, Lord, as we stay awake; watch over us while we sleep.*

I also got off on a mental tangent (distraction?) thinking about us not being lemon meringue, nor are we devil's food cake. And I thought a lot about that, and even had the inspiration, I think is the word, to mention this to Sr. Gerard this afternoon when I found her sitting alone in the rocker by the picture window overlooking the cemetery. Sr. Gertrude used to sit there a lot. I pulled over the other rocker and sat with her.

"Devil's food cake, you say? I wouldn't have said people think we're lemon meringue, but 'angel food cake.' Both are wrong, of course, but both are here, you know, under this new roof we're sitting safely under."

"What do you mean, Sister?" This was always a dangerous question to ask Sr. Gerard!

"Well, you know…the good angels are here; there's all our guardian angels following us around, and probably some wonderful angelic beings assigned to watch over the place, although I wonder where they were when the fire broke out! But, you know, Sister, there are also a multitude, I would think, a multitude of bad angels, fallen angels, demons that hang out here too. Sometimes I think we should read the reading for Tuesday night Compline every night: '*Be sober, be watchful, your opponent the devil, is prowling like a roaring lion looking for someone to devour.*' That's why we get sprinkled with holy water every night during the *Salve*; the devils flee from holy water."

"Yes, I know that. I don't always think about it though. Blessing ourselves with holy water entering and leaving the chapel becomes routine. I used to have a little holy water font inside our cell, but I let it run dry." (After a moment of silence…) "Do you think the bad angels outnumber the good angels?" This was, again, a question one could ask Sr. Gerard and not feel embarrassed.

"I don't know, Sister. But I will tell you this. Of late, for some months now, shortly before the fire actually, there has been a coldness in the house, a spiritual coldness. There's a demonic presence here that wasn't here before. But you probably think I'm ranting and crazy like the other Sisters do."

"I don't think you're crazy, Sister Gerard. I've noticed a chill too, not just in the air, but among the young Sisters. I can't put my finger on it. Nothing horrific has happened. Nobody's…" I stopped before saying too much. I was exaggerating in a humorous way, but remembering to whom I was talking. Sr. Gerard had blessed candles in every night table of the infirmary in preparation of the three days of darkness predicted at Garabandal. "Nobody's been hurt or killed." (I almost said 'murdered,' but that would have been too macabre.)

Sr. Gerard had her serious half-smile. "The fire wasn't exactly an accident, given the circumstances. And it did take the life of our Sister Agnes Mary, may she rest in peace. I heard about the light crashing on the altar; on the altar, mind you. If you look up you'll see it is not directly over the altar but almost a foot in front of the edge. The Evil One manifests in stupid ways for being so intelligent." And she almost laughed out loud. I wondered if she spoke from experience or just reading.

"But those things could be explained away in a natural way; things don't always fall straight down; the gas had been turned up high in the kitchenette oven…Sister Agnes Mary had very weak lungs to begin with, it was just a matter of time."

"That may all be true. Like I said, Old Red Legs is an evil spiritual intelligence greater than our misguided thoughts, temptations, and negative feelings. Look beyond the obvious.

There's a spirit of division creeping into the house which I don't ever recall. Sister Bruna, may she rest in peace, and a couple of the old Sisters spoke of a demonic presence back in the early fifties. There was a fire at that time too; remember talk of the old furnace blowing up and the refectory ceiling collapsing, killing old Sister Whatshername? She was from Russia; you've heard the Sisters talking about her…Sister Anna?"

"Anastasia."

"You're right, Sister Anastasia. It was terrible. I don't even want to think about it."

"But that was over fifty years ago. Things have been peaceful since."

"Yes and no, Sister. Yes and no. Look at the world and the state of the Church. You know what they say when Good Pope John opened the windows? The smoke of Satan billowed in."

"So I've heard, maybe not quite in those words."

"Sister," Sr. Gerard sat up a little straighter and spoke emphatically. "We are always engaged in the spiritual battle. The world only sees the superficial façade of life, especially our life, the Church, the priesthood, certainly, and the ordinary cultural or ethnic-colored family life; they do not see the battle being waged for souls, and how much the Evil One is out to destroy everything good, everything united. He brings division, discord, dissent—all the 'd' words…disease, disasters, divorce…"

"Drugs," I added to Sister's litany. Sister nodded affirmatively.

"Strange things can happen under the guise of the good."
She stopped for a moment looking out at the cemetery where
the shadows were long and dark forming over the graves as
the sun was going down.

"I can give you one little example to think about."

"Please." One never knew what Sr. Gerard would come
up with, but surprisingly she wasn't sounding off on her
usual apocalyptic track.

"There's that lovely actress on retreat here, what's her
name. Linda Rosewood, or something?"

"Rhonda Lynwood."

"Whatever. Her staying a month and living in the Cave
would never have happened years ago, but you know that.
She's not breaking into the enclosure, but even Papal Enclosure does not prevent the Evil One from coming in; I'm
not implying that, regarding her being here, on the con-
trary, we are, you might say, protected, because of this Linda
Rosewood."

"Rhonda Lynwood."

"Yes, Rhonda Lynwood, because this Rhonda Lynwood is
here under the blessing of the prioress. While it is highly con-
troversial, given her celebrity and all the secrecy surrounding
her being here, she's being obedient to a prompting of the
Holy Spirit to do this. I'm sure it has not been easy for her.
But obedience, Sister, is always the key to what we do. After
all, it was high disobedience that caused the Angels to fall,
and that caused Adam and Eve, and everyone since to fall,
except Our Lady, of course. And Our Lady is the Queen of
Holy Obedience. That's a new title I think should be added
to her Litany, but that's another subject."

"So, you don't think Rhonda Lynwood has brought the Devil here with her?"

"No, not at all; she's brought her sins in with her, but then we all have. There's a greater force at work in our battle, and if anything, this Rose Lynwood has spurred on the forces of good. She's here under an act of charity, and charity united to obedience is a powerful force. It's not the actress I'm concerned about; if anything, I see the work of grace changing her whole appearance from when she dragged herself in here weeks ago. I've only caught glimpses of her sitting alone in the chapel, sometimes in the middle of the night." (Sr. Gerard was known to keep the night guard from 3:00-4:00 a.m.) "I also know you've been a channel of that grace, to sound a little Franciscan. Bless you for that. But something or someone else has opened the window, as Pope John put it. Look for disobedience and dissension. Another 'actress,' but not the real one." Sister giggled at her own play on words.

"What did the Sisters do fifty years ago that you just talked about? When Sister Anatasia was here. Did they do anything?"

"They had the place exorcised, of course. They doused the place with holy water and blessed salt, every room, every nook and cranny. Sister Bruna was a young Sister, maybe even a novice, but she remembered that they did it at the beginning of Compline...blessed the water and salt, went through the whole house singing the psalms, and ended in the chapel with the Nunc Dimittis (*Canticle of Simeon* sung at Compline: *Now Lord You may dismiss your servant in peace*) and the *Salve* procession and Litany of Our Lady which took the community around the whole cloister. Remember, we

are always sprinkled with holy water during the *Salve*. There
was never a disturbance since."

I've been thinking about my conversation with Sr. Gerard
all evening, Lord. Maybe I should mention it to Mother, but
she might think I'm getting like Sr. Gerard, or the talking
with Rhonda at night, after Compline, is doing strange
things to my head. I wish I could talk to someone else first,
Lord, like Ezra or even Gwendolyn, but Mother has forbid-
den us to speak of Rhonda's being here, and I don't want
to be disobedient, especially after all Sr. Gerard said about
it. Lord, I know You'll open a way for me. Mother would
probably give permission for me to talk to Ezra. He knows
all about her; for heaven's sake, he has heard her confession
by now and absolved her of her sins in a way I couldn't.

And, as you know, Lord, Rhonda and Sr. Gerard haven't
been my only unusual encounters since Lent began. There
was the Mitzie visit last Sunday. Sr. Paula made a face at me
when she handed me a note saying I had company in the
little parlor. I thought it was strange for Sister to make a
face. I knew she's been ill, and in and out of the infirmary,
but she's usually very cheery. Maybe because it's Lent, and
we shouldn't have visitors, and sometimes she thinks I'm the
exception to the rule and it isn't fair. Dear Sr. Annunciata
said as much to me yesterday on her feast (the Annunciation)
when she couldn't have the visit of an old former neighbor.

I quietly asked Sr. Paula who it was. And she just said, "I
think it's that friend of your sister." I'm thinking, Mitzie?
By herself? Or maybe Rivka Stein? Well, whoever it was, I
knocked on Mother's door, grateful she was in her office.

"Come in, Sister. *Praised be Jesus Christ.*"

"*Now and forever*, Mother. I'm glad you're in; I just wanted to get your permission to see someone in the parlor; Sister Paula just gave me a note that there's someone there—a 'friend' of my sister."

"I see. Well, it's unusual, isn't it, and that your sister isn't with her. You've been over-talked-to by our secret retreatant. Are you up to it? Or would you prefer not to?"

"Either way, Mother, I'm up to it, as well as very curious, but don't want to do it without your permission."

"You have my permission, Sister. It's also Sunday, so we can bend the Lenten rules a little out of charity." And Mother smiled. Her years as infirmarian made her very compassionate, thank You, Lord. She must've had her reasons for refusing Sr. Annunciata. Poor Mother, having to balance all this.

I made a quick visit to the chapel and blessed myself three times with holy water, and said the Prayer to St. Michael, remembering he was my special patron for the year. I guess Sr. Gerard's talk made an impression in my thick skull.

Thirty-One

Last Sunday

*O men, how long will your hearts be closed, will you love
what is futile and seek what is false? It is the Lord who
grants favors to those whom he loves; the Lord hears me
whenever I call him.* (Psalm 4, Sunday Compline)

GOING INTO MY side of the small parlor, I saw Mitzie sitting
there by the grille, looking very Sunday casual in her woolen
camel hair color pant suit with a dark brown silk scarf in full
bloom around her neck.

"Good morning, Mitzie. This is a surprise. Is everything
all right? Is Sally okay?" It didn't hit me till just then that she
could be here to tell me Sally died in the night or was in an
accident, or was bitten by one of the mutts and had rabies,
or something.

"Sally is fine, Sister. She's actually in Atlantic City for a
Barnard Class Reunion."

"My, it's kind of cold for a trip to the shore; it's the middle
of winter."

She laughed. "They don't go for the beach, but the hotel
and casinos. There's just a couple vans full of them. I could've

gone with her, but those things bore the living day lights out of me. So I thought I would take advantage of visiting with you alone."

"Isn't that lovely, such a blessing for me during Lent." I hope she didn't catch the sarcasm in my statement, and I immediately felt guilty for being sarcastic, and during Lent and everything. Fr. Wilcox once told me in confession that I had a "sarcastic streak" in me, and that I should nip it in the bud. (Nipping things in the bud was his pastoral solution for all our temptations.) The problem is the flower's already bloomed before you think about nipping it. Anyway, I smiled a big Feinstein smile, and was surprised and happy and just a little anxious to talk with Mitzie. And I secretly said a prayer that this visit would be grace-filled.

"When Sal told me she had a sister who was a real Catholic nun in a nunnery, as she put it, I didn't believe her. I knew she was a secular Jew who didn't believe in much, spiritually speaking. My leanings in, well, what you call, 'new age' spiritual practices, like yoga, transcendental meditation, reiki, and even diet, used to really bother her. In a funny way, she didn't take my spiritual practice seriously, and always referred to you as the real thing, even though she didn't know what that all meant for you. But you were the genuine thing, and without her saying it, she was implying that if anyone had something to say about spiritual practices it would be you. How do you like that for a non-practicing New York Jewess?" Mitzie looked intently at me, but smiled and seemed just for a second like a little girl asking her mommy for a favor. I wondered if she might suffer from a mild case of sarcasm too.

I smiled back, leaned back in my chair, and without thinking, blessed myself saying, "My goodness, Lord, have mercy on us."

Mitzie thought that was very funny and all the tension held tight above the silk scarf relaxed.

"It's a funny thing, you've reminded me of. I'll tell you a secret that not even Sally knows, at least I don't think she does." Mitzie's eyes opened wide and she shifted her chair closer to the grille, all ears.

"My entire family was quite opposed to my converting to Catholicism, as you can imagine. We were not Orthodox Jews who would have totally disowned me, covered the mirrors in the house, and sat Shiva for their lost daughter. Dead to them. Nor were we agnostic secular Jews in name only; we were regular, 'devout Jews' who kept Shabbat, the high holy days, especially Passover and Yom Kippur, and Chanukah, which had strands of Christian threads in it, like a Chanukah tree, and once a Jewish Santa Claus at a Hadassah party, of all things." We both laughed.

"But we were never, I don't know how to say it, religious enough at home that what you call 'spirituality' was a real influence in our lives, or at least in my life. It wasn't so in Ruthie, Sally, certainly not in David, and only in an ethnic kind of way with Mama."

A slight knock on the extern door, and without saying 'come in', Sr. Paula came in with a pot of coffee, two mugs, and a couple slices of banana nut bread. Her disapproving frown had disappeared, and she was her old jolly self. She also handed me a note which I looked at while Mitzie poured the coffee. Gwen was hoping to see me this afternoon for ten minutes. *Oy, no wonder Teresa of Avila started a reform movement in Carmel!*

Settled back with coffee and banana nut bread, I went on. "The only one who had a real spiritual thread, as you put it, was my father. He prayed before meals, and on the holidays, like at Passover; it seemed to me that we had our very own rabbi living with us. I think he recognized the spiritual attraction I was going through even before I did. My attraction seemed like curiosity; my best Gentile friend was dying of cancer, and her faith was definitely her comfort and strength."

Mitzie hummed a few times, but was intently listening, and enjoying the coffee. "French roast, right?"

"Yes, from Solomon Deli's down the street. It's a continuous donation since 9/11. Mama used to stop there when she'd visit, and rave about Zabar's up near her, but Solomon's was so much more convenient, and family-like, so she started buying French roast coffee and a nosh from them. Sometime after 9/11 Mr. Solomon himself came to see me, asking for 'the Jewish nun whose Mother visits a lot.' When he learned she was at Windows on the World on 9/11, he sends us a donation of coffee every month in her honor. It's very kind of him, isn't it? It's kind of like having Mama here."

"It's such a blessing." Coming from Mitzie!

"Indeed it is! I haven't told you the best part, and this is the secret part. Papa used to come here every week to meet with Mother John Dominic, the prioress. They would sit in this very parlor and talk about Jesus and the Messiah, and the life of prayer and living united to Him by grace."

"Meaning?"

"Meaning, by the very life of God, the Holy Spirit. All that I talked about with you and Sally about the soul, there's so much more, because God Himself comes to dwell within us, in our souls. This is the Divine Life of the Holy Spirit."

"How does one get this holy spirit? Do you chant a mantra? Or sit in a certain position and breathe slowly or count your breaths?"

I didn't laugh because I knew she was serious. "No, none of those. I think for me, let me only speak of my own experience, when I came to know and believe that Jesus is truly God who came among us as a man, became our Passover Sacrifice, and rose from the dead, and lives today, and is present right now…that was the first 'grace', but I had a deep desire to be united to Him. There's almost something 'nuptial' there, without the physical part, it isn't sensual, but spiritual…mystical, some call it. And the Lord Himself, you see, provided the ways for us to be joined to Him."

Mitzie stopped eating, stopped drinking, and put her coffee down, and just looked straight at me. "Go on…"

"The very first way is being baptized. It's the most incredible 'mystical happening' because it literally changes your soul, you could say. It annihilates all sin, and thus joins you to Christ in the state of sinlessness. He fills us with His very life, and joins us in love to Himself, and thus to the Father, God the Father with whom Christ is one."

"And then what happens?" Mitzie was, as they say today, 'in the zone.'

"The life of grace continues; it transforms the soul; it is united intimately to the Lord at Mass and Holy Communion; it is given supernatural gifts when anointed at

Confirmation. These are all what we call 'sacraments.' They involve both the body and the soul. Even marriage, you see, for us, is a sacrament. It's really the first sacrament given by the Lord Himself to Adam and Eve. The end is union with God, an exclusive deep bond with each other, which symbolizes or is a sign of that union of God with every soul living by His grace, His life. And, like Him, to pro-create children." I stopped for a moment. My coffee was very luke-warm, but wet, and wet was good.

"Sal thinks that when I tell her I want to practice celibacy that I'm just giving in to 'the rules.' That it's against the rules to do lots of things, and religion has a lot of rules that keep people inhibited and feeling guilty and repressed."

"Wow, that's a lot to unpack, as Sister Leah Marie says. I always wanted to get to unpacking some of that with my brother the psychiatrist, but, well, God had other plans for him. I don't know if Sally can identify with or understand this, but I've thought about it a lot over the years, especially in the early years, even before I entered. My Jewishness already had me attuned to the Torah. I am a bat-mitzvah, you know, a 'daughter of the Law.' This so-called Law is not a Rule Book or 'rules' like Sal, and most of the world, think. It's rather in the nature of our souls, you see. It's in the nature of our soul to be united to the Creator, even if potentially. That, again, is our end, our purpose. There is a law that belongs to our nature, as all nature, all creation, has within it their own law, making them to be who or what they are. Gravity is law of nature. Animal instinct is full of laws of nature. We don't call these 'rules.' It's not sinful, or against the rules, for a tiger to kill and eat an antelope. So...and here's the big difficult part for many, especially in our day and age. Within human beings there is a 'natural law' which tends to human flourishing in grace, as we talked about, for union with God. All things have an end, as we've said. If I ate a plate of ground glass, it would be against the natural law, as my body cannot digest ground glass, and it would probably kill me besides. To kill another, to lie to another, betrays the natural end for the human mind, or intellect, to know the truth. The sacrament of marriage also has a built-in natural law whose end is conceiving new life—pro-creating, as it were, with God. Male and female He created them, for this end, and has built it into their natures."

"I see that; I understand that, and I can also understand how my kind argues against it, but then, one has to deny this whole understanding of what you call 'natural law.' But if one is honest and thinks about it, it is the way it is."

"My sister Ruthie and I never got to this level of discussion, mind you, but she would argue that God doesn't really care what we do with our bodies; they are made for pleasure, so we eat, drink, have sex, and bathe, and primp, and even decorate them. She was defending her tattoo against Mama's objections. But isn't that the so called 'world's' understanding of pleasure? I remember the slogan back in the late sixties or seventies: 'If it feels good, do it.' I'd have all Sally's Barnard's alumnae screaming at me if I said that's what the Devil said to Adam and Eve about the apple, which is really about being disobedient to the 'law', the single one command of God—do not know evil, for it separates you from Me, and you are made for Me. I am your Father."

"But honestly, Sister, isn't it unnatural not to have a family, children perhaps, love and affection; don't you miss all that? Isn't that part of our nature as women? And...I can't believe I just said that! "

I kind of laughed, not because it was so humorous, but because this seems to be the "problem" many people have or imagine when they think about our life.

"My dear dead sister used to think our life was 'sad.' I suppose in many ways she thought it was that because we didn't have all that you mention, plus a lot of other things like television, movies, vacations, new clothes, shopping, eating-out, cocktail hour, going to the theater, and all that. All the things she loved which I suppose made her life meaningful or gave her some purpose. Now, to be honest with you, Mitzie, of course we—or I should just speak for myself—I miss having love, affection, children, a family, and even all the freedom of a career, and well—just living in New York City! These are sacrifices I'm willing to make, and really, I don't think of my life here as un-natural, but super-natural. That's the big piece missing in the world's looking at this life. It's a supernatural life because it's joined in a real way, an intense way, you could say, with Christ. If Christ isn't all we say and believe He is, then what are we doing here? We're certainly not a club of spinsters or old maids who are unhappy with life! Or just find it convenient living together." *Calm down, Baruch, don't get too loud here!* Taking a breath, I continued, "We're— well, to use again an old fashioned way of talking about it— we're in a nuptial relationship with the Lord; you've heard it said that nuns are the 'Brides of Christ.' It's bridal in that we give ourselves exclusively to Him, our bodies and souls, and we believe that in the Mystical Body of Christ, that is, the Church, such a giving is fruitful. So there is really a maternal dimension to our lives, without the obvious here and now consolation of that. It's a supernatural fruitfulness which we will only realize in Eternal Life."

Mitzie sat silent and immobile. I don't think she was ready for such an answer. But I think she was also quite moved by it. After taking a couple deep breaths and a swig of luke-warm French roast, I went on.

"Unless that sounds too flowery or romantic or highfalu-tin, even too pious, I should add that we are also many times dry as the desert sands. I think there are two biblical images that describe our life very well: the mountain and the desert. The mountain is the most wonderful image: cool, refreshing, high above all the noise and business of the world below, a place where one meets God, like Moses and Elijah and Jesus on the Mount of Transfiguration. And the other image is the desert. If you've ever spent time in a real desert, which I haven't, but I've heard tell, it's like Hell on earth, pardon my French." Mitzie laughed.

"I have spent time in the desert. Not counting Las Vegas, of course, I have been on desert expeditions, and I was miserable. I do not do well in heat and blazing sun! Even my eyes burned, and you get kind of dizzy from looking at nothing but sand. We had cases of spring water with us, but my throat dried out so quickly and my lips cracked. My niece (my brother's daughter) and her family live in Ari-zona, and even that is unbearable, but we run from one air-conditioned place to another. And water is like a precious gem. You don't dare waste an ounce of it. But I don't think that's quite what you mean."

"Well, yes, in that the spiritual life can be very dry, monotonous, with only a few cacti to look at. And so thirsty. Again, I'm talking in a spiritual sense, or a 'supernatural' way, analogous to the natural—we thirst for God, for the truth about life and death, for the grace of the moment, for the graces to purify ourselves of our pride and lust and greed, and vanity…all those things." I kind of laughed. Mitzie laughed with me.

"Tell me about it! I thought getting old would mean one could let go of all that, looking around at the elderly, mind you, but some of us seem to get more obsessed over our looks."

"I suppose so. I guess that's another blessing of the habit; it hides a multitude." We laughed like we were old friends. Then we got quiet again. And Mitzie brushed away the crumbs from the banana nut cake, fallen onto her camel-colored sweater, and without looking at me, she mumbled, "This sweater cost me over 400 dollars, on sale. I've got a chest of drawers full of sweaters; I've got more shoes and clothes than places to put them. I've got everything I thought I ever wanted. I've got a job I love, friends, lots of money, and I've been around the world and back with your sister who underneath all the doggy-talk is still a journalist. She gets us into places most tourists don't even know are there. And I read spiritual books, of sorts, have even meditated on the Himalayan Mountains, but I feel so old and empty, and haunted by the question: 'Is this it? Is this all there is?' I don't have that deep peace which I've seen here,

and in you, since that first time I met you." She smiled with
a sad longing in her face.

"I remember that first time very well. You asked me to
share with you about celibacy. I didn't do that right away,
because it can only be understood, I think, with the supernatural foundation I just spoke of. Oh, I know many people
live celibately without a relationship with God; it's for the
sake of a career, or they just aren't in a relationship with
anyone; and I know, the stirrings of life change and dimin-
ish with age. Well, you know what I mean. If one has had
a spiritual life—a relationship with the Lord—it doesn't
have to be the desert; there are oases and air-conditioned
comforts in old age. I've always loved being with our Sisters
in the infirmary for that very reason. Not the physical air-
conditioning, although in July and August that's such a
blessing, but in the spiritual sense; they're 'really cool,' to
use another phrase my sister Ruthie used to say. She had a
fan club, you know, among the old Sisters who followed her
career. You might've thought she was Rhonda Lynwood."
Oops, watch it, Baruch. "Anyway, celibacy is a gift in the
end, it's all a part of the gift of yourself to the Lord. Living
chastely, whether one is in here or out there, brings an interior peacefulness, I think. I can't explain things too good,
but do you see what I mean?"

"I do, Sister Mary Baruch, and I thank you for sharing
all that so candidly with me. It's a big help. I think, well, I
mean, I guess, well, I don't know where this is coming from,
but I wish I could get to know the Lord like you talk about
Him."

I silently heard a choir of angels break into "alleluias" and dance for joy. They're in Sr. Gerard's multitude surrounding the place and hanging out in the rafters of the chapel.

"Well, isn't that something. If my mama were here she'd be saying, 'Such a conclusion you should come to here in this place; such a blessing, dahling, you should thank the Lord.'" Mitzie laughed a full open-mouth laugh.

"But if my papa was here (and maybe he is), he would tell you to simply begin to read the Gospel of John and his Letters, and to talk to the same Lord. It may seem kind of silly or childish, but just talk to Him, introduce yourself, and tell Him all about your life, and ask Him to show you how to become His best friend."

Mitzie's raucous laughter had suddenly turned into a flood of tears. I hope it was her moment of grace, Lord, for I know You were right there with us. I asked her if, and this was my moment of grace, Lord, I asked her if she thought Sally loved her enough to let her come to know the Lord and live chastely for Him? And she said they already lived chastely; she wasn't sure how she would react to her having a "supernatural relationship" with Jesus Christ, but if all I said was true, then He would provide the grace. She was ready "to climb the mountain."

Thirty-Two

A Late-March Afternoon, After None

*You will not fear the terror of the night nor the arrow that flies
by day, nor the plague that prowls in the darkness nor the scourge
that lays waste at noon.* (Psalm 91, Sunday Compline)

I WAS FEELING JUST a little guilty, Lord, during None, that
I hadn't spent much time with Gwendolyn. She's been here
over two months now, and we hadn't had much time to simply chat. She thinks I've been tied up with the novices, but
it's been Rhonda Lynwood more than them, and she's been
dealing with her own medical treatments and trips to the
hospital. So I fixed a little tray of cookies, banana nut cake,
and English tea, and asked Sr. Paula to boil the water after
None.

Gwen was at None and got to the parlor ahead of me. She
was sitting by the grille when I arrived.

"Look at you, Lady Putterforth, you're skinny as a model."

"I know, M.B., I'm a penguin in captivity. Speaking
of penguins, look at my latest." She stood up and turned

around revealing an artic penguin on the entire back of her ice-blue sweater."

"Oh my, it's certainly big." She laughed her old laugh.

"It was a gift from my insane sister who arrived yesterday."

"Oh my, I didn't know she was coming over. Where is she staying?"

"She's at The London on West 54th Street. It's really a luxury hotel; she's got a suite with a great view of uptown. She's only here for a few days. She says she's here to see a show and check out a couple cabaret acts and wants me to go with her, as I'm the expert on cabaret. But I think she's really just checking up on me. She thinks I'm dying, but then, I am, but then, aren't we all?"

I didn't answer that, but changed the subject. "How are the treatments going? I'm sorry I haven't had a chance to talk to you about all that. Do you feel like a guinea pig?"

"Thanks for asking, love. I'm very tired by midday, but the doctor seems pleased with things. My appetite is getting better, which is a good sign, according to him. So we'll see. I'm not up much for running around Manhattan checking out cabaret acts, I can tell you that. And…" She stopped, as Sr. Paula arrived with our tea and nosh.

"Oh, how lovely, biscuits during Lent with delicious looking nut bread. Whoever made this?" Sr. Paula blushed, and with a grand smile said, "T'was I, your ladyship." And she curtsied. Then they both laughed. I could see it was a game they had been playing, realizing they've become good friends over the past couple months.

After futzing with the cups and biscuits, she went on. "So, the main reason I wanted to chat, besides telling you about

Jacqueline, is that Mother Bernadette has told me I need to move on, very nicely, and not, well, like immediately, but hopefully before Holy Week. I understand perfectly, and am so grateful for these months here, but I'm also ready to move on, you know. But I don't know what to do, and wondered if you knew anyone nearby who might have a flat to let? I thought of moving to Manhattan, closer to Sloane, but I've come to love the Heights, and would still want to be close to you and the Sisters."

"I'm sorry to hear that. Mother didn't mention it specifically. She mentioned at a Council meeting that we have a few aspirants coming for Holy Week, and she didn't want them inside, which is normal. Besides…"

"Besides what?"

"Oh, there's a negative feeling right now in the house about a lot of things, I guess, and we're actually thinking of having a kind of exorcism of the place. We thought Holy Week would be a perfect time, right before the Triduum, you know."

"I know. Well, not so much about the aspirants and such, but about the spooky feeling in the place." She said this like it was normal chatter, and it didn't bother her.

"Spooky? I didn't say spooky, just a kind of negativity creeping in."

"Hmmmm. This nut bread is quite good. Well, if you're looking for an exorcist, you've got one living right here with you."

"You?" I laughed at the insinuation.

"No, of course not. When it comes to spooks, I couldn't say boo to a goose. It's Father Matthew."

"Ezra?"

"Yes, my dear. He wasn't lighting candles and praying rosaries at the shrine in Lancaster; he was all over the place expelling demons. He's been doing that since his days in Africa."

"Uh. I never knew that. How do you know that? Are you sure?"

"Yes, I've assisted him. Well, not like a priest does, but I've been present and pray during it. England is full of spooks and demons, you can just imagine."

I just sat silent for the moment.

"I'll tell Mother that, if that's all true. Maybe I should talk to Ezra first."

"Oh, Mother already knows, love. Ezra says she hasn't mentioned anything to you, yet, as you've got a lot of things on your plate. Those novices must keep you hopping, eh?"

"Yes, hopping. I've been hopping up and down the stairs with our secret retreatant whom you aren't supposed to know about." I smiled.

"Oh, you mean that little nun who sits in the corner of the chapel?"

"Yes, little Sister Solange." Gwen, of course, knew all about it, and probably chatted with the 'little Sister' a few times after the Office. She knew I couldn't talk about it, and honestly, that's good, as I can't talk about any of it, except what foods she liked, and that she baked great cinnamon buns, which Fr. Kelsey, our regular confessor, knows all about too.

"Well, I'm sorry you'll be moving out, and right at this time too. But…let me think about it. My sister Sally and

Mitzie are friends with a couple, the Steins, who live here in the Heights, just a couple blocks away, and I think they have a large house with lots of empty rooms. They've been here, so they know who we are. I'll ask Sally."

"That would be jolly good. You're not eating the nut, oh I forgot, you're fasting. I'll just wrap these up and take them to my room. And how's that nephew of yours doing? You haven't mentioned him in ages."

"Sharbel? He's off on a cross country trip visiting monasteries. He's been to France, you know, to visit a friend he met on the Camino, who entered a French Benedictine monastery, and now Sharbel's been bitten by the monastic bug. He hasn't given up on the Dominicans, I don't think, but either way, his mother is not happy. I don't know if she knows he's visiting monasteries. She thinks he's just being a little rich kid with lots of time and money. The rich young man." She didn't quite catch my biblical reference.

"Lucky, kid. Listen, I've got to take a nap before venturing out for dinner with Jackie and checking out a place called The Lions' Lair. Sounds kinda spooky to me."

"Maybe you should take Ezra with you, just in case." We laughed. Her artic penguin jiggling as she made her way towards the door.

"Ta ta." And she was gone. I was tired myself, Lord, but grateful I had the rest of the afternoon to just sit in the chapel and quench my thirst.

Thirty-Three

Palm Sunday 2007

O come, bless the Lord, all you who serve the Lord, who stand in the house of the Lord, in the courts of the house of our God. (Psalm 143, Sunday Compline)

WE HAD A lovely Mass this morning, with a procession around the cloister. The guests in the extern chapel can't come in for that, of course, and Rhonda didn't come to Mass at all. I think she's getting weaker and was very tired. Sr. Paula told me later that Fr. Matthew took Holy Communion down to her after Mass. Her retreat will come to an end on Easter Sunday. Fr. Oyster is flying in for the Triduum, although he'll be staying at St. Vincent's, and be here for the day Mass on Sunday.

I'll be relieved when she's gone. That's not very charitable, I know, Lord. But she has been draining. Listening takes a lot of energy. I don't know how You do it! Only kidding, Lord. It's amazing that you listen to each one of us as if we're the only one speaking to You. I wonder·if more people would pray if they realized that. Of course, You can listen without our even using words.

We had a long Council meeting yesterday. It was to help us prepare for Holy Week by giving us a few crosses to carry in prayer this week. Two of our monasteries have closed recently, well one is in the process. It will be their last Easter together, then the Sisters will disperse to other monasteries of the Order. The happy news is that we are receiving two. According to Mother, one is for the infirmary and one in the professed community. The really sad news which Mother wants us to pray for is that we are not doing well financially, ever since 9/11 actually, and the maintenance of our buildings is "through the ceiling." Mother's expression. We may need to look for a smaller place, which could mean even leaving Brooklyn Heights. We all gave a little gasp at the thought of it. I can't even go there in my thoughts, Lord. How could we ever leave here? Queen of Hope, bring us hope!

We also have one aspirant coming on Easter Monday who will live inside for a month. Her name is Emilia Hopkins and she's from Alabama, although she's been living and working in Manhattan for the last three years as a copywriter for some advertising agency.

I was finally able to get Mrs. Sanchez on the phone. She had been away, as I surmised, in Puerto Rico. She's coming for "tea" early on in Holy Week, probably on Tuesday. But the strangest thing, and maybe it was lost in translation, but I invited Havana's grandmother to come too, and she said Havana's grandmother has been dead for ten years. I didn't think to specify, as we all have two grandmothers, but there is no grandmother living with Mrs. Sanchez. When I mentioned it to Havana, she just shrugged and said, "It's the other one." And I didn't ask where she lives. Maybe it's best just to meet the mother first. Strange, because sometimes Havana sounds like she's just been talking to her grandmother last night. And strange because postulants are not allowed to use the phone without permission. My poor head has been on over-load with Rhonda, and Sr. Elijah Rose who came to see me last week, on Wednesday, our usual day for meeting. She kind of slouched in with a sad face.

"So, Sister, this is probably your last Holy Week in the novitiate. This time next year you'll be solemnly professed and won't have to do all the work." I was trying to be funny, as she seemed a little down to me.

"I know. It's been a funny Lent for me. I haven't been able to get into it like in past years. I don't know why. I know you think Leah and I aren't getting along, but that's not true. She just gets on my nerves more, and probably vice-versa."

"Why do you think that—that she's getting on your nerves?"

"I don't know. She seems more into doing her work, which she loves, you know, making habits and aprons, and slee-vettes (sleeves worn over the habit sleeves, only to the elbow, to protect the regular, fuller, sleeves). Maybe it's because I don't have a job that I really love, like she does."

"You're doing wonderfully in the kitchen."

"Yeah, it's not a bad job, but peeling potatoes and making vats of tapioca pudding are not the most fulfilling jobs."

"Ah, I see. You want a *fulfilling* charge."

"No, I want to do whatever the Lord's will is (catching my implications), but it would be okay if it was a little more fulfilling, you know. Like my mornings in the infirmary, I really love that and I'm trained for that. I never thought I'd say I love giving shots to old nuns, or taking blood pressures, and talking about meds, but I do."

"I see. Of course, you are a nurse and are good at what you do. We're blessed to have you, otherwise we'd have to have a lay person come in the mornings. You've been a big help to me, Sister, watching after Rhonda's medications. She's told me you're the best nurse she's ever had because you seem like you really care."

"Thank you, Sister. I haven't heard that from anyone, except Rhonda, of course. I'll miss her, but I think she's going to need more care than she can get here. Poor thing."

"Yes, but you know, she'll be leaving us on Easter Sunday."

"She told me. I hope she'll be okay. Her cancer is spread to her lungs, you know, and she's scared of suffocating to death. But other factors kick in before that, which isn't the happiest news to have either!"

"She has three houses, not counting a cottage in Switzerland. I think she'll go to the large estate in Rhode Island first; she says the air is best there, not far from the Ocean, and certainly the quietest. But back to you…I can't imagine Sister Leah Marie purposely wanting to bother you. You've always gotten along so well."

"I know. It isn't really Sister Leah who's getting on my nerves; it's the other one."

"Sister Kateri?"

"No, the postulant. *Señorita Cuba*, we call her. Oh, I'm sorry. I shouldn't have told you that; it's probably very uncharitable, but that girl's got attitude. Ummm."

I had to laugh, not at the "diagnosis," but the way Sr. Elijah Rose delivered it. Her whole body kind of jiggled with the "Ummm." And she waved her hand and rolled her eyes all at the same time.

"Havana does have a way about her, doesn't she? You're not the only one to have problems with her…her 'attitude' as you put it, so just be patient for a little while longer."

"Un hun; we'll try, Sister, but that's all the good Lord's doin', cause I done run out of patience, ummmm." Jiggle, jiggle.

"Let's give it all an extra fifteen minutes of silent prayer with the Blessed Sacrament, okay? I'll join you in that."

"You mean together?"

"No, we can each find the time when we have the time, but we'll both be looking to do it for a special intention… we can include Rhonda in that intention too."

"Sounds good to me. Lord knows I can use all the time I can get before the Blessed Sacrament. That sounds very good, actually. Thank you, Sister…" And with that Sr. Elijah Rose took off with a happy face on.

Thirty-Four

Palm Sunday After Compline

They shall see the Lord face to face and bear his name on their foreheads. The night shall be no more. They will need no light from lamps or the sun, for the Lord God shall give them light, and they shall reign forever. (Revelation 22, Sunday Compline)

"DUNKING THE EARL in boiling water brings calm to a haridan's haggarded nerves." Rhonda had a way with words, that's for sure. We only had one class with her which Sr. Gertrude would have called "Elocution 101." I don't think it made any difference in the way any of us read.

"Well, Sister Myrtle, this is our last night of 'therapy.'"

"Sister Solange Marie, Sister. Myrtle left the world, remember? And the whole forest of Pines."

I laughed. Despite the drain, she was also quite delightful. The early weeks were the most cathartic, as Ezra would say. After her general confession, I noticed that her spirits were up, despite the ongoing take-over of cancer and loss of energy. I wondered if he (Ezra) prayed an exorcism over her, but I didn't dare ask. She spent more time in the chapel, just sitting in the Holy Presence of the Blessed Sacrament. I kind of envied her for that. Maybe I should spend more time after Compline with the Lord. Adoration therapy.

"So, tell me, what are your immediate plans? You mentioned going to Newport when you leave here."

"Yes, at least that's what I want. Easter Sunday night, when I leave, Fr. Reggie wants to take me to an old swanky restaurant I used to like in Manhattan. It was Jimmy's favorite too. But I told him when we spoke earlier that my swanky days were over. And I'm not ready to face any crowds. So we're flying by private jet from Islip Airport to Narragansett or Block Island, I'm not sure. But a quick flight from Long Island to Rhode Island, and there will be a limo service waiting to take us to Waters Edge. Reggie has hired a full time nurse, a maid, and is flying in Dr. Kilanowski, my Beverly Hills oncologist, for an initial checkup. I'm hoping I can stay at Waters Edge till I die, but it's all in God's hands, and Dr. Kilanowski's, in that order!"

I smiled, pleased that she was surrendered to God's will and seemed to be at peace with everything, which really was her purpose in being here. "So, it's been a good retreat for you?" That was more a statement than a question.

"Oh, Sister, I can't tell you how much it has meant to me, and all that you have done; all the time you've spent with me, and let me chew your ear off. I'll be forever grateful. I wish there was something I could give you."

"Thank you, Rhonda, but you've given to all of us an example of fortitude and courage and prayer, really. I know from you that when the 'chips are down' as you put it, life changes and we see things differently. You've helped me to see my life more intently, as it can become rather, what, routine over the years. Your being here, has enriched my own time of prayer, if that makes any sense." I wasn't as eloquent as Rhonda was with words.

"Speaking of prayer, Sister, I have just one last request to ask of you."

"Yes? Whatever I can do, Rhonda." (*I'm thinking she probably wants me to light a candle or two; I'm good at that.*)

"Would you pray over me? Not the regular prayers, but just your own words. I went to a few charismatic prayer meetings when I came back to the Faith; it was very popular at the time, but not really my kind of thing, and it wasn't possible because of the celebrity thing, but I liked it when someone prayed over me; it gave me strength."

"Well, I'm not very good at that—praying spontaneous prayers over anyone. Greta and I went to one prayer meeting once at a church on the West Side, and it was good, but Greta thought it was too Pentecostal. She knew more about those things than I did. But when would you like me to do this?" (I was already thinking I needed days to make up some well-worded prayers. And I didn't want to say anything heretical. I took to heart a class we had had on *lex orandi, lex credenda* (as one prays, so one believes; literally: the law of praying is the law of believing).

"Well, I'm ready right now. This is our last night, you said, and I don't want to disturb you when the Tivium begins."

"Triduum."

"Oh, yes, thank you. I always get that mixed up."

(I'm sorry, Lord, here's a poor woman on the threshold of death, humbly asking me to pray over her, and I'm correcting her Latin. It's so arrogant of me. What difference does it make?)

"I can see you're a little anxious, probably worried you'll say the wrong things, so I think, if you're willing, we could do it right here and now. Think of it as a formal way to conclude our months of 'tea therapy.'"

"Okay, that's fine. It's an honor and its humbling, Rhonda. No one has ever asked me to do this."

We silently finished our Earl Grey, and Rhonda moved her chair to right in front of the grille, sat down, folded her hands, and closed her eyes. I wasn't quite sure how to go about this, but silently prayed to the Holy Spirit to help me. I stood close to the grille. My hands folded in prayer.

"Dear Mother of Perpetual Help and Comforter of the Afflicted, thou art the dispenser of all the gifts which God grants to us miserable sinners, for this reason we come to you and ask for your most powerful intercession. I pray, dear Mother, for our friend, Rhonda, that you will be with her every moment of every day, and that you will be her refuge in times of suffering and distress and lead her always to your beloved Son, Jesus.

"Oh, Lord, have mercy on us and hear my prayer. Take care of Rhonda and give her the grace to unite every suffering to Your sacrifice that it may be for her a way of holiness and redemption for herself and all those whom she loves. We thank you, Lord, for all the graces and blessings you have given to Rhonda. Bless her now, Lord, and heal her of any distress and anxiety as she goes back into the world." (I felt a sudden urge to pray even more intensely, and without deliberation, I opened my hands in the orans position facing Rhonda.) "Oh, dear Lord, if it be Your holy Will, heal Rhonda of all fear, heal her from all anxiety and worry. Lord, heal her from every sickness she carries; take away her pain; take away her cancer; take away every trace of illness in every molecule of her body, Lord. Give her time to make amends for all that weighs on her heart. You have absolved her of her sin, Lord, give her time now to make amends and be healed of the wounds of sin, and remembrances of the past. Give her peace and time to prepare her soul to see You face to face, and to join all her loved ones, and all the glorious saints in Heaven. Help her, now Lord, to let go of all that gets in the way of her peace and communion with You, for You are our Savior, our Salvation, our Joy and our Lord." (I closed my hands again, thumbs crossed, fingers pointing up.) "Holy Angels, St. Michael and all Archangels, all the saints and holy ones, come to Rhonda's aid. Holy Father Dominic, St. Catherine, St. Sharbel, and St. Joseph, come to her aid, and when the time of her Passover comes, accompany her through the Red Sea of Your mercy, and bring her into Your Promised land of Heaven, in the Heart of Jesus. Amen, amen." There was a silent pause, and I sat down still facing Rhonda. "Let us pray together to Our Lady as we pray to her every night at Compline: Hail Holy Queen…"

Rhonda prayed with me. She put her fingers through the opening of the grille, and I put mine on top of hers when we prayed: "*And after this our exile show unto us the blessed fruit of thy womb, Jesus. O clement, O loving, O sweet Virgin Mary.*" Tears flowed down her cheeks. She stood and without a word, blew me a kiss through the grille, and silently left the parlor.

I stayed seated for a few minutes, and put my face in my hands, which were very warm. "Oh, Lord, help us all to prepare ourselves to come to You. Thank you, Lord…thank You." I got up and quietly left the parlor, glancing up to the corner of the ceiling to where I imagined the tabernacle was. The Cave…*Out of the depths we cry to You, O Lord, Lord hear our prayer.*

I came silently to our cell, and here I sit in Squeak at the beginning of Holy Week.

Thirty-Five

Wednesday of Holy Week

*Upon you no evil shall fall, no plague approach where you
dwell. For you has he commanded his angels, to keep you
in all your ways.* (Psalm 91, Sunday Compline)

I DON'T KNOW IF dunking the Earl was going to work at this
"tea party," but it was the only day before Holy Thursday
that we could meet. I thought it would be good for Mother
to be a part of this. I also invited SCAR as a member of
Mother's Council. And she's got more hidden wisdom than
any of us.

Mrs. Sanchez was ten minutes late. We were just ready to
leave the parlor ourselves when Sr. Paula opened the door
and Mrs. Sanchez came in. She was a slight woman, probably in her fifties, too much makeup, especially rouge and eye
shadow which didn't match, several junk jewelry bracelets,
dangling earrings, and a couple over-sized rings. She was a
little wobbly on her feet. Sr. Gertrude once told me I would
have made a perfect assistant director or a police detective,
as I noticed all these details. I think I inherited the "charism"

from Mama, who remembered what every Hadassah woman was wearing and every hair out of place, who had a wig and who didn't, and whose shoes didn't match her bag. Hannah of a Thousand Silver Hairs.

I was thus distracted as we made our introductions. Mrs. Sanchez seemed nervous, like she was being sent to the principal's office and was going to be told how naughty her daughter was, smoking in the girls' locker room, or something.

Mother introduced me as Havana's *immediate superior*, an expression we never used; it seemed very odd.

"I'm her postulant mistress." This sounded even more odd; we always just said "novice mistress" for everyone.

"We thought it would be beneficial to Havana and to us to meet you and to let you know that we don't think the life is a good fit for her." I figured there was no sense beating around the bush.

Mrs. Sanchez just stared at us for a moment. Perhaps she was translating things in her head, but then, she spoke with very clear, but broken, English, "I told that to Vanna from the very start; I don't know where she get the idea that she should be nun. You probably uncovered fact that she not very religious. I surprised, to be honest with you, that she still here."

Well, that was certainly not what we were expecting to hear, but it was also a great relief, and confirmed us in our decision to let Havana go.

"She speaks a lot about getting advice from her grand-mother, with whom she seems to be speaking to a lot. Does she live nearby?"

"Her Nonna, my poor mother died over ten years ago. She was very close to Vanna. I'd even say closer than I was for different reasons. Vanna took it very hard when Nonna died. She lived with us all of Vanna's life, and when she was gone, Vanna would sit in her room, on little stool, and talk to her like she was sitting there in chair where she always sat. I no stop it, I sorry to say, because I felt so sorry for her, and because I had to go to work, and Vanna, she, no have many friends, and she was hoppy to sit for hours in room of Nonna, you understand?" (I'm thinking to myself: She should be so "hoppy" here.)

"I thought she grew out of it. But she go to prayer meeting where people, they talked about dead people, you know? After while Vanna, she stopped going into room of Nonna. She got involved in all her school activities, you know. And she have new boyfriend every week, you know how boy crazy girls can get."

We just smiled, kind of like. It had been a long time since I thought about the world of being boy crazy. I'm not sure that I ever was. SCAR never cracked even a smile, and simply said, "Tell us more about Havana's activities in high school."

"I dunt pay attention to a lot of it; I was working two yobs, and not see her much. She hang out with girlfriends, I think. She go through all crazy things girls go through, you know, like smoking and sneaking drinks, and going shopping. She go through different fashion in clothes, you know. She was Goth for while…all black clothes, black eyes, purple lips." I glanced over at SCAR who was looking at her like she was speaking a foreign language.

None of us reacted like we knew anything at all about that. I made a mental note to ask Sr. Leah about it; she would've gone through it, but I don't remember her ever coming here with black eyeliner and purple lips. Oy. In my day, we thought double gym socks, saddle shoes, and poodle skirts were pretty radical.

SCAR, skipping over the Goth-age, asked, "Did she go to Mass?"

"Uh...well, not really. We both, uh, don't have no time, you know. I work two yobs to put food on table and pay rent. But, you see, that is why I so surprised Vanna want to become nun, and locked-up like diz." She looked at the grille like she was in a maximum security prison.

"What about her other grandmother; is she still living?"

"Vanna never know her. The mother of my husband never come to diz country. They both die years ago in Cuba. Nonna is only grandmother Vanna know."

That seemed to be all we needed to hear. We made some polite comments about the weather and the flowers coming out. We hardly finished our tea when it seemed we were saying goodbye to Mrs. Sanchez and thanked her for coming. We would be talking to Havana, and she'd probably be coming home for Easter. We waited till Mrs. Sanchez left the parlor, and the three of us kibitzed about our meeting, concluding very quickly that Havana should go, and I, as her "immediate superior," would be the one to tell her. I supposed that meant "immediately." Lucky me.

But there was no reason to drag things out, so after dinner dishes, I pulled Havana aside and told her to meet me in my office in ten minutes. That gave me a couple minutes to recollect myself and to ask the Lord to give me the grace to be kind and gentle. I wasn't sure how Havana would react to this news.

Fifteen minutes later she knocked at my door and came in before I could say "Come in."

"Sit down, Havana."

"You've probably got a list of more chores for me to do, right? Whadda you gonna do if I say 'no'? Huh? Little prissy Leah never gets any extra chores. And Elijah the prophet gets away with murder…"

"Sit down, Havana, and don't open your mouth till I say you can." She was silently shocked and noisily plopped down in the chair. Her once purple lips pursed out in a pout.

"The formation team (another made-up term) and I met this morning with your mother. She confirmed what we've been considering for some time now, Havana, that this way of life just isn't the best for you. Perhaps another Order with an apostolic outreach would be more amicably suited for you. The enclosed life, as you've seen, can be very restrictive. Have you been contemplating this yourself?"

"I think you're using a bunch of big words to confuse me, and that you don't like me, so you're aiming to kick me out, that's what I'm thinking. But your favorites, including the little Injun with her silly bags, can't do no wrong."

I was rather taken aback by such a strong reaction. I could feel my hand trembling just a little under my scapular. The animosity in her voice frightened me, but I went on. Why was she filled with so much anger, or was it fear? I tried to be calm and gentle.

"Well, we think it's all for the best—for you. You don't have to do any of your usual chores, but gather your things together; you should be ready to leave after Mass tomorrow. We're having a special blessing at Compline tonight; it will be good for you to be there." I looked around thinking I had left the window open, as there was a sudden chill filling my office.

"Tell me, Havana, how do you keep in contact with your grandmother? With Nonna?"

"None of your business." She snapped at me and left the room, banging the door. I must say I was a bit shook up by her nasty reaction to everything and just sat back down at my desk bewildered by it all.

* * *

About ten minutes passed. I was going through the file for the usual papers we had when a postulant departs. A knock at my door and a "Come in" brought SCAR bounding in with something bulky under her scapular.

"*Laudetur Jesus Christus*," she began in the former manner. "I took it upon myself, Sister, after that meeting with Havana's mother, to take a look in her cell. I was, shall we say, suspicious. And look what I found on her desk." And with that she pulled out from under her scapular a wooden Ouija board. She placed it on my desk and from her tunic pocket, pulled out the piece that moves on the board spelling out words.

"Meet Grandma!" Sr. Catherine Agnes announced, pointing to the board. "From the looks of it, I'd say little Havana has continued talking to Grandma for years."

I didn't know anything at all about Ouija boards; I never played with one nor did I know kids or adults, certainly, who did. I think Ruthie may have tried it once, but that was years and years ago.

"I've told Havana that she would be leaving us tomorrow after Mass, and she should come to our special Compline tonight. I'd better put this somewhere before she discovers it's missing. She's probably wanting to fill Nonna in on all the news. Put it in the bottom of the closet there, Sister. I don't want to touch it."

Before Vespers, I saw Mother in her office, along with Sr. Rosaria and Sr. Anna Maria. I filled them in on my talk with Havana and Sr. Catherine Agnes's finding the Ouija board in her cell.

"Leave it to Sister Catherine Agnes to march right into someone's cell," Sr. Rosaria was chuckling as she said it.

Sr. Anna Maria chimed in, "Well, remember she's a former postulant mistress; they always had the right to go into one's cell whenever they wanted. Usually to make sure you're making your bed with hospital corners." We all laughed, as we had all experienced SCAR's boot camp regimen.

Mother also had to sign a "release paper" which we have on file for anyone who leaves or is dismissed. We are not held accountable for wages accrued from work done during one's stay here. Mother was upset about the Ouija board and said we should tell Fr. Matthew about it, and dispose of it however he suggested we do that.

"What's so dangerous about it, Mother? I thought it was just a game children play, like telling ghost stories. It's like playing séance, not that that's okay, but isn't it relatively harmless?"

Sr. Rosaria again jumped right in. "Oh, they're very dangerous, Sister. They are portals for the Evil One to enter under the guise of a game and make believe séance, as you called it. And the Devil can take the form or voice of a deceased loved one, to make sure you come back, and let him in. There are any number of so-called ports or portals, especially in Latino countries and with Santeria, which is really like another religion; it was big, as I recall, in Cuba and spread to the U.S. after the Cuban revolution. I wouldn't be surprised if Havana's grandmother was involved in all that."

"Are you saying her grandmother could be communicating with her through this board?" I was getting disturbed by the whole thing. And to think it's been right on our novitiate floor for months. *Oy, such a thing should be just down the hall?*

Mother jumped in. "I doubt that Grandma was talking to her; that Havana *thought* she was is the disturbing part."

"But don't underestimate the influence of the Devil and his legions. If Havana has been talking to Grandma for ten years, she may have actually heard her voice, which was not really Grandma." Sister Rosaria spoke again, this time with an air of authority.

"Well, I'm glad we're having the entire monastery blessed this evening." Mother added, "And best to remain discrete, Sisters, about all this. We don't want to alarm any of the more sensitive Sisters in community."

"I told Havana she shouldn't miss Compline tonight, mainly because the young Sisters would all be upset because she's not there; they don't know she's leaving yet, unless Havana has told them herself. Besides, the special blessing will be good for her." Ha! Little did I know then!

Thirty-Six

Compline

Upon you no evil shall fall, no plague approach where you dwell. For you has he commanded his angels, to keep you in all your ways. (Psalm 91, Sunday Compline)

COMPLINE BEGAN AS it always does: after the introductory verse, we kneel for the examination of conscience. I usually trip over the "and what we have failed to do" part, wondering just what I missed today. We stood for the hymn and sang Psalms 31 and 130. Then we substituted the reading, using the one from Tuesday night Compline, from 1 Peter 5:8, *Stay sober and alert. Your opponent the devil is prowling like a roaring lion looking for someone to devour. Resist him, solid in your faith.*

A vat of new water was in front of the grille, next to our communion window. Fr. Matthew came in through the sacristy door. He was wearing a surplice and stole. And blessed the salt and water. We all listened attentively to the words:

"*I exorcize thee, created element of water, in the name of God + the Father Almighty, and in the name of Jesus + Christ His*

Son our Lord, and in the power of the Holy + Ghost; that thou
may be made water from which the evil spirit hath been driven
out for the banishment of every power of the enemy, that thou
may be able to uproot and cast out entirely that enemy himself,
together with his rebel angels, by the power of the same Lord
Jesus Christ, Who will come to judge the living and the dead
and the world by fire. Amen."

Father mixed the exorcized salt and water together and
prayed:

"...wherever it shall be sprinkled and Thy holy name shall
be invoked in prayer, every assault of the unclean spirit may be
baffled, the poison of the serpent cast out, and the presence of
the Holy Ghost everywhere vouchsafed to us who entreat Thy
mercy..."

Then he lifted the aspergillum and began sprinkling the
grille first, then he turned to all of us and started sprinkling
us. I was standing on the end in the front row, closest to the
grille. Havana was right next to me. When the holy water
hit her she let out a blood curdling scream: "OOOOWW-
WWWW!", and her voice suddenly changed to a harsh deep
woman's voice with a Cuban accent. And she grabbed me
around the neck and pushed me out of the stall, my veil
pulled back and half torn off.

"Tú, vieja judía; Odias a mi nieta y quieres despedirla.
No te dejaré. Morirás primero." (You old Jew; you hate my
granddaughter and want to send her away. I won't let you.
You will die first.)

I was being choked and couldn't scream or get away. I
could hear the Sisters screaming around me. Havana's face

became all distorted and growled at me, "Vieja judía, vieja judía."

Her grip was getting tighter, and I thought I was going to pass out, or simply die—this was it; I'm going to meet the Lord. *This is it. Lord, have mercy on me. St. Michael, Archangel, help me.* And louder than I've ever heard his voice, Ezra shouted, his words reverberating the light fixtures and candles: "***I cast you out***, *every unclean spirit, every satanic power, every onslaught of the infernal adversary, every legion, every diabolical group and sect, in the name and by the power of Our Lord Jesus Christ (holy water splashing on me), I command you, begone and fly far from this Church of God, from the souls made by God in His image and redeemed by the Precious Blood of the Divine Lamb.*" (Another splash of water, my face and bandeau were soaked.)

"*In the name of Jesus Christ, Our Lord and God, by the intercession of Mary, spotless Virgin and Mother of God, of St. Michael the Archangel, of the blessed Apostles Peter and Paul, St. Benedict, St. Dominic, and all the saints, and by the authority residing in our holy ministry,* **we cast you out. Begone!**"

Suddenly released from her grip, I fell to the floor and on my side. I could hear the quick swishing of tunics, as Sisters grabbed me and lifted me up. Havana, I'm told, collapsed on the marble floor, her arms and legs flailing about in spasmodic contortions. It was the most frightening thing I've ever seen! Then she let out a deep guttural whoosh and lay perfectly still and limp. It was over.

Sr. Lucy, at the direction of Mother Bernadette, intoned the *Sub Tuum*, and the whole community belted it out louder than I've ever heard: *Sub tuum praesidium confugimus, sancta*

Dei Gennetrix; nostras deprecationes ne despicias in necessitat-
ibus, sed a periculis cunctis libera nos semper, Virgo benedicta.
(We fly to your protection, holy Mother of God; do not
despise our prayers in our necessities, but ever deliver us
from all dangers, Blessed Virgin.)

I could feel the perspiration mixed with "buckets" of
holy water rolling down my face. I opened my eyes and saw
SCAR blotting my face with her scapular and patting me on
the cheek, "You're okay, Sister Baruch, you're okay." I smiled
up into her face, and she gave me the biggest smile I've ever
seen from her, with tears rolling down her cheeks.

I turned towards Havana who was still limp and now
weeping, but speaking in her normal voice. "Help me, some-
body, help me." Two Sisters lifted her up.

"Havana…Havana…you're okay." I was repeating SCAR's
words to her. She fell into my arms and cried. Sr. Elijah Rose
and Sr. Kateri came over by her side, and let her fall into
their arms as well.

I looked over at Ezra, who was still frozen in a pose with
his right arm stretched out; His cheeks were sunken and his
eyes closed till he heard our voices, and then he too went
limp, and sat down in the choir stall nearest him. He was
pressing his chest and breathing heavily, but looked up and
smiled.

After the *Sub Tuum*, there was a peaceful calm that filled
the chapel. Standing arm in arm at the grille separating us
from the extern chapel were Gwendolyn and Rhonda, our
two long-term guests. Their eyes were as big as saucers. It
was dear Gwendolyn who spoke out loud and clear, "Glory
be to God, Ezra, you cast the bloody 'ell outta 'er."

Fr. Ezra, a little woozy and wobbly, stood up and straightened out his surplice and stole, and in a pure youthful voice, intoned the *Pater Noster* and we all joined in with full loud voices, forming into two choirs as we did so. It was as if we had programs we were following, which we didn't. Sr. Leah Marie and Sr. Antonia led the procession out of the chapel with lighted candles, down the east cloister, while Sr. Lucy and Sr. Cecilia began the Litany of the Saints. Havana remained behind, sitting on a bench, with Sr. Paula in attendance, keeping a sharp eye on her, and speaking very gently to her. The last to leave were myself, Sr. Catherine Agnes (SCAR), Mother Bernadette, and Sr. Elijah Rose who was holding the holy water bucket for Fr. Matthew who was last, sprinkling every corner and entrance way he passed. He had to stop about midway round, at the bottom of the stairway leading up to the novitiate. It was like he was knocked over by a strong wind. He had to hold on to a window ledge, and sat for a moment on the window seat. He raised his eyes, squinting like a bright light was turned on him, and he shot the holy water at the stairs, and muttered something in Latin. The procession ahead of him stopped and turned towards him, and he whisked the aspergillum in circles, sprinkling everything surrounding him.

"Mother and Sister Baruch, come with me. All of you pray over and over the Prayer to St. Michael till we return." And he bounded up the stairs, casting holy water on the steps in front of him. Mother and I behind him, pulled ourselves up with the help of the railings; it was not windy, but there was a heaviness in the air.

Pointing to the exact place, he said, "That's Havana's room, right?"

I responded, "Yes, it is." And he told us not to go further, but he went to the room alone and held up his crucifix in his left hand and doused the hall and door with holy water.

Returning to us, he said, "Let us go on; the infestation is too great for now. Be careful going down the stairs." The candles at the lead of the procession flickered and went out; we heard a distant crash, and remembered it, from the time the light fell down on the altar. Passing by the refectory entrance, the portrait of Pope Benedict flew off the wall and crashed against the opposite window frame, nearly hitting two Sisters in the head.

"Just stand quietly, Sisters. Pay no attention to anything… this will pass; angels of God assist us…this will pass…angels of God, be with us. (I was thinking, he's got to pray: *angels of God unfreeze us*.) We were all dead silent not moving a muscle. It passed, as he said. And we continued in our regular awkward pace invoking every saint and blessed that we ever heard of.

When it was all over, we returned through the ante-choir in the rear of the chapel, singing the *Salve*. Mother announced that Great Silence would begin in an hour. In the meantime, everyone deserved to retire to the large parlor for a cup of tea, or a glass of the chardonnay being saved for tomorrow night's supper. It's tonight that we needed a little cheer. Rhonda Lynwood and Gwen were invited and happily accepted. (Rhonda had also donated the chardonnay!) It was also the last time everyone could say goodbye to Rhonda, and after such a night, she would be a welcome distraction.

Although I doubt the conversation would be about her movies or the happily ever after of Sr. Solange Marie.

Mother, Sr. Catherine Agnes (SCAR), Sr. Rosaria, Sr. Anna Maria, Fr. Matthew, and I met with Havana in Mother's office. It was somewhat surreal, as Havana looked and sounded like a normal young girl. She told us about contacting her Nonna every night and said she felt like she was under a spell.

"I don't know how I got here, Sister, really. It's like I've been sleepwalking or something. I think you're all wonderful ladies, but I don't want to be a nun…why am I here?"

We let Fr. Matthew, who was sitting in Mother's chair, do most of the talking. I'm not sure Havana understood all that he was telling her; I'm not sure I did either. According to him, she had been the object of a demonic attachment for some time now, possibly years. The Evil One, who gained entrance to her through the Ouija board, possessed her and used her, obviously, to gain access to the monastery. He said she probably didn't even use the Ouiji board after a while, but had what she thought were conversations with her grandmother, and she would do whatever Nonna said. Havana nodded her head.

Father said he has dealt with other demonic possessions similar to this, and that she was clear of the effects; he could see that, but we would need to "do more" with her room, so no one should take her room for now. We all mumbled in total agreement, looking back and forth at each other in amazement.

"Some demons are expelled immediately by holy water; others need repeated prayers and other holy objects we've found helpful. The presence and power of Christ is a billion times more powerful than the Devil, which is one reason he hates places like this and will try every trick to frighten us and to creak in through whatever means he can. We should not be afraid. He went on to say that there was probably not a single demon, but legions of demons, as it was easy access once they knew a way. Sometimes there are very obvious entrances...portals." He was sounding like Sr. Gerard, who slept through the whole night, thank you, Lord.

Havana didn't remember the fire except what others talked about it the next day; she kept saying she didn't know why she was here.

She was relieved and thrilled to know she could leave, and wanted to leave right away and not wait till the morning. She had the number of a girlfriend in Manhattan where she could stay. I told her we had taken the Ouija board, and she said she didn't want it; she never wanted to see it again. (Holy water has pretty powerful side effects.)

Mother suggested she might want to call her mother and stay with her for the night, but she said no, that would not be good. It was her mother who gave her the Ouija board, and many times they would talk to Nonna together. Besides, she didn't know if her mother would be alone, or was work-ing, or wanted her home. She would let her know later that she had left us. *How sad*, I thought. Sometimes we just don't know what young people go through. I think I loved Havana for the first time in that moment, and prayed God would protect her.

Sr. Anna Maria said she would help her get her things together, make the phone call to her friend, and would give her some money, and taxi fare. And that was that.

After she left, Mother, SCAR, Ezra, and I went over to my office. I opened the closet and pointed to the Ouija board. Fr. Ezra picked it up with both hands and told me to clear the corner of my desk. Then with a karate-like chop he banged it on the edge of the desk, breaking it in two; he repeated it with each half, and taking off his shoe, he smashed what he called the planchette into pieces. He took a plastic waste-basket bag and put the pieces in there and left them outside the enclosure door; he would dispose of them. Ezra told us then that he believed that the demons used the Ouija board to get to Havana and through her and that board made their way into the monastery, after which she didn't really need the board. He told us that there may have been other already present infestations here for many years.

"The monastery is over a hundred years old, you know. You are a prayerful and faithful house, and so the battle is real and will go on, but the Lord has won the battle. We celebrate that, do we not, the next three days!"

After the Triduum, he would celebrate a private Mass in Havana's old room each day of the Octave. And our Eucharistic procession tomorrow night would go the entire round of the cloister, not just to the altar of repose. That should take care of things.

In the meantime, he was to join us in the large parlor for a little refreshment, which was highly unusual, but it would help to calm the nerves of the Sisters and let him give a short version of what he told us. After all, this was a highly

unusual night. *Why is this night different from all other nights?*
Our Jewish Passover question came to mind. It was certainly
appropriate in its own way—we had been through a Passover of the Evil One, and passed through the holy water of
salvation, and as our Fr. Matthew said, we would be litur-
gically celebrating it all for real beginning tomorrow night.

I went with him to the large parlor for a couple minutes, but was too done in to stay longer. I spent a quiet fifteen minutes in the chapel, came to our cell, and sprinkled
everything with Fr. Ezra's newly made holy water, and settled
down here in Squeak to say "good night, dear Lord. And
may Your holy angels dwell here to keep us in peace. Amen."
I smiled and thought of Samwise in the *Fellowship of the
Ring* when he saw an Oliphant and exclaimed, "What a life!"
(J. R. R. Tolkein, *The Lord of the Rings*).

Thirty-Seven

Holy Thursday Night 2007

> *Lord, we beg you to visit this house and banish from it all the deadly power of the enemy. May your holy angels dwell here to keep us in peace, and may your blessings be upon us always. We ask through Christ our Lord. Amen.* (Final Prayer, Compline)

(Squeak) Lord, it almost seems like I'm breaking silence while writing in my journal, but I know I'm not. It's been quite a Holy Week so far, and we are now plunged into the Sacred Triduum, the three "high holy days" of the Faith.

I met with the three simple professed after breakfast this morning. I knew they would need to talk about everything for a half hour. They were relieved that Havana had left and were actually anxious on this Holy Thursday to get busy with all that needed to be done. Sr. Kateri is assigned to the sacristy all day. Sr. Elijah Rose to the kitchen all day—not her happiest assignment—and Sr. Leah Marie to help Sr. Paula mainly cleaning the parlors and making sure the guest rooms are ready. The young professed Sisters are all busy too, chanting, cooking, cleaning…the three "c's" of our life!

One could literally feel the difference in the house. The Sisters all had smiles and seemed to actually be happy to work. I remember one Triduum they were grumpy about having to work on Holy Thursday, but there's always a lot of preparations, and with less Sisters in community, the younger ones get more "chores" to do. I went downstairs to the Cave.

I presumed Rhonda Lynwood would be packing and probably cleaning her rooms. I rang our little bell to let her know I was in the parlor. She appeared a bit disheveled but all smiles. I told her not to bother cleaning her rooms; we cleaned up the place before she came; we can clean it up when she leaves. So she sat down instead.

"That was some night last night, wasn't it?"

Rhonda laughed. "You're telling me! I thought, boy, I've never had a Holy Week like this one; it will pack a wallop to renewing our baptism vows and renouncing Satan at the Vigil Saturday night."

"My gosh, Rhonda, you're right. I haven't even thought of that."

"Well, at the time, I'm sure you were thinking of other things!" Chuckle.

"Honestly, I was thinking *this is it, Baruch...Lord have mercy on my poor soul.* After she let go of me, I saw you and Gwendolyn at the grille looking like, I don't know what!"

Rhonda laughed. "That was all rather scary, but actually I feel more energetic this morning than I have the past couple weeks. I'm looking forward to the Trid-u-um. I hope Fr. Matthew is as revived as I am!"

"Have you ever been to an exorcism?"

"Not quite as real or dramatic as last night. Once, probably twenty years ago, I found myself at a so called 'party' which turned out to be a drug-fest. I've never seen demons 'manifesting' as they say, but that night they were in full swing. A ceiling light fell out of the ceiling and crashed on the coffee table which destroyed the pizza but didn't touch the coke, and I don't mean Coca-Cola. Pictures were falling off the wall, and people...well, I don't want to even tell you. I had the good sense to high tail it out of there. This was before cell phones, and my driver had taken off, so I walked down this abandoned street which would take me to Hollywood Boulevard, and a surly looking man stepped out from a doorway, and stuck a gun in my face. I lost my bag, my ruby necklace, a diamond dinner ring, and my shoes—800-dollar Manolos, I'll have you know." (I had no idea what she was talking about.) "He knocked me down and took off. Some teenagers were walking down the street and nearly fell over me, but helped me get up, and nearly carried me to the boulevard. I got a cab and got home without being recognized. I never carried a house key with me. Rolex, my driver, had that, but there was a hidden key under a stone flower urn which weighed a ton. I got in and got the money for the cab. The cabbie was not at all shocked by any of it, like it was a normal Saturday night in Beverly Hills."

"Weren't you scared to death with the gun in your face?"

"Only for a second or two. This is going to sound strange, and I've never told this to anyone, but I can tell you, Sister, Lord knows I've told you all about my creepy life. I think I saw a fog-like mist moving around me, protecting me. I

didn't analyze it at the time, I just felt safe, even giving over
my stuff wasn't so scary. I think…I think it was…"

"Your Guardian Angel. Oy. He should've showed up five
minutes earlier."

Rhonda laughed. "I think he was busy getting me out of
the house and got distracted." We both laughed. Funny, how
we deal with serious stuff. We can't really handle it all, so we
turn it into humor. Mother Rosaria once said that when we
were talking about trivial tragedies.

"Well, it doesn't happen all the time, thank God, but it
does bring one back to the faith and realization that the
Devil and all his pomp and works are real." That was all we
said, and without much ado, Rhonda pirouetted back into
her rooms, in $19.95 black slippers from Walmart.

Our evening procession, Lord, was unlike any from all the
years past; it was the night after we had processed around the
cloister sprinkling every room and corner with holy water
after our traumatic experience in the chapel. We all stayed
for the entire holy hour and sang Compline quietly at the
altar of repose. Ezra did not stay, but told Mother to move
the Blessed Sacrament to the temporary tabernacle in our
sacristy. I only got a glimpse of him when he was leaving the
altar of repose; he looked white as a sheet. I was afraid he
would pass out.

I don't meditate very much, Lord, on Your passion and
death as conquering the forces of evil, and defeating the Evil
One for us, but last night a lot of us did, even if we were like
your old sleepy disciples who have just come from their First
Mass and ordination, and didn't understand that the Paschal

Lamb was going to be sacrificed. Tonight was different from all other nights. Amen.

* * *

Holy Saturday

Gwendolyn was here for our extraordinary night; I think Fr. Ezra may have told her about it before time. His, what he called later, his "Deliverance Ministry" was a chapter in his life which I knew nothing about. Gwendolyn was certainly good in keeping it a secret from me too; she was probably told to do so. I went through a twinge of jealousy about it, for a couple days. That she would share something so spiritually unique and a sacred ministry, really, which I did not, even to the extent of not knowing about it. I can see how "spiritually childish" it is to be jealous of a good someone or others do, and God did remind me, in His own quiet way, that I was a part of it all the time by the penances I offered, sometimes, routinely in the Morning Offering, for the "salvation of souls." The hidden life of prayer and penance is a powerful "blood stream" pulsing through the Mystical Body of the Church, which we "white corpuscles" forget. We hear it preached; we read it; we imagine it; but for the most part, we take it for granted or simply are unaware of it, or forget it, or simply don't believe it, because we rarely see the fruit of our maternal labor pains!

Gwendolyn had herself undergone a kind of deeper conversion; I noticed it when she first came back from England. She accepted the cross of her illness with a fortitude I hadn't seen in her before, and she was prayerful and at peace in a way that the younger Gwendolyn didn't have. I thought maybe it was just the effects of illness and old age and whatever wrinkles she had to iron out with her only living relative, Jaqueline. She hid behind the penguin obsession, and it kept her rooted in her life. It kept her joined to her son in a daily, non-morbid way besides giving her a persona outside herself which could hide her true self where she surrendered herself to God. I guess that could be said of all of us too. It's how "the life" allows us to be hidden beneath the exterior things to surrender interiorly to God, especially when that surrender is found to be a mystical kind of death to our self.

So it was significant that Gwendolyn was here, and standing arm in arm with Rhonda at the grille. The two cancer-ridden ladies among us who knew my best friend, Ezra, in a way I never knew. It was Gwendolyn who told Mother about Ezra at the very time when we needed to know that. And Rhonda who poured out her sinful soul to him in the Sacrament of God's merciful forgiveness.

Both were here for a short time and both leaving us. For Gwendolyn, the Rivka and Aaron Stein arrangement worked out perfectly, and with a little help from her friends, she moved out of her two rooms and into the Steins furnished basement apartment. She had her own entrance, a kitchenette, bath and shower, and a "studio apartment" with an old-fashioned murphy bed, and a round table in the corner, a lazy boy recliner, and a place for a television, which she would get. The Steins were thrilled to have her and remembered Penguin Pub, and had been there twice. They knew Sr. Gertrude who told them about "Ruth Steinway." It also helped that she, Gwendolyn, loved dogs. Something I never realized. She was quite done in by it all, however, and said she wasn't sure she'd make it to Holy Thursday or Good Friday, but would be here for Sunday Mass. We'll see. Dear Gwendolyn. I must pray for her more.

The first voice mail on my office phone this afternoon: "Well, you've gone and done it now, Rebecca Feinstein. All Mitzie can talk about is Jesus and some beloved disciple. She wants to go to Mass at your place on Sunday and wants to know what time, and would we be able to see you afterwards. Don't count on me being there. I should never have gone to Atlantic City and let the two of you alone."

Oy. Sally is not a happy Jewish camper this Passover. But isn't it interesting, Lord, about Mitzie? You do have Your ways! I know Sally is a pip, but You are the Lord of Lords and the Lord of Pips.

I called the pip back and spoke to their voice mail as well. "Sally and Mitzie, I got your lovely message. Easter Sunday morning Mass is at 10:00 a.m. I'm sorry I won't be able to see you afterwards, privately; the parlors are all taken, but the big parlor is where we greet everyone after the Mass. It's noisy, and as one Sister says, 'A bit like Grand Central.' But I could at least say hello. By the way, thanks for all you did for Gwendolyn; she's moved into the Steins and loves it. She should be here for Mass; you'll get to see her. Happy Easter."

The second voice mail. "This is for Sister Baruch Mary; it's Olivia, Sharbel's mother. Sister, have you heard from him or have any idea where he is? I haven't heard since last month. He was somewhere in Colorado and heading west. I thought I'd hear something before Easter, but not a word. If you have any news of his whereabouts, please let me know. I worry. Thank you, Sister. Oh…Happy Easter. It's Olivia Ghattas."

I called her back immediately, and to my surprise she picked up.

"Dr. Ghattas, please."

"This is Dr. Ghattas. Is this Sister Mary Baruch?"

"Yes, how did you know?"

"Caller-I.D. Thanks for getting back to me. Have you heard from Sharbel?

I was hoping he'd be home for Easter."

"No, I haven't heard recently. I got a postcard, hold on a minute, it's here in my desk drawer, from Colorado…this is what he wrote: 'Love C. Going I. in couple days for hw. Then U, pray I don't b-c a M. Maybe LV b-4 Cal. Then Or. S.' It's like reading a secret code!"

"Well, at least he writes to you in code. I got one email from a café in Nebraska, I think. Can you de-code your postcard?" I laughed.

"I think he's saying: Love Colorado. Going to Iowa in a couple days for Holy Week. Then Utah, pray I don't… this is the b-c a M. The M is capitalized, so I think he's saying, 'pray I don't become a Mormon. Maybe LV'…I thought it may be another religion, like Lutheran something or other, but Sister Paula said she thinks its Las Vegas, before California. Then Oregon. I imagine Sister Paula hit it on the head."

"Oregon? Why would he want to go to Oregon? Vegas, I get, but what's in Oregon for Heaven's sake. And Nebraska and Iowa; I'm not even sure where they are!"

I didn't breathe a word about any monasteries. The main one was in Iowa. I'm also sure the "M" stood for "monk" not

"Mormon." "Well, if I'm right, he's still in Iowa till Easter, I would imagine. Maybe he'll call you for Easter."

"Well, I hope so. He does worry me a lot. Winona hasn't heard from him either."

"Try not to worry, dear, and if by chance he calls here, I'll let him know you're worried and tell him to call you. He must've inherited his father's travel gene."

"I reckon so. Thank you, Sister, I'm sorry to bother you. Have a wonderful Easter."

"Good bye now...God bless." I hung up. 'I reckon so?' A sophisticated, neuro-surgeon living in the Hampdens on Long Island, and she says: 'reckon so.' Oy.

I checked on "the girls" in the afternoon, and they were all happily at work. Sr. Kateri was polishing candle sticks, Sr. Elijah Rose was mopping the refectory floor and getting the table covers ready, and Leah Marie was arranging flowers in the work sacristy. I was going to clean out Havana's cell, but decided to wait till after the Easter Octave; after Ezra's little admonishment, I wasn't going near the place. I kept the door closed, as if that mattered! I had already fixed a cell for Emelia Hopkins. I had the afternoon free, so I visited the infirmary. I wanted to fill Sr. Gerard in on our little rendez-vous with Old Red Legs.

"I knew there was something going on, I could feel it." Sr. Gerard was all ears. "Our Lady is our Protectress, I'm sure. She tells us over and over to pray the rosary for the conver-sion of sinners. Sometimes it's so simple, yet people get all dangled up in other things."

"I know, Sister. How true it is." I had a flashback in my mind of giving Sharbel my rosary. "What do you mean, Sister, that you could 'feel it?'"

"Oh, I don't know in theological terms or anything, it's just a feeling, like there's trouble in the house. We had a retreat master once who told us that a sign of the Devil was division. The Holy Spirit unites us, but the Devil divides us. He does it in little ordinary ways, mostly, I think, in gossip and criticism about others, and in our getting impatient and flustered with others. That's when the Devil gets his foot in the door."

"And you could feel that in the house?"

"Oh sure, I've felt it in myself, but ain't it funny, something like our terrible fire, which probably had the Devil behind it, brought us together at a time when we were all at odds with each other. The old Sisters were getting grumpy and impatient; Sr. Paula was coming down with stuff; Sisters were fighting over things…there was a chill in the air, I felt it."

I knew what Sr. Gerard was talking about; I felt it, too, in how the young Sisters weren't getting along, how disgruntled they were, and negativity was creeping in where we used to find a lot of joy and peace. I thought it was the gaps left by the deaths of Sr.s Gertrude and Sr. Benedict, but it was around the time when Havana started coming around. It was the "strange thing" Sr. Paula and I couldn't put our finger on…maybe. Well, it was all over now.

"Thank you, Sister Gerard, and keep praying the rosary for us, okay? Oh, and please remember my nephew, Sharbel.

He's driving across country to Oregon." *I hope he has my rosary in his pocket!*

Thirty-Eight

Easter Sunday

> *Alleluia. Resurrexit Dominus, alleluia, sicut dicit*
> *vobis, alleluia, alleluia.* (Nunc Dimittis antiphon
> for Easter at Compline. Alleluia. The Lord is risen,
> alleluia; as He said to you, alleluia, alleluia.)

MOTHER BERNADETTE WAS right; it seemed like we shouted out our renouncing Satan at the Vigil Mass with greater gusto than ever before! We also sang our *Alleluias* with more fervor and joy than I can remember.

We also had two seminarians helping out, which was a great help to Ezra. Then this morning, Fr. Oyster appeared for the morning Mass. He met with Mother in the parlor the hour before Mass. I don't know any of what was said. I couldn't see if Sally and Mitzie were out in the extern chapel. When I asked Sr. Paula if they were there, she only said, "The other one, not your sister." I don't know why she can't remember Mitzie's name. I made it to the large parlor for maybe ten minutes. Long enough to introduce Gwendolyn to Mitzie, and then I had to leave. I went down to the Cave to see Rhonda for the last time. It was a bit warm, after all it was spring, but she was carrying her mink coat.

"I'd give this to you as a present, but I know you'd never wear it."

I laughed. "Couldn't you just see me walking in the *Salve* procession, wearing this?"

"Wanna try it on?"

"I thought we renounced all temptation, but…okay." She folded it and put it on the turn. I put it on and felt all snuggly and Upper East Side. I strutted up and down the parlor, which is like four steps in each directions, and got Rhonda in a fit of laughing.

I quickly slipped it off and "turned it over" to her. "Well, I think it will serve you better in Rhode Island, besides it clashes with my shoes."

Rhonda's laughter suddenly turned to tears. "Oh, Sister, how can I ever thank you for all you've done for me. I don't think I could've gotten through without you and our 'tea therapy.' You'll always be my Sister Solange."

I couldn't say anything. There was suddenly a frog settled in my throat. But she could see, I hope, from my own teary expression how grateful I was and moved by her words…the great Rhonda Lynwood grateful to me. "I'm grateful too, Rhonda, you take care of yourself, and pray for me…for all of us."

"I will, Sister, I'm feeling more energetic this morning than I have in a long time, must be all those alleluias!"

She didn't have a farewell from the community; we kind of did that last Wednesday night, but Mother did come down to the Cave and said her goodbyes. Rhonda quietly

SISTER MARY BARUCH

made her way out the enclosure door where Fr. Oyster was
waiting for her. She gave Sr. Paula a big hug too as Sister
helped them with her luggage, and I'm told outside the main
entrance was a gaggle of photographers waiting for her exit.
Someone had tipped them off. I suspect a Dominican from
the Oyster Bay area who didn't quite "get it." Nonetheless,
he was taking care of her and getting her safely to Water's
Edge near Newport. Her impending death will no doubt
make the headlines, but her faith story will go untold.

* * *

Mother was all aglow at recreation. The Sisters from the infirmary were present. Sr. Bertrand had a headband over her veil
holding up two bright pink velveteen bunny ears. And she
was passing out little netted satchels each filled with a chocolate bunny, a yellow marshmallow chick, and assorted candies and jelly beans. The novitiate presented Mother with a
large wicker basket filled with varied colored eggs each with
a Sister's name on it.

 After everyone was settled down with something warm to
drink and a piece of Easter cake, Mother quieted us all.

 "Sisters, the *Lord is Risen, Alleluia.*"

 And we all shouted back, "*He's risen indeed, Alleluia.*"

 "Thank you to the Sisters in the novitiate and in the infirmary for your most thoughtful gifts. We have much to be
grateful for this year as the Lord has certainly been with us
and brought us through His Paschal Mystery, not just the
last three days, but all year. It is a year we will long remember. And now I have something very beautiful to show you.

It is a parting gift from Rhonda Lynwood with her gratitude for your prayers, your hospitality, and your sisterly care for her."

And with that, Mother pulled from a gold velvet bag, a beautiful Faberge decorated Egg. It was at least six inches high, and was sealed in a glossy metallic blue, with an icon of Our Lady of Tenderness framed in golden ringlets with rubies and sapphires all around the egg. It rested on its own matching pedestal also encrusted with rubies and sapphires.

"It once belonged to the Imperial family of Russia and was given to Rhonda thirty years ago by an anonymous fan. It was destined for a museum in Washington, D.C., but Rhonda changed that and wants us to have it. It should remind us, she said, of Mary, Queen of Hope, and Mother of this humble monastery hidden in the shadows of New York. I dare say, Sisters, it is a treasure we shall keep in safe keeping, as Our Lady, Queen of Hope, keeps us going for years to come. For now, it will be on a little stand in the chapel next to Our Lady's statue. You may all look at it closely to see the intricate work involved, but please do not handle it."

We ooohed and aaahed at it and chatted quietly among ourselves. When the bell rang, we put away our things and silently made our way out to the chapel for Compline, happy to add our Paschal Alleluias to the *Salve Regina*.

How good and how pleasant it is when sisters dwell together in unity. I realized in a unique moment of peace how much I love this house and these Sisters with whom I live day in and day out. The Lord is Risen indeed and continues to send out His peace.

Compline ends every night with the same blessing: *May the all-powerful Lord grant us a restful night and a peaceful death. Amen.*

After Compline, I passed my office door on the way to our cell and saw the red light blinking that I had a message. I thought for the moment, I should just let it go till the morning, but I went in to check it. Maybe Sally has forgiven me and is calling to wish me a happy Easter!

"Sister Baruch, this is Olivia Ghattas. Sharbel has been in an accident near Des Moines, Iowa. His friend in the car was killed. Sharbel is unconscious and in critical condition. I'm leaving in two hours for the airport. Please pray."

* * *

I'm sitting in our cell with St. James' Scallop in my hands, trying to pray.

(squeak)